BLACK WATER

A Novel

KERSTIN EKMAN

BLACKWATER

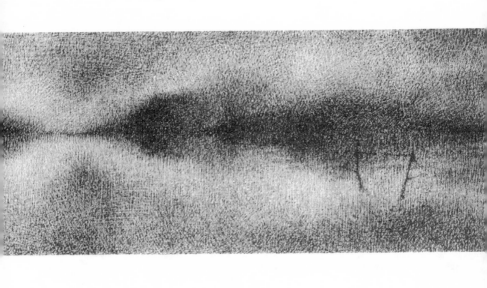

Picador USA
New York

BLACKWATER

KERSTIN EKMAN

translated by Joan Tate

Picador® is a U.S. registered trademark and is used by
St. Martin's Press under license from Pan Books Limited.

Book design by Gretchen Achilles
Illustration copyright © 1996 Samantha Burton

Library of Congress Cataloging-in-Publication Data

Ekman, Kerstin.
    [Händelser vid vatten. English]
    Blackwater / Kerstin Ekman ; translated by Joan Tate.
        p.   cm.
    ISBN 0-312-15247-7
    1. Communal living—Sweden—Fiction.   2. Mothers and
daughters—Fiction.   3. Sweden—Fiction.   I. Tate, Joan.   II. Title.
PT9876.15.K55H3613   1997
839.7'374—dc20   96-31790
                                                                    CIP

First published in Sweden by Albert Bonniers Forlag as
                    Händelser vid vatten

First Picador USA Edition: February 1997

10   9   8   7   6   5   4   3   2   1

Translated with the support of
the Nordic Council of Ministers

Principal Characters

Annie Raft

Mia Raft *Annie's daughter*

Birger Torbjörnsson *the district doctor*

Åke Vemdal *the district chief of police*

Roland Fjellstrom *campsite owner*

Lill-Ola Lennartsson *owner of fishing tackle shop*

THE BRANDBERGS:

Torsten Brandberg }

Gudrun Brandberg } *the parents of Johan*

Johan Brandberg

Per-Ola }

Björne }

Pekka } *Johan's half brothers, by Torsten*

Väine }

Harry Vidart *neighbor who shares enclosure with the Brandbergs*

THE STARHILL COMMUNE:

Dan Ulander

Lotta

Petrus and Brita

Sigrid and Gertrud *Brita's daughters*

Bert and Enel

Pella *Enel's daughter*

Marianne Öhnberg (Önis)

Mats *Önis's son*

BLACKWATER

ONE

A sound woke her. Four o'clock in the morning. 4:02 in the red digits of the clock radio. There was a gray light in the room. The windowpanes were streaked with rain and outside damp was rising from the grass.

She wasn't frightened, but alert. Now she could hear what it was: a car engine ticking over. No one would come up here to see her this early. Saddie was still asleep on the sheepskin below the bed. She was thirteen and rather deaf.

A car door slammed. Another. So at least two people. Then this silence. No voices.

She slept with a shotgun beside her. There was a gap between the bed and the wall, and the gun lay in this space. A very neat weapon, Spanish. A Sabela. She kept the cartridges behind the clock radio. It took her twenty-two seconds to broach the gun and put in the cartridges. She had practiced and timed it. But she had never had any serious need to load it.

The house was locked. She had never forgotten to lock the front door, not even by accident. Not in eighteen years.

She lay with her hand on the finely carved butt of the Sabela, feeling its dull, greasy surface. Rigid and a little cold.

She didn't want to go out into the kitchen to look because she would be visible through the window. Instead, she got up and stood listening by the door. Saddie followed her, but collapsed on the rug under the low table and started snoring again. No voices could be heard.

In the end she went out into the kitchen after all. Without the shotgun. That's probably what you do. You think it will be all right.

The rain was now pouring soundlessly down the windowpanes. Beyond the veil of glass and water, Mia was standing in front of the car, her body welded to another.

They were very wet. Her jacket had been soaked through across the back and shoulders; her hair lay plastered to her head, looking darker than it was. He had really dark hair, brownish-black and straight. There were leaves in it, dwarf birch twigs and fern leaves. Mia must have put them there. She had been playing with him. They were so close, it looked as if he had penetrated her out there in the rain. But that was not it. What she saw was something equally primeval, as if a wound were opening itself in time. And then closed, was gone. As the faces detached themselves from each other, she recognized him.

She leaned against the worktop, standing there in her old nightdress, oblivious of the fact that they might see her. Her heart was moving inside her like an animal. After a while, her mouth had filled with saliva and a violent nausea forced her to swallow.

The same face. Firmer and coarser after eighteen years, but it was him. The rain was streaming as if down a window in time, and he was there, in flesh and blood.

She backed away from the window. They couldn't have seen her. By the time Mia had put the key into the lock, she was already back in bed. She heard Saddie plodding out to the porch and her quiet delight as her tail struck the coats in the hall, making the hangers jingle. Mia went out into the kitchen and the car started up. She was presumably waving to him. Then she went upstairs with Saddie at her heels, not bothering to go and wash. It was not difficult to understand why.

Annie's feet had turned cold and the chill spread upward. But she didn't dare go out into the kitchen to light the stove, or even hunt out a warm bathrobe. She did not want Mia to hear she was awake.

They had made love. Perhaps outside, in the rain. He was that boy. Though much older. With budding leaves in his wet hair, he also looked like something else. Something she had seen, an image perhaps. In spite of herself, she pictured a knife. She could see the knife in those strong young bodies.

Now Mia was lying up there in the smell of him, not even wanting to wash. She wanted to keep him with her.

4

What should she say when Mia came down?

You're twenty-three. There must be fifteen years between you. Keep away from him. He's dangerous.

It was eighteen years since she had seen that face, a young face then, and the agitation on it had been of another kind. But it was the same face.

The bed above creaked. Mia couldn't sleep or didn't want to. His presence was throbbing inside her, in her thighs, stomach, vagina, and her kiss-bruised lips. While Annie lay frozen dry in her bed, stretched out stiffly.

She reached for the telephone. It was not even half past four yet, but she wanted to hear his voice although she perhaps shouldn't talk for long. She might be overheard up there.

He must have been totally closed off at that moment, sealed into sleep like an envelope. But he answered at the first signal and she thought about how used he was to being woken and that he ought to have been allowed to sleep this Saturday morning.

"Only me. Sorry. I woke you, of course."

"Doesn't matter. Are you ill?"

His voice was indistinct.

"No, no."

"What is it, then?"

What should she say? He waited.

"I've seen him. You know. The one I saw that night."

He said nothing, but he must have known whom she meant because he didn't ask again.

"That's impossible," he said finally.

"Really, I've seen him."

"You couldn't recognize him."

"I did, though."

She heard him breathing heavily through his mouth.

"I don't know who he is," she said. "But I'll find out soon. I can't talk anymore now. I'll phone later."

He was reluctant to put the receiver down. She realized he wanted to calm her down, perhaps persuade her she'd been mistaken. But she said good-bye. She could still hear his breathing as she replaced the receiver.

His voice remained with her, as if he had spoken with his lips to her ear. The warmth in it, the moistness in the whorls on his chest. A valley with night mist, birds in the leaves.

All she could do now was wait.

Mia didn't sleep late. Annie was having a cup of tea when she came down. Mia's lips were bruised and the look on her face was absent. She ought to be embarrassed because she hadn't phoned to say she was coming.

But she probably hadn't been coming to see Annie. She had come in that man's car. It was clear she was thinking about him all the time. He wouldn't disappear like the squalls of rain over the mountain this cold morning. They would have to talk about him.

"What a lot of flowers," Mia said finally, probably not realizing that it had been the end of the term. "I didn't phone. We just drove up. It just happened."

We, she said, as a matter of course.

"We were going to stop overnight at Nirsbuan."

"Did you give up?"

"It got so cold. There's only that little stove and there wasn't much wood. But we saw the blackcocks. They're playing in the marsh."

"Still?"

"There's snow up there. In some places, anyway."

She had sat down opposite Annie and was holding the hot mug of tea between her hands. Her hair was dry now, curly with reddish tints again. She had found an old tracksuit in the attic, a faded blue with COUP DU MONDE across the chest.

"Johan Brandberg drove me up," she said. "You know who I mean?"

"No."

"No, of course not. He hasn't been living at home. Not for many years."

"Eighteen."

She looked up.

"Then you do know who he is?"

"I've seen him."

Mia could know nothing of what her mother had seen that day. She had been deep down in the grass, her face pressed so hard against the ground that a pattern of grass and moss had been left on her soft skin afterward.

The telephone rang. Annie answered and heard it was from a pay phone. The voice asking for Mia was light, far too light for his age. Had he seen her, slid down into time?

Mia left after the conversation. Annie needn't drive her down, she said. He had rung from the pay phone down by the store and was waiting for her there with the car.

Mia had been with her when it happened. Annie had tried to keep it secret from her and it was unlikely she had any memory of it. But of course she had heard all about it afterward, ad nauseam. Whenever she said she had been brought up in Blackwater, people would exclaim, Oh, there!

In the early 1970s, Blackwater had been a dying village among many others. Rain fell on the faces around the Walpurgis Night bonfire. The air smelled of diesel oil. They filled coffee cans with oil-soaked sawdust and set them alight. The roads glowed from those lanterns for a few hours on one single evening a year. Otherwise nothing.

Since then this village had become a black jewel. Visible. Full of power.

Yes, it was here. Or, rather, four kilometers up from the village, by the water called the river Lobber. It had had other names and would be given more. In places it was a fast-running river, hurtling over precipices farther up and forming rapids. But here several large, deep patches of calm water opened up between the racing stretches. The banks were boggy and tangled with bluish willow. Alpine sowthistle and northern wolfsbane grew above head height, and you could fall into beaver holes trying to make your way through it. All around the river was inaccessible marshland crisscrossed by animal paths. The place had no name.

Midsummer Eve almost eighteen years ago. A hot day. They had traveled to Östersund by train. She knew that. But how did she know?

Clear and irrefutable memories were actually very few. She had stood with the telephone crank in her hand. That was a fact and she remembered it, but not much more. The heat. Later that day, the asphalt outside the Tempo store had been soft.

She couldn't remember what they had been wearing or what time the train had gotten in. They had to wait a long time at the bus station. The bus to Blackwater left at half past two, then as now. Over all those years, the timetable had never changed.

It was Midsummer Eve, so it was a Friday. The old Midsummer Eve was not until Saturday. She had looked it up. There was nothing about their journey in her notebooks, because they hadn't existed then. Her loneliness had not begun, everything was still hectic, her head, her whole body singing. She was to start a new life.

And she had done so. When she tried to wind the crank of the taxi telephone, the handle came off in her hand. She might have thought that a bad start. But she didn't. The song inside her was too powerful.

She got hold of a taxi in the street and they spent a long time walking around Östersund. In the afternoon, they sat on a park bench and ate some kind of junk food. For the last time, she probably thought. They boarded the bus with all their luggage from the train and the goods shed. Mia began feeling sick at Gravliden. A horrid name, burial grove, so she remembered that it started there. An old man smelling of goat had gotten on. The heat rose in the packed bus and the air grew oppressive. The smell of filth and goat hung all around the old man, spreading in irregular waves, perhaps from the movements on the bus. People got on and off with shopping bags. They had been shopping in Östersund. It occurred to her that she would not be able to shop like that anymore.

She had a paper bag ready, because Mia kept feeling sick all the way. They got out for a while at every stop to give her some fresh air, but it was suffocatingly hot that afternoon. An hour later, the old man got off and things were better. Hot and exhausted, Mia fell asleep on her lap.

"It'll be better now," said the driver.

"How much farther is it?"

"Going to Blackwater, are you? You one of them Starhill people?"

"No."

That had nothing to do with him.

"On vacation, then?"

She thought that a silly question. But he couldn't know she was going to live a new life. To escape any more questions, she agreed she was on vacation. Mia was asleep so she couldn't contradict her. She never found out how much farther it was. He did not speak to her again.

Then the forests began, and the major areas of felling. The bus no longer stopped so often. At every village, crates of milk and other perishables were set down on the stand by the store. The postwomen came out and opened the door for the driver and he carried in the mailbags. People were waiting in their cars for letters and the evening papers, many of them beery, helloing at the driver and each other.

"What are they saying?" Mia whispered.

But Annie didn't understand what they were saying either.

They were traveling in a foreign country. When a large, cold lake was glimpsed between the trees, that was only a break in the monotony that would soon disappear and be replaced by another. She didn't know they were traveling upward along a system of lakes extending right up to the high mountains in Norway, where it ran out of marshlands and mountain streams. In the felled clearings the great network of water had been cut off and the ground had dried to dead flesh in the body of the landscape. Nor did she know that the felled clearings they could see from the road were only the small ones, that larger and larger areas had been cut off from their links with the clouds, making them incapable of giving anything back when the acid rain trickled through them.

They didn't reach Röbäck, where the church was, until evening. They were to register in the parish there, but the rural district was large. She had no idea how far it extended. They got off and looked at the church while the driver unloaded at the store. The church walls were dazzling in the strong evening sunlight. The church stood on a tongue of land stretching out into Lake Rösjön, a white fence running out toward the water like the railing on a boat. The whole church on its spit out into the great mountain lake resembled a ship. Perhaps the idea had been that on the Day of Judgment it would move out from the shore with all its dead.

The water looked cold. The shores were covered with dark spruce forest, with no greenery nearest to the water. Rocks and bare, smooth stones ran down into the lake. She knew it was cold. Twelve or thirteen degrees, Dan had written.

"Look at those funny kids," said Mia.

A small column of children appeared by the bus. Only four of them, but they were walking in a line, three girls in long skirts and braids, carrying bark baskets, and a boy in a knit cap, the ear flaps dangling as he walked. They stood talking to the driver for a moment. Then the whole troop set off slowly down the road. They appeared to her as a projection, an extract from an old film or from a different age as the milk crates thumped on to the stand outside the store. Or weren't they children?

"Maybe they were the little people, the wee folk?" she said to Mia, immediately regretting it, for with great seriousness Mia watched the little troop disappearing around the bend of the road.

The driver waved. Time to leave.

Blackwater was the last stop. The lake was bright that evening, the shores below the mountain reflected in the water, blue-black, every detail of the jagged contour of firs as clear as the original. It no longer looked like a reflection in the water, but like another atmosphere, with depths continuing downward in long, wooded slopes toward a bottom they could not see.

They were stiff-legged when they got off. Mia's lips were dry and cracked, all her fruit drink long since gone. Annie looked around for Dan so that he could stay with Mia while she went into the store to buy her something to drink. It was half past seven and the store was closed, but the storekeeper was there while the goods were being unloaded. Cars were coming and going all the time, people fetching their mail and newspapers just as they had in the other villages.

She could see neither the VW Beetle nor Dan. Mia was unwilling to wait alone outside the store and grabbed Annie's hand, her small triangular face pale and gray under the freckles, her hair plastered at her temples and forehead as the sweat dried. She needed to pee, and something to drink, then perhaps something to eat, but Annie could do little for her until Dan came. She had to make sure the driver included everything that was theirs as he unloaded. He was a quarter of an hour early, he said, and she presumed that was why Dan had not yet put in an appearance.

After all the cars had driven away and the storekeeper had locked up and gone down to his house on the headland beyond the store, they were left alone on the graveled patch with their suitcases and cardboard boxes. The silence was violent after the noise of the cars. It was strange to experience the stillness she had longed for and feel uneasy at the same time. Dan ought to be there by now.

On Midsummer Eve, Johan Brandberg was sitting at his desk in his room. It was afternoon and it had grown very hot. He was reading about the Antarctic expedition with the *Maud* in the 1950s. He was free. Since the end of the term, he had been working with his father, clearing in the forest. There had been no talk of any other job. Later on in the summer, Väine and he were to plant. He wondered what it would be like to be out all day with Väine. His half brother was scarcely a year older than he was, but he was stronger, and not just physically. Johan thought about the Lajka dog, and that disgusted him so much, he began to feel sick in the stuffy room.

He leaned over the desk and opened the window. Down there he could see the yard and the barn, the enclosure and some of Vidart's goats. They had grazed it bare inside, but on the other side of the fence the grass was thick and full of flowers. He recognized the globeflowers.

During the October elk shoot, the Lajka had come back twice and sat on the steps. On the Saturday, the day before the share-out of the meat, Torsten shot her. The body lay in the woodshed over the weekend, then he had told Väine to bury it.

Johan remembered the sound of Väine hacking into the grass behind the barn with the spade. The ground was already frozen hard. He had been at his desk, as now, but with a social studies textbook in front of him. Suppose he'd asked me, he had thought. Suppose I'd vomited into the hole.

On the Monday he had been on the school bus again, leaving it all behind him. Now he had to stay. All week. All the weeks up to August 22.

He was to clear eight hectares of pine forest and then they were to plant contorta pines in the clearing above Alda's.

But now he was free and was sitting there with a book, free thanks to Gudrun. He might become a vet, or a surveyor. There were books and books. Not everything was the same muck, not even for Torsten. Per-Ola worked in Åre as a crane driver. Björne felled for the Cellulose Company and Pekka had as well this last year. But now he was talking about the mines in Spitsbergen. Or an oil rig. But that was probably just talk. Or dreams.

Pekka had dreams in that mess called brain tissue. And what had he in his testicles? Mine look the same, he thought. And I have the same kind of matter in my brain.

But not the same genes.

Those thoughts were coming again. He kept having them, and wanting to have them, but he would never have dared ask Gudrun. Not straight out.

He had had those thoughts once when he was out skiing with her, when he was eleven or twelve, old enough anyhow to manage Bear Mountain. They were on their way up the last steep slope when they heard a scooter. At first they couldn't make out where the sound was coming from, and then it was suddenly deathly quiet again. But they zigzagged up a bit farther and had just taken off their skis to climb the last bit on the ice crust, when they saw the man on the scooter outlined against the sky.

Johan was able to call up that sight at any given moment. A tall man. Orange sweatshirt and worn black leather trousers. Belt with silver studs and a knife in a horn sheath, bigger than any knife he had ever seen before and fiercely curved toward the tip. The man had taken his cap off and put it on the scooter seat. His hair was black with streaks at the temple that looked silvery. Narrow slits of eyes in the strong light, black inside. And behind him all the spiky white Norwegian mountains.

"He's looking for his reindeer," said Gudrun. And when they got up there, he cried out, *"Bouregh!"* and then they had gone on talking to each other in their Sami. Johan understood no more than every tenth word and was deeply embarrassed when the tall man said something to him and he couldn't answer. The man ruffled his hair and touched him.

He could visualize the scene at any time. But he was thrifty about doing so. It must never get worn out, nor must the sight up there against the sky of the tall man who was his father.

That was it. There was no other explanation.

Then he heard Vidart's car, a Duett with a faulty silencer. The dogs had heard it long before he did and were already barking.

Vidart repaired and sometimes bought and sold used cars. He used the Duett only to carry the milk churns in. His wife always used to drive it across Torsten Brandberg's yard up to the enclosure. But a stop had been put to that now.

Gypsy bastard, Torsten said. That cripple who can't work. Assessed disabled at fifty thousand. Of course he's stealing.

Torsten had himself bought four brand-new Hakkapeliitta tires from Vidart. Given eleven hundred for them. And don't think he kept quiet about it, either. He had told them all over the kitchen table that Vidart had simply phoned the insurance company and said, "I had four new Hakkapeliitta tires stolen last night. And what's worse, I've promised them to someone who's driving down to work today. So you must get a move on over settling that claim."

"Is Vidart a gypsy?" Johan had asked Gudrun afterward, but she didn't know. Torsten said that people called that were that. "Why does he hate him?" Johan asked. What a word! But she had let the needle stop in the cloth, as if testing out the word on Torsten and Vidart. "He's always disliked Vidart," she said in the end. "Probably because he's new here."

Vidart had lived in Blackwater for only seventeen years. That was longer than Johan's lifetime. The goats in the enclosure were Harry Vidart's. They leaped about between the wrecks of cars and had gnawed all the tree trunks clean. Torsten had told him to remove a rusted-up Volvo PV and shift the electric fence farther in. The bit of the enclosure facing the road was the Brandbergs'.

Torsten had told him long ago. Vidart had bought the property from the widow of old man Enoksson and she didn't know about the enclosure situation. Most people said the road up there was public, but Torsten said the bit from the barn was his, as was the bit of the enclosure where the Volvo was. It glowed fox-red with rust and the goats clambered on it to get at a willow that still had some leaves on it. Apart from that, the enclosure looked as if it had been sprayed with defoliant.

In the presence of witnesses, Torsten had told Vidart for the last time to move the wreck and the fence. It was to be done by Monday at the latest, he had said. That was the same week as Johan's term ending.

Vidart had moved the fence a bit farther in and removed everything loose from the wreck. He was going to take the rest in the front loader, but there was something wrong with the hydraulics. So that week went by.

On Tuesday morning, when Vidart's wife came with the Duett loaded with churns for milking, there was a gate right across the road. She got out and saw it was just fastened with a twisted wire. She didn't dare open it, but turned around and drove away. After that, Vidart took the tractor across the hay meadows up to the enclosure and the goat shed every morning and evening.

Naturally all this could not go on in the long run. He couldn't do the milking twice a day when he had his workshop to run, and his wife couldn't drive the tractor. He was clearly fed up now. He didn't send his wife in the Duett, but came himself.

He left the engine running as he got out and opened the gate, fiddling for a long time with the wire. As he drove in and the car disappeared behind the barn, Johan's heart began to thump. He knew his father and brothers must have long since seen Vidart. It had become quiet downstairs. The radio had been on in the kitchen before. The dogs were quiet, too, once the Duett had disappeared.

Then Per-Ola came out. Johan saw him as he strode out of the shade of the porch. He had already changed and was wearing white trousers and a white shirt. The others were obviously still indoors and it was still absolutely quiet.

Per-Ola crossed over to the carpentry shed and came out with a chain and a padlock, then went across and padlocked the gate to the gatepost. The timber in it gleamed yellow in the sun.

When he had finished with the padlock, he went back in. Now they're having coffee, Johan thought. No, liquor. Or liquor in their coffee. Gudrun had put out a coffee cake before she had left. She was in Byvången visiting Torsten's mother at the old people's home. All the brothers were at home, down there waiting, and Torsten was the one to decide what was to be done. So far, he had sent out only Per-Ola. But Johan's heart was still thumping.

It took Vidart an hour to do the milking. The yard was silent. No one seemed to move or speak down in the kitchen. Johan wanted to break the silence but didn't dare switch on the radio. It was best if Torsten didn't know he was up in his room, sitting there looking down at the enclosure.

He sat there in silence, and his legs, turned sideways because he could no longer get them under the desk, had long since gone to sleep.

Both the new Lajka and the Jämte hound started barking madly from the dog pen. Watching Vidart driving out from behind the barn and stopping the car was like watching a film. Johan knew everything in advance. Now he would find the chain and padlock. Shake it. Then look up toward the house.

And then?

Vidart walked past the gate along the edge of the ditch, where there was no fence. The enclosure began a little farther on. Torsten had put the gate like a boom across the road.

As Vidart came out into the gravel yard, he slowed down. That made the dogs even more furious. Then Torsten came into Johan's line of vision. He had a rake in his hand and started raking the yard gravel.

"Open the gate!" Vidart shouted.

"Quiet!" Torsten yelled. The dogs abruptly fell silent. The only sound now was the scraping of the rake's teeth in the gravel. Then Vidart called out:

"Open the gate! I've got the car."

But Torsten didn't answer. Johan got up. He had no desire to listen anymore. He stood leaning against the door. Vidart was talking loudly and shrilly outside, but when Torsten finally answered, only his words could be made out.

"I can't see no man to open up for."

Shrill talk again, the goat voice Vidart's. If only he would keep his mouth shut. Why didn't he understand that the only thing he could do now was to go away? Leave the car there. Fetch the milk with the tractor from the other side.

Johan heard a strange noise. Something cracked. He ran over to the window and looked down. Torsten had half the rake handle in his hand, splintered and sharp at the broken end. He must have broken it across his knee. Vidart was standing quite still, glaring at him. When he said something in that high, chattering voice, Torsten took two long steps toward him and thrust the handle against his throat. The goat voice bleated, then they both ran into the enclosure, Vidart ahead, dragging his polio-damaged leg, Torsten following stiffly. Yet it all happened very quickly. They ran past the barn and disappeared behind it.

The dogs had started barking again and didn't stop until Torsten came back, now without the rake handle. He disappeared out of Johan's sight as he reached the veranda, yelled at the dogs to be quiet, and they obeyed. Vidart should have done the same if he'd had any sense. Then the glass in the veranda door rattled.

Through the floorboards, Johan could hear Per-Ola asking something and Torsten answering. Then Per-Ola said something that made the others laugh. Vidart had been cowardly and fled. That was why they thought it funny down there. But if he headed homeward, he ought to have come out into the part of the enclosure not hidden by the barn. He would be visible all the way as he slanted across the hay meadows on his way home.

Or had he hidden? It was quiet in the kitchen again and Johan had a feeling that like him, they were all waiting for Vidart to appear. It was quite still in the heat, the dogs silent. Through the window, Johan could smell the grass as well as the birch leaves from the branches Torsten had put on the steps.

Johan sat quite still, glancing occasionally at his watch. Eleven minutes had gone by since Torsten had come back. Then the veranda door rattled and his father came out with Per-Ola behind him, followed shortly by Björne and Pekka and finally Väine. They didn't walk toward the enclosure, but vanished behind the house. After a while Johan heard two cars starting up.

As soon as the sound of engines had died away, without thinking Johan ran down, simply racing down the stairs and out. He was behind the barn in less than two minutes. Vidart was lying on his back in the sun, blood on his throat. It had run down into the hollow of his throat, where he had a disc or a coin on a silver chain, now resting in a shallow pool of blood, glinting like a small crescent. A little way off, the entire flock of goats stood staring at Johan. After a while they started grazing.

Johan lightly touched Vidart's hand and cheek. His stubble was gray and he looked older than usual. His peaked cap was behind his head, a large, sweaty brown patch on it. He had just milked the goats—that was obvious. His body and clothes smelled strongly.

There was no point in going back for help. The house was empty. If Gudrun had been at home, she would have seen to Vidart. Again he touched the pale gray cheek and thought it was like touching a big ewe.

He ran off again, taking the route across the hay meadows toward the nearest farm, Westlund's. Elna met him on the steps, caught him, and he didn't know whether he was crying or vomiting. It felt as if he were doing both.

Birger had set off for Blackwater together with Åke Vemdal with the idea of going fishing. Midsummer was the time to start. But somehow it had become the usual from the very beginning—raising the man's eyelids and looking at the cloudy globe, its iris turned upward. Feeling his pulse at his wrist. He couldn't touch the man's neck until he had washed.

Anyhow, there was no flow of blood to be stemmed. That had run down into the hollow of his neck and coagulated. He showed Åke how close to the artery it had come from. The wound had ragged edges as if it had been made by some jagged tool.

Vidart regained consciousness after a while. He had been knocked down, he said. By Torsten Brandberg.

"What did he hit you with?"

"His fist."

They helped him to his feet, and he had some difficulty standing. "Head's going around," he said. "Everything going black."

Birger got him upright. He had a feeling Vidart was acting a bit, hoping to show Åke Vemdal how bad things were, since he had been so bloody lucky that the police chief in Byvången had just happened to be there. The doctor, too. But he had been unconscious for quite a while, so Birger was taking no risks.

"You must go to the hospital," he said.

Vidart had no objections, but he was worried about the milk. The sharp look had come back into his eyes and he looked cunning, apparently himself again as soon as he got his cap back on. Hell, why did I have to be here right now? Birger thought. He said as much as soon as they had gotten Harry Vidart into the Westlund kitchen. They had dropped in on the Westlunds because Birger wanted to hear how Elna was. He had sent her to Östersund for her gallstones two weeks earlier. Assar Westlund had phoned for Ivar Jonssa. No ambulance was needed. Ivar's big taxi would do.

While they waited, they went out onto the veranda for a smoke. Birger had thought of telling Åke something about Vidart and Torsten Brandberg, but Vidart's wife came while they were there. They had phoned for her, of course, and she had her hair in big curlers and was sobbing as she ran. When Ivar had come with his Mercedes and they had helped Vidart lie on the lowered seat, she called out:

"But what shall I do about the milk? And the car?"

Assar Westlund said he would take the milk back for her with his tractor.

"Best to leave the Duett there for the time being," he added. "But I'll have a word with Torsten."

Then the taxi left and Birger and Åke went in to the boy lying on the dark-red sofa in the parlor. Elna had pulled down the blinds, and the bluish light made his face look even whiter. He was no more than sixteen and had coarse black hair and narrow brown eyes. When he got up, he turned out to be tall and gangling. Otherwise he looked more like Gudrun than like Torsten. They shook hands, and once they had sat down, the boy glanced at the bucket Elna had put in. He had vomited a little into it and now he shoved it behind the sofa, looking both frightened and embarrassed.

"How are you feeling?"

He made a movement but didn't reply.

"Vidart's gone to the hospital," said Birger. "But he's in no danger. He can stand."

The brown eyes widened. Had the boy thought Vidart was dead?

"This is Åke Vemdal. Do you know who he is?"

The boy shook his head.

"I'm the new police chief in Byvången," said Åke.

"Who . . . who reported it?" said Johan.

"No one. We were here in the Westlunds' kitchen when you came. We were going fishing."

"What happened?" said Åke.

"I don't know."

He had his arms propped on his thighs, his head forward, so they couldn't meet those brown eyes.

"But you ran for help?"

"Yes."

"Did you see him being knocked down?"

He shook his head.

"But how did you know he was lying there?"

"I saw when he came."

"And Torsten went after him?"

The boy didn't reply, but looked around for the bucket, swallowing several times as if wanting to show them he was nauseated. It was certainly hot in the room, but Birger wondered whether he was really feeling sick. Maybe he was acting to avoid answering. Åke waited a moment, then spoke again.

"Did you see your father going after him?"

"I don't know. I didn't think about it."

"Did you see him? Had he any tool in his hand?"

Johan said nothing.

"We found one," said Åke. "A kind of sharp stick. Broken off."

The boy made an almost catlike movement with his long body and the next moment was lying curled up on the sofa with his back to them.

"Wait," said Birger quietly. "Let's go out into the kitchen, and I'll tell you what's behind all this."

"Do you know?"

"Everyone knows."

But they hadn't time. Loud voices came from the kitchen, then the door opened and Gudrun was standing on the threshold with the light from the kitchen behind her so that her face looked almost black.

"What are you doing?"

She went over to Johan and touched him.

"He's got nothing to say about this," she said. "He just went to get help for Vidart."

"We have to ask him what happened."

"To hell with that," said Gudrun. "Nothing's happened that he's seen."

She was small. It looked odd as she pulled the tall youth off the sofa and hustled him out with her. He walked with his head down. Åke followed.

"You must know there'll be an investigation into this."

"You carry on and investigate. But Johan's not testifying against his father."

She shoved the boy out, slamming the kitchen door behind her. Åke took a step as if to stop them, but Birger said:

"Leave them. You can't question him now, anyhow."

They heard Gudrun's car starting up and driving away. Elna and Assar were sitting beside each other on the sofa, looking like guests in their own kitchen.

"Let's go outside," said Birger.

It wasn't all that easy to tell Åke, who knew nothing, about Torsten Brandberg and Vidart. Åke had not even been to Blackwater until then, but he belonged to the district. He had come to take up the post a month or two earlier. They had been out together once, a case of suicide up toward the border. Åke had had no one to send and no car available. An alcoholic living with his parents had gone up into the attic and killed himself with a shotgun. As they were going back in the car a few hours later, Birger thought he heard a bird screeching. He hadn't realized until later that it had been the mother.

Birger had looked in on them earlier in the summer when he had been out on a call nearby. The mother had been admitted to the Frösö clinic at the time, and he had found the father sitting in the kitchen. He had been living on coffee and cigarettes for some time, and he collapsed when Birger came. That was the first time he had wept since the son's death. Birger had gone up to the attic to see if they had cleaned up. But the stains were still there, and dried brain matter and marks from the shot could be seen on the ceiling, a shattered lightbulb still hanging from the wire. He cleaned up as best he could with a scrubbing brush and scraper, then arranged for a woman to go in to cook for the father, now on his own.

Åke and he had gotten to know each other on that first visit and the long car ride back.

"I know Johan," said Birger. "He's at senior high in Byvången in the same class as my boy. He's bright. But his mother Gudrun is the only one who thinks he should go on. The other boys are sons of Torsten and his first wife, Mimmi. She died of a cerebral hemorrhage giving birth to Väine. Then Gudrun came and helped him with the boys and the household. She's one of a large Sami family. But on the poor side. She worked for Torsten, then became pregnant and Johan was born. That was hardly a year after Mimmi's death. So Väine and Johan are practically contemporaries."

"Are they all Sami?"

"No. Only Gudrun. And Torsten has never been a friend of the Sami. Lapps shouldn't live in the village, he says. That's his opinion, and he is not alone in that. Torsten's been a damned great fighter in his day. When he was younger and got drunk, he went and asked people: 'Anyone here want beating up?' He could go all the way to Byvången to knock a man down. I don't think things have ever been good between Johan and the half brothers, not really any good between him and his father, either. But you saw Gudrun. They daren't touch a hair on the boy's head when she's looking. So you see Johan may have trouble if they start thinking he's told on Torsten."

"That can be explained, can't it? He didn't know we were here."

"I'm not sure they'd listen," said Birger.

When they got into the hall, she indicated with a movement of her head that he should go straight up to his room. A quarter of an hour later, she brought him bread and cheese and a glass of milk. Johan was sitting on the bed and hadn't even dared go to the lavatory, he was so afraid Torsten might hear him. But she told him they hadn't come back home yet. Then he went to the toilet on the landing and peed for what seemed to him a quarter of an hour.

Gudrun was at the desk, staring out at the enclosure, when he came back. She was looking unhappy, nibbling bits of skin off her lips. He had always felt uneasy when she was unhappy, because it was usually his fault. He irritated Torsten and annoyed the brothers.

"I didn't know the police were there," he said.

"You've done nothing wrong," she said, but it sounded mechanical to him. He wondered what she was thinking. It struck him that she knew everything about him, almost, anyhow, but he knew nothing about her. She was his mother and everything she did down there in the kitchen and out on the farm was predictable. Nearly everything she said, too. But he didn't know any of the important things. Nothing about the time she was pregnant. Nothing about her and the man on the scooter. Or why it was Torsten she had married.

"If he's charged with assault, they'll take his guns off him, won't they?"

"We don't know if he's been charged yet."

"I only meant if he should be. Then he won't be able to lead the shoot?"

"Stop it now," said Gudrun. She seemed to think he wanted Torsten to lose his license. Then he started telling her what he had really seen from the window, but she didn't want to hear it.

"Stay here for a while," she said. "I'll talk to Torsten later."

She looked tired as she got up. She was all dressed up in a white cotton cardigan over her flowery dress, and she had high-heeled sandals on. But her face was looking ordinary again. She had nibbled off all the lipstick as she sat there on his bed.

A little later he heard her in the kitchen, a cupboard door slamming and the clatter of china. She was emptying the plate rack, ordinary sounds, and they calmed him.

At about half past six, the cars came back. The brothers' voices were loud and raucous. They had clearly taken quite a lot on board. Torsten was laughing at something Väine had said. Gudrun had started frying fish and the smell wafted up to John, but they ate their delayed evening meal without her calling up to him. He was shut in his room as if he had done something criminal.

He was the only one of the brothers never to have been thrashed by Torsten, and it was Gudrun who protected him. But although he had never been thrashed, he was the one most afraid of it, and they knew it. Her protection made him look foolish.

He got up and went down. But halfway down the stairs, his fear returned, not of them hitting him, but of Torsten's half-closed, heavy eyes, the way he waited for an opportunity when drunk. Of the swift movements of the brothers, intended to frighten him. He decided to go fishing.

On these early summer nights, he fished at Dogmere, just by the path up to the outfield buildings. There he could see if anyone went up to the peregrine falcon's nest by the river Lobber. He didn't think the attacks would come from the main road. Henry Strömgren saw every single car up there. Two chicks had disappeared the previous summer.

His jacket was hanging in the hall and his rod and boots were on the porch. He was careful not to clatter with the rod, but when he got outside and started up the moped, he revved up loudly so they wouldn't think he was running away from them. He knew they were watching him from the kitchen window.

He fetched bait up at Alda's, as he usually left the moped there and then walked up to Dogmere. The old woman was in a long-term ward permanently now and the grass was already growing in great clumps around the steps. He usually dug for bait behind her woodshed.

He found a can on the garbage heap just inside the forest, and an old potato digger in the woodshed. He hadn't been digging long before he heard a car. It skidded on the grass as it took the corner. The doors slammed almost the moment the car stopped. He listened for voices and footsteps.

The brothers had surrounded him before he had time to decide whether to run or not. He stood with the digger in his hand and they were all around him, apparently in a playful mood. They shifted their feet like soccer players waiting for kickoff. As they came closer, he could smell aftershave and beer.

They must have gotten up in the middle of the meal to come after him. Gudrun had not been able to stop them. She was sure to have tried.

He realized something quite new was beginning now. It had begun the moment he left the house, taking the moped, and also when he revved up to show them he didn't care if they did see him.

He put the digger down on the brown soil full of nettle roots and bits of glass. He picked up his rod and the can of worms and started up the path to the hut. They followed, shoving him from all sides and asking what he was scared of. He started half running, although he wished he hadn't. Väine caught up with him and tripped him up. Pekka grabbed his arm and hauled him back onto his feet.

"Stand up, for Christ's sake."

"What do you want?"

Björne drove his fist into his stomach, though not with full force. Johan doubled up as if bowing and they all laughed. Through his nausea, he caught the scent of the forest, but there was no way out in that direction. They were all around him. Per-Ola and Pekka had lit cigarettes. Björne shook his head when they offered him one and put a dose of snuff under his upper lip, which now bulged and looked swollen. He had his mouth open as usual, and was staring at Johan, but he didn't appear to be going to hit him again.

"What are you scared of?" Pekka asked. "Aren't you going to call the police?"

"What the hell's the matter with you? Afraid of pissing in your pants?" said Väine, and the others laughed. Väine would be regarded as a man after this. He struck out, but playfully and not at Johan's face. They left him alone, perhaps because of their clothes, for they had all changed into light jackets and trousers.

Hoping to show the others what he could do, Väine grew more and more annoyed when Johan ducked without defending himself. He started making karate blows with stiff hands, checking them just in front of Johan's face.

Björne and Pekka had moved away from the others for a moment. Something rattled farther up in the forest. When they came back, Pekka said to Väine:

"Get the tow rope."

They're going to tie me up, thought Johan. They'll tie me to a tree. Then they'll go. That's all. They daren't do anything else because of Gudrun. Or the police.

Pekka didn't tie him up once he had the tow rope, but just put it around Johan's body under his arms and pulled. It felt like a noose. Then they pushed him ahead of them. They made a detour off the path, and in among the trees he saw a decayed wooden lid leaning against a stone. They kicked him ahead to the edge of a round stone-walled hole. Then he screamed.

As they let him down through the opening he resisted as best he could, kicking out, biting one of them in the arm, and received a blow on the back of his neck. Falling, he felt a violent pain as the rope tightened around his body from its own weight.

He was hanging, the rope cutting deeply under his arms from the weight of his body and legs. He could feel no water. Above, he could hear their voices, but not what they were shouting. Then he fell.

When he came to again, he was at the bottom of a well. It had dried up, he realized, and perhaps never been used in Alda's time. He was half sitting in muddy clay with the rope around his body. At first he thought he had broken something, but when he cautiously moved his limbs he noticed it hurt only where the rope cut in. He had a thick sweatshirt on, and thanks to that, the rope had not cut in too deeply, but he could get at neither the knot nor the end of the rope. They must be on his back. He tried to sit down properly in the narrow space, then looked up. The well opening was almost white in the light of the summer evening. No face was visible up there, and he couldn't hear anything.

He was sitting in loose mud and water, stones underneath. He wriggled to get away from one hurting him, then began fumbling for his knife to cut the rope. Once he had gotten hold of it and cut through the nylon rope, the pressure lifted and he struggled into an upright position. Nothing was broken. It was difficult to know how deep the well was. The circle of light up there had now turned blue and he could also see a little more of the well wall. The water came just over the foot of his boot.

At least they hadn't put the lid back on. They would soon be back to let a rope down. Fairly soon. They wouldn't want anyone else to hear his calls for help.

But he was not going to call out. They were probably sitting in the car waiting for him to begin shouting for help. They had always thought him a coward. He just used to walk away when they started picking a fight, hating to look on when people got knocked down. But down there at the bottom of the well he felt he had something in him they knew nothing about. He would not shout. They would not have that pleasure. The bastards.

He tired of standing and tried leaning in various ways with his backside and lower arms against the well wall to lighten the pressure. His legs and back ached and prickled. He wouldn't be able to stay standing in the long run.

How long were they going to leave him here? An hour? Or right into the night? The worst would be if they drove back to the village and got so drunk they forgot him—he wouldn't be brought up until long into Midsummer Day. Gudrun would look for him if he didn't come home. She would spot the moped if she drove around in the car. So presumably it was no use starting to shout until early morning. But he was not going to do that. This time Gudrun was not going to take him home. He was finished with that.

She took Mia by the hand and walked down toward the shore. There was a house by the water, an unpainted old wooden house eaten away by rain and age. A confusion of growth surrounded it: clumps of wild chervil flowering together with columbines in beds where the soil had sunk away and dried to a mouse color. Currant bushes had grown into each other and put down a tangle of shoots that had rooted. On the slope toward the lake, raspberry canes had grown together into an impenetrable tangle. The grass came up to Mia's waist and there were great clumps of nettles by the steps. She had no desire to go any farther into this green mass, humming with insects, the smell of spices and venom rising from it.

Annie lifted Mia up on the concrete lid of a well and left her there while she went down to the water to fill a flask. But Mia refused to drink lake water, shook her head, and clamped her mouth tight shut. The water was perfectly clear, like glass right down to the brown bed of immobile stones. But she wouldn't drink.

The store was painted white and had the pennants of the two countries above the door. It wasn't far from the house with the nettles. The patch of ground where the gas pumps stood ended at the remains of a fence that had rotted away, probably once belonging to a cottage now gone. A long, narrow wooden building, painted green, a parish hall or a community center, had a collapsed timbered barn next to it, its shingle roof fallen in. The house on the other side was clearly occupied, with puckered nylon curtains in all the ground floor windows. But the attic window had a big hole with a rag stuffed into it, a sheet of hardboard replacing the other pane.

The village was very quiet now that the rush at the arrival of the mail bus was over. Annie found it hard to make it all out, the decay and desolation jarring against the new buildings and improvements. Why couldn't they be bothered to pull down the collapsed and decayed buildings? Didn't they see them any longer?

Perhaps the villagers saw only what looked like urban developments. They saw modernity where she saw decay and neglect, and where Dan saw simplicity. For neither in his letters nor in his brief telephone calls, presumably made from the phone booth by the store, had he described the village as she now saw it in the clear evening light.

The greenery was obscene. It made her think of bushy pubic hair (seen in bathhouses, before turning away). She hadn't expected this, but rather some kind of barrenness. But all the preconceptions she had vividly held during the weeks of expectation and anxiety had now evaporated.

They went over to their suitcases and sat down to wait. On the other side of the road, grassy slopes were gleaming in the sun, the colors of the meadow flowers brighter than she had ever seen before. Opposite the store was a modern house, boxlike, painted green and dark brown. As the house was on a steep slope, the basement was high. In it was a small fishing-tackle shop with the name Fiskebua in pokerwork on a board outside and a Swedish flag hanging from a flagpole protruding from the wall. They could just see a man inside, so Annie took Mia's hand and crossed the road.

The door was locked, but he opened up when she knocked. He had no soft drinks for sale, but he said Mia was welcome to some homemade juice. He refused to let Annie pay for the juice and buns he fetched from the kitchen upstairs, but she had to satisfy his curiosity.

He had graying hair brushed forward, long at the back and around his ears, and his trousers were flared. She thought he looked idiotic, almost indecent in those tightly cut trousers, but the fashion had penetrated all the way up there, and she hadn't expected that, either. He looked exhausted, with slack, baggy creases under his eyes, his nose big, the pores on it enlarged, his eyelids heavy. But he seemed anything but tired.

She told him as little as possible—that they were to be picked up and that they were on their way up to Nilsbodarna. He asked if she meant Nirsbuan. What was she going to do there?

"We're going to live there," said Mia abruptly. Up to then she had drunk her juice and eaten the buns without a sound. He laughed. Annie never forgot that laugh.

"Are you one of the Starhill people?" he said suddenly.

"We come from Stockholm," she replied. But his guess wasn't far wrong. It was thanks to the commune at Starhill that Dan had found Nilsbodarna.

"Oh, so you're taking Nirsbuan from the Brandbergs. That won't be easy, I guess," he said, grinning. She didn't understand what he meant. She didn't like him, and now she didn't want to talk about their circumstances anymore.

They heard a car and Mia rushed over to the window, but it wasn't Dan. Four men got out of a large Volvo that had driven up by the house, the tires scattering gravel. They were really three young men and a boy who was driving. He looked scarcely eighteen. A smell of aftershave and liquor wafted from them as they entered the shop. One of them was dressed in white and had muddy marks on his trousers, as if someone had kicked him. The trousers were tight, the material thin. Annie could see his genitals quite clearly outlined against his thigh and had to avert her eyes when he looked at her. They were dressed for the Midsummer events; once again she saw that fashion was being followed here, and she felt childish with all her preconceived ideas.

They filled the little shop with their large bodies and loud voices, but fell silent when they saw her, as if no longer aware of what they had come for. They weren't interested in fishing tackle, nor in the rack of chocolates and evening papers.

"Yes, well, then," said the man behind the counter, looking straight at Annie. She realized he didn't want them in there any longer and that made her feel ill at ease. She took Mia's hand and went out. The moment she had closed the door she heard the voices raised again.

Mia wanted to pee and they went down among the currant bushes. There was still no sign of Dan, and it wasn't as quiet as before. A bus had driven up in front of the community center and musical instruments and large amplifiers were being unloaded from it.

She had considered sitting with Mia on the porch steps of the abandoned house to wait, but insects kept emerging out of the grass, almost invisible creatures that stung like sparks from a fire. Mia started crying. Annie picked her up and ran off into the tall grass, every step she took raking up a cloud of the stinging insects. Up near the store it was relatively free of them. They seemed to stick to grass and foliage.

Buttercups and red campion glowed in the evening sun on the grassy slopes. The lake was still just as calm, but the color had deepened. From the community center came the thump of an electric bass and keyboard riffs hugely amplified through the loudspeakers. The four men came out of the little shop, got into the car, and started drinking beer from bottles, leaving the car doors open and their legs outside. The youngest stayed on the steps of the shop and belched ostentatiously after emptying his bottle, which he threw down on the gravel. The others laughed. The shopkeeper came out and said something in a low voice, then took the bottle back in with him, after a glance at Annie on the other side of the road. She presumed he had no proper license, so the purchase had been illegal.

More cars came skidding onto the gravel at the roadside, nearly all of them full of men, young men. She couldn't make out what they were shouting at each other, but could hear some were Norwegians. Most of them appeared to be good-naturedly drunk.

Cars were also drawing up at the community center and the instruments were rasping and thumping inside as they sound checked. Outside the little shop, a couple of Norwegians were teasing the young driver of the Volvo. He was now quite drunk, stumbling and swaying as he headed back to the car, singing in a slurred voice a short song she found it hard to catch. Anyhow, it caused some amusement and so he kept singing it again, over and over as he strode around in his tight trousers. In the end she could make out the words:

> "What the fuck
> Dad's cock's in front
> Just as well
> Mum's got a cunt."

He pirouetted clumsily like a bear and almost fell over in front of one of the cars containing an older man in a cap on which it said RÖBÄCK'S GA-RAGE.

"Bloody hell, Väine, you don't have to tell Evert about your dad and your mother," shouted the shopkeeper, causing loud and long laughter from the other cars. There was an abrupt silence when one of the men got out of the Volvo, the fattest of them, a large man with curly brown hair that looked sweaty under his peaked cap. He wasn't dressed like the others, but in jeans and a thick blue sweatshirt. Strange, wearing that in the middle of summer, she thought. She noticed a sheath knife dangling below the bottom at the back.

He strode up to the steps. It was just like watching a film. He raised his hand and she saw they were to witness a show of strength. The hand was rigid, the little finger and the outer edge turned toward the flag hanging out from the wall by the door. He struck out with the rigid hand and the flagpole snapped with a crack. The shopkeeper vanished inside and closed the door. The man who had snapped the flagpole strolled back to the Volvo and crawled into the back. Another man pulled in the youth who had sung the song, started the car, and drove down toward the community center. The other cars followed.

The music had started up properly now. More cars kept appearing. But Dan did not come.

It was not easy to get hold of Torsten Brandberg and his four older sons. Åke Vemdal and Birger Torbjörnsson gave up after an hour's random driving around and asking, but they found them when they returned to the campsite out at Tangen. All five were drinking beer in Roland Fjellström's office. Nor was questioning them particularly profitable. Torsten did not deny hitting Vidart, but said it was in self-defense. As far as the rake handle was concerned, he said he had held it out to protect himself.

"He was unconscious for over twenty minutes," said Åke. "At least."

"And you believe that? Anyway, he was on his feet when I left."

The sons grinned. Torsten looked calm, almost amused as he sat there, his hand clasped around a beer can. The boys standing around him were muscular, and not one of them had yet acquired the stigmata of the forestry worker. Väine, the seventeen-year-old, appeared to be drunk, breathing heavily, his mouth open. He was as beefy as the others. Birger felt fat and flabby before all this looming muscularity.

Åke again asked about the rake handle, but was given the same answer. Torsten didn't budge. In the end that great hand around the can looked rather forced. He was still sitting in the same position when they left and did not reply when they said good-bye.

By then they were both hungry, so they went to the cabin before leaving. They had counted on fish for the evening and hadn't purchased much more than beer and bread. But Birger had bought a sausage ring in case the fishing was bad.

"Isn't there a bar or a hotel here?" said Åke.

"No, not here."

They ate slices of sausage on crispbread. Birger thought it was good. That was what he ate more and more frequently whenever Barbro was away, though just as frequently he thought he really ought to start cooking properly. He wondered what Åke did. He knew he lived alone, though not whether he was divorced or a widower, or simply a bachelor.

Birger felt just like some old bachelor as they got into the car and drove up to the Blackreed River. People were heading for the community center. The music thumped. They watched girls in summer clothes hurrying down the hill, perceiving them as moist fragrance despite the thick glass of the windshield. He wondered what Barbro was doing. She was out organizing an information meeting on the uranium prospecting on Bear Mountain, and he didn't think she would want to join in the Midsummer celebrations. Last year she hadn't even wanted to celebrate Christmas.

There were cars outside Lill-Ola's fishing-tackle booth, and when Åke saw the shop was open, he said he wanted to get some more flies. But Birger managed to steer him away. Åke would discover that the men in the cars were drunk and at worst he would realize that Lill-Ola Lennartsson sold other things as well as fishing flies and licenses. And Åke would not be able to ignore drunk driving. At this rate, they would get no fishing at all.

A young woman was sitting outside Aronsson's, a small girl beside her. Birger thought they looked old-fashioned, perhaps because the little girl had braids and the woman was wearing a long blue skirt. They were sitting on suitcases just below the loading stand and appeared to be waiting for someone. But the woman seemed resigned. For a moment he thought of asking her where she was going and whether anyone was coming to fetch her. But he had no desire to be officious.

He tried shading his watch so that he could see the hands, but the light from above was too bright and at the same time too poor at the bottom of the well to make out the numbers. He had no real idea how long he had been down the well. The sharp stones and the smell of mud, the rough shale and the circle of light above dazzling him—it was a shaft right down into timelessness, a vacuum for him and him alone. He found he had to sit down in the mud. The seat of his jeans was already wet, so maybe that didn't matter much, but he was cold. After he had gotten down, had shoved aside a few stones, and was sitting with his forehead against his knees, he thought he felt a movement just by him.

He sat dead still. This was silly. There couldn't be anything in the well. No rats. He considered hallucinations—was he so weak he was already having them?

He could feel nothing with his foot through his stiff boot, so he had to grope with his hand among the stones. He distinctly felt something quiver against his palm, something cold and smooth. Then a strong movement like an arm striking out. He screamed.

He stood up, stamping and kicking, yelling insanely up at the circle of light.

"Help! Help! Get me out!"

Finally he was just screaming, no words. But the hole up there stayed light, like a blue disc. Nothing moved against it.

His voice cracked. He was standing with his back pressed to the sharp, knobbly wall of the well. There was something down by his feet. Larger than a snake. He felt cold again. He had forgotten it when he was yelling.

Whatever he did, nothing changed. The well wall and the blue lid in the sky were the same. And that powerful thing hitting out down by his feet.

He tried shouting again, but that only hurt his throat. He had damaged something by screaming. For a moment it seemed to him as if the bottom of the well was being raised and he was being pressed up against the hard blue-white disc.

He got his knife free again, a small sheath knife, rather blunt. He used it only to gut fish. And how could he slash with it in the dark?

He started stamping and kicking among the stones on the bottom, stirring up a smell of mold from the water. But no movement. He started stamping systematically around and felt the same movement by the wall, though more evasive this time. Then he kicked out so water flew and he stubbed his toes on the stones, but he ignored the pain. He was going to go on kicking until it was still. Kick it to death. Whatever it was. I'm bigger, anyhow, he thought.

Something—was it a smell?—made him think of fish. And then there was the memory of a feeling like a snake against his hand.

Eel.

There's an eel in the well.

He knew that in the old days they used to let eels into wells to keep them clean of worms and insects. He wanted to piss and he was very tired. If I piss in the water, I can't drink it, he thought. I must have a drink first. What if I'm to be here a long time? Maybe it's not harmful to drink piss. It'd be diluted. Eels can live for a hundred years. Maybe it's white. I can't stand here much longer. Then I'll have to sit with the eel. That doesn't matter. But the water, the cold. How long has this well been dry or almost dry? How the hell can an eel live in so little water year after year?

He had begun shaking with cold, so he kept beating his arms around his chest, but he couldn't stop his body shuddering. He tried to get warm by stamping, though more cautiously this time. There was no need to stamp on the eel. Foul, pissing in the water, too, but he had to in the end, his bladder bursting. Then he sat down to rest. He fumbled among the stones and felt the eel. It wriggled away but couldn't get far. Fucking tough on the eel! And how often had it been hit by a stone?

Pekka and Björne must have thrown stones to check how much water was down there. He didn't think they'd wanted to drown him. Or dared.

The chill of the water made him get up again. He could hardly see the well wall in the darkness, but he could feel moss in the cracks. It must be a long time since there had been any water down there.

The wall was made of shale, of course, like all the old stonework in the area. The slabs of shale had been displaced by the frost. It must be a crooked old well shaft.

He tried standing absolutely still, listening for cars or voices, but he could hear nothing, not even birds. Up there where time and light existed, it was Midsummer Eve. People had had their meal. The Norwegians had started coming. Cars were skidding in toward the community center. There would be much talk about Torsten and Vidart and that Torsten's own lad had gone and reported him. Or whatever they made of it.

The music had begun thumping away and they were dancing inside— or was it already over? He had lost all sense of time. Gudrun had washed up, of course, and put her white cardigan on over her dress. Had they gone down to the center? Torsten wouldn't care a fuck about the talk.

Did Gudrun know that when he was young, Torsten had knocked down men he didn't even know? And that with two others he had taken the Enoksson boy out and beaten him up because he'd left their lumber team and gone to work for Henningsson? That they'd done that at least twice?

Had she known that when she married him? Was there something deep down in sweet little Gudrun, with her courses in English and natural dyes, that liked all that? In the dark of the night? He felt sick. Maybe it wasn't right to think in that way. But all the same, it was her fault he was down a well.

The light didn't reach down there. It was up above. He could see it. But it had no effect down there. The well shaft was too deep. Someone had dug and dug, confidently hopeful at first because the divining rod had turned down just there, then in sheer rage. Eventually, he must have dug on from sheer pigheadedness, whoever it was. Not Alda's husband. It must have been whoever had cleared the forest and built the cottage. He would have returned from the forest for a meal, saying nothing, taken his cap, and gone out again. And if he had sons, they had to haul up the rubble. When at last he reached water, he had proved that he couldn't have been wrong. Then the wall was built with shale, thoroughly, first-class work.

But the water had retreated.

Johan sat down with the eel. He couldn't do that for long because he soon froze, but he found it almost as cold when he stood up. The seat of his trousers was soaking wet. He dozed off with his head against the sharp slabs of shale, a kind of sleep, although he knew all the time where he was, and that he had to rest and keep moving alternately until they came to get him out.

He woke thinking someone was touching his hand, but the hand and arm had gone numb. He was sitting heavily on one side with his arm underneath him and could no longer feel the cold. His body was stiff and chilled through and through. When he tried to ease himself up, his legs refused to obey.

Then he remembered the eel and was more frightened than he had been before. Not of the eel, but of what might happen. His thoughts had touched on that occasionally. That anything could happen. And that things didn't always go well. They could go badly. It'll be too late.

The worst thing could happen. The kind no one can think to a conclusion.

Old man Annersa had lain dead in his cottage for five weeks, his horse dying of thirst in the stable.

The goldeneye with a hook through its beak, and its soaking wet, semi-rotten feathers.

The Enoksson boy sawing straight through his thigh with a chainsaw. How? No one knew. Things just went badly.

I must get up. The eel woke me.

He started moving his toes and fingers, and slowly feeling came back even in his calves and lower arms. In the end, he heaved himself up with his back to the wall, feeling like a collapsed hay-drying rack that had to be raised. He hooked his fingers in the protruding shale slabs and hoisted himself into an upright position, at last succeeding and stamping again to get warm. Then it struck him, like an electric shock.

Shale protruded from the wall, probably all the way up. The well had settled. Get the toe of his boot in far enough for support. Dig out the moss farther up with the knife if he couldn't find a bit of shale far enough out. Climb.

Bloody hell! Heave himself up step by step. Dig out. Prop his backside against the wall and hoist himself on up.

He started at once and soon found a foothold for his boot, then another, which was not so good but enough if he pressed his back hard against the wall. He was no longer standing in water.

Suddenly he remembered the eel. He knew it was a kind of madness, recklessness anyhow, but he did it all the same. He climbed down again and squatted down to rummage around in the water and muddy leaves until he got hold of the strong, slippery body skulking among the stones.

It was a bloody big eel! It twisted and turned in his grip. He fumbled for his knife, but then thought perhaps the eel was a hundred years old. Over fifty anyway. For Alda's husband had probably not been the well digger.

If only he had something to put it in. He tore off his sweatshirt and shirt, quickly putting the sweatshirt back on, for it really was cold. Then he put the shirt down in the water and, once he got a hold on the eel again, he wrapped the material around it, knotting the sleeves hard into a firm package while it trembled and thrashed around inside. He fumbled for his belt and tied the shirt package beside his knife. The wriggling wet bundle was heavier than he had thought.

He started climbing again. He found three footholds before it became really difficult. There were no shale slabs protruding far enough to get a foothold. It would be better if he were barefoot, but he hesitated to sacrifice his boots. Barefoot, he would have to get back home along the verges. And he didn't want to go home. He had no intention of returning to his brothers' scornful grins or Gudrun smuggling glasses of milk and sandwiches up to his room.

Then he remembered the tow rope they had tied him up with. He climbed down again, and as he stood rooting around in the water for it, his excitement faded. Everything seemed to be happening slowly, like in a dream. He would never be ready. Something else always got in the way.

But now he had his boots tied firmly around his waist and he made the two steps up on the three first footholds. They were sharp but he went on, resting on his haunches, leaning forward and clinging to the wall in front of him, his muscles trembling, each new foothold hurting his toes. But he pressed them in. He couldn't use the knife, as he didn't dare let go anywhere. Sometimes he had his whole weight on one elbow or one knee.

He hauled himself on up until he felt the light on his face and his arms could almost reach the edge of the well. He hoisted himself up the last bit with his backside. His sweatshirt got caught and his back scraped against the sharp shale, but he ignored the pain and pressed on. The eel thrashed wildly in its shirt bundle, as if making one last effort to get back into its prison. As he tumbled over the edge of the well, the bundle got in the way. I'm squashing the eel, he thought. But he couldn't help it. He gave one last heave, kicked out as hard as he could against the wall, then hauled himself up the last bit and was over the edge, lying in the grass, the eel wriggling beneath him.

He was not going to stay lying there. They're not bloody going to find me here, he thought. The sky was blindingly bright, but Alda's cottage and the forest behind it were in the shade from the ridge. He trotted silently on his bare feet down to the woodshed and went in behind it, untied his boots, and put them on. It was twenty to twelve. I left home at seven, he thought. They got me ten minutes later, at the most fifteen. Then they fooled around a bit, perhaps for ten minutes. I was down in the well before half past seven. I've been down there for over four hours.

All his joy had gone and now he was simply cold. He remembered the intoxication of his recklessness when he had realized he could climb. But that hadn't been a very remarkable idea. In fact, it was strange that he hadn't thought of it at once.

Before leaving his hiding place, he listened carefully for any sound of car engines. He hurried up the path. Where to, he didn't really know. Away from the village, anyhow.

The insects were tiny, smaller than a pinhead and invisible until there was a cloud of them. They stirred them up as they walked through the tall grass, but as soon as they came to the open space in front of the store, the insects were swept away by the current of air from the lake. There was no real wind and the evening was warm. An hour or two later, insects sought them out up there as well, finding their cheeks and necks and crawling into the corners of their eyes, their stings like sparks. Mia kept crying and thrashing around. It was hard to bear. They had to run across to the little shop and bang on the door, but the shopkeeper and his wife were now watching television upstairs, and it was some time before they heard.

He wasn't surprised to see them again. He or his wife must have peered around the curtains. He was humorous about the insects and implied that you had to be born there to cope. They were called stingers, he said. She said she doubted anyone could cope with them. At that he grew rather heated and said people who worked in the forest couldn't go home just because of the stingers. You just had to get used to them.

She asked whether they could sit in the shop and wait, though she would prefer to find a place where they could get something to eat.

"There isn't anywhere. Not in this village."

He sounded almost triumphant. His wife was in the living room, only half her attention on the television screen. They had been sitting together on a green velvet sofa, coffee and a large assortment of small pastries and cookies on a tabletop made of flower-decorated tiles. They were drinking something brown in wide glasses. Cacao liqueur?

"Wouldn't you prefer to rent a room instead?"

"Roland said the campsite was full," his wife called. There was malicious pleasure in her voice.

"There are private cabins, but they're probably all taken until after Midsummer," said her husband in confirmation.

Then it occurred to Annie that perhaps Dan had thought Midsummer Eve was not until the next day. On the Saturday. For it was, really. The old Midsummer Eve.

"My boyfriend's probably up there at Nilsbodarna," she said. "There's been a misunderstanding. Do you know anyone who could take us there by car?"

"There's no road."

"I know. But there is up to where the path begins. I have a map with me. It's not far to walk after that."

Husband and wife looked at each other. Annie could sense their criticism. This was not aversion but something more subtle. They seemed to have agreed on something and now it had been confirmed.

"I need to buy some food for my daughter," she said, though she hated saying it. From the living room, the wife said nothing. She was staring at the screen.

"That's all right," said the man. "Though we want to watch the feature film first. Perhaps you'd like to watch it as well."

So Annie had to sit down in an armchair by the coffee table. Mia clambered up on her knee and soon lost interest in the film. Instead, she looked around this room full of objects that must have seemed strange to her. Lots of animals, embroidered, carved, or made of glass or pottery. As the woman fetched a cup and poured out coffee, she tried not to take her eyes off the screen, where a familiar actor was moving around in a cassock. Mia started systematically eating the pastry, cream puffs, and sugared buns in small pleated paper cups. Annie sat crookedly in the armchair to be able to overlook the area in front of the shop. A car went by now and again, but none stopped. Mia fell sleep after a while, curled up on her lap, her long legs hanging outside and her thumb in her mouth. Annie hadn't seen her take to her thumb for a long time.

Once the bizarre drama on the screen was over, they went out into the kitchen and the woman made something she called bilberry gruel for Mia.

She took the bilberries out of the freezer and boiled them up in water, then whipped some flour into them. Of course, Mia wouldn't touch it. It looked like purple glue. But she ate some bread and salami and drank some milk.

Annie looked into a room alongside the kitchen. It was full of pictures. Above the bed was one made of short-pile plush, brightly dyed in shades of pink, yellow, and brown. It depicted a naked girl. She had tight, fluffy breasts with budding nipples like large eyeballs gazing at whoever came in. They must look at the wife every time she went in with the dustcloth. For everything was certainly very clean.

They thought Annie ought to stay in the village, but she was beginning to suffocate in the long, narrow kitchen. Besides, something might have happened to Dan. He was all alone up there. But the man whose name was Ola dismissed that.

"What the hell would happen to him there?"

"He might have broken his leg?"

She noticed they thought she was peculiar.

"Living in the Nirsbuan," the woman said, snorting through flabby lips like a horse.

In the end, Annie managed to persuade him to drive them there. They were allowed to leave their belongings in his garage, where they changed into boots. Ola said they had to wear boots, as they would be walking over marshy ground.

"Won't you stay?" was the last thing his wife said, though not saying where. Hands in the sleeves of her cardigan, she watched them leave from the steps. It was growing chilly out, but was still just as light.

Ola had told them to walk on ahead. They wouldn't take the main road that went on into Norway, but a turning off in the middle of the village. He would follow later and pick them up.

Annie felt great relief as they left the village. They walked uphill almost immediately, but they didn't have to go far. Ola came in the car when they were just beyond the last houses.

"Why did we have to walk the first stretch?" she asked him.

He grinned. But she persisted. It wasn't exactly frightening that he wouldn't pick them up until no one could see them. His wife knew he was going to take them. But she was ill at ease.

"Well, no need to tell everyone you're giving Red Guards a lift," he said.

She was so astonished by his words that she couldn't bring herself to ask anything more. It sounded so idiotic. Or old hat. She remembered

Elmer Diktonius's poem about Red Emil, the mother with her hand around the throat of the bastard child. What did he know about the Reds in Finland's civil war? She didn't ask any more questions, but she said:

"I think my boyfriend will come and meet us. He's probably just got delayed."

"Is he your boyfriend, then?" he said mockingly.

"Yes."

"Oh, I thought you didn't have special ones. I thought it was just anyone."

I'll say nothing more, she thought. Whatever happens.

All the way was forest, no buildings at all. They came to a clearing, where he told her to turn and look down toward the lake. You could see the high mountains in Norway from there, and they were black and blue-shaded, the peaks streaked with snow. There was a turquoise patch in the great lake that seemed to have no connection with the color of the sky, the water all around a deeper blue.

The forest took over again and the road rose steeply. Crooked birches with veils of black lichen mixed with the spruces. When the forest opened out she could see a small lake glinting far down below the road, almost black with the reflection of the spruce forest. Only in the middle was there a lighter oval, which again did not reflect the pale blue color of the sky. Instead, it was golden, like old red gold. Ola stopped on the roadside, saying this was Strömgren's, an old homestead really. She didn't know what this meant. Dogs were barking wildly and hurling themselves at a wire-netting fence. She caught a glimpse of someone in a window, but no one came out when they stopped.

A number of gray timbered buildings lay scattered far apart on the hillside. He showed her the path leading from a woodshed up to a small gray house.

"It goes on down toward the stream, and you have to follow it up to the last barn. Then you'll come to the path down from the village. There you must turn left. Otherwise you'll find yourself coming down again."

A red car was parked on the roadside, a Renault 4L. It didn't seem to belong to the farm, because there was an old Opel parked there by the barn wall. So there must be people out there somewhere. That made her feel good. People who had a little red car.

She had a rucksack with her for their sweaters and the sandwiches Ola's wife had wrapped up for her. She had already taken out the map in the car. Ola helped her find the cottages he called Nirsbuan. On the map they were called Nilsbodarna. She realized now they were farm outbuild-ings. The path ran on eastward across the marshes and toward a river called Mountain River on the map, but which Ola called the Lobber. They had to cross that. There was a ford there and it was easy to find because it was just before the river ran into the Klöppen, a large mountain lake. The path went on up to Starhill. But for their part, they had to turn east toward the little black square marked Nirsbuan.

"Thanks for the lift," she said, feeling she had to, but not daring to offer to pay. She was quite simply afraid his answer might be indecent.

"Why doesn't Dan come?" said Mia as soon as they were alone.

"I don't know. He's probably got the wrong day."

She couldn't hear the sound of Ola's car, but he must have gone. Now there were only birds and even they sounded hesitant. Perhaps most of them were asleep, although it was so light. It was past midnight. A bird kept calling on the same monotonous note and there was a strong scent of birch leaves all around them, the leaves not as far out as down in the village. The grass in the pastures was also shorter than on the slopes down below.

The homestead consisted of a modern red building and a barn, a couple of dog runs and a group of small gray cottages on a slope. The light was so uncertain now that the houses farthest down by the lake seemed to be moving. Mia held Annie's hand as they trudged along, listening atten-tively in toward the forest.

"The way he goes on," she said. Annie realized she meant the caper-caillie whistling on its one note. The pasture sloped down to a stream, and in the dip the path divided where there was a small building with a collapsed shingle roof.

"We go left here."

The path curved, then climbed again. After a while they could see the woodshed again and the house from the back. Annie was uncertain. The map told her nothing about the network of paths across the pasture, nor about the numerous small wooden buildings gleaming in the night light. To make sure, they plodded back to the stream, and at the little house they set off in the other direction.

The path seemed larger now, apparently leading somewhere and tak-ing them away from the little gray timber houses. They came into a forest consisting almost entirely of twisted birches hung with lichen. Some had fallen and were slowly rotting; gray fungus grew like tumors out of them.

Ferns protruded from the ground beneath the birches, their hairy brown tips still curled up. The forest with its hanging black lichen and fallen trees was full of bird calls, whistles, clicks, and flutings. But they saw no birds.

They had come up into upland terrain and she thought this odd, for they ought to have been nearing the lake. Now they seemed to be going up to a ridge and the path had joined a much larger and more used one. She suddenly realized they were going in the wrong direction. Ola had said to be careful not to get onto the path from Blackwater. That would take them down into the village again if they went on.

"We must turn back," she said. Mia gave her a look that made her seem adult.

"Or . . . hang on. We've probably come on to the right path from the village. But we're on our way down. We must turn around, not go down the way we came, but take this big path to the lake. Wait, and I'll show you."

She sat Mia down on a tree trunk and started unfolding the map. It was difficult to see the details, for the light was gray under the trees, and she realized she needed a compass. But when they had left Ola's car, she had had no idea the landscape was so full of paths branching off and dissolving into long, wet streaks of marshland, diffuse gray buildings, and human installations where there should have been wilderness, heights and hollows she had not expected. Not even the names matched those on the map.

She had been in a hurry to get away and had felt pressured by Ola's unpleasant, semi-aggressive curiosity. He was nothing like what she had imagined people here would be.

"Shh!" said Mia. She was listening intently. Then Annie could hear a sharp, regular sound and a thumping. It was coming closer, and she realized someone was moving along the path farther up and coming toward them. She put her arm around Mia and almost pushed her down behind the tree trunk. The girl landed on the map, which rustled. Then Annie heard the noise again and realized the sharp sound was someone breathing. Panting. But she couldn't make out whether it was an animal or a human being. She held Mia pressed to the ground, but the tree trunk wasn't high enough to conceal Annie, too.

He never even saw her. He was lumbering up the slope, looking straight ahead, his mouth open, his sharp breathing coming in small labored gasps. He was very dark, with long, dead-straight hair he had tucked behind his ears. His eyes were narrow and black and he was carrying something in his arms. She had no time to identify it, seeing only that it hindered him as he hurried on. Then he was gone.

She had frightened Mia and was now regretting it. But getting her down out of sight had been an instinctive action.

"It was only a boy," she said, trying to talk away the fear she saw in Mia's face.

"Are there animals here?"

"I don't know. We must hurry now. It's not far to Nirsbuan. We might meet Dan. He'll realize he's got the wrong day."

She walked quietly, listening as they went on. The tall, dark-haired boy might turn and come back. Mia noticed she was tense and no longer let go of her hand.

It was colder up there, so they escaped the insects. To start with, the path was clear and easy, leading down into lowland ground that became wetter until it finally ran into a long marsh, white flowers looking like tufts of wool gleaming in the night light. There were thousands of them in a layer of air moving just above the shifting reddish-yellow and green of the sedge. Their boots squelched and it was heavy going. Once or twice the path divided, but Annie had no difficulty distinguishing which was the most used.

The forest had withdrawn to the higher slopes. They got farther and farther away from it as it grew darker. She figured it would soon be growing lighter. Mia said nothing about being tired and Annie didn't dare ask. They had to go on. But the path was much longer and rougher than she had imagined, the marshy soil sucking at their feet and dragging them down.

They came to a little stream and crossed it. They thought of having a drink of water, but the mosquitoes attacked the moment they stopped. After balancing on stones and crossing to the other side, they found the path divided into several indistinct branches. They trudged around for a while to find the right one, getting farther and farther away from the stream. When they went back to find the fording place, it had gone.

Stones and clear water rippling with a chattering sound over the fine sandy bottom. Marsh marigolds, not yet out. Some woolly greenish-gray clumps of willow leaning over the water. Twisted birches festooned with black veils. It looked much the same everywhere. She couldn't tell where they had crossed.

"You know what," she said, trying to sound decisive. "I think it's difficult finding the path up here in the marshland. Suppose we go straight across and try to find the river instead?"

She couldn't see the water, but it must be the river there behind a broad belt of green clumps and occasional birches. To start with, they followed the stream, but walking there with no path was quite another matter. The ground was uneven, and large, hard tussocks of grass grew nearest the stream. She wondered what Mia was thinking as she swiftly glanced around. The tussocks looked like scrubby skulls sticking out of the earth; the birches were twisted and full of knots.

On the last stretch down to the river, they cut across some marshland that swayed under their feet. They could hear the water now, a murmur as talkative as the stream's, but with several voices. According to the map, the river ran down from the mountain, its winding bends ceasing at the Klöppen. As they rounded a little island of birches in the marshland, she caught sight of the lake. A white sheet, a metallic gleam lighter than the sky's.

The same fuzzy gray willows grew along the river as on the banks of the stream, but the undergrowth was higher, apparently impenetrable. The ground was firmer among the birches, but very uneven. She was beginning to feel really tired. With her much-shorter legs, how long would Mia be able to cope with walking up and down dips and uneven ground?

Quite unexpectedly, the undergrowth thinned out, leaving a slope running down to the river. Something blue glinted, and once past the last obscuring bushes, they could see two twisted spruces close to each other and beside them a small tent. A circling bird with its wings outspread suddenly dived, its wings pressed close to its body, and they heard a whistling sound that was perhaps a call. It looked like a projectile as it dived through the air.

The tent was not big enough for more than two people. It had been pitched close to the water, which raced along between smooth, round stones. At first she felt a tremendous relief. Whoever was sleeping inside would have walked there and must know where the path led and where to ford the river. Then she saw Mia's eyes fixed on the bright blue little tent, and they were wide with fear. She ought to tell her everything was all right now. They had found people. They would soon find Nirsbuan and their journey's end. But she said nothing. She took Mia's hand and pulled her slowly behind the undergrowth.

"Let's go," she whispered, though it was totally unnecessary to whisper. Inside that tent no one could have heard anything above the noise of the water.

A silvery light was gleaming around the cottage, which lay high up, and through the screen of wild chervil Johan could see how everything seemed to rise and fall in the uncertain light—like the earth breathing.

He didn't go in by the door. The key to the cottage always used to be kept on a nail under the eaves on the gable facing the lake. But Torsten had said that if the Starhill people occupied it, he would report them to the police for breaking and entering. Then he put an iron crossbar across the door and locked it with a padlock. Nowadays, he kept the key at home.

It was possible to ease out the nails that held the hingeless bedroom window in place. Once he had climbed inside, he threw the eel parcel on the kitchen table and at once started the lengthy process of lighting the stove. It had to be started with methane, so he soaked some old newspaper, stuffed it inside, and lit it. At first there had been a rustle when he pulled out the damper, as if something, perhaps the body of a bird, had fallen down a bit. Then a thick cloud of yellow smoke came billowing out as he set fire to the sticks and firewood. He almost started crying, as if he had lost ten or twelve years of his life as he crouched down in front of the stove, chilled to the bone and shaking. Acrid smoke soon filled the cabin.

He opened the window, pulled out the burning wood, and put it into a basin. Then he started from the beginning again, the methane flared up this time and the roaring sounded different.

Running along the path, he had been thinking about the warmth of the cabin, hot cocoa, and the old quilts he would wrap around himself. He would be in a nest. But once he got the stove going and the smoke had more or less dispersed, there was much to do before he could curl up and think. He wanted to think. He had to. But first he had to fetch a bucket of water from the lake, and to do that he had to climb out through the kitchen window. Then he had to put the bedroom window back into its frame and slot the nails back in. He had to hang his wet jeans over the stove and could find nothing else to wear while they were drying. There were some old jackets, but no trousers. He wrapped a blanket around his legs and stumbled around as if in a long skirt.

There was some cocoa left in the packet, but only a few yellowish lumps remained of the dried milk, sticky with damp. The cocoa he made was watery, but at least hot. The cookies tasted of the cottage.

What a bloody hassle just to get a bit of warmth and something to eat! The sun had risen as he crawled under the quilts. All this time, the eel had lain writhing in its shirt wrapping; Johan forgot all about it until he was well bedded down. He got up, untied the shirt-sleeves, and let the eel down into the bucket of water. For a while its long, glossy body thrashed around and the water swirled from the force of those hidden muscles. Then it lay still in a circle at the bottom of the yellow plastic bucket and Johan was too tired to watch it anymore. Or to think. That had to be postponed. He had to get some sleep.

But he was so damned cold, he couldn't sleep. It was too light, and he could hear the noise of the birds through the ill-fitting window, especially a great tit constantly repeating two shrill notes. Behind his tightly closed eyelids his eyeballs were still smarting from the smoke, and he could relieve that only by opening his eyes.

After a while he got up and put some more dry birchwood full of mouse droppings into the stove. When he thought about Torsten being the one who had chopped the wood, who had hauled the beaver-felled trunk with the scooter, he felt panic-stricken. Torsten had made the warmth for him. Everything he had eaten since he was born, Torsten had provided. He could see him in front of his eyes, bare torso, work trousers sagging. Brown skin with powerful bunched muscles. Black hair growing in a cross on his chest, the foot of the cross rooted firmly in that invisible area in his loins.

He was wide awake now, shuddering with cold under the damp quilts. The sun was shining brightly through the east window, the great tit persisting.

He had wanted to think. But not like this. Thoughts and images were forcing their way into him like the sunlight from outside. He couldn't shut them out or sort them.

He could see Torsten by the washstand, snorting in the water, his powerful body leaning forward, spots and blotches on the skin of his back. He pictured Gudrun's hand on that back, her fingers sliding over the spots. How the hell could he see that so clearly, something he had never seen?

He was trapped. Caught in a web, captured. The food he ate was Torsten's muscular strength. Everything he knew, truly deep down knew, came from the minds of Torsten and Gudrun. They loaded their programs into him. And now his mind was exhausted and heated from the mass of data he wished to shut off but could not stop as it all went on racing through his skull.

He got up and switched on the radio. It was hanging on a nail in the ceiling to escape the barrier made by the hillside behind, but the batteries were low and all he could hear was crackles.

Perhaps he'd feel better after he'd had something to eat. He found a can of baked beans, opened it, and ate them without heating them up. They tasted sweet and revolting. Afterward, a warmth gradually began to spread from within, especially in his loins and thighs. Together with a kind of drowsiness, this feeling often crept up on him in the afternoons, making him horny. He took hold of his member and it felt warm and large. Then he forgot it and could no longer hear the great tit. Sleep fluttered in his mind, using no force, but nonetheless he would have been unable to resist it.

There weren't many midges by the Blackreed River. The evening was warm enough, but maybe they hadn't yet gotten going that year. Nor were the salmon trout rising. In three hours they managed to get twelve, though only five of any size. They saw a beaver swimming, the last glint of sun on its head. It turned with a great slap of its flat tail and vanished almost simultaneously with the sun. Then it grew rapidly colder. The fish stopped rising, so they went back to the campsite. It was past one o'clock when Birger fried the small salmon trout. The cabin filled with gray fumes, but it smelled good. Åke had poured out whiskey and put out crispbread and beer.

After they had eaten, exhaustion hit them and they went to bed without clearing the table. As Åke started snoring in the upper bunk, Birger was suddenly overwhelmed by the poverty of it all; the smell of frying fish in the cramped cabin, the sound of cars driving onto the site, the drunken shouts, and the squeals of girls. But those skidding around out there had at least gotten hold of women. Here were two old bachelors lying scratching themselves under the blankets. Not so much as a flower on the table, although it was Midsummer Eve. I must pull myself together, he thought. Tomorrow I'll cook a proper meal.

The moment he made the promise—it was a promise he would gradually come to keep—he realized he no longer believed she would come back.

The very ground itself frightened her. They kept falling into deep hollows. Mia was crying. They followed paths that tunneled through the thick undergrowth or disappeared into large holes, and in the end she realized that these paths hadn't been made by people. But she found the place where the river ran into the lake and they heard the small rapids between the stones talking and murmuring.

The stony riverbed made it difficult to get across with Mia, and she stumbled several times, water getting into her short boots. Once they were across, the path was distinct even where it was hard going, the undergrowth thick all around it. They stuck to the path almost without raising their eyes from the narrow strip, slippery with pine needles. At last they came to Nirsbuan, on a slope where buttercups were flowering in the thousands in the light of the night.

Small timbered gray buildings. Not until they started walking up toward what must be the actual cottage did she understand why the mat of grass and flowers was so thick and high. No one had mown it. But someone had recently walked through the tall grass.

The cottage was locked on the outside, a padlocked bar across the door. She felt it and was unable to open it. Someone had been there and walked through the night-wet grass up to the cottage. But not through the door.

She climbed up on a pile of bricks and peered through the window into the kitchen. Everything inside was low, the stove almost down on the floor. The light fell in so that she could see the maker's label on the oven door. There was an empty sofa in there, perhaps called a bed. You could pull a drawer out from underneath and at least two children would have room to sleep in it. A rickety-looking table, two broken ladderback chairs. A yellow plastic bucket. On the wall, a framed picture of Jesus in his crown of thorns. Some refuse—a can and a torn newspaper—on the table. A soot-stained bowl. Nothing else. As she went around the house to look in through the other windows, she heard Mia crying. The moment she stood still, the mosquitoes and midges attacked.

The curtains, blue checked and rather dirty, were drawn across one of the windows at the back. She could see only a small section of a wall of blue floral wallpaper, on it a new pattern of brown patches of damp. A piece had loosened and hung down off the wall farther down. Then there was a bit of a bed. It must be a bed, because she thought she could identify a faded quilt. A foot sticking out at the end. So Dan was there!

It was dim inside behind the drawn curtains. She knocked on the windowpane to wake him and saw the foot swiftly disappear.

She waited, but nothing happened. Silence. She looked at the quilt. It was still and flat. Nothing moving. She didn't dare knock again.

A foot. Quite white in the thin, uncertain light. Must have been Dan's. Why was he hiding?

She went around to the front again, involuntarily walking quietly, creeping along, trying to avoid treading on anything that might make a noise.

Mia was crying like a baby now, her mouth open and tears smearing her face. Annie couldn't explain the inexplicable to her, that Dan was there but didn't want to come out. She couldn't imagine how Mia would cope with the long walk back; indeed, she was hardly able to imagine how she would herself.

She carried the little girl into the forest again, out of sight of the cottage. Was it Dan in there? Why had he pulled in his foot? She sat down on a tree stump with Mia in her arms, waving the midges away with a sprig she had broken off. She whispered that they would go back, but only to the blue tent. They would wake whoever was asleep inside and ask for help. Maybe they had a paraffin stove and could make some tea for them. Or cocoa. Then they would be sure to take them to the road, and if one of them was a big strong man he would carry Mia. They would drive them down to the village in their Renault 4L, for they must be the owners. And soon, quite soon, in only an hour or two, they would both be tucked up in a warm bed. Mia's tears had abated and turned into hiccups. She put her thumb in her mouth again and slept for a while.

The morning sun was coming through the trees as they started walking, the birdsong soaring. Everything seemed so much easier now that the sun was warming up. They crossed the river at the same place. She didn't dare try anywhere else. Once on the other side, they were to make their way back to the tent, but it was not easy to walk along the riverbank. The undergrowth was tangled and the ground churned up by animals. They had to move farther up, to the edge of the marshland.

At last she recognized the two spruces storms had twisted together into a knot, but she couldn't see the tent. There couldn't possibly be two other deformed spruces like those by the river. She was having trouble finding landmarks in the marshland, for in the uncertain light it looked as if both trees and undergrowth had moved.

"You stay there," she said to Mia. "It must be down there by those spruces. I'll go down and look. Then you won't have to walk that last bit if I'm wrong."

She gave Mia the rucksack to sit on, and a birch sprig to keep off the midges. But the insects appeared to have given up in the morning sun. Mia was anxious and tearful.

"I'm only going down to the river. You'll be able to see me all the way."

It was the right place. As she came down to the spruces, she saw the jeans hanging over one of the branches. But the tent had collapsed. That was why she hadn't been able to see it from up in the marsh. She went closer.

What did she actually see? Afterward, she didn't know. So many hideous descriptions appeared. She had probably read some of them. She couldn't remember later.

For a long time there was a great empty space there. She saw her own hands under the water, white, even whitish-green. She saw the spruces. They had knotted together to form a great nodule, grown together where one of them had been bent by a storm long before. The wet jeans were hanging over a branch. The swampy patch of small birches on the other side of the river—always softer, greener, and more secretive than the side you are on.

She wanted to run away. But she must have gone on a few steps more. She felt sick and her legs refused to carry her. Then it struck her with great violence. She fell to her knees, the palms of her hands propped against the swaying ground. When she got up, her hands were blood-stained. She rubbed and rubbed them against each other, then tried to wipe them on her skirt, but that wasn't much use. She staggered away, crawling at first, then dipping her hands in the water. It was cold. Strong current. Swift transparent water. Her hands were clean. She vomited into the water and the current took away the mess she had heaved out of herself. The water was soon clean again, clear and swift-running. With her head averted and without looking at the tent, she went back up to Mia.

"They weren't there," she said. Roughly she grabbed the girl's arm and hurried away toward the marsh. The sun was coming right through the white woolly tufts now, floating, apparently hovering above the sedge. The tent was no longer visible. She saw the river and its swift water, dark, foaming in whirlpools. And the ground on the other side.

Afterward, she was no longer sure of the place. It was not marked, had no boundaries. It wandered like a sunspot between shadows of clouds. It was an event, an event by water. As everything is.

He had read that an eel could live for a long time without food, making its way through shallow ditches to new waters and down toward the sea.

If trapped in a pool with no connections with streams or lakes, it could wriggle its way through damp grass to reach freshwater.

It was now lying quite still in the yellow plastic bucket.

Early morning and clear sunny weather, warm indoors, so he had no need to get up and light the stove. He had been scared by the banging on the window, but that had gone now. As soon as he'd heard it was a woman's voice, he had calmed down. Gudrun was looking for him. She could go on doing so for a while. But he couldn't go back to sleep. That didn't matter much; he wasn't particularly tired now, and he needed to think.

But he couldn't. He was too hungry. He got up and rummaged in the cupboard above the sink. A packet of pancake mix. White pepper. Cocoa. How idiotic, the whole house at home was stuffed with food; both freezers, the larder, the fridge, and the cold cellar. He would have to go back home without having done any thinking.

Well, that wasn't the end of the world. He had lain low in his room before, hunched over his desk. He could say to hell with them for hours on end. And it was only over the weekend that there would be as many as five of them. Five towers of muscle. The smell of aftershave and cigarette smoke. Drinks. Soccer on the shimmering blue screen, drawn curtains.

Racing off in cars. And the unease that spurted out now and again. Gudrun like some kind of bloody incense in the room.

Where did hatred come from?

He got up and pulled on his jeans. They were dry but stiff from the clay. He stirred some water into the pancake mix and cocoa. It did not dissolve, sticky lumps swimming around, the cocoa dry on the surface. He lit the stove to heat up the unappetizing mess.

He had to climb out of the window to take a leak. It was all so silly, so much trouble. He had never liked things that wasted time and were tiresome. Like camping.

As he was climbing back in, the cocoa gruel was boiling over, thick now and burnt to the bottom of the pan. He ate it once it had cooled a bit, then cleared up after himself. No point going on with this. Gudrun had probably been really worried. She must have woken the whole household. No one had moved at first, he was sure of that. He wondered whether she had had to go and search on her own.

They would grin a bit when he got back, then say nothing. Nor would he dare say anything. He would have to go on living there, curled up, one year at a time. Then military service.

It struck him it would be the same then.

Torsten and his real sons fitted in. They belonged, only sometimes they went a bit too far. Then there were fines to pay.

It would be the same doing his military service, and at college. Though there he would have a better chance. There he could be just as confident as Torsten was up on the tractor and perhaps occasionally go a bit too far himself.

He hunted out a cloudberry pail with a lid and put the eel into it. It didn't thrash around, but he was afraid it was a deceptive old devil, so he firmly clipped down the lid before climbing out of the window.

The sunlight was bright over the Klöppen; he could hardly keep his eyes on the water. Before he left, he had to go to the privy down by the trees on the shore. The planking was silver-gray and faintly green, covered with a thin coat of decay. Insects were clicking inside and it smelled of rot. He began to read an old magazine, the paper yellow around the edges. It was difficult to find anything he hadn't read before.

There was a serial he had ignored before, thinking it was about love, but now he found it was a political story—though with love in it. A weeping wife who was an alcoholic. The husband had gotten drunk and the pretty young girl he was out with in his car had been killed. The worst thing would be if her brother found out. And the newspapers.

Chappaquiddick.

The word popped up in his head, meaningless at first, then he remembered, Edward Kennedy. He started shuffling through the heap of magazines to find some more episodes of the serial.

Yes, it was the story of the president's brother, though they had changed all the names. The beginning and the end were missing, but he read what he could find.

Outrageous, really.

Edward Kennedy was still around and active. He had only gone a little too far. But it had worked out.

Things always worked out for them.

His revulsion rose like the smell of shit from the torn paper. He ripped out a page with a picture of the president's sister-in-law on it—tears, staring eyes, pearl necklace, a red mouth that had yellowed—and rubbed it soft before wiping himself with it. Shitting had made him even hungrier.

The lake looked peculiar, oily in the stillness, as if the water were sticky. He could see no one on the other side and was pleased, though it didn't matter. Soon he would be up at the Strömgren homestead and would meet people on the road. They would wonder what he had in the pail.

Then he noticed the canoe, a light metal one glinting in a willow thicket.

What actually happens when you decide?

Afterward, Johan realized he never had decided, not when he fetched the paddle from the cookhouse, nor when he picked the lock on the chain. He had thought it would be good not to have to walk, that's all. He would come out by Röbäck if he paddled down the length of the lake. Then he could hitch home. That was better than trudging on sore feet all the way from the homestead carrying a pail.

The water enveloped the slim body of the canoe. As he dipped the paddle in and took a stroke, it seemed to him that muscles were trembling under the skin of the water.

Christ, how fast it goes. A puff of wind brought the smell of resin and grass, and the water smelled of water as the paddle broke it up.

I am kept away by Norway's mountains
from the King's war and my dear home

as Grandmother used to read. All those things in that old head. Listen to the soughing in the trees. She had been to Östersund twice in her life, but never farther.

Suppose people were forced to travel like the eel to mate. In an involuntary eternal arabesque. Go to Sargasso. The wide Sargasso Sea. Go to Sargasso.

He was sitting like innards inside the shiny shell. He had always felt at one with a canoe. Torsten went fishing with as many as thirty nets in October storms howling with ice and mist, and he said it was a bloody silly craft. But had he ever dared get into one? That tower of muscle? That great lump of fat?

He had to think. The lake narrowed down toward the Röbäck and the headland thrust out its arm. The canoe glided the last bit, the blade of the paddle dripping. As he was about to pull the canoe up on the grass, it occurred to him they would find it down there below the sawmill in Röbäck. Gudrun would chase around, asking, of course.

He must have decided then. He grabbed the canoe and shoved it with full force out into the water, flinging the paddle after it, regretting it almost at once. The canoe would dance down to the sawmill and lie banging against the stones. That was stupid, but it was done now.

He ought to have realized there wouldn't be many cars around just after four in the morning. The sun had deceived him. He sat down on the roadside grass. All he could hear was the roar of the stream, like a train, or a gigantic toilet permanently flushing. He could hardly hear the birds, which was why he was surprised when a car came along at last. He leapt into the road with the pail and thrust out his thumb. It was a woman in a white Saab. She braked so the gravel spurted.

"Going to Norway?"

She said it. He just nodded, but at the same moment thought about Oula Laras on his scooter. He and his family lived in Langvasslien.

He had to put the pail on the floor in the back. She didn't even ask what was in it. She hadn't said much yet, but he thought she talked like the Finns who used to come and do clearing work for Torsten. There were chocolate wrappers and rubbish all over the car and a plastic container of duty-free liquor on the backseat.

"God, it's beautiful here," she said as the road ran along Blackwater. "I've never been this way before. I usually go via Östersund and Trondheim."

When they got into the village, everything seemed silent and sleeping, but then he spotted Vidart's old Duett on its way down toward Tangen. He crouched down so he wouldn't be seen.

"Oh, dear, dear," said the woman. She had a harsh laugh, not exactly jolly. She sounded sarcastic and he felt uncertain beside her.

"Good," she said as they crossed the border. "That's enough of Sweden. Quite enough. Or are you Swedish?"

Of course, she hadn't heard him say much. He shook his head.

"Norwegian?"

"No," he said. "Not that either, actually." And it was true. It might be true. Everything was giving way. He felt something new coming on, something other than being stuck in his room. But he had no money on him. As long as I get through the weekend, he thought. It was an ordinary Saturday here. Or was it? As soon as the weekend was over, he could get some clearing work. Or planting, anyhow.

When they banged on the door, it was almost half past four in the morning. Birger hadn't slept and his head began to ache the moment he raised it from the pillow. He got out of bed with some caution. When he opened the door and the morning air poured in, he realized the smell of frying was still there in a cold and musty blend of tobacco smoke. Roland Fjellström, who owned the campsite, was standing outside saying something had happened up by the Lobber.

Åke Vemdal pulled on his trousers and set off toward the office. Birger stood with his forehead against the windowpane. His face felt swollen. He would be able to sleep now.

The deep, narrow bay between the Tangen and the crown lands was bright, and a low cloud was caught on the mountain ridge on the other side, torn by the spruce tops and floating like milk in the water. The sun was coming from the wrong direction, the unusual light making him feel strange and exposed. He saw some goldeneye rising, streaks trembling in the water behind them. Far away, the water was moving. Then he saw it was a boat. Dark.

It was being rowed evenly at a good speed along the east shore, toward the Tangen. He stood there for a long time, watching it, and he knew he could sleep soundly now, at last. But perhaps he ought to make some coffee for Åke.

Someone was rowing with an otter board, the board visible far out on the left, the long line with its small lines and hooks a silvery thread between the boat and the board. What a nerve! But if you were fishing that way, it was a good idea to do it before five in the morning on Midsummer Day, when the site was sunk in a heavy, hung-over sleep.

He could see the otter board dancing on. There was only one man in the boat and he must have been holding the line around his forefinger as he rowed. What he would do if he got a bite was hard to imagine.

The man stopped rowing and the boat glided on with the force of the last strokes, then slowed down. The man was pouring water onto the oarlocks. The oars had probably been creaking. Birger couldn't hear it, but he heard footsteps in the gravel outside. Åke Vemdal was running back.

The otter board sagged and swung crosswise. With a soft jerk, the oarsman got up speed again to keep it at a distance. It was Björne Brandberg. Birger could see him now. Clever old boy, too. Making the most of it while the others slept, slack and dry-mouthed. And he must have the line between his teeth.

Åke flung open the door.

"Come on, you, too," he said. "We're going up to the Strömgren homestead."

She was wearing a blue denim skirt smeared with blood down the sides, the hem wet and dirty. Her hair was fair and fell quite a long way down her back. Both she and the little girl were exhausted. The child had braids that had come undone, and her swollen, battered face made him at once hostile to the mother. He hadn't believed a word of what she had said, it was all so unbelievably insane. Out with a six-year-old on the marshlands up toward Starhill in the middle of the night. In a long skirt.

But when he examined the child, he saw the swellings on her face had been caused by insect bites. Oriana heated some milk for her and tucked her up on a sofa in the bedroom. The mother was sitting bolt upright on a kitchen chair, staring at the blank television screen.

They really needed Henry Strömgren with them to find the place, but Åke did not want to leave Oriana alone with the girl's mother, so he asked Henry to keep an eye on her. She was not to leave, and she was not to go anywhere near any kind of weapon. No knives on the table. He had phoned for reinforcements. But it would be an hour or two before they got to Blackwater and up there.

Åke and Birger set off down to the Lobber and found the place after some wandering around. There was a tent, and it lay on the ground just as she had said, slashed to pieces and soaked in blood that had begun to dry. The canvas was molded around the two bodies. One body lay half over the other. Everything was quite still.

They carefully turned back the canvas and had to loosen the light metal pegs in one or two places to be able to lift it. But Åke wanted them to touch the tent as little as possible.

The sunlight flooded a head of long hair. It had been dark and curly, but was now sticky with blood, and there were feathers stuck to it. There were feathers everywhere, stuck in patches of dried blood. The sleeping bags had been slashed to shreds and the feathers poured out of them whenever the canvas was touched. Fine down floated away on the mountain breeze.

A face. Lips drawn back. The upper lip had dried over the teeth. A young woman. She lay underneath. Perhaps the man, lying half over her, had tried to protect her from the knife. He was fair. At the back of his neck was a cake of coagulated blood.

Birger put two fingers where the pulse in the neck had once throbbed. He found the woman's neck under the tangled hair and feathers. Her flesh was still and colder than his fingertips.

"Just leave them where they are," said Åke. "The technical boys are on their way."

They had pulled a bit of the canvas aside to reveal a transistor radio. A hand that must be the man's looked as if it had stiffened as it reached for the handle. Beside it was a pair of rolled-up socks, fluffy with down, a large, unopened bar of chocolate, and a whole lot of small polished stones that looked like uneven beads. She must have been wearing a necklace. The face had a pallor that had already begun to turn gray.

"Sit over there," said Åke, pointing at a fallen birch. The top of it was green and dipping its first leaves in the water. They were already eaten by larvae, which disgusted him. The water was racing along in a web of many sounds, rustling, murmuring, and tinkling. Sometimes someone seemed to be talking in a monotone out of the water.

He watched Åke crawling around the tent and moving the blue canvas with a very light hand. A bird of prey called above them, as if complaining. Birger felt cold.

"Maybe you should go on up there," said Åke. "Those two are both in shock."

"No, for Christ's sake."

"He won't come back now."

"You don't know."

No, they were beyond what was knowable, and the morning chill paralyzed his thoughts as well as his movements. His mind was blank, no guess or speculation as long as he sat there. Listening to the racing, transparent water that had nothing to say. It just talked. The web of sounds woke an echo in his mind, and his mind made it chatter. But for a moment he thought he was listening to what had happened there, that it had been engraved in the bright night and was being reproduced by the waves and the whirlpools in the water. And that he nevertheless could not distinguish anything more than chattering and small cries. Sometimes it sounded like mewing.

I don't know where Barbro is, he thought. I didn't even ask. Some kind of demonstration against the uranium mining on Bear Mountain. They were going to camp, she had said.

But where?

They were standing over by the sink.
They had put her striped yellow rucksack up on the work surface and one
of them was removing the contents, putting the items down one by one
after thoroughly inspecting them.

He was the chief of police, stationed at Byvången. The other man was
a doctor. They had just returned from the place by the river. The knees of
the police chief's trousers were wet. He asked her what her name was.

"You saw that on my driver's license."

He ignored her reply and went on to ask when she was born and
where she lived. On one of Dan's letters, now lying on the work surface, it
said Annie Raft, Karlbergsgatan 121. She wished he had been satisfied
with that.

"I was born in 1941, on October 21. And I was on my way up to
Nilsbodarna. I'm going to live there."

Silence fell. She was expecting the next question. Have you rented it
from the Brandbergs for the summer? But perhaps they didn't know who
owned the cottage. She hadn't known, either, twelve hours earlier. Then it
would somehow have been easier to answer. But the question didn't come.
Instead, he said:

"You've stated you were on your way *from* Nirsbuan."

That was the first time he had used the word "stated." The odd thing
was that she couldn't remember saying anything at all, but she must have.
Otherwise Henry Strömgren wouldn't have phoned for them.

"I had been to Nirsbuan," she said. She found it difficult to pronounce the name and regretted having used it. The conversation was full of traps, not really a conversation at all. She hadn't slept for twenty-six hours. I'll say it exactly as it is, she thought. I'll say I had been up by the outbuildings, by the cabin. In the cabin. No, I shan't say cabin. The cottage? I was on my way away from there because it was empty. I needn't say what I saw. That's of no importance.

But the police chief asked her what her profession was.

"I'm a teacher."

When he said nothing, she felt he didn't believe her.

"I was trained at the teacher training college in Stockholm. And I went to the College of Music."

"Where are you employed?"

His questions were precise. This one was impossible to answer. She had a sudden attack of faintness and asked if she could rest for a while.

"Where are you employed?" he said.

"I've given it up. I was at Mälarvåg Further Education College. I taught Swedish and music. As well as literature. That's a separate subject. I stopped working there in the spring. Though I ran a summer course in choral singing. For two weeks. So I couldn't get away until now. Dan had gone on ahead."

She was saying too much. She ought not to accommodate them. They were solid in their system, dressed in their sports trousers with pockets on the thighs. Quasi-military garb. Deadly assured. But they were both un-shaven. That made it more difficult to see them as Dan would have seen them.

"Dan Ulander," said the police chief. Either he knew Dan or he had seen the name on the back of the envelope. "Where is he now?"

"I don't know," she said. "He was supposed to meet us. He didn't come. Then I thought he was up there. So I walked there."

"You walked there."

He had a map among his papers, took it out and looked at it.

"How old is the child?" the other man said. He's beginning to put on weight, she thought. A fat doctor. She said Mia was six.

"You walked with a six-year-old up to Nirsbuan last night? And back again?"

That was it. She couldn't deny it. She might have said she hadn't known how far it was. But they knew she had a map. The rucksack lay on the drainboard and everything she had put into it was lined up on the stainless steel surface. As they had taken the things out, they had asked her whether she had a knife. That had made her think about survival. Knife, matches, groundsheet, a box of pastilles, the letter from Dan, a pack of tampons, the sandwiches, Mia's Ken and Barbie dolls and their nylon clothes and tiny shoes. Annie's red wallet was also there. They had examined her driver's license and placed it next to the wallet. When they had first arrived, the police chief had asked Oriana to stay in the kitchen for a while. Then he had told Annie to take off her denim jacket and he had gone through the pockets while the doctor felt her body under her top and skirt. A professional fumbling. She had been made to take off her boots. But she had neither taken in anything of what was happening nor reacted when they had searched her rucksack. Only now did she understand the question about a knife.

"Have you no photograph of Dan Ulander on you?"

She replied that there was none. He wouldn't be photographed.

"What do you mean? Doesn't he go to a photographer, or won't he allow anyone to take photographs of him?"

"I don't know."

She considered that to be the only sensible answer she had given that morning.

"You were at Nirsbuan. And were you frightened?"

That statement was unexpected. She didn't know where he had gotten it from. Had she said so herself? Or had Mia? Mia couldn't have realized she had been frightened, could she? She had been on the other side of the cottage.

"Tell my why you were frightened?"

She told him she had seen a foot. She now had more control over herself. The attacks of dizziness that were a kind of second-long faint, or nodding off, were coming less frequently. She wouldn't say too much. So she just said she had seen a foot when she had looked through the window.

"And that frightened you?"

"It was pulled away. I knocked on the window and it was pulled back."

"Did you recognize the foot?"

She didn't want that question. She had already thought about it. A couple of months earlier she had told Dan she would recognize him even if she saw nothing but a little patch of his skin. A strand of his hair would be enough, or the nail of his little finger. She would recognize the smell of his body among other bodies in a dark room.

"Yes, I recognized his foot," she said now. "Dan's."

"Do you live with this man?"

"Yes."

"Did you live with him when you worked at Mälarvåg College?"

"Yes."

"Where did you live?"

"We lived there."

"What was his job?"

"He didn't have a job."

"He lived with you but didn't work?"

"We didn't live together," she said, her voice thinner now, ending in a whimper.

"You said you lived together."

"Yes. We were together. We were to live together here."

"What are you going to live on?"

"I'm going to teach. And he's going to work."

She foresaw the next question, so added:

"I'm to teach the children at the Starhill commune."

"You've stated you don't belong to the Starhill commune," he said.

There was that word again: She had stated.

"Whom would I have said that to?" she said, and was prepared for what he would answer: I'm the one asking questions here. But he said almost in a friendly way:

"The bus driver."

The police had tracked down the bus driver and woken him. Something really had happened. But she no longer knew what she had said when she came into this house. She must have talked about what she had seen. But what had she seen?

Two people were dead. They had told her that when they had come back from the river. Knifed.

The kitchen in the glaring sunlight so early in the morning was a peculiar place. Its triviality hid false or genuine depths, impossible to tell, as if in a dream. This was where the Strömgrens led their warm, tobacco-smelling lives, of which she knew nothing. The place didn't smell of goat. They had a shower and left their clothes in a bedroom next to the bathroom. They were goat farmers in different conditions from those of the Starhill people. She had deciphered their life despite her exhaustion. The television set in the kitchen. The avocado-green refrigerator. Green cowpat-patterned wallpaper. Henry and Oriana put out no signals of their origins or aspirations. But she had immediately realized they were kind people.

"What was the time when you arrived at Nirsbuan?"

"Two, maybe. Or just before."

"Can you remember a moment when you definitely looked at the time during your walk?"

"By the river. No, by the cottage. Before we left there."

"What did your watch say then?"

"Past two."

"Then you'd seen the tent just before?"

"Yes. It was upright. Nothing had happened there then."

She heard dogs barking outside and the sound of cars. The one who was a policeman looked as if he hadn't noticed. He had propped his chin lightly in his left hand, the forefinger and thumb forming a fork. He had light bluish-gray eyes that held hers firmly. She was his route into all this raw mist and blood, but she wriggled away. You can't look another person straight in the eye that long if you haven't practiced it, she thought. And yet he appeared slightly preoccupied. Or tired. She had to look away after a while.

"You walked to Nirsbuan and when you got there, what did you do then?"

"Looked in. I looked in through the kitchen window. And then through the window around the back."

"You didn't knock on the door?"

"No."

"Why not?"

It had been barred and had a large padlock hanging from it. She didn't want to say that. Then they would make out that Dan had broken in. While she had been walking all that way with Mia during the night, everything she had done had seemed to her necessary and obvious. Now it seemed confused. Impossible to explain.

For the rest of her life she was to preserve the memory of that walk. But how much of it would she have remembered if he had not forced her to describe it over and over again in that warm kitchen? There must be tangled events, illogical or utterly insane actions in all lives. To forget. They refused to allow her to forget. They forced her to bind them together into a pattern. But it was a false pattern.

She felt ashamed. They made her feel ashamed. The doctor's questions were the worst, and he didn't ask many. He asked only about Mia. And then the police chief.

"This man. The man you were going to live with, he didn't show up. Had you arranged for him to come and meet you off the bus?"

"That's fairly obvious, isn't it?" she said.

"But he didn't come."

"No."

"How long did you wait?"

What could she answer? Then she remembered the television film and said that it had begun when she went up to Ola and his wife.

"Had you any idea why he hadn't appeared?"

"Yes, I thought he had forgotten it was Midsummer Eve. Or that he thought I had meant the old, the real Midsummer Eve. He was lying there asleep. So that must have been it."

"But why do you think he drew back his foot when you tapped on the window?"

"How would I know that?"

"You know him."

"I don't know."

"Why did you run away? Why didn't you try to get into the cottage?"

She said nothing.

"What were you afraid of?" he said.

Yes, what had she been afraid of? She no longer knew. It had all shattered. A greater terror had wiped it out.

"Why did you walk back?"

"I don't really know. Everything was . . . creepy."

"Did you think he had someone else there? Another girl?"

Neither of them had any expression any longer. Not even features.

"Did he?" Their faces were nothing but two discs of pale, moist flesh. They said nothing. They were looking attentively at her. But she held out and did not reply.

The policeman got up. He was red-eyed and looked tired, but the other man seemed sleepier, his mouth occasionally dropping open and his eyelids drooping. He had pale, creased eyelids. He pulled himself together and followed the policeman out of the kitchen. A little later, Oriana Strömgren came down from the top floor, where she and Henry had been banished with the children.

She looked swiftly sideways several times at Annie as she made the coffee. When it was ready, it was a pale brown, slightly sour drink. She offered Annie thin crispbread with soft goat's cheese on it. Annie ate it at the time, but was never again able to eat that cheese. Mia went on eating it, not connecting it with what had happened.

Mia was asleep in Oriana and Henry's bedroom. No one had said they had to stay at the Strömgrens'. Annie didn't even know if she was allowed to leave the kitchen. She had no car to get down into the village. She could decide nothing.

Now and again she dozed off as she sat there on the kitchen bench, and Oriana said she should go to bed. But she wanted to stay up. She didn't want to go to bed. She thought if she fell asleep and slid away from this event that was no longer an event, she would wake up to something irretrievable.

Eventually a policeman in a gray coverall with badges and reflectors on it came in. She was to go with him down to the river. A question of identification, he said.

"But it can't possibly be anyone I know!"

He didn't reply, just stood with the kitchen door open until she joined him. The doctor and the chief of police were waiting outside. There were lots of people and cars now, dogs barking incessantly. She said she couldn't look at the bodies in the tent. That was impossible.

"We must request you to," said the police chief. He said he had to ask but he didn't ask. He had gone through her belongings and the other man had fumbled over her body with his hands.

"We want to know if you know one of them."

"Why should I? Why just the one?"

"We think we may know who the girl is," he said. "We want you to look at the boy."

She vomited on the way down. They waited patiently, the doctor even holding her up. But then they hustled her on to continue along the path that disappeared into the wet of the marsh. She was weeping as she approached the river, the men pushing and shoving her.

"It won't take long, it won't take long," said Birger, whose name she did not know then.

"I know it's not Dan!"

"Good," he said. "Then it'll be quick."

The tent canvas was lifted off. They were lying side by side on their backs. But they were stiff and the bodies had not been properly straightened out, knees and elbows bent, fingers splayed. The girl's back was hunched, her head apparently raised from the plastic sheeting and stiffened like that. She had a wound with brownish-black edges on her cheek. It looked like a mouth, another mouth, and it was open.

It was not Dan. They were two alien, whitish-gray, dried-up faces with sticky hair all around them. And there were more men around the tent. They had rolls of plastic strips and kept moving the camera tripod and light metal cases around. There were feathers everywhere. Unruly white down. Behind her clenched teeth lay the taste of vomit, acrid and pungent.

They drove her down to the village. She said she wanted to wait for Dan and they took her to the campsite. She was given a cabin to creep into with Mia, a cabin lined with red wood and with a small veranda. It looked like a playhouse. There was only one window; it was dark inside and smelled of tobacco smoke and old blankets.

It was late morning. She was not really sure what the time was and couldn't find the energy to look. They both fell asleep curled up together on the lower bunk. When she woke there were faces at the window.

The site was crowded with people. Cars drove up to the office and the people who got out were handsomely dressed, but Annie could see no faces, only eyes. She and Mia finally had to leave their hiding place because Mia was hungry. Annie felt sick. They went into Roland Fjellström's office and he gave them sausages and a bag of instant macaroni. He had black hair and brilliant blue eyes. She saw nothing but his low hairline and thought he looked as if he had come from the planet of the apes. She couldn't make him out at all, and perhaps it was the same with all the other masks of faces—she could make nothing of them, seeing nothing but their glances crawling over her own rigid face.

Word had leaked out that she had seen someone on the path up there and they knew she had told the police it was a foreigner. They thought he was the murderer and she believed that herself. Yet she hesitated to say what he looked like because that was so poisoned. He looked like a Vietnamese. She hesitated so long, it never got said. She couldn't stand the campsite any longer, and when Mia had finished her sausage and maca-roni, she took her small hand and they walked up the road. Cars slowed down and people stared at them through the windows. She had thought Dan would find them more easily if they walked on the road. He must be coming.

In the end, she realized they couldn't go on wandering up and down in the village. They had read the posters on the bulletin board by the store several times. Bingo at Vika Parish Hall. Midsummer party in Kvæbakken. Cream porridge, a Norwegian delicacy. Buy your boots at Fiskbua, Three Towers brand—bargain prices! Midsummer service at Björnstubacken. White flour—special offer.

She didn't want to go back to the site. She had seen two houses on a hillside and Mia had asked why it said COTTAGE on a notice when you could see perfectly well it was a cottage.

It never occurred to her that the only vacant cottage in the village might perhaps not be the best one. She just went up the slope with Mia and asked an elderly woman in the house at the top whether they could rent the cottage by the road. It cost thirty krona a night.

She couldn't remember what Aagot Fagerli looked like when they came out of her house, only that she had given her thirty krona. They fetched the rucksack from the campsite and set off for the cottage, but the police caught up with them. She was not to leave the site without telling them. She showed them the cottage and she was driven in a police car to Ola's garage by Fiskebuan so that she could fetch her luggage.

Once they were left alone, she locked the door on the inside. It had a simple skeleton key with an e-shaped bit, so the lock wouldn't give them much protection. The entrance hall was lined with pale green paneling and bright blue wallpaper; behind a door, steep stairs led up to the attic. She went up to look and found it contained preserving jars, old clothes, and rolled-up rugs. Otherwise it was empty.

The cottage was flooded with daylight and you could see right through it from the windows. Quite a big kitchen with pine walls and bright blue wallpaper. Windows on three walls. The bedroom had no door, only an opening with old and beautifully shaped molding. It too was light and visible from all the windows. There were two large cupboards in the kitchen, and when Annie opened the yellow hardboard doors, she was there were Swedish woolen blankets on shelves in one of them, and hard feather pillows with striped pillowcases. The other one was empty apart from some ancient hangers. There was an iron stove, rusty on top, a long kitchen work surface covered with self-adhesive plastic patterned like tiles, white with small blue windmills. There was a table by one of the windows and two wooden chairs. In the bedroom was a bed with a green bedspread patterned with irregular small rectangles and black and yellow lines. This had been audaciously modern in the 1950s.

Mia sat in silence in the kitchen on an iron bed with a flock mattress, and when Annie saw her face she thought: What have I done?

"There are people around in the area," Åke Vemdal said. "We must get those two out."

He had spread the map out on Oriana's kitchen table and told Birger he could go down to the campsite if he liked. More police had come from Östersund. The forensic squad, too. So he needn't stay.

"We must cover all movements in the area. Check lists of those leaving it."

He had begun to use the same language as the technical chief, whose squad was now installed in Henry's barn. The man kept holding up a finger and saying, "Yes, sir! Eyes right!" whenever he wanted to make a correction.

"Barbro's still there," said Birger.

He was not allowed to go and look for her. The police had taken over. He had asked to see the lists, but Vemdal said not many people had come out and they had been noted down. Three. They had been questioned when Birger and he had been down by the river with Annie Raft. None of them had been anywhere near the place where the tent was, or the ford.

Birger's memory was silent, as if a lid had closed over his ears. A wide, stony riverbed glazed by thin water, mobile, silent.

Åke thought he knew who the dead girl was. They had found a passport made out to Sabine Vestdijk, thirty-three years old, studying. Or student. Åke was not certain of the exact meaning of *étudiante*. The red Renault parked up at the homestead had an NL badge with the owner's name on it, and the name was the same as that in the passport. The girl's appearance matched the passport photograph. There was a tent in the car. Two things were unclear; the man's identity and the tent. Why had they had two tents in such a small car?

Birger was hardly listening. He was thinking that Barbro must still be out there somewhere. The other demonstrators had come shambling back with their rucksacks an hour or two before the church service. They had come from Byvången in a minibus that had stopped at a timber-loading bay about a kilometer from the Strömgren homestead. Most of them were teachers. A couple of elderly women, silver-haired and in old-fashioned outdoor clothes. He recognized them from the Peace and Freedom movement and from Amnesty. Barbro used to hold their group meetings at home.

The commune from Röbäck came in an old Volkswagen bus. They brought with them the Starhill people, who had stayed overnight with them so that the children would not have to walk the long way down from Starhill in the morning. They were wearing Inca caps, patterned shirts, pointed Lapp shoes, and had leather backpacks. They had left their placards on the bus after they had been told there would be no service at Björnstubacken. But the police brought with them two placards they had found up there.

URANIUM PROSPECTING BEGUN
TAKE A MIDSUMMER WALK!
EXPOSE LOCAL AUTHORITY LIES!

Birger had seen a great many variations of the texts on Barbro's drawing board. *Midsummer walk with us. See with your own eyes. The authorities are lying about the uranium. The council is not telling the truth. Come and see it on Bear Mountain.*

He had asked what they would see. Stakes, she had replied. You could hardly walk on Bear Mountain at Midsummer, for the snow had not yet melted. But she had explained that a great many people would come to the open-air service. That was the only opportunity they had. Some people would go on up with them and the others would at least see the placards.

The two men Vemdal had sent up the path had seen neither the doctor's wife nor any tent. The demonstrators didn't know where she was. They hadn't even known she was coming up the evening before. Birger had thought the whole group was going.

I hardly asked her anything, he thought. And why don't the other demonstrators know anything? He thought they had answered evasively when he questioned them, or else they were lying outright.

The hours were long, a long, dazzlingly sunny day full of voices and the tramp of feet, starting cars and barking dogs. The feeling would not leave him. Fear. Guilty conscience. Whatever it was. Whatever was inside him was hurting, anyhow, a fierce and lasting pain. A kind of force. He wished he could scream in the way that pale woman in the denim skirt had. For there were people left in the area. Barbro Torbjörnsson and Dan Ulander. Perhaps others they knew nothing about.

"Who is Dan Ulander?" he asked Vemdal.

"One of the demonstrators."

Vemdal was short of staff. He was considering the local riflemen, in case there was a maniac on the loose out there. Birger watched him bending over the outspread maps. They wanted to turn it into a military operation in the area.

A maniac. That too was a name for a kind of force. You had to have names for things. There was something they called the Area.

What area? Where did it end? On the map it looked like lichen in faint shades of green, yellow, and brown. But there were mountain peaks and marshlands. Right up to Multhögen. There was a road there, but miles upon miles of roadless countryside in between. Heathland, swamps, peaks.

Some of the demonstrators were still outside. Inquisitive people had come up from the village, several carloads. One or two had seen the Dutch car outside Fiskebuan on Midsummer Eve.

"We'll cordon it off," said Åke Vemdal. "Close it off down in the village and make sure all this lot go away."

They were called inquisitive. But why had they really come? When Birger was a boy, it had been wartime and everything had been bad. Even the toilet paper had been thin. Thin and shiny, often tearing. He had never been able to resist smelling his finger when that happened. They were sticky and smelled bad. But you wanted to feel all the same.

It was wrong to say these people were inquisitive. They wanted to feel. Henry and Oriana's children's faces could be seen in the top windows. They were inquisitive. Henry had lugged the television up there and pulled the antenna in through the window. But they preferred to see what was going on down in the yard. And the dogs barked all day long, barking themselves hoarse.

Lill-Ola Lennartsson came up in a police car. He was wearing a brown plush tracksuit. Lill-Ola had been a Swedish champion athlete when he still lived in Byvången. His clothing looked implausible until Birger remembered Ola sold all kinds of leisure wear in his shop, playsuits and slippers made of reindeer and rabbit skin. The tracksuit was tight around his thin buttocks, revealing that this former long-distance runner was beginning to lose his ass.

Åke wanted Birger to go with him into Henry's barn, but Lill-Ola was looking very shaky. That was when Birger realized that it had been wrong to make the woman in the denim skirt go down to the river to view the corpses. That had been cruel and done in a hurry. It could have waited. I ought to take a look at her, he thought.

The legs of the tracksuit were wide at the bottom and flapped around Ola's ankles as he went up the barn steps, his shoulders hunched up and his head thrust forward. He stood in the same way as he looked down at the bodies. They looked older now. Grayer. One was on the back of the pickup. Ola nodded.

"That was the girl. She came into the shop."

They showed him the man's corpse lying on a police stretcher on the floor.

"Never seen him before."

"Was she on her own in the shop?"

Yes, she had been alone and she had said nothing about a man. Vemdal asked him to look carefully at the man. He coped well with it and didn't hurry. Birger looked away. Clothes and objects they had found in the collapsed tent were lying on an old baking table in sealed plastic bags. He could see the beads that had been among the feathers. They had found the thread and put it into the same bag. It was white, but a few centimeters had been stained brown by the blood. Small objects that weren't at all obvious in a tent: beads, a barrette, a notebook with signs of the zodiac on the cover: Sagittarius. They had no meaning now, nothing immediately obvious, anyway.

A faint twittering was coming from the table. He went closer and saw it was a small cage with a brown rat inside it. He retched. The rat twirled around once, then sat dead still, looking out with black eyes like glass beads.

Ola had finished. He was quite certain, he said. He recognized the girl, but not the man. He had never seen him before. Now he wanted to leave.

But he had coped well. When they got out on the steps, he said the girl had bought some fishing gear from him—lines and a couple of small spinners. And she had borrowed his tent.

"Well, rented," he added. "She had a damned great camping tent with her. I happened to see it when we went out to the car to look at her rods to see what size lines she wanted. They couldn't have put up a tent like that by the Lobber."

"Why was she going there in particular?"

He didn't know. He had sold her a fishing license and given her the usual map.

"Did she know the place?"

"I don't know. She spoke nothing but English."

He had to go back into the barn to look at the tent and see if he was sure he recognized it.

"It's easy to recognize," he said. "It's blue with a black and white sticker on it. A penguin. That's the brand mark."

But Åke wanted him to look. He lumbered back in, gray hairs and dandruff on the shoulders of his plush tracksuit. Birger had a feeling he had been surprised in bed or something equally private. He had never seen him in anything but very modern sports outfits before.

When Ola saw the tent, he let out a cry and took a step or two back. He clearly hadn't known they had been stabbed to death as they lay inside the tent. He turned away to avoid having to look at the slashed canvas and brown bloodstains.

Then he collapsed. It was so unexpected, they hadn't time to catch him. He lay in a small brown heap on the floor. His longish hair had been brushed forward, and when it was disturbed, they could see he was going bald. As they carried him out, Birger spotted the Strömgren children in the top window.

"You must get everything out of here," he said. "It can't go on like this. You're scaring the kids."

But they took no notice of him. What a bloody mess, he thought. And where was Barbro?

There didn't seem to be anything wrong with Lill-Ola Lennartsson's heart. It was just an ordinary faint.

"But I'll examine him properly," he said.

"We'll drive him back home. Come on down with us."

Birger had no wish to, but it was hard to refuse. As he drove behind the police car down toward the village, he was thinking they were carrying out Barbro, that they had had her hidden behind the barn down by the river. Sheer madness. But his heart was thumping. Irregularly, as well.

When he took his doctor's bag out of the trunk, his eye fell on the salmon trout he and Åke had caught in the Blackreed. Maybe they aren't too far gone, he thought. If they're all right we'll have them tonight. There are lemons in the fridge.

It was an incantation. Barbro and he and Tomas would have fried salmon trout for dinner. Everything would be just as usual. For a while, anyhow. Then he had to try to think about what all this meant. Why had she gone off earlier than the other demonstrators? And why hadn't he bothered? Not even asked.

At the Lennartssons', he got the same feeling he so often had when he was called out, that he was looking into something far too private, something they ought not to have to show. It often surprised him how badly people's external appearances corresponded with what their homes looked and smelled like. They equipped themselves in the chain stores in town and the discount store in Byvången and looked like everyone else. But inside their own homes they had a whole lot of peculiarities. Big safes though they were dirt poor. Stacks of cardboard boxes. Tons of old home-made furniture. Lill-Ola's long, narrow bedroom held only one picture that Birger figured had been bought, a picture of a naked girl. The rest, and there were many, were knotted in wool like rugs. He recognized them from other places. They all had motifs from nature: deer by the water, eagles in flight, mountain landscapes in the sun. Presumably he had made them himself together with his wife. A great many men worked on such things in front of the television at night.

Naked ladies, deer, and waterfalls were nothing peculiar, nor was sleeping alone. But he wished he hadn't had to go into this room. It was furry and intimate like a kangaroo's pouch.

Anyhow, there was nothing wrong with Lill-Ola's heart. But he had had a shock, a powerful mental shock. He had stretched out on the bed and he was cold. Birger told his wife to fetch a blanket and make a hot drink for him.

"Not coffee."

He gave him a tranquilizer tablet to wash down with water and left six more for him in a small white envelope.

"Take one when you need it today and tomorrow. But no more than three a day."

Ola's wife stood beside him, watching. She looked inquisitive. Or whatever you call it. As if she'd seen a road accident. He had to ask her again to go and get a blanket. Then she started heating up some milk in the kitchen.

As he was leaving, he asked if he could put his fish in their freezer so that they didn't go bad. She nodded. Hitherto she had said nothing at all. He had a feeling she wouldn't remember what he looked like once he had left the house.

He fetched the package of fish from the car and went back to put it in the freezer in the back kitchen. It was far on in the year and the freezer was half empty. But packages and plastic boxes were still neatly if somewhat sparsely stacked in it. She kept berries on the left side, wild mushrooms and fish on the right, and meat evidently at the bottom. There were two bulky paper packages labeled CAPERCAILLIE, UNPLUCKED. When he took an ice cream carton filled with cloudberry preserve to put on top of the fish so that they would freeze more quickly, he knocked down a pile of boxes of berries. The freezer rattled and she looked out from the kitchen. Lill-Ola appeared the next moment.

"What the hell are you up to?"

His voice was a shrill cry, the same as when he had seen the tent in the lodge at the Strömgrens'.

"I'm only putting some fish in," Birger said. "Your wife said it would be all right."

He said good-bye and went down to the campsite to look in on the woman who had found the two dead bodies. He still had a guilty conscience about her. But he couldn't find her.

By the time he got back, they had brought up a large police bus with radio antennae. The squad had found moped tracks on the path to the outbuildings that ran up from the village. But they hadn't found the moped. Nor Barbro.

"Are you sure she came here?" said Åke Vemdal.

What could he answer?

Johan had intended to stay awake and think up something to say to the woman driving the Saab. She was smoking and whistling quietly, and it was making him sleepy. He kept dozing off for longer and longer periods and didn't even wake as they drove through the villages. She didn't appear to slow down at all, and when she finally braked sharply, he was thrown forward with no time to brace himself.

"Oops!" was all she said, then added as she was halfway out of the car, "Just going to buy some cigarettes and a few things like that."

They had stopped by a coop store in a village he didn't know. They must have driven far, past the first familiar places across the border. He could get out now. The simplest thing would be just to push off, then he wouldn't have to say anything. He didn't really know why, but it would have made him uncomfortable to say that he wasn't going any farther with her.

Cigarettes and things like that, she had said. No food. Or was she going to buy something to eat? He had no money on him and was getting hungrier with every waking minute.

People were doing their Saturday shopping and a man was loading plastic shopping bags into the trunk of his Ford. The man went back to get a six-pack of beer he'd left on the steps, and, having put it in the trunk, he slammed it shut, leaving a shopping bag on the ground beside the car. The man went straight around to the front, got in, and drove off.

The bag looked as if it held containers of cream. Heavy cream. Whipping cream. And other things. If he hasn't far to go, he'll soon be back, Johan thought. When he notices he's left one bag behind. Or someone will come out of the store and notice it.

He didn't decide to do it, he just did it—got out of the Saab, took three or four steps, and picked up the shopping bag. It was quite heavy. He clasped it to him and carried it like that so that it couldn't be seen from the store as he crossed the road. He walked straight into the forest along a small dirt road. He could hear a car coming up behind him and felt his back stiffen as he tried to hear whether anyone had come out of the store. After a while the road curved and he knew he was no longer visible from the store. He ducked under a gate and ran straight up into the forest with his burden, the fir trees closing around him.

It was a steep, dark forest, silent in the heat. His back to a tree, he sat down in the moss and started unpacking the bag. A leek. Twelve packets of yeast labeled Gjær. The man had been going to make a mash for home brew. What had looked like a half-liter container of cream was rodent killer. Ordinary yellow boxes of rat poison. A metal cake tin. Salt. Greaseproof baking paper. A box of detergent.

The leek was the only edible item. The devil himself had packed the shopping bag. As he had been walking up, he had thought about fried fishcakes, vacuum packed, or a whole lot of cream intended for porridge. After all, it was Midsummer. Chocolate cakes. Potato pancakes and cheese.

But there was nothing. He couldn't eat the leek. Stealing the bag had been quite pointless, and now he'd lost the eel. The pail was still in the car and the woman must have long since driven on.

Only now did he feel ashamed. But he couldn't very well take the bag back to the store. He hid it behind the tree, but down by the road he changed his mind and went back to get the boxes of rat poison. He stuffed them into the container intended for parking fees. At least no field mice would have gastric hemorrhages.

Before heading back to the main road, he had considered staying in the forest for a while to think about which direction he should hitch next. Maybe it would be just as well to go back home. But he was hungry, so hungry he couldn't think straight. All he could do was walk, walk and walk until his stomach stopped tearing at him.

The Saab was still there. At first he thought it was another car the same as hers, but she was sitting inside, that woman in the blue-and-white-striped cotton top. It scared him a little. That was silly, of course, but it was rather strange that she was still there, peering at him as if she had known all the time he would come back. She was eating a banana.

"Still here?" he said.

"Yes."

A pack of Marlboros and a large bar of chocolate lay where he had been sitting.

"I didn't think you'd leave your eel," she said.

So she had opened the lid and looked in. Foolishly, he turned scarlet, a hot wave rising from his throat. He got into the car and she started up. When he put the chocolate on the dashboard, she said:

"Go ahead. Have some if you like."

He ate, and she started laughing.

Vemdal came over to him, holding out his palm. He was wearing a thin rubber glove. A piece of paper lay in his hand. It looked like a crumpled bit of a paper bag. It was printed with a picture of the head of an Indian in a full feathered headdress and the word *pow* in large letters. Just where the paper was torn, he could see the Indian's raised brown hand.

"Do you know what this is?"

Birger shook his head. Åke Vemdal put the piece of paper down on a notepad and took out another piece of paper folded like an envelope. Carefully he started poking it open with a pair of blunt pincers, then spread it out. It held a few grains of white powder, and a closer look revealed some transparent crystals among it.

"No medicine you know of?"

"No. Have you found a syringe?"

"No, I haven't."

Then Birger saw the pad of paper underneath the torn bag.

Antaris Balte on motocross bike. Reindeer herdsman. 8/15. Barbro Lund with son. 9/30.

"But that's her!"

Vemdal didn't understand.

"That's Barbro. And my boy."

He pointed.

"What the hell is that about?"

"They're the people who came out this morning. From the Area," said Vemdal.

"It's Barbro. Her name's Lund, was. Her maiden name."

"Why would she have given her maiden name?"

"She uses it when she signs her tapestries."

"She was questioned and then they left at about ten," said Vemdal. "The car was up at Björnstubacken."

"Can you take a car up there?"

"It's really only a tractor road. But obviously it was possible."

"That was Barbro. Good God!"

When the shock of relief had settled, he thought of the boy. How had she gotten him to go with her? Tomas hadn't even wanted to come fishing. For him to go demonstrating against uranium mining was incredible. But he had been there. Barbro Lund and son, it said on the list.

"Come back home," she said when he phoned from the Strömgrens' kitchen. Nothing else.

His stomach had troubled him from the moment he had seen her name on the list. He could feel the pressure on his bowels, but didn't get a chance to make use of Henry and Oriana's toilet. As he was on his way into the village, his guts rebelled and he had to get out and squat down behind some trees. Got no farther. A police car passed and slowed down. Birger tried to wave as he relieved himself.

This had never happened to him before. It happened when you were really frightened. Shit scared. In the trenches. When people were assaulted. It hadn't happened to either of those two in the tent. But it had happened to him afterward. After the fear.

Thick, dark-gray smoke was billowing out of a chimney farther down in the village, dispersing very slowly in the gleaming sky. He stared at the cloud of smoke as he squatted there. Everything had gone so quickly, he hadn't brought any paper with him from the car. He took a handful of birch leaves. It felt unpleasant afterward, and he had to wash, so he drove to the Westlunds'. Elna tried to give him some coffee, but his stomach was still queasy and he declined. Assar went with him out onto the steps. Birger saw that Elna had hung out the wash although it was Midsummer Day. Blue-gray longjohns and floral quilt covers. He had grown up in a work community outside Gävle, and when he was a child, no one ever hung the wash out on Sundays. You didn't even rake the gravel path when morning service was being held.

"Has Vidart come back?" he said.

The Duett was standing in rusty majesty down by the road, just up Vidart's drive.

"He's still in the hospital. The Duett came back sometime last night." Birger thought that was good.

"The Brandbergs want to play it down," he said.

"I suppose they hope the police have other things to think about."

As he got into the car, he thought he could smell burning rubber. There was something else, too, something nauseating. The grayish-black smoke was flickering in the heat above the houses. He had a neighbor in Byvången who burned butcher's waste and old tires on his Walpurgis bonfire. This was something like that. At first he thought it was coming from the Brandbergs' chimney, but then he saw it was the Lennartssons'. That reminded him of his fish.

When he knocked on the back door, no one came. He knocked again and finally pushed open the door and called out. It was quiet. He felt a vague unease, went on in, and opened the door to Lill-Ola's bedroom. Ola was lying on his back and the room was almost insufferably hot and heavy. She had put a checked car rug over him. A half-empty glass of milk stood on the bedside table. The envelope of pills was crumpled up. The man had taken all six.

Birger opened the window. The sun was baking at the front and the air almost hotter outside. The stench of burning he had noticed outside the Westlunds' came in. He felt Lill-Ola's pulse, but it was regular and calm. He was asleep, would sleep for a long time and probably wake with a headache. The large-pored skin was pale gray and moist, sweat oozing out of his throat and forehead. Birger removed the rug before leaving.

He was going to take his fish out of the freezer, but had to search around for a while before finding it. The stacks of cartons had been mixed up. Plastic bags of buns and vegetable packs lay among the meat. I didn't leave such a damned mess behind me, he thought. Lill-Ola must have been rummaging in the freezer. Did he think I had stolen something? Is he that crazy?

He heard sounds from the basement, the heating pipes echoing. He had to go around the house to find the basement door, and when he opened it, evil-smelling smoke poured out at him. As it cleared, he saw Bojan Lennartsson poking around in the boiler. Flakes of soot and feathers were swirling around in the smoke. She was bent double, raking in and out of the bottom of the boiler.

"Can I help?" he said.

He frightened her. She swung around with the rake in her hand. She almost looked smoked herself, grayish-black, and she was angry when she saw him. Or afraid.

"I'm heating up the water," she snapped.

"Yes, can I help? You've got backdraft. You've probably forgotten a damper?"

She didn't reply, but closed the boiler door. Now he could see she had been stuffing cardboard boxes into the boiler. She had cut them up into large pieces, and pale brown and white feathers lay trampled in the soot.

"It's done now," she said. "Ola is all right. You can go."

"He's taken all those pills I gave him. That wasn't exactly intended."

She wiped her dirty hands on her coverall and shooed him ahead of her as she went out.

"Is that dangerous?"

"No, I didn't give him that many."

She poked her head forward and trotted off toward the stairs. Upstairs she slammed the door behind her so that the windows rattled. She had had enough. So have I, he thought.

He found a bag of mint toffees in the glove compartment and ate them all as he drove along, telling himself it was best to eat all of them so that he could throw the bag away. He didn't want Barbro to find it. He was getting far too damned fat.

When the toffees were finished, he found himself again and again falling forward over the wheel. His eyelids kept drooping and meaningless pictures rose before his eyes. He saw the flesh of disintegrating fish in muddy water. He was forced to stop in Laxkroken. He called home from the phone booth by the store. Tomas answered.

"I must get some sleep," Birger said. "I'll park somewhere. How are things with Mom?"

"All right."

"What about you?"

"What d'you mean?"

"I thought perhaps you found it creepy up there."

"Where?"

"Where it happened. You were quite close."

There was silence at the other end.

"What?" said Tomas finally. "I wasn't there. I was at home last night."

It was past six by the time Birger got home. He had slept heavily and was aching from sitting leaning back against the headrest. Before driving the car into the yard, he stopped to look at the latticework above the veranda and on the balcony.

Behind the house was the hill with the dead aspens. Ten years before the site had been a sea of wild chervil and summer flowers, a forested hill behind. Abandoned cars had been half buried in the sea of flowers, as well as broken glass, old shoes, and rotting timber. The ground had been water-logged and heavily churned up. The madman they had bought it from had had dreams that had never materialized. But there had been red and black currant bushes, twenty-one of them. In among all that garbage, the poor soil had been generous.

After he had driven in, he again stood for a while, looking at the balcony latticework, letting his eyes wander down to the fine fretwork details around the veranda—still not scraped—and following them around a window. Too late, he discovered Barbro's face on the other side of the pane. As he raised his hand, she vanished.

She was already on her way upstairs when he got in, and didn't stop when he hailed her. He felt bad about having failed to notice her at once in the window.

"I was looking at the white paintwork," he said. "It looks quite good on the balcony."

He didn't hear her reply; the light steps continued up the stairs.

"I'll start on the veranda next weekend. I'll have to take a week of my holiday."

She had disappeared into the bedroom. Something had changed again. He knew these imperceptible shifts of ground by now. At first he had perhaps not been sufficiently observant. Or sufficiently wary. But he re-membered when she had begun to take to the roads.

That was two and a half years ago. She had taken the kick-sled and gone out, instead of sitting at her loom. That was after the meeting with their neighbor and his brother in the forest. Karl-Åke and his brother had marked the trees in the line along the neighboring patch. They had sold their parcel of land to the Cellulose Company.

Barbro had gone out on the kick-sled in the twilight after lunch and stayed out as long as there was still a little red left in the sky. Then she had started doing the same thing in the dark. Birger had checked the sled and nailed on reflectors so that at least she would be visible.

"Grief grows like a fetus," she said. "What will come of it all?"

He thought her words were too grandiose. Especially for a parcel of forest. Perhaps also for a miscarriage in the ninth week. She should make pictures of it instead. But the threads were just hanging from the cloth. It used to look industrious with all those multicolored threads of wool hanging from the tapestry. But now it looked dead. Day after day the same threads hanging in the same way.

At the end of February he had prescribed an antidepressant for her, but it made her feel bad and she soon stopped taking it. She also stopped going out on the kick-sled.

"They're going to clear-fell the whole lot," she said. "They're taking down our forest."

"It isn't ours and you know it."

"When Karl-Åke is free he drives into town and goes dancing at the Winn or else he flies his seaplane. Britt has never set foot in these woods. And I bet Astrid Åke hasn't been there for twenty or twenty-five years. She used to go there once in a while to pick berries. But Karl-Åke and Britt take the trailer and go to Norway to pick them. On a grand scale. The home forest is just something to clear-fell. So that we can have more advertising bumf from supermarkets to throw into the trash. So that Karl-Åke can have a bigger Mercedes."

"A concrete manure pit. That's what it's about. He wants a system for liquid manure. And the patch up here is actually ready for felling."

"They used to coppice it. They just took what was mature."

"That's not allowed anymore. Now you get a felling plan from the Forestry Department and you have to follow it."

He had thought they would begin to talk factually about forestry. He didn't approve of the clear-felling either. But it could at least be discussed. Barbro was sitting with her head turned away.

"Grief is growing," she said. "I don't know what to do with it. I feel bitterness and hatred. Maybe that's good. Maybe not. Hatred can be a strength."

"Psychobabble," he said, smiling. Perhaps that was rather harsh, he could see from her face. But it had been meant as a joke. They used to be able to joke with each other.

"Up in Alved, they're prepared to freeze to death for their river. The police pulled down their tents. The company takes my forest and Karl-Åke gets a bigger car."

"You can't call the forest yours," he said, so good-naturedly that she had to understand he thought she was partly right. She knew where the fox lairs were and where the mother elk used to stand with her calf when listening for their footsteps. She had taken him out with her when the Arctic raspberries were ripe and had gone straight to the plants down by the shore. She had made him drink water from the stream because it flowed northward. Got him out one chilly June night which she said was Trinity Sunday. There had been veils of mist over the wetland meadow by the shore.

"You should weave it," he said. "You should weave mouse holes and fox lairs and Arctic raspberry plants. That'd be great."

"It doesn't help. Tapestries can't stop other forests being felled. The stone where I usually sit and look at the lake has had moss on it as long as moss has existed. Until now. Now the moss will dry out and die. The aspens will die, too, although the company doesn't want them. They'll take them down and let them rot. They're going to fell timber across the stream. Pollute the water with engine oil."

Later on, all that had taken place, and the aspens had died. Some remained, swaying over the felled area behind the house. But, of course, the autumn storms would bring them down, one by one. It was not good to see. It was damned bad luck and there was nothing they could have done about it. You don't expect people to cut down trees around dwellings. When Barbro and he bought the old house, there had been one owner in between; Karl-Åke and Britt had built their villa fifteen years ago.

Toward that summer, two years ago, Barbro had fallen silent. That was long before they arrived with their machines. She would get on with her chores when he came home. Cooking, washing the dishes. Some tidying she hadn't had time to do during the day. But he didn't know what she did during the day. She didn't say much and sometimes just seemed morose, but occasionally she poured out wine for him. She didn't drink much, never had. But she sat opposite him with her glass of wine and then she talked. Held him with the wine but not with her eyes.

"Soon time now," she said.

At that stage, he always knew what she meant, but he skirted the issue. "Time for what?"

"They've begun clearing the forest road for motor vehicles."

"That can take years. This little bit is nothing to the company. They'll wait and do it together with something else. That might not be for ages."

"To think the alders are going to die," she said. "The alders and the birches and the big spruces and pines up by the ridge. The rowans by the sandpit, the willows, the heather, the whortleberry scrub, the bilberry scrub, the ferns and bracken, the wood sorrel, the little woodland mere, the great incredible swaying violet forest of *Geranium silvaticum,* the horsetail, the wrinkled prickly cap. All of them will dry out. Be burnt off. I was allowed to have it for ten years. Now it's finished."

"You always say that you know what you're party to merely by living in a Western country," he said.

"Maybe I don't want to be party to it any longer."

That was the worst; he never knew whether she was declaiming or whether it was real pain. He could never decide. Previously he had believed her when she said things hurt. And were hurting now. But was she hurting in the way she said?

"They have the law on their side. They're even rewarded for it. Big Mercedes, house, seaplane."

She refilled his wineglass and he grew sleepy. But she became angry if his eyelids began to droop. He tried to pull himself together.

"Do you remember what it was like when we came here?" he said. "Remember the first redcurrants we had here among the garbage? Do you remember how churned up the ground was? Ripped to pieces."

She was looking past him, somewhere above his ear. He could get angry, too.

"Those wounds are healed now," he said. "The cat's foot and the melancholy thistle have come back. You said so yourself the other day. The grass and trees are growing. It's healing. The clearing will, too. It takes a few years. Then it grows green again."

"I remember what it was like when we came here," she replied. "Astrid wondered why on earth we had come. 'What can a place like this be to people like you?'" she said. Both she and Karin Arvidsson phoned to ask if they could come and pick currants. Helga's old mother appeared on the steps one morning with two pails. "They're too much for you," they said. And we let them pick. We were full of how the soil just gave and gave. We wanted to be the same. But I got hardly any redcurrants for the freezer and I had to pick those from all twenty-one bushes, wherever they'd left some. Then we heard nothing from them. But Norrås almost broke Bonnie's back with a stake. And Wedin shot our cats. Picked them off one by one. And no one has ever said a word about us healing the wounds in this ground. Presumably they don't see it. But if I had gaudy petunias or evilsmelling marigolds in plastic pots or cartwheels painted pink and cream for nasturtiums to wind their way around—then they would see it and I would be praised."

There was hatred and contempt in her voice. Not only pain.

"I've made pastries for their parish evenings and taken English classes and given books away as Christmas presents—imagine! Books! But, of course, you reported Norrås for cruelty to animals when he left his sheep with no water. It makes me sick to walk along the road in case I meet that animal tormentor or that cat killer. And since the miscarriage, I've been afraid to meet anyone at all. Before, I thought I had life in me. Then they took it off me. Like the redcurrant bushes."

"They?"

"I had a miscarriage after picking cranberries under the power lines."

"This isn't sensible, Barbro."

But she didn't hear him.

"I didn't dare use the road after the miscarriage because I didn't want to meet anyone. But I had the forest. Pretty soon I'll have no forest. It belongs to them, according to you. The forest is Karl-Åke's. *Geranium silvaticum* is the name of that mauve mist under the elders."

She drank great gulps of the wine and he thought, What if she takes to drink?

"The midsummer flower. It has its image imprinted in its cell. But human beings don't carry their image within them."

"Genetically I suppose we do . . ."

She went on without listening.

"A human being can become anything, can grow askew. But there is a template of the midsummer flower within the plant itself, a small, clear image. The flower doesn't go beyond that. It can be crossbred, shift from deep purple to pale pink or pure white. It can be streaky or all one color. But it doesn't go beyond its image which it has deeply imprinted inside the innermost nucleus of its cell."

"That *is* an image," he said. "Weave it instead. Don't just talk. It's not good for you."

He meant it seriously. There was something wrong with talking in that way, apart from what she said. Long periods of silence alternating with moments of chat. Talk. No healthy person talks like this, he thought. She sits brooding for days and thinks all this out. Then she talks. She doesn't weave. Doesn't design any pictures, no patterns. Talks. It's great sometimes, but not really healthy.

"No! I can't weave. You want me to replace the forest with images. The county council would put them up on hospital walls. But I want to have the forest. The sick want the forest. They want to live."

That March, one of the saviors of the river had come from Stockholm to give a lecture in the parish hall. Birger didn't get there until it was all over because he had been out on call. The parish ladies were washing dishes. In the main hall, all the lights were out except the one above the rostrum. In the semi-darkness below the stage, Barbro was sitting with the river saver at a hardboard table from which the ladies had removed the paper table-cloth. Barbro and he had their heads close together, a yellow light from the rostrum casting a halo around them. The environmentalist had dark blond hair falling below his shoulders, parted in the middle. He was wearing a striped carpenter's shirt and Lapp boots. All those who had stayed to wash dishes were standing in the doorway watching, when Birger caught sight of them.

"Was it him?" he asked her now. "The river saver? The one with the Jesus hair?"

And it was.

"But why in the name of heaven did you say he was your son?"

"It was a joke."

She was in the bedroom putting rolled-up stockings and thick socks into a box. He didn't know whether she was packing or cleaning out drawers. She went on with a box of sweaters and cardigans. When she went to fetch another box from the wardrobe, he followed her. He knew he ought to say something that would stop her, if she was packing. But if she was just tidying up, it would be unnecessary and perhaps even risky to say anything.

"Shall we get a bottle of wine?" he said. "I think I've got a Moselle cooling."

"No, thanks."

That was when he had really understood that the therapeutic wine drinking was over.

"You must phone Vemdal," Birger said.

"Oh, we weren't even anywhere near."

"Where were you last night?"

"Up at Starhill. I didn't see anything."

"You'd better phone him anyhow."

"Why?"

"They're looking for him."

She snorted. It couldn't be called a laugh.

"They'll have to sort that out themselves."

H e told her how he had found the eel. But before he talked, he was given something to eat at an inn in Steinmo. The woman ate a little, too, and drank yellowish wine, but most of all she kept looking at him. And she was amused.

He had salmon trout with cream sauce and morels and boiled potatoes, large and yellow, real pebble-shaped ones. When the proprietress had brought the menu in its plastic folder, the woman had waved it aside.

"The salmon trout," she said. "And wine."

They hadn't exchanged many words in the car. He had been ashamed of his muddy jeans as well as his shirt, which he had dried above the stove in the cottage. It smelled of fish in the heat.

"It's the eel," he said, so then he had to tell her. She kept calling him Johan every other sentence. He must have told her his name in the car. Although he was horribly embarrassed, he asked her:

"What's your name?"

"Ylajali," she said. "Ylajali Happolati."

He was sitting in a ray of sunlight from the window, hot and drunk from the food. There was a smell of grass and cattle dung coming through the open window, and below the hay meadows he could see the river, a sluggish ribbon of colorless, gleaming water. She poured more wine into his glass. He would have preferred milk, as he was still hungry. She must have understood, because she asked and a girl brought some in a glass jug. He was also given maize pudding with cloudberry preserve and thick yellow cream. The woman had no dessert.

When they had finished, he had to go to the toilet, of course, and he felt ashamed of that, too. But he said he had to change the water in the eel pail. In the car, he fell asleep at once and when he woke, his shirt stank so much, he noticed it himself. He pulled it off. It felt strange sitting there naked to the waist, but he couldn't very well put his thick sweatshirt on in that heat.

They were driving westward, so she must have been heading for the coast. They had not discussed how far he would go on with her. When he was awake, he thought he ought to say something, but he couldn't come up with anything except to ask whether Happolati was a Finnish name. No, it wasn't, she said, apparently making fun of him.

"I thought you had a Finnish accent."

She burst out laughing.

"Never say that to a Swedish Finn! My name's not Happolati. I just said that because you were so hungry."

He could make nothing of it all.

"What about your other name then? Ylja . . ."

"You can call me Ylja. That's good."

Good? He didn't have to call her anything. She kept using his name. "Are you hot, Johan?" Silly, really. Ordering without looking at the menu, and wine and two desserts, then eating only a little of the salmon trout, that was upper-class. "Let the seat back if you like, Johan. Did you sleep well, Johan?"

They got out when they had reached the high peak and walked down across the marshland to look at the river running below the steep precipice, a hundred or two hundred meters down to the water. The small falls in the perpendicular cliff on the other side looked immobile at a distance. White clouds, stiff water spraying from the foam of greenery on the mountainsides.

She had changed into boots and was standing on the crowberry scrub at the edge, just in front of him. He didn't know if he would dare stand like that with someone behind him. With Gudrun perhaps. But the woman stood there in her jeans and a smart but shabby pullover, practically leaning over to look down into the depths, where the water rushed out with no sound audible to them up there.

He had put on his sweatshirt, for the wind from the mountain heath was cold, but when they got back into the car, he had to take it off again. She looked at him once or twice.

She's old, he thought. Her fair hair was coarse. Up on the mountain she had fastened it into a short ponytail with a rubber band at the back of her neck. She had a straight nose and a clean-cut chin, her lips pale, with no lipstick. She had painted her eyes. He felt peculiar when she looked at his naked chest.

"Do you want a shirt?" she said.

He didn't know what to answer. He couldn't have gotten his shoulders and neck into any shirt of hers. She said nothing more and he fell asleep again.

When they had gotten down level with the river and started along the winding roads north, she stopped by a building with the coop sign on it. It was closed but she managed to get a man to come and open up the gas pump. After filling up, she went inside with him and came back with a shirt, toothbrush, a cake of soap, and a towel with Betty Boop on it.

"I haven't any money," he said, and he heard himself sounding angry. Nonetheless, he went down to the river and washed. The shirt was ordinary, brown-and-white-striped flannel, and he felt at home in it. She had also guessed his size right. He checked that the eel was still alive and changed the water in the pail again.

He now realized he was running away but he didn't know where they were going. She seemed able to be silent for any length of time without being embarrassed.

"You've been up to some mischief," she said abruptly after he had been half-asleep for a long stretch.

Mischief was a silly word. But it meant she didn't believe him. He had told her about the well.

"You didn't want to be seen in the villages," she said. "But you're beginning to feel safer now."

He didn't reply.

"If you want to think things over, you can stay with us for a while."

Who were "we"? Did she have a husband? They drove all that evening and finally he dared ask:

"Have you got a cabin up here somewhere?"

"My family has a place."

She drove fast and quite fiercely up all the hills, taking them up into the mountains. He looked at the dashboard to see if the engine was about to boil. She was sure not to have thought about that. But the Saab kept an even temperature. The car was fairly new, the seats already shabby. Everything she was wearing and the stuff flung in the back seemed to be the kind of thing you paid an unnecessarily high price for. She was wearing shoes with straps around the back of her foot and leather heels scuffed at the back. Gudrun would never have worn shoes like that when driving. Nor would she have smoked. She knew that made him feel sick in a car.

Annie had locked the door, having no intention of going out anymore. But they had to fetch water. There was a well in among the trees diagonally behind the house. The privy was directly across the road in an old barn, but they didn't have to go over there because there was a chamber pot in the cupboard under the sink. They brought back great bunches of flowers when they went for water. She had found jam jars in the attic and in them they put wild chervil, red campion, and buttercups. Mia worked with her lips pressed tight together. She was pale.

How much did she know? That there had been an accident. That was what Annie had said. Two people had been killed in an accident and they didn't know how it had happened.

She thought Mia would ask after Dan, but she didn't, just asked what they were going to have for breakfast. They had neither bread nor milk, and the store was closed.

They found some groceries left behind or forgotten in a cupboard by the stove, including a box of waffle mix, so Annie said she would make pancakes for breakfast. And rosehip tea. Now they would have some cold macaroni, then go to bed.

"It's not night yet," said Mia.

"Yes, it is. But it's light like this up here."

"The sun's shining over there."

On the slope where the houses above Fiskebuan were, the grass was gleaming in the sun.

They dragged the iron bed into the bedroom and put it next to the other bed. There was also a rickety bedside table. Annie draped her Palestine shawl over it and put a jar of flowers beside the alarm clock. They both liked having the sound of the radio once she got it going. Then they crept into bed.

Mia lay with cold little paws on the covers. Annie rubbed them and tucked them in. The electric radiator ticked. It would soon get warmer.

The child fell asleep, pale even in her sleep. Evensong came over the radio. A clergyman said you should deliver yourself unto the night. God was in the night. In the daytime we have problems to solve, he said. At night we deliver ourselves unto God. She thought about the two young people who had gone to bed in the tent and delivered themselves unto the bright night and its god.

Then came the weather forecast and she could relax a little, it was so ordinary. The whole of this long, wet, windy country with its mountain regions and coastal areas, its lighthouses and headlands, its thousands of islands and great lakes, was now having a few hot days and mild nights. The forecast slowly ascended to the spot where they were now and went on past them to the northernmost point, to the light that never went out.

She couldn't sleep. There were no blinds to pull down and it was still daylight inside. If she fell asleep, someone might come to the bedroom window and stand there, looking in at their faces. She had drawn the cotton lace curtains across, but they were no protection, the pattern too open. She got up and hung the bedspread over one window and the Palestine shawl over the other. It wasn't long enough. The beds could also be seen from the kitchen window.

She thought about Dan not knowing anything about what had happened. They were looking for him. They were also looking for a woman called Barbro Torbjörnsson, the doctor's wife. When they found Dan, he would come to her.

Then she noticed everything was quiet within her. She had always talked to him. That had gone on ever since they had been together.

At first, when they had not yet exchanged a single personal word, he had often said things that made her feel uncertain. She had been unable to answer, but afterward she had thought up a continuation. She found ingenious replies and it became a conversation. A kind of conversation.

That didn't stop when they really started talking to each other. Not even when they became lovers. On the contrary. Nor when he distrusted her. He occasionally said she was playing with him, like a mother playing forbidden games with a son. But she never showed him it was serious.

When they decided to go to Jämtland, he ought to have believed her. But the letters and telephone calls were sometimes so strange. She could hear the chill in his voice and she wept and carried on to find out what it was. Then the coins ran out at the other end.

Sometimes she thought she had had some kind of fever. She was hot and heavy from going around carrying him inside her. Whenever they met, the fierce tensions in her slackened. That was happiness. Or, anyhow, freedom from torment.

That was now silent. She hadn't turned to him for over twenty-four hours. She hadn't even noticed that the state she had lived in was over. She couldn't believe there was any other explanation than that he was no longer out there. Was not alive.

Nerves and muscles hurt. Turning over in bed gave her a few moments' relief, but after a while it was just as bad again. Her ear started aching if she lay on her side. She dozed off and woke thinking someone was standing over her. She screamed and Mia woke. There was no one else in the room.

"You were dreaming, Mom," Mia said.

Annie could still see a blurred gray face leaning over her own. A lined, wooden face. It took a long time for her to realize it didn't exist. She tried to think about other things; her cases of books that would come later, the big suitcase containing her linen, and the crate of china. Dan would think she had brought too much with her, and maybe the wrong things. But there was a great deal she had not been able to throw away.

She tried to think through the contents of her crates and cardboard boxes, thinking about them piece by piece and picturing them in front of her. That gradually made her doze off again. But she woke once more, her mouth dry and her head aching fiercely.

All she could see was fractured images from the night and the day that had passed. They were meaningless, yet seared behind her eyes. The police officers' boots with reflector bands on them. White sleeping-bag feathers. Oriana Strömgren's egg timer—a chicken made of white and yellow plastic. The face lay in wait for her all the time, that lined, wooden, primeval face. She woke Mia and put a blanket around her.

"We must get out of here. We'll go to the lady up there."

She put the other blanket around herself and they went out into the night of the birdsong they had heard through the rough window glass in which the light trembled. The sounds were loud now, pressing in on her, and she could no longer defend herself against either sounds or light.

The slope was very steep and the house up there had blank, empty windows. Mia banged on the door, thumping with her little fist. Aagot Fagerli stood there with a pullover over her nightdress, at first without her teeth in. She let them in and went ahead of them into the bedroom. Once there, she turned her back on them and took something out of a glass of water on the chair by the bed. Then her face looked filled out again. Mia looked on very carefully and asked about it afterward. Annie would never even have noticed had she been alone.

She was cold. Great shudderings ran through her body. She seemed to be seeing details sharply, as if she had the vision of a bird of prey. But she could no longer find any order in why she was there. Why had she come to all this light. Mia's face was so small.

"Lie down, now," said the old lady to her. "Darn it, girl, how *sprø* you are." Annie would become familiar with Aagot's voice, with its half-Norwegian speech and fairly innocuous American oaths. And the smell of spices in her privy. Spices and mustiness. A blanket and a sofa in knobbly checked material, yellow and brown. A small ornamental lamp. There was a faint smell of paraffin. She switched on nothing electric. That would have been pointless in this room flooded with light. She pulled down the dark blue blinds and let Annie lie on the sofa with the little orange dome to stare at. Aagot gave her some hot milk with some kind of liquor in it. She had sweetened it with brown honey.

Sprø. She thought that meant frail. Inside she was like the glass in a thermos.

She could hear the stiff rustle as Mia and the old woman turned the pages of a big picture book on the kitchen table, then she dozed off.

T here was a rumble as the car crossed a bridge. She stopped, opened the door, and he could hear a waterfall. The sun was low, swollen, and red, almost hidden by a mountain ridge. They must be very high up. Down below the road was a forest of birches with moisture-filled black and green lichens. Birds were busy everywhere, thousands of them. Their calls soared below and above the small waterfalls of the rapids and the murmur from the great metal pipe running under the bridge.

He felt afraid. It must be because he had woken so abruptly and didn't know where they were. The road appeared to continue on up toward the high mountain. Worried that his voice might sound childish and angry, he didn't say anything. Foolishly enough, he could feel his throat thickening. He had to wake up properly.

She had a rucksack with a frame in the trunk. She took it out and started stuffing into it everything lying around in the car, putting the soap and toothbrush wrapped in the Betty Boop towel on top.

He took the rucksack and heaved it on. They climbed down the steep slope to the rapids and started following a path along the river.

"Is it far?" he said.

"Fifty-five minutes."

Idiotically exact. She might just as well have said an hour. He imagined she always wanted to appear certain.

"Then I can't carry the pail in my hand," he said, stopping to tie it onto the rucksack.

They left the river and came out into rocky terrain where there were parched old spruces that were barely alive, some of them with sickly witch's broom growing wildly in them. The path sometimes ran across bog channels smelling fermented from the springy mass beneath them. She walked ahead of him and they rested only twice the whole way. Then she smoked. The last bit sloped downward. He saw a dull surface of water through the trees, clouds of mist swirling above it, reddish in the morning light. The lake lay in a round bowl of mountains. The water was utterly still.

"We're there," she whispered, though he could see no house. She seemed to him to be slinking like a lynx the last bit down to the shore, where she sank to her knees and scooped up some water in her hands. She rinsed her face and sat for a long while with her head down.

After a while she seemed to rouse herself, and signed to him to come after her. If she had resembled a lynx, he felt like an elk, a clumsy yearling crashing down and breaking dead branches. A diver was making its way across the lake with a silvery-red plow of water behind it. Johan frightened it and it started rising, its wings flapping and feet kicking and tearing the water.

"You can let the eel go now," she said.

He shook his head.

"But what are you going to do with it?"

He didn't know. They started walking again. The path along the shore branched off and ran up through the forest, where the sow-thistle had started appearing. It was very light now and the heat rose as they moved away from the mere and the raw mist. He caught a glimpse of a house between the birches, a large brown timbered building with a glassed-in veranda. He was amazed to find a house like that there. No car could get along the path, though possibly a tractor could.

The glass in the veranda windows was flashing orange lightning in the morning sun. The roof ridges had black wooden bird silhouettes on them and the whole house had tarred weather-boarding all over it. Then he realized it was a shooting lodge, the kind bigwigs had had built at the beginning of the century.

She didn't take him up to the big house, but went on into the birchwoods to a wooden outbuilding beside a riverbank.

"You can sleep in the grouse shed." That wasn't as bad as it sounded, for when they went in, he saw it was equipped with bunks and a table in front of the one window. It smelled of foam rubber. The mattresses had begun to smell in the heat still shut in the closed cottage.

She vanished without a word, but he knew she would come back. His towel, toothbrush, and soap lay on the table. A mosquito window was propped against the table and he started putting it up. When she returned with a glass of milk and two sandwiches, cool air was pouring in through the netting. He sat down on the bed, leaning forward because of the upper bunk, and ate the food. She stood smoking by the window, looking out. When he had finished, he kicked off his boots, crawled into bed, and pulled the quilt up over him. Then she turned around. He couldn't see her face, it was almost black against the light behind.

"You and I have something to do," she said. "Then you can sleep."

She came over and pulled the quilt off him. Leaning over, she put her hand on the front of his jeans. She gave a little laugh, like a snort. She must have felt his dick throbbing.

When she pulled down the zipper of his fly, he was scared. He felt she was handling him carelessly and he was afraid his foreskin would get caught in the zipper. But of course the trousers were tight and she had to make an effort to get them open. Anyhow, he had nothing there when she got it out, only a soft handful of skin and slack muscles.

"So soft," she said, and now she sounded like ptarmigan calling far away in the birch woods. His dick started rising again. Her breath smelled of spirits. She had gone straight to the duty-free liquor up there. Not that surprising. She had driven a long way and was perhaps not feeling too well. But she hadn't brought the bottle with her to offer him some, and that angered him. The anger, small as it was, did him good. For a moment he had been really frightened, not just anxious but really frightened. Her mouth was slightly open, her tongue playing in the corner of it. She kept fondling him all the time. ,

He had given quite a lot of thought to an occasion like this. That it would come. But he had thought about a girl, a faceless girl, yes, but soft. He was the one who was going to do all sorts of things. He had worried about not finding the way, not really knowing, or being clumsy and hurting her. But not like this.

She was holding his testicles, her middle finger far in, embarrassingly close to his asshole. He wriggled a little, but the fingers were firm in their grip, a strong hand, short and broad.

Then she rose slowly and he followed, not really knowing if that was from her hold on him. She fumbled at the bunk above, pulled, the foam rubber mattress came tumbling down and she flung it onto the floor. Then she turned him with his back to the mattress and the next moment he was sitting on it. She stayed where she was, undressing.

That went quickly. She had nothing on but a pullover and slacks and a pair of rustling pale blue panties. He was sitting with his knees drawn up, his hands clasped over them. He couldn't make up his mind to do anything. His ears were ringing and the light was getting stronger and stronger. He could hear the water in the river and the birds.

She pulled off his trousers and underpants, now so filthy he was ashamed. The slimy mud from the well had penetrated through the material of his trousers. He had stood by the road in a shirt smelling of fish, a faded sweatshirt under his arm. She could think what she liked.

Once he was naked, she stood astride him and he had her bush of curly hair right at eye level. But he closed his eyes. He had a hardon now and it was throbbing.

He sat leaning slightly back, propping himself on his hands, and he didn't have to do anything. She parted her legs and threaded herself onto him. It was a little awkward, his dick grubbing about in the small lips and flaps. But it was moist and he slid in and she sank down, heavily, far too heavily onto him. For although the pleasure made his nerves tingle, it hurt. She twisted his dick back as she leaned away from him, and he came with a pain that made his upper lip curl back from his teeth.

Then he recovered, grimacing and leaning back. She slid off him and he felt it run and run. But she ignored it, took the quilt off the lower bunk, and drew it over them.

They hadn't kissed. My fault, he thought. I did nothing. It just came for me.

He leaned over her and with his lips explored the now-pale face. He felt the coarseness of her hair, but everything else was very soft. Her lips were quite small, like the lips down there. And her tongue had a lively little point. She was like sand, soft and harsh and pale. As he lay leaning over her, he felt how very much stronger he was, that she was not a large woman. Small and fair.

After a while she began to finger him again, and when there was a response, she pulled. This was not as he had imagined. He had thought all this kind of thing went like a dream, almost imperceptibly. Not purposefully like this.

Then she did it again. Though this time he lay on his back as she sat astride him. He was more assured now. He had put his hands on her thighs below her hips. If she bent too far back, he would pull her toward him. This time it was good in a dreamy way, almost as if in his sleep. She closed her eyes and he saw her teeth gleaming with saliva as she drew up her upper lip. He could see the thin skin of her eyelids quivering and her jaw muscles tightening. She's enjoying it, he thought, and I am the one doing it. Move slowly. He gathered strength in his strange, torpid state in order to raise his back and turn them both over. But then she opened her eyes and said:

"What's your god called?"

He didn't understand the question, and echoed:

"God?"

He wasn't even sure he had heard right. Perhaps he was making a fool of himself by asking like that. But that was the word. She repeated it and it was there, like a stone in your mouth.

"You're sensitive to disturbances," she said quietly, and slid away. Everything about him had softened. But she was still expecting him to answer. She lay on her side, propped on one elbow, looking at him quizzically. His head was empty. Called? he was about to echo, but didn't. What is God called?

He remembered a preacher with a voice that had sunk from the first syllable so that it sounded like singing: "Jeesus is waiting for you! Jeesus!" And his grandmother beginning to tremble. He had felt her body shaking inside her coat, and he had withdrawn from her, ashamed and wanting to pee.

"The god of your forefathers," she said, helping him, and at last he understood.

"Peive, one of the Lapp gods," he said uncertainly.

That was school knowledge. His teacher's enthusiasm had made him feel just as embarrassed as he was now.

"I thought Tjas Olmai was your man, otherwise."

She could see from his face that he knew nothing and she laughed.

"The water man," she said. "The god of the fish."

"A fleeting moment stole my life away." It was a popular song. Or a poem. Birger didn't really read poetry, but he might have heard it on the radio. Anyhow, it fitted. More than a moment, of course. Twenty, twenty-five minutes. Or beyond time. It had probably been happiness. Or in any case the most powerful thing he had ever experienced. He ought to tell her about it. But he couldn't. He should have done it right away.

Or now?

He slowly drained the last of his drink. The liquor was very diluted, the ice melted. Then he went up to the bedroom and stood outside the door, actually fearful. He thought about how much had happened in a year, eighteen months. Slid away and been displaced.

Then he opened the door and she sat up suddenly in bed as if she, too, were frightened. Her face was pale in the night light, her dark hair in a thick braid tied with a ribbon.

Did she think he should have knocked? Had yet another displacement taken place without his noticing?

"This is my fault, too, Barbro," he said.

And realized at once what a bloody stupid thing it had been to say.

"I mean, I know it's my fault."

She stared at him, her eyes quite black; the pupils must have been enormously enlarged. Her mouth was tightly shut and colorless. He realized he couldn't tell her. What should he say? I was involved in a peculiar thing; it was at the Sulky, you know, that little hotel at the end of Rådhusgatan. It was the strangest thing that's ever happened to me, and then things turned out this way. That's why I seemed to sadden.

But he didn't say it, for he already knew she wouldn't ask what it was he had been through. She would just look. Her pupils were as large as crowberries now. He had to touch her instead and do it now, take her.

He really had thought he was going to do it. Then the moment when it was at least possible had gone. She twisted around, lay down with her back to him, her body quite still under the covers, her face invisible.

Then he did a hell of a stupid thing. He took hold of her when it was wrong, although he knew it. He sat heavily down on the bed and put his hands on her shoulders, pulling her up around toward him. Her body twisted unnaturally because she neither cooperated nor resisted. He ran his lips over her hair and forehead, felt the knitted eyebrows, sought her mouth, and at that moment her arms shot out and she pushed him away, making a sound like a groan or a grunt.

At first he thought it was because he smelled of whiskey; then came the true, profound humiliation. He knew he had been frightened of this all his life. In one way or another. He got up and went over to the door. She didn't move.

Talking crap about the forest and the river and the guilt of the west. I have a double chin and sandals. That's all. Stomach, belly. That's it.

But she was in a bad way. Perhaps worse than she realized. He stood for a moment with his hand on the door handle, looking at the hump under the duvet. Not a strand of hair was visible. He felt calmer now. It was as if he were looking at a patient.

"Which one of you thought up that joke?" he said.

"What joke?"

"That he was to pretend to be your son?"

"I don't know. He did, probably."

He was lying on the bed with the star pattern of the net curtain on his bare brown skin. There was sun in the room, body heat and moisture. The scent of him that used to come to her in her sleep rose from the bed, although nothing there was moving. A new pattern appeared to prevail, the light picking out other strands of hair among the ash blond. A movement could endanger the equilibrium in the room. Nor did it seem a movement as she slid down and the moist skin on his upper lip met her tongue, but more like a displacement of time, a slow movement of a wave bringing them together after weeks of cold and haste and hours of terror.

She whispered, "Dan, Dan," thinking, I oughtn't to, anyhow not now, for the cottage is bright with sunlight and there are windows in all directions. Mia had spotted the Volkswagen Beetle when she woke. It had been driven down behind the barn on the opposite side of the road. They had rushed down from Aagot Fagerli's house to see if he had come.

But Mia had immediately gone out again. Perhaps it was the memory of that time. She ought not to have such memories, let alone be given any more. It's only natural, Dan said. Annie thought she could just see Mia's face up on the slope, hidden by birch scrub, then appearing again. But thinking was not possible now, sorting out what was good or not good. "How did you find us?" she whispered, and he said it was the rucksack they had left on the steps. He had recognized it. The striped woolen rucksack from Crete.

"Why didn't you want to open the door?"

She said it into his ear at the very moment he entered her and she felt her nerves tingle. A tree of light branched all over her body. She forgot the question, but repeated it when he let her rest in a moment of calmer breathing, in restraint, while he whispered: "Don't move, don't move." And then:

"Open the door?"

For he knew nothing.

"Were you asleep? In Nirsbuan? It was you, wasn't it?"

She had no desire to talk much about it, not now anyway, and she couldn't bring herself to describe that terrible walk all over again. Nor did she need to, he said. Everything was all right now. Everything was just the way it should have been when she got off the bus. He said she enclosed him like a tight, soft, wet glove and so everything was all right now and she had no need to wonder. But she did think one thing was strange.

"But I knocked on the window."

He knew nothing about that, but probably because he had been asleep, sound asleep.

"Why didn't you meet the bus? Did you think Mia and I were coming on the old Midsummer Eve?"

That was it. Nothing that had happened had anything to do with them. She had just happened to walk past. It was like being a witness to a train crash. It had nothing to do with you, but was simply terrible. They were free now.

She had been ensnared. A fish in a net. A thousand stupid things, people, regulations, papers, and things, things, things. Like the car battery. In the winter it had to be taken out, carried indoors, and left on the drainboard if it was more than ten degrees below zero and if the car was to start at a quarter to seven.

The baby-sitter took tranquilizers because she needed to lose weight, but the truth was she couldn't even vacuum-clean without them. So on some days her face was like a pale moon with spots, and she had to be sent home. For Annie it was back to the car, the road, the black ice, lamplight. And at college. "Sit down and draw now, Mia. I'll get you some cookies."

Eight lessons with cookie crumbs and chalk dust and the smell of sweaters and exhalations, Mia wanting to pee and being bored, her chatter dispersing whatever concentration there had been in the class-room, if any.

Dan had come to the college during the revolution. The revolt, anyhow. It had been slightly ridiculous, because he was so slim and his words so powerful. Beautiful little body, dark stubble. He never cared what he ate. To revolt. That presumably really meant to roll around. Just as we rolled around. It hurt a little at first. "Isn't it a little nice as well?" he whispered. Oh God, oh God, oh God.

At first in town, at an artist friend's of his. Those friends. Sometimes a three-week acquaintance: share everything, Kropotkin. But this one was the kind who still bought chips. Cans of beer, bottles of turpentine, bags of potato chips, flattened tubes of paint, paint on cardboard plates, stained mattress. To revolt! With a pupil.

Grandmother Henny baby-sat in Karlbergsvägen, thinking Annie was taking a course. Then Mia and she had begun to stay overnight in Mälarvåg, the second winter. That was the car battery. But Dan as well.

Out there, though, the atmosphere had turned gray around them. The revolt was sluggish in a county college of great brutes who wanted to be policemen and put rebels up against the wall. And little girls wanting to be nurses and dental receptionists and put on bandages and mended people as well as rebels.

In the corridor it always smelled of cake baking and hair spray. The pupils exchanged magazines and drank beer. Dan was a storm petrel but the storm was a long time coming. They were still washing their nylon shirts and hanging them up to dry.

She would never have broken free. Although three colleagues had ceased talking to her, she would never have had the energy, never dared (Mia!), if he hadn't come in one morning when Mia was asleep and crept under the covers and made love wonderfully and sweetly as if in a summer cottage.

She would never have broken free if Mia hadn't woken, seen them, and run out, still quite silent but crying, and met Arlén, who taught social studies.

"Dan's hurting Mommy!"

Then it was the principal, his light office with its tapestry pictures and woodwork bowls.

"Your presence here is no longer a matter of course."

Trembling chin. The ballpoint to hold on to. He was more terrified than she was. God, how she had longed for a reprimand, a few gobs of words, real language! These academics on the staff, councillors and female volunteers.

Dan was like a dog shaking itself, not even wet. But my life.

It was the test. He must realize that.

Mia didn't want to come. That was already quite clear when they started driving up. She curled herself up into a ball in the back, put her hands over her face, and said something inaudible in a sharp little voice. Anna asked Dan to stop.

"Want to go back home."

Annie tried to explain, but she wouldn't listen.

"Want to go home. Want to go home."

She was speaking doggedly behind her hands. Annie got out and went to sit in the back with her.

"We're going up to Starhill now. We're not going to Nirsbuan at all. And we can take another road to Starhill. We won't be going past where we walked before. We're going to live up there. There are other children there."

Dan had started driving again while Annie was talking. Mia threw herself backward, arching her back and screaming.

"Stop, Dan!" said Annie.

But he drove on, very slowly along the bumpy timber track up toward Björnstubacken. When they stopped at a loading bay by the road, she tried to take Mia in her arms, but the girl had grown big over the last year and she was strong when she resisted. Dan had gotten out of the car and was standing watching them. He's thinking I'll give up now. He damned well looks as if this is just what he expected.

Anger flared up and died away just as quickly. She grew angry when she was under pressure and could say idiotic things. But she had never before felt under pressure like this with Dan. Mia was sobbing now, though she sounded slightly calmer. Outside, Dan was tying up the rucksack, looking rather absent, and she thought he was pale. The police questioning had presumably been more unpleasant than he had let on.

"Do you still want to?" he had asked her when they left. She had simply nodded.

"You're not afraid?"

It had nothing to do with them. It was something that had happened during Midsummer drunkenness—tourists, a foreigner. It was horrible, but it was over.

"We're a whole gang up there," he said. "No one is alone."

Packing up their things and paying Aagot Fagerli had gone quickly. Aagot had asked about Dan. They could have coffee before they left. She seemed to want to see him. But Annie said no thank you and that they were in a hurry.

"Hurry" was a word from the old days, but when it slipped out of her she thought it all right. At least it was something people understood. She felt the same powerful relief as she had the first time she had left the village. But Dan set off toward the store.

"I've got to make a phone call."

His words seemed to remain hanging in the car. She had thought they had left all that behind. He sounded as if he were tied up, fully booked. Perhaps he was phoning home? But where, in that case? He had said he no longer had anything to do with his parents.

But there had been a murder. She herself had phoned her parents from Aagot Fagerli's house and told them everything was all right.

He spoke earnestly for a long time. She could see him through the glass and it hurt inside, the nerves in her stomach cutting like knives. It hurt so much, she realized with a kind of astonishment that she was jealous. Suspicious. I am destroyed. Perhaps I can never live any other life but this complicated one.

He said nothing about the phone call when he came back. Perhaps he hadn't time. The police car slid out from the space behind the gas pumps the moment they set off up toward the road to the homestead and the mountain. It must have been there all the time, and now it passed them and flagged them down before they had gotten out of the village.

She thought it unpleasant, but Dan was openly scornful. He told them that the faded red VW had been outside Aagot Fagerli's barn since early that morning.

"You could have come in at any time," he said.

They took no notice of what he said, only asked him to go with them to the campsite where they had an incident room. Annie had to have coffee with the old Norwegian woman after all, afterward roaming around the steep slope with Mia until he came back two hours later. By then they were hungry and she ought to have gone back to the cottage to fix something, at least for Mia. But she thought it would take so long to explain to the old woman why they had come back. And to go shopping for food, then clean up the cottage again after they had eaten. Anyway, Dan had some fruit in the car.

He had two ways of being. He was mostly turned on and energetic, a field of force surrounded him, and he inspired others. When he moved around a room and spoke, everyone looked at him. She had thought of intellectual and sexual energy when she had seen him for the first time, thinking it was zest for life.

But it was more a gathering of strength, willpower, defying boredom, and loss of energy. Dancing. Keeping himself visible.

His other way of being always started with pallor, his lips turning thin, his voice slightly irritable as he retreated into himself, and he seemed to turn gray. She wondered whether that was coming on now. He walked around the car without looking at them. In a quiet voice, she tried to explain to Mia that they were going to walk a totally different way. They weren't going to wade across the river. There was a small bridge higher up and then an easy path through the forest all the way to Starhill.

"All our things will go there later."

"How? Cars can't go that way."

Yes, how? They would presumably have to be carried up.

"I don't know," said Annie. "But we'll have all our things there."

When they reached the bridge late in the afternoon, she saw it was quite big and the path was broad with tractor tracks along it. Dan said the bridge was new and they were making a road for timber trucks, so presumably they were going to start felling soon. The commune felt threatened, but still didn't really know what was going on or how close to Starhill the felling would come.

"Petrus doesn't want us to use the bridge."

"Because it belongs to the Enemy?"

But he seemed to dislike her joking about it.

It took them a long time to get up there. Usually it took about an hour, Dan said, but they had heavy rucksacks with them and often had to stop to let Mia rest. The much-used path ran steadily upward, the bark on spruce roots worn away by feet, paws, and hooves. Occasionally they saw a deep, clear hoofprint where the ground was dark and muddy. Annie knew nothing about tracks, but such large cows didn't exist, so she told Mia elk had been there, leaving their round and oval spheres of droppings in big heaps.

They came to a plateau and Mia had to rest again. Annie was worried Dan might think they were being too slow. But he let Mia look through his binoculars and talked encouragingly to her. The spruces were sparser now and there were no pines to be seen. Birches had taken over with their black banners of lichen and pale green clouds of foliage.

Dan whistled under his breath as he walked. Annie realized it was quite unconscious, a toneless whistling through scarcely pursed lips. She could distinguish two tunes. One was a popular song from the fifties of which she remembered only the chorus:

"We'll go far
we'll be fine

in the back
here in the car."

The other was a song of yearning. They had been walking for over an hour when she realized what it was: *The Umbrellas of Cherbourg*. Film music. She couldn't connect either of the tunes with Dan. Of course, that was because she knew nothing about his previous life. Things hadn't been good for him. That was all he had said. Had they been so poor? Were there any really poor people nowadays? Her own background never felt so petit bourgeois as when she thought about his past. She didn't even know how to ask the questions.

Her head was aching and she thought it must have something to do with the pressure of the rucksack straps on her shoulders. After a time she couldn't think about anything else. She had thought they would talk to each other, but they did so only at the beginning, then fell into a kind of vacant plodding and got out of breath on the uphill stretches. Her headache settled above one eye, where it kept exploding and flickering. As soon as the going was more or less level or went downhill, Dan started whistling again. She wished he would stop, but was reluctant to say anything. In the end she began to lag behind with Mia in order not to have to hear that hissing little whistling, just out of tune.

After two hours, the birches started thinning out. They walked down into a hollow where the path turned darkly muddy, thick clumps of globe-flowers growing in the grass, the buds still tight, hard, and green, only faintly turning yellow. She remembered they had bloomed at Nirsbuan and realized that there they must be very high up, almost in another season. She also saw the grass was grazed where the slopes rose after the hollow. When they reached the first hilltop, Starhill became visible.

A handful of cottages, red and gray. One with a stone base. The nearest cottage was wooden, the color of the timbers alternating, gleaming in gray, silver, and gray-green. Beyond it were red-painted houses, the paintwork eroded by the wind. They look natural, she thought. Sensible.

It was all washed over by a chilly mountain breeze, carrying neither smells nor warmth. Tasteless and odorless, the breeze washed over their faces as if they were stones or grassy slopes, the sound of birds rising and falling from the birchwoods.

A stony mountain rose behind the pasture, a perpendicular precipice down toward the belt of birches collapsed into a rectangular pattern. The meaningless straight lines and angles frightened her. In the other direction, the pastureland was encircled by blue-black mountains with irregular white patches, unmoving and distant to the north, west, and south. The ravine of the river Lobber ran in a wide curve around the foot of the mountain, separating the forested hillside and pastureland from the mountain. But it was really their height that made them so distant.

They all had different characteristics. Farthest north stood a long, sloping mountain that appeared to have been halved like a loaf of bread, the perpendicular sliced surface gleaming blue. It looked unreal, a piece of scenery. Diagonally behind it rose another which was white and gleaming with ice. It resembled the top of a pyramid and must have been very high and far away.

Fallen, shattered shapes, inhuman proportions. This chaos of stone appeared to have been recently petrified in the wind.

She heard a low grunting sound, and when she turned to look at the pastureland down below the mountainside, she saw a flock of ewes with their lambs. They were watching, standing quite still, their silvery heads and long, curved noses raised and turned toward the path. Their ears were pink, the sun coming through them. She felt they were waiting for one of them to move or say something. Mia looked scared. Then Annie took a step toward them and without her knowing where they came from, a few words appeared, a childish rigmarole.

"Oh, little sheep, oh, little sheep, we won't harm your babies . . . such lovely babies, such lovely babies you have, you little sheep . . ."

Mia giggled, the tip of her tongue between her teeth. The ewes resumed grazing. Of course they hadn't recognized her voice, but she hadn't frightened them.

A dog started barking. She should have known how quiet it was up there from the whispering of the grass. She could hear the tinkling of the waterfall in the stream far away, but she first heard the silence when the barking of the dog broke out and sounds came from the mountain. They were dull, regular, and of frightening strength. At first she couldn't connect them with the figure silently but rhythmically raising and lowering an ax at the corner of one of the houses. Then she managed to make out the dry real sound of the ax blade and the echo from the perpendicular mountainside.

She still knew nothing and was accepting everything as if it were reality. The primeval wielding of the ax. The security of the rhythmical sounds of a blade striking wood. The eternal barking of a dog.

They came closer and she realized that the long, cloven beard of the ax wielder was not white around his mouth but yellow, his eyes not faded and watery, and he was not ancient as he had first appeared to be. Petrus. She had the impression that the wood chopping had been staged the moment Dan, she, and Mia had come into sight from the cottage nearest to the path. The dog must have come out at the same time as the man. Otherwise it would have started barking much earlier.

Then Brita appeared in her long home-woven skirt and an apron raised by her stomach. She was in an advanced state of pregnancy. Her braid lay curled into a knot at the nape of her neck. The braids of the two girls were hanging down in front. Annie could see the braids were glossy, but only because they were greasy, lying close to their heads and divided into strands. Confused, she felt a sense of disgust. Mia had stiffened.

Children are like strange dogs. Alert almost to the point of terror. So she didn't hear or see much more than Mia and the strange children as they were taken into the timbered cottage. She was also more tired than she cared to show, and she knew Mia was very hungry.

Porridge, it was. Brita ladled it out of a saucepan on the iron stove. Porridge with husks and seeds and small hard bits in it. Petrus thoroughly analyzed it in his melodious voice, names of grasses and herbs, kinds of seed, fruits, and nuts slowly enumerated and repeated. Mia pushed her bowl away so that the milk slopped.

"It smells nasty," she said. "Like inside shoes."

Blank looks. Everyone looked at her. Brita said it was goat's milk and that was the milk they had. Annie was panic-stricken, not just a rapidly passing shudder, but panic that would rule her for a long time. What if Mia wouldn't drink the milk? What if she refused to eat?

They were there. It was serious. Dan had disappeared outside. Above the stove built in between slabs of shale, a pair of socks was drying. She had such a bad headache she couldn't look out of the window, where the light was hurtling in. No one mentioned what had happened down by the Lobber. No one asked her what she had seen. The lilting voice was talking about species of wild seeds and growing things. Mia sat there with her mouth clamped shut, avoiding looking at the two strange girls.

They were to live in the sensible building. She thought that was probably better. The ceilings were higher. But it was hideous and connected with something called the cookhouse. She couldn't really make out what that was, but they didn't cook food in there. Farther away was a goat shed of corrugated iron and planks.

Petrus and Brita did not go inside with her. Dan showed her the room and the first thing she saw was a head of untidy hair. Whoever was in the bed had pulled the blanket up so far that only the hair showed. The head did not move.

"Lotta!"

Dan said it appealingly, as if to a child. The face appeared and gradually the body, thin and rather bowed. This was no child. Lotta was a grown woman and she looked ill. Mia stared with attention and held on hard to the Cretan rucksack.

There were two bunk beds made of metal tubing. The room had only one window. Beneath it a piece of hardboard served as a kind of table, and on that stood a paraffin lamp, another hanging from a nail in the wall. The room was papered with wallpaper painted over in a grayish-blue color, buckled and split in a couple of places. There was an iron stove by one wall and a mirror with a broken plastic frame by the door. She felt it. Not plastic. Celluloid.

Lotta was using one of the two chairs as a bedside table. She had arranged a nest for herself. Some pictures of cats were on the wall, but otherwise she hadn't bothered about the room. Nothing remained of the curtains except a pelmet of loosely woven cotton, once white but now yellowish-gray, the stripes still red and green. The curtain material roused a sense of childhood in Annie, as did the frame of the mirror—forties style. The rag rug running from the door up to the table by the window was so dirty, the colors could no longer be made out.

It was incredible. Perhaps she would have started planning—white curtains, jars of meadow flowers, clean rag rugs—had she not had such a headache. She was also feeling sick now, so she just sat down on the vacant bed, careful not to hit her head on the upper bunk, and stared at Dan. She was waiting for him to say something, explain, but his eyes avoided hers. He seemed to be busy untying the rucksacks and talking to Lotta.

"I'll go now and you two can settle how you want it here," he said. But he did not sound calm, so he must have noticed after all.

From the very beginning Annie had said that she couldn't live in a commune. That was really the only thing she had stated with any conviction. Otherwise her life was open. She wanted to change it. But never to live with other people. Not after Enskede.

She hadn't told him about Enskede, though. It had seemed petty to complain about overcrowding in an ordinary house. The sounds from the lavatory. The stock exchange quotes on the radio. The roar of the vacuum cleaner. The neighbor's circular saw. Perhaps it would have been paradise to Dan. A house.

He had promised to find a house of their own, and had finally written about Nirsbuan in his letters. But it wasn't possible to occupy it. He must have realized that. It belonged to someone, even if it was only a summer place. She had thought he was putting it in order for them, that it was almost ready. He hadn't written that, but he had surely said it over the phone?

"Is this bed free?" she said, unable to stop herself sounding ironic. That happened to her when she was under pressure. Lotta nodded. She was hunched up on the edge of her bed, looking cold.

"You two don't want to live with anyone else."

Annie was forced to look at her gray face. The girl was like a dog waiting to be kicked out. Mia had climbed up on the top bunk. There was no ladder and Annie never even noticed how she did it. Now she was sitting up there with the striped rucksack in her arms, pouting and frowning so that she looked like a watchful, intelligent monkey. I must go carefully, Annie thought. With them all.

"Who else lives in the house?" she asked. "Well, I know who lives here. But I don't know in which house."

"There's only this one. And then Petrus and Brita's. There are two more rooms here. And the kitchen. Bert and Enel live in one and you know they have a little girl. And Önis in the other with her Mats. Though they've got only one bed. I mean two. One like this, I mean."

She had a Stockholm accent and was anxious about being thrown out. Her options were limited: here or with Bert and Enel. She smiled timidly. Mia said from above:

"Why are her teeth so gray?"

It should have been a whisper, but it was shrill. Lotta flung one arm around her pillow, snatched up the blanket, and rushed out. She came back shortly afterward and started tearing the cat pictures off the wall, the thumbtacks scattering down on the bed. I must remember, Annie thought. So that no one lies on them. How cold I am. I ought to stop her.

"Don't rush off like that," she said, but not very convincingly. Her headache was so bad now, she was afraid of throwing up. If so, where? There must be some kind of privy somewhere.

Lotta pulled out a suitcase and two bags from under the bed, noisily, scraping and shoving. Clearly she had found some courage and was pleading with all this racket. But Annie had lain down and closed her eyes. She could smell mold from the pillow. The smell of old foam rubber must come from the mattress. One movement and I'll puke. Dan will have to do something about this. She heard the door slam and the frame of the mirror rattle against the wallpaper. They were alone.

She must try to sleep for a while so that her headache would lift. Dan came back and Annie knew a long time had passed, but she couldn't look at her watch. The light from the window squeezed its way in even when she closed her eyes. Her headache rocked and crackled. He said they were to eat and she asked him to take Mia with him.

"Egg," she whispered.

"What?"

"She eats eggs."

In her torpor, images from the night had returned. That lined wooden face. A hood. Dear Lord, what was it? How could your mind produce images of things you'd never seen? Evil. Dry. A head that was dead and alive. Like rotting wood, crawling with life in the cracks.

Mia had come back and begun to unpack the Greek rucksack, where her Barbie dolls and their clothes were. Ken had nothing on but a pair of white gauze underpants. Barbie had a pink bra and matching panties. Mia was dressing them. Dan wasn't there. But the two girls were standing in the doorway. Annie knew they were nine and seven and called Sigrid and Gertrud.

It was like watching timid animals. She vaguely pretended to be asleep so she wouldn't have to make the effort to talk to them. Mia was chattering away, but Annie heard it was to the dolls, or they were talking to her. Her voice rose to a falsetto when she was Barbie wanting to wear her silvery evening dress. But Mia was sensible and said it was windy out. Ken rumbled.

"Why weren't you on the bus?" she heard one of the girls say from the door. Annie didn't know whether the child was speaking to her and hoped it was to Mia, but Mia didn't answer, either.

The pathetic little troop by the bus! The Inca hoods. They believed we'd be coming, she thought. Well, we did. Though we were in the churchyard then.

The smell of foam rubber came and went in waves. I must borrow some sheets, Annie thought. Until my own come up. And something for this headache.

———

She woke in another light. Must be evening. Her head felt muffled but better. She could see without it hurting.

Yes—the rug was dirty, like the curtains. Everything was threadbare, dingy, stained with smoke and decades of damp. The house had belonged to Wifsta Fishing Club, she remembered now, in the days when Wifsta shipyard had owned the forest around Starhill. It had long ago been sold to another company and their employees never came there. Perhaps they had another place.

She had come there to work. To make it beautiful. Not to step into something completed. Mia was mumbling away above. Ken and Barbie were no doubt being ticked off for their pretensions.

That evening there was a meeting in the main cottage. Brita gave them herbal tea with honey. Petrus explained to Annie that they planned the work for the next day at these meetings. Then each person could bring up his or her problems.

"Problems?" said Annie stupidly, and Petrus looked thoughtfully at her. There was a silence. Dan had tipped his chair back and was chewing on a piece of grass he had brought with him. The rosy light from the evening sun through the window fell on his face; he was made of gold. She felt a small movement in her loins and a wave of blood spread into her thighs. She felt like doing what he was doing, leaning back and closing her eyes.

Enel and Bert were on the kitchen sofa with Enel's daughter, a five-year-old or thereabouts. She was called Pella, a name that had made Mia snort through her nose.

Enel was thin and sinewy, Bert rather gaunt, his jeans loose on him. He was going bald and had brown eyes. They were both divorced and had moved here. Dan had written that Bert was an architect but that was not true; he had been a draftsman employed at the town architect's office in Nynäshamn. Enel had worked as a nursing assistant at the hospital there.

Marianne Öhnberg was called Önis and she was the only one from Jämtland. But she had lived in Stockholm for several years and had Mats. She had worked for the social services in a home for severely disturbed children. She was fat and her face was beautiful. She had bitten her nails so far down that the lacerated flesh on her fingertips had swollen. Lotta was sitting next to Önis, hunched up, a sweater over her shoulders. She had been crying; her face and eyelids were puffy, her lips sore.

They were talking quietly about boiling. Annie gradually realized they were talking about goat's cheese. They discussed food supplements. Bert thought the lambs should be given extra. Melodiously, Petrus said the grazing was enough. The grass was lush enough, green and wonderful. Woooonderfoool, he said. His voice was remarkable. It sang, as if he were speaking an old-fashioned dialect. But which? Everything he said sounded calm and reflective. And he smiled into his light brown beard which was yellow around his mouth. Annie was terrified Mia would say something about that. It somehow looked as if he had been eating something that had stuck there.

When I've had a rest I'll think all this is wonderful, Annie thought. All these people wanting to help one another. The calm.

They all spoke in very quiet voices, though Dan said nothing. That was unusual, too. He was sitting in the flood of light. She couldn't make out whether he was pale, whether he was in one of his difficult moods.

He was probably just tired. Tired and golden. When Mia had fallen asleep, they would make love, quietly and intensely—the way it could be almost only when you were very tired or slightly feverish.

"Lotta . . ."

Petrus sounded pleading. Annie realized they had come to the problems. I must put away my irony. It is a defense. Dan used to run his fingertips lightly over her face, as if to take away the pain. You won't need that irony up there, he had said.

"It's difficult to talk when there are new people here," Lotta said, and Annie thought—that's one in the eye for us.

"Try."

"I've been going crazy for several days now."

She was sitting on the floor, propped up against the wooden wall, but then she roughly drew up her knees, flung her arms around them, and hid her face.

"Annie," said Petrus.

"What?"

They all looked at her.

"We want to get to know you," said Petrus. "Tell us why you're so tense."

They waited. She simply had to say something, but it was obvious what was worrying her. So why did she have to say it? And she didn't want to say anything while Mia was there, not when the children were listening. They were sitting quietly and attentively beside their parents, and all of them were looking at her.

"It's what happened," she said. "The accident by the Lobber. I saw them."

"Annie," said Petrus, leaning over toward her, so close she could feel his breath. It smelled odd. Like an animal's. Was it the goat's milk?

"You mustn't think about that anymore," he said, the smell wafting over her, sour and mild at the same time. "It's in the past now. It has nothing to do with us up here."

"But I saw . . . you have to think about how . . . well, how it happened. That it'll be solved, I mean. We live so near."

"No."

What a fantastic thing to say! No. We don't live near. But she had no time to protest.

"You've left that now," said Petrus. "The tabloid world. You're here now."

"Lotta, dear!"

Brita had put her arm around the bony back. Lotta looked like a child curled up on the floor. She raised her face and it was wet. Wet and swollen.

"What is it now?"

"It's hopeless because everyone notices it at once. I'm doomed. It's always like this. Everyone can tell by looking at me."

"I don't think so," said Brita.

"Yes, they do—even that kid. The new one. 'Why has she got such gray teeth?' she said. I can't take it. She saw it right away."

Annie looked at Mia, who had stiffened, pouting out her lips. She knew Mia was clenching her teeth hard. Her eyebrows shot forward and her face crumpled. The little monkey had appeared. Jesus, now she's really going to blow her top, Annie thought.

"Mia didn't say quite that," she said quickly. "You said just now you've been . . . troubled for several days. And we only came this afternoon."

Cool and sharp. Oh, Christ! She had also spoken loudly, as if in front of a class. All of them except Lotta looked at her.

"You don't have to defend yourself, Annie. Not here. We're friends," said Brita. Annie wanted to say she wasn't defending herself, but didn't because she had seen from the corner of her eye a flash of something unbelievable—Dan tittering.

"Has anyone got anything else?" Petrus asked. He talks like a book, Annie thought. Like a damned Bible. No doubt he had noticed that everything was going off the rails.

Sigrid with her gleaming braids drew a deep breath.

"Yes?"

"The girl plays with Barbie dolls," she said.

"Mia?"

She nodded repeatedly.

"Yes, well," said Petrus. "We're going to forget about that here. There's so much else. There are lambs and kittens, Mia. Alive and a lot of fun."

He sounded kind, even very kind, but Mia's face was expressionless. He went on in his singsong voice as if at all costs he had to influence her. That wouldn't work, Annie knew. Not when she had that expression on her face.

"Barbie dolls are dead," he said. "Aren't they?"

Now there'll be hell to pay, thought Annie. But to her surprise, Mia replied almost dispassionately:

"Then I suppose they should be buried."

"That's right, that's right," said Petrus. He gave Annie a smile and quite a genial look. It was the soft cloven beard that did it.

Then they broke up. It was warm outside, but they couldn't stay there because the stingers had emerged. She knew their name now, those almost-invisible insects. They gave her an excuse to go into the house with Dan. Mia bustled in, fetched Barbie and Ken, then vanished again.

Annie registered that the mattress on Lotta's bed had gone. Perhaps she ought to straighten that out now, but it could wait for the time being. They could have one night to themselves. Dan disappeared again. She didn't know what he did when he was gone, but things would become clearer. She went out and looked into the kitchen. There was an iron stove, a table covered with oilcloth, one cupboard on the wall, and some wooden boxes on the floor, apparently used as cupboards or shelves, for there were bags of groceries in them. Everything was clean and bunches of herbs were hanging drying above the stove. Önis and Enel, she thought. They're sure to be clean people. This'll be all right. But Dan must make some cupboards.

Wailing sounds of singing came through the window, and to her surprise she saw it was Mia, with Sigrid and Gertrud joining in. A drift of flowers lay heaped on the slope above the house and Mia was squealing away, waving a sprig of birch about.

Going out, Annie saw Barbie's bare foot sticking out of the heap of flowers. The rigid little foot filled her with unease. Mia was burying Ken and Barbie with great enthusiasm. She had fashioned a cross with sticks, neatly made and fastened together with tacks. She must have had help. Perhaps Sigrid was already capable of that.

"Eaaarth to eaaarth, duuuust to duuust, God is deaaaath, deaaaath, eaaarth to eaaarth, duuust to duust," Mia was chanting, and Annie wished she would get it over and done with.

"The bird shall come, the great bird, strike dust in deeeath!"

Sigrid and little Gertrud were trying to sing along but had no idea what to do with the words, or the tune, either. At last they had finished, as definitively as if it had gone according to the book.

"Now they're asleep," said Sigrid quietly.

"They must have a tent," said Mia, and bustled inside. She seemed quite untroubled by the insects, but Annie couldn't stand them any longer. Moving to the kitchen window, she watched Mia put a handkerchief like a tent over the dolls and the harvest of flowers. Sigrid helped her prop it up with sticks, and as soon as that was done, Mia left the other two without even looking at them.

She fell asleep the moment she was up in the top bunk. She ought to have washed, but Annie didn't really know how to go about it. Tomorrow, she thought. That's when we'll make a proper start. Dan had come in and stretched out on the bed. His face was very pale.

"What was it about Lotta that everyone saw?" she asked him.

"What?"

"That gray-teeth business."

"We'll take that up when Lotta's with us."

He had closed his eyes, his skin moist and grayish. He isn't well, she thought. He's having a bad time again. Yet she couldn't help asking again.

"I want to know."

"Amphetamines."

"Uh-huh . . . you've taken care of her? To help her."

"We have taken care of her," he said. "You, too."

Before she went to bed, she went out to fetch Ken and Barbie. The cross was still there, and the handkerchief supposed to be a tent, and the flowers.

But the dolls had gone. Damned kids, she thought. Hypocritical little monsters. Though it was human. They wanted nothing greater. And tomorrow I'll stop thinking bad things and talking sharply. They're only children.

Petrus and Brita had already gone to bed. Annie was embarrassed when he opened the door in a gray-striped, almost full-length nightshirt. She whispered quietly that Sigrid and Gertrud had taken Mia's dolls with them. He pulled her in through the door, for midges and mosquitoes poured in toward the warmth when it was open.

"The girls didn't go and get them," he said. "I did. Mia won't miss them. You heard that yourself. She accepted they were dead."

"Maybe so," said Annie. "But I think it'd be better for us all if they've been resurrected from the dead when she wakes up tomorrow morning."

He stared at her with round blue eyes. There was sorrow in them.

"Give them to me," she said.

Slowly he went across to the wood box and opened it. As he handed her the dolls, he was looking infinitely sad. But she felt she already knew him. He isn't sad, she thought. He's just damned annoyed.

H e should never have told her his name, should have said something else, as she had done. Now she knew his name was Johan and she had turned it into Jukka. Well, they did call Per-Erik Pekka at home, but Jukka was much too Finnish.

"Jukka, Jukka, Jukka . . ."

She said it as she sat astride him and moved with him inside her. He was ashamed, but the shame was sweetish, and she laughed.

He had slept far into the morning and woken soaked with sweat with the sun directly in his face. He felt anxious, not really afraid, but apprehensive. Would she tell him it was time for him to go? He had no money. He had to stay at least until after the Midsummer holiday was over. Or borrow some money. But would she lend him any? Maybe she would laugh at him, or give him a lot, several hundred. He didn't know.

She had brought mugs for tea and a teapot in a basket with her, and sandwiches. Everything seemed ordinary, almost normal. At first he thought it was soft goat's cheese spread on the bread, but it was peanut butter. She ate nothing, but she drank some tea. At first she had spoiled it by putting milk into it. She might have asked him first.

"I'll go and make some more," he said.

"You're not allowed out," she said, laughing.

"I have to go out!"

"All right, but don't go and pee where they can see you from the house."

When he was down by the river and the birch leaves were moving, glittering above him, he remembered a dream he had had just before he woke up. He had been flying over vast forests. It was a blue twilight, his body flying without causing him any surprise, nothing below him except the tops of trees. He was flying low and saw smoke and swirling sparks from fires glowing down in the felling areas.

Back inside, he remembered she had told him something as they had lain on the mattress. Europe had once been covered by vast forests from the Caucasus all the way to the Atlantic, though the Caucasus had been called something else then, something that had been forgotten. People had lit fires at the Midsummer solstice all over Europe, throughout the forests called Europe.

The strange thing was that he had dreamed about it and seen deciduous trees in the twilight. Chestnuts and oaks, dark elms, limes and ash trees. Thick hazelnut bushes. The guelder rose. Dogwood. He wasn't even sure he had ever seen all those trees in reality. She had said the words and he had dreamed he had seen them.

When he had finished eating, she locked the door, went over to the window, and drew the curtains. He thought of saying he wanted to brush his teeth but didn't dare. He was afraid she would laugh at him. She pulled down the zipper and got out of her jeans, leaving them on the floor with the holes from legs and feet still there. He thought about a cartoon film—if she stepped backward they would roll back up her legs and close around her slightly protruding, firm little bottom. She's not as old as I thought yesterday, he thought. For then she would be flatter there. Or was she swaybacked?

She flung away the striped pullover and again he saw her breasts, like the kind of pale, pointed jam muffins Gudrun used to make. That thought put him in a good mood and his anxiety vanished. He felt like saying, Do you want to greet an old acquaintance? That raced through his mind once they were down on the mattress on the floor and he was about to enter her. But he was afraid it would sound stupid. She still had her pants on, and when he pulled at them, they tore. She ripped them off and flung them impatiently away.

"They're made of paper!"

She didn't reply. But he almost forgot what he was doing because he was looking at the soft little heap of pale blue paper. That was good, because in that way he could hold back longer.

She was more pleased with him now, though she had a strange way of showing it, slapping his bottom so that it stung, patting and slapping alternately on his right and left buttock.

When she had dressed again and went to pull back the curtains, she called over to him and they looked through a crack.

"Can you see him?"

He saw a man with quite a few silvery-gray streaks in thick hair that had once been black. But he probably wasn't all that old. He was sitting by the river looking out over the water, in green windproof trousers with flap pockets on the thighs and a green checked shirt.

"He mustn't see you. Don't forget."

Johan said it was impossible to hide for a whole day in an old grouse shed. She said he didn't have to do that, as long as he just kept away from the house.

"It doesn't matter much if the others see you at a distance. But watch out for him. "He's daangerous," she drawled.

It was impossible to tell whether she was joking or not. But he had to stay all the same.

Sunday was another hot day. He roamed around without going anywhere near the house. There was a large dog run but no dogs. The kennels had been broken up by the birch scrub, pale shoots making their way out of the entrances. He found the icehouse, which was empty and likely to have been so for decades. It would have been really good to have found some ice under the sawdust, for there was no electricity there. In a shed full of old tools and rusty fish buckets, he found a rat cage. He rummaged among the trash and finally found a long otter line in a wood store. He fetched his soap and the pail with the eel which he had put by the river, and in the shelter of the forest he made his way down to the little bowl-shaped pool he had seen the morning they arrived. He went around to the north side of the mere, where the banks were steep and rocky.

The eel was exhausted, motionless in the too-warm water, so it wasn't difficult transferring it to the rat cage. He lowered it under the water for a moment to revive it, then hauled up the cage and looked carefully at it. Long fins ran along its body, its head narrowing toward the front, its nose flat and glossily black. Its body was one long, powerful muscle. Nothing but willpower. Or instinct. Just a strong embodiment of will. Its belly was white.

If what he had read was true, it could make its way to the sea even from there, wriggling through the dew, climbing along channels. A traveling eel moved as fast as a human being on foot. It always knew what it wanted. Perhaps it didn't know anything else.

He tied the line firmly to the wire netting and then threw the cage out into deep water. He felt he was tormenting the eel, but he didn't want to release it. The line ran in the crevices in the rocks up to where he tied it to a pine root.

When he had finished with the eel, he took off his jeans and underpants and started washing them. They were difficult to clean with nothing but soap and water so cold his hands froze. When the clothes seemed more or less rinsed, he hung them in a birch, then lay down on a flat stone to wait for them to dry.

It was too warm for the tiny stinging insects and not even the mosquitoes had really gotten going. He struck out with a birch switch at a horsefly. The sun was baking on the stone and the breezes wrinkling the water sent a shudder through him, but he soon relaxed as it grew still.

He fell asleep, his cheeks flaring in the heat of the sun as if he had a fever. The soughing from the birches in the breeze penetrated into his torpor. Clouds started trotting across the sky like driverless horses. He sensed their shadows like shivers, and as they passed by, the light rose and pressed in through his closed eyelids. The smells of the forest came right into his sleep.

He was lying with one knee bent, his dick resting against his thigh when he woke. He thought he had dreamed that something or someone had been standing looking at him. As he let his gaze wander along the shore, he could see nothing but a jumble of green upon green. Finn the green hunter came into his mind, something Grandmother had told him, or he'd read in a magazine. Green in green among green. He felt strangely empty inside, a green jumble of oblivion, and his skin felt licked by eyes.

He got up and scrambled into his wet jeans. He was cold now. He didn't know where Ylja was or when she was coming to find him. He was hungry again. He had to go back to the grouse shed to lie down and wait until she appeared and gave him the right to exist. This was all bloody stupid shit and he must have been crazy to have left home. Torsten knocking down Vidart behind the enclosure wasn't the third world war. Letting him down Alda's old well had been a cruel thing to do, but since he had gotten himself out on his own, he would have had an advantage if he had stayed.

No, not an advantage. Possibly the right to exist.

What an expression. He had gotten it on the brain. Before he left, he hauled in the rat cage and looked at the eel. It was a big bastard. With a better knife than his little fish gutter, he could have cut its head off, gone up to the house, and been king for a while. There must be a smokehouse somewhere.

He threw the cage out and carefully hid the line with stones.

There was nothing to do but sleep, sleep away his hunger. Women's voices penetrated through to him in the cottage, many of them, light voices, occasionally shrill. He could see no one through the window facing the river. Cautiously opening the door a crack, he saw a whole group of women around the green-clad man. As he closed the door again and lay down on the bunk, the voices sounded like the screeching of gulls.

The man was like a fox. A silver fox. Slim, slightly pointed nose, slanting eyes. And his voice could clearly be heard through those of the women. He had a Finnish accent, too, though you weren't supposed to say that.

Ylja did not appear until long into the evening, but then she had food with her. Smoked reindeer heart, only a little bit carved off it. Wholemeal bread. Salt butter and cold fried salmon trout. Almond-shaped boiled potatoes, still warm. And Finnish Koskenkorva vodka.

It was strange she should drink that, because everything else about her was upper-class. He told her so, though politely, he thought. But she said it suited her best and caused the least hangover. It all sounded like quite a habit. She offered him some, and he tried to drink it as if he were used to it, too, or anyhow didn't think all that much of it. Though it was hard to see how much he was given as she poured it straight into his tumbler. He had already had a rather acid Norwegian pilsner, and next time he was thirsty, he went to fetch water from the river.

He ate all the food, which must have been the remains of dinner up at the house. She laughed to see him put away the entire reindeer heart. Then she pulled him down on the mattress.

He was bewildered and dislocated, now and again even momentarily frightened, sometimes totally exhilarated, beyond everything—then there seemed to be nothing else but her soft body and the light coming from the window. Birdsong and murmuring water. The intense, almost unbearable pleasure when she held something under his testicles and made the orgasm continue although it had begun to fade, on and on, to the borders of pain, until in the end he realized it was the vodka bottle. They cooled it in the river every time either of them had to go out to pee.

He didn't know where he was when he woke, but he was horribly thirsty. She gave him some water and told him he was in the grouse shed at Trollevolden, that his name was Johan Brandberg and he was born on February 21, 1957. So he had told her when he was born? What else had he said?

She gave him a splash of vodka in his glass when he had finished the water. He asked her when she was born, thinking he had a right to know. "I'm a Scorpio," she replied, and he got no more out of her.

She whimpered slightly when it was good for her. He thought he would do anything to make her whine and whimper like that. She seemed young and sensitive then, and as if clinging to him. His head spun, though perhaps that was the liquor. And exhaustion.

He presumed she was going back up to the house after he had fallen asleep, so thought it best to ask her some questions while he was still able to keep his eyes open. He wanted to know why he wasn't allowed to be seen, and when would she be coming back? She replied only that he wouldn't be seeing much of her during the day.

"We're going for a long walk."

"Where to?"

"To the Stone God Cave, if you must know."

"Who's going? All those women? And the Silver Fox?"

She laughed at his name for the man in green.

"The Stone God Cave? Is it a real cave?"

"It certainly is," she said in some kind of Norwegian.

"Why can't I come, too?"

"It's complicated," she said. "Come on, Jukka. Forget the cave. Forget those females."

But he persisted. He wanted to know who they were. As well as the man in green.

"Why is he dangerous?"

"He's not that dangerous," she mumbled sleepily against his throat.

"You said he was."

"Only dangerous to you, little Jukka."

"I'm not little."

"No, so big, so big," she said caressingly, softly taking his dick, and it responded although he didn't want to at that moment. He was thirsty from the reindeer heart and that helped him maintain his concentration. He lay on top of her and grasped her upper arms, firmly, but not hurting her. To make sure, he asked her.

"No, you're not hurting me. You do me good. But hurry and come on in. You're cold."

"Not now."

He really wanted to know.

"Are you sure you want to know?"

"Yes, of course."

"But once you know, you'll be caught, little Jukka."

"Know what? Who they are, do you mean?"

"They're women from the old tribe," she mumbled. "He's the Traveler. And you are the new."

"New what?"

"The new Traveler."

He let her go and she wriggled over toward the bottle and cautiously poured a little into their glasses. When she had drunk hers, she lay on her back with her eyes closed and there was no tension in her body, her fair hair sliding roughly like sand between his fingers. Her lips were pale and she had red blotches on her breasts and throat. Perhaps he had rubbed too hard against her. She was also slightly red around the mouth.

"The Traveler always comes walking with a living animal. Like you. Then you know it's him. The animal is his companion. That's how they recognize him. Or some of them do. The others will soon know."

"Who?"

"The women. Then they take you instead of the old Traveler."

"The Silver Fox?"

She laughed, her eyes closed.

"Yes. He came with a fox. That's right. You, Johan, you have talents."

"What kind of women are they?"

"They belong to an old tribe."

"Like Finnish Sami, or something like that?"

"No . . . not so northern. They existed in the great forest between the Caucasus and the Atlantic."

"There aren't any tribes like that left."

"In a way, no. But all the same. They were matrilinear."

He tried to find some meaning in the word, but felt stupid. Matrix, he thought, and then linear. But no meaning came from them.

"They trace their origins down the female line," she said, almost whispering. He didn't want her to fall asleep now. He wanted to know. He slid into her again and woke her up with small movements. She was almost too moist. They were wet together. He had created much of it.

"And then there was the secret," she said. "They protect it."

"What?"

"Their secret. Of the Traveler, and that they belonged to the old tribe. The tribe was dispersed, you see. They were abducted. Married off. Had daughters. But they told their daughters the secret. And they never told anyone else—because that was dangerous. Perhaps someone said something once. But that went wrong."

"How?"

"Guess."

"But you're telling me now."

"You, yes. You're the new Traveler. He's the only one who's allowed to know. In the past he would kill the old one and replace him."

"As what?"

"Priest. King . . . chieftain. Whatever you like."

"You mean a sect? And he's the leader."

"No. He's just the Traveler. He's theirs."

"So they don't marry?"

"Of course they do," she said. "They marry and have children and become wives and get an education and become professional. They live normal lives."

"Whereabouts?"

"Everywhere. They're all over the place—dispersed, perhaps. But they keep the secret. And occasionally they meet him and have their rituals. He travels around, meets them at one of the sacred places, whichever is nearest to where they live."

"So they never meet all at once?"

"That's impossible. Some live in Israel. In America. But most of them live in Europe. Whenever they can, they try to go to the place where he is to appear. Like here."

"That's all piffle," he said, gripping her upper arms, almost too hard.

"Of course," she said lightly. "But watch out for the old Traveler. If he realizes you're going to replace him, he may kill you. Such things have happened. In the old days the old one killed all newcomers who threatened to take his place. Or else he himself was killed. Nowadays the old one just gives way."

"What do you mean, gives way?"

"Goes away. Tries to find a new life. A normal life, or whatever. But that's not all that easy these days. He has never worked."

"What has he lived on, then?"

"The women. Some of them are wealthy. They donate money. For the other ones' travels, too."

"Are they going to the cave?"

"Yes."

"What are you going to do there?"

"You won't be told that until you've been initiated. You mustn't show yourself until this festivity is over. We'll let the old one know afterward."

"You're lying," he said. "You think I'm childish enough to agree to this."

She laughed. It sounded soft. She had become much softer, much kinder. He was not so afraid of her as he had been at first. But he didn't like her teasing him.

"Tell me what you're going to do tomorrow. Seriously. And who those women are."

"We're going to the Stone God Cave."

"I don't believe it exists."

"Oh, yes, it does, up on the high mountain. The path past the icehouse. You can look through the gap in the curtains tomorrow morning and you'll see the whole company crossing the river."

As she lay on her back with her eyes closed, he could look at her properly. He looked and felt with his tongue. Her skin was so thin at the temples, he could see blue veins through it; those were thin, too. Her breasts flattened as she lay like that, the teaspoonful middle rosy brown like the sweet spoonful of jam on top of a pastry; there were blue veins on her breasts as well. She had been vaccinated on her left arm, but otherwise had no scars. The fair, curly hair in her loins was even coarser than elsewhere, tickling his nose and smelling of the sea. She was kind now. Perhaps she wasn't teasing him, but just amusing herself. Tomorrow she'll tell me who she is, he thought. Tell me things that are real, about herself. She likes me now.

After she had left him, he couldn't sleep. He had slept nearly all day. He no longer knew what day it was, Sunday or Monday. The two had merged into each other. He was tired and his eyes were smarting, but he went out into the bright, clear night and its birdsong. That was better than lying on the bunk, counting the timbers in the cabin walls.

They were all asleep in there now and he could wander around the house, looking at it. He stared at the rough wooden shingles covering the walls. Silhouettes of dragon heads crowned the ridges, and there was an iron weather vane shaped like a three-tongued flag. The glass in the windows was old and distorting, gleaming reddish in the morning sun, and all the curtains on the upper floor were drawn.

He wondered where the cave was, if it actually existed. She had said it wasn't far. The path began at the icehouse, crossed the river over a footbridge of two logs, and went on across a marshland sloping upward. The path was easy across the marsh between islands of firm ground with birches and one or two small spruces. He took that way and enjoyed moving quickly without having to think. His body warmed and all his anxiety vanished. Hundreds of birds were calling and whistling all around him, thousands, he thought, thousands of birds calling and I just keep on walking.

The path appeared to lead up to the high mountain. After he had walked for twenty minutes, it became steeper, over stony ground extending in what must be an east–west direction, long rocky offshoots from the mountain. In the end he was balancing on a very narrow ridge and approaching the hillside. Or the mountainside, he thought. Norwegians called every bump a mountain.

The path ran along ledges in the mountain, and pretty soon he had to climb. He turned around when the going got slower on the cliff face and what he saw was incredible. The sea. The whole sea, misty blue in the morning sun, the mist on the horizon reddish and glowing. Out there was the sun, and above the mountain ridges the clouds had begun building up.

He had thought they were far up in the high mountains toward the Swedish border, but they were close to the sea, at the most a few kilometers from the shore, and he could bloody well see all the way to America. The ridge he was balancing on probably extended from northeast to northwest. He decided to climb right up and look.

On his way up, keeping to the crevices, he regretted his decision as the precipice began to frighten him. The path was still clear, but zigzagged up the cliff. Below was a ravine where he could see birds flying. When the first puffs of cloud came drifting, his face turned wet, then for a few moments he could see clouds below him, floating in the ravine, ragged and steaming. He could just see the tops of pines in the watery mist, from above, as the birds saw them.

He decided not to look down anymore, but just continue up from ledge to ledge, being careful before stepping off a safe place, checking whether a stone was loose under his foot. Onward and upward. He'd have to find a better path down, a less steep one. There was no sign of any cave. That was all just bloody nonsense. He had gone on walking as if drunk and was now stuck on the mountainside, clouds drifting below and above him, soaking him with their moisture.

As soon as he got to the top and found firm, lichen-covered rock beneath his feet, squalls of rain came racing in and he could no longer see the sea. He hunched down and waited for a better view, but the air thickened more and more and he found himself sitting in the cloud, dripping wet. He realized he would never find a better path and the risk was that he would lose his way, so he started down. His stomach pressed to the rough, cracked mountainside, he felt with his foot for loose stones below and held on until his fingers ached whenever he had to shift his weight.

A squall brought a cold shower over his back, but then another came and seemed to sweep away the worst. The sun flashed. He dared to look over his shoulder and could see right down. The sea was there again, boiling with light.

When he had gone so far that he could walk upright without the support of his hands, he noticed a thick rope fastened to a pine tree and hanging down the other side of the cliff. He went over to it and looked down. The rope had knots in it and ended just above the worn and trampled ground, a path apparently beginning where the rope ended.

He realized that you were supposed to let yourself down. The path led into the perpendicular mountainside, and opened up into a large, almost oval entrance.

The cave. So it did exist after all. As he slithered down the rope, he realized that he'd done the worst part quite unnecessarily. The cave wasn't all that high up and the path to it was easy. There were ferns in the entrance, hanging from the roof of the cave inside, the dark rock covered with lichen, but not far inside. Then it became sterile. The mountain had crumbled and cracked when the cold had lifted in the spring, and he was now standing on stone and gravel.

Only the first part was smooth, the ground beginning to slope steeply down into the darkness. Must be a damned big cave. He would tell her he had been there now—she wasn't expecting that of him. But he had to go a little farther in. There must be something there he could say he had seen so that she would believe him.

It was too steep to walk down, so he had to sit and slide through the mess of gravel and mud beneath him. That's the end of my jeans, he thought when occasionally he had to brake quite hard against the ground. Large rocks protruded, firmly rooted in the ground, and he could hold on to them. His eyes soon got used to the dark and the meager light from above. The smell of rock and mud was harsh and lifeless, the smell of the underworld, nothing but stalagmites and stalactites in the roof. Not a single patch of moss.

Finally he came down to more level ground. To test out the size of the space around him he tried with his voice, but his throat locked and it hurt to call out. The damp and cold went right through him and he became clumsy, wishing he could squat down and just wait. But nothing would happen. He was alone with this harsh odor, with the darkness and cold that was the mountain's.

When he turned his head, he could see the cave entrance and it dazzled him. He had to sit for a while with his head turned away to get his night vision back again. He picked up stones from the cave floor and flung them around, bouncing them off the walls. He threw systematically, like fly-fishing, fanning stones out from where he was standing. On their way down, the stones didn't strike the wall at right angles and he heard them hitting the ground far away.

So there was a path there—the cave went on, but how far? He didn't want to know. He would turn back now. He would tell her this, anyhow, in which direction it went.

He had closed his eyes as he threw, to be able to hear the stones landing. When he opened them, he could see a bit farther in front of him.

It was a rock. High and rough, upright, narrowing toward the top, taller than a human being.

Quite suddenly he was frightened out of his wits, fear coming without warning. Before he had been uneasy, but now it was terror, so great that he didn't think of being careful. He rushed back up, gravel and stones falling below him, then slid down again. Against all his instincts he made himself calm down to be able to get out, thrusting with his feet into the ground, sliding. When he finally reached the cave entrance, he pressed his face into the harsh crowberry scrub and moss, and after a while was aware of the taste and smell of earth that was alive.

He didn't know what had frightened him, nor did he want to think about it. That served no purpose. All he knew was that he must get away, at first down to the hunting lodge, then out to the road. Hitch.

The women came along the path just above the river. He heard them from a long way away and leaped up to hide behind one of the mounds, ducking right down behind a thick, fungus-clad, rotting birch trunk from where he could peer out at them.

The Silver Fox was in the lead. They were all talking and laughing loudly, clad in flashy sportswear. Ylja was somewhere in the middle, apparently elated, hallooing away, her hair tied up with a cord in a short ponytail.

He calmed down once they had disappeared. Presumably he had plenty of time before they returned, so he decided to go back and rest. His fears had vanished as soon as he saw and heard the little troop of walkers. They looked ordinary. Everything was ordinary down there, but all the same, he was determined to leave.

He fell asleep and woke too late, he thought, but rested. He would have to hurry, but couldn't leave without any money. He needed at least enough to be able to buy some food and rent a cabin until he got some planting or clearing work. He thought he would take some from her handbag, that long brown thing, made of something knobbly and stiff. Crocodile skin, she had told him when he asked. He didn't want to wait until she came back, or ask her for money. Then he would never get away.

The house wasn't locked and there were paraffin lamps and a board game on the veranda table. Someone had been lying on the faded sofa cushions. What if any of them were still there?

Well, so what? It couldn't be forbidden to go inside. He went into the dark hallway. The floor was littered with running shoes, boots, dog-chewed balls, a shotgun leaning in one corner. Bits of polystyrene, an otter board. The framed photographs on the walls looked as if they were taken at the beginning of the century, all men. Men in tweed caps and lace-up leather boots. One posed with his foot on a bear's head, a thick stick jammed into its mouth to hold it open. Torsten had a similar photograph on the parlor wall at home. In one photograph, two men were carrying a salmon on a stake between them. Another showed a whole company with their dogs in front of heaps of dead birds.

The glass in the frames was dusty and two were broken. Some of the frames contained large sprigs of dried flowers. It all looked as if no one bothered about the pictures any longer; they simply hung there, the men's faces staring rigidly down at the mess in the hall.

He could see a kitchen, which looked relatively modern and was very small. They must have had a cookhouse outside. Leftover food lay everywhere, and wine bottles. They must have carried a lot in their rucksacks. There was a smell of garlic and the acid smell of spilled red wine. He spread some overripe dessert cheese on some bread and quickly ate three or four pieces, then put some bread and cheese into his pocket.

The dining room had a rustic table and a whole lot of stuffed animal heads on the walls and birds on the sideboard. They looked moth-eaten and decaying, noses withered and claws missing, only the glass eyes clear.

He wasted no time on the ground floor. The bedrooms were upstairs, sleeping bags all over the place, three or four in each room—there must be fifteen or twenty women. He found Ylja's room at the south end of the house. Why was she allowed to sleep by herself? The Silver Fox didn't seem to have a room up there. Perhaps he slept with one of the women? Though in that case he must sleep with three or four of them? Or with Ylja? Were they married?

To hell with it, he thought. I'm going. I'll never see any of them ever again.

He felt different as he picked up her handbag, half anxious again. It was on the chair by the bed. On another chair lay a number of packs of those pale blue paper panties. The bed was unmade and smelled of her, though more faintly, and the sheets were also paper.

When he first opened the bag, he thought of looking for her driver's license to see what her name and age were, but then he thought hell, it didn't matter. He would never see her again, perhaps never even think about her again.

He found a wallet with Finnish banknotes in it and in one compartment some Norwegian ten-krone coins. At first he thought he was stuck and would have to stay, but then he found the center compartment in the bag, closed with a zipper. There was a whole wad of Norwegian hundred-krone notes, and the exchange certificate. She had gotten almost eighteen hundred Norwegian kroner. She wouldn't notice if he took two hundred. Not even if he took three. In the end he took five hundred. It happened so quickly, he had no time to think it through.

There was a folded pharmacy's bag in the handbag as well, flat but not empty. He looked inside and found several packets of condoms bought at the drugstore in Byvången, the receipt still there. But they had never used them. He couldn't understand, and it filled him with anger, though he couldn't really work out why.

He had just closed the bag when he heard voices. Shortly afterward, a door downstairs rattled and the house filled with women. They were laughing as they thumped up the stairs—several on their way up. He was caught like a rat in a trap. There was only one door, and that led straight out to the stairs.

Without thinking, he had backed over toward the window. Now he turned around and glanced down at the ground. It looked soft and wasn't too far down. He opened the window and wriggled out. At first he intended to hang on to the windowsill and drop down once he was hanging straight. That would shorten his fall by his length. But he hadn't time. He thought he heard someone at the door, so he jumped.

He immediately realized it had gone badly wrong. The ground wasn't soft; the tall grass had deceived him. He felt a sharp pain in his hip, but soon found it was his left foot that had landed really badly. Something had happened to it. His fall was still shuddering within him, from fear as much as shock and pain, and he couldn't feel his foot at all.

He could hear nothing from above. He was lying almost hidden in the tall grass and birches. Slowly he started getting up, his foot throbbing, not hurting all that much except when he put his weight on it. He slithered over to the wall of the house and hauled himself upright, then hopped clumsily around the house, clutching at the tarred wooden shingles. He didn't once turn around as he limped out into the birch woods down toward the river, then made his way to the grouse shed from one slim tree to the next.

She didn't come until late that evening, bringing with her cold breast of hazel-grouse, still sticky with sauce, which had solidified and was rather greasy. She also gave him some dessert cheese, the same kind he had taken up at the house, but he hadn't eaten that. His foot hurt so much he felt sick. His ankle had swollen and reminded him of his grandmother's ankles every time he looked at it—bluish, puffy, though the skin wasn't as rough as hers.

Ylja didn't say much, as if her thoughts were still up at the house. She poured vodka into his glass, broke an egg into it, then peppered it. Beside his plate lay four yellow tablets.

"What are those?"

"Vitamin B."

She's nuts, he thought. But he should have realized that from the beginning. He was afraid of her now. Perhaps she had noticed some money was missing. It would be like her to say nothing. To wait. He didn't dare do anything except empty his glass. The egg and the liquor slid down surprisingly easily.

She left without having sex with him. There was something wrong. Had she tired? Or had she already opened her handbag?

He said nothing about his bad foot, just stayed lying on the bunk with the blanket over his legs. Nor did she ask him anything. Not until after she had gone did he realize that now he couldn't leave. He was her prisoner. But perhaps she didn't know that?

If the phone went at night, he always thought the worst, that it was an abdomen or an accident. Possibly a heart. Sharp voice over the phone, shrill with fear. It aches. It thumps and flutters. I have red flashes. The thigh. The artery. It went in deep. "Bandage it up. Bandage it tight, but not too tight."

And eleven suicides in six years, four of them messy.

On county fair days, he usually did conjuring tricks, coins coming out of people's ears and crotches. No one had expected that of him.

He never risked ignoring an abdomen. But on this June night, it was a retired teacher up in Tuviken with palpitations. She often had them. Although he had done an ECG on her and knew it was a benevolent arrhythmia, he gave in. That was idiotic—she would demand more and more house calls—but he fell for the temptation of the road, the emptiness of mind, the roar of the engine and the radio on low. Mile after mile, as far as he liked—for he could no longer sleep.

Barbro had not said a word about Midsummer Eve. She had remained silent, busying herself with her clothes and working materials, some packed into cardboard boxes and suitcases. But they had still been in her workroom when he left.

He lied to the teacher in Tuviken and said he happened to be passing on his way to a call nearby. She wanted to know where and her curiosity stabilized her heart better than the quinine. He was given a cup of coffee, unable to refuse since it was real coffee and dark brown, and that banished any last thoughts of sleep. Anyhow, the murky hour would soon be over.

Streaks of mist were floating, lit through in the watercourses. He saw elks munching, though sometimes they turned out to be lichen-covered blocks of stone.

He would be home again in less than an hour, and Barbro would be lying in the bed he was to lie in. That was why he was driving through forests and marshlands, driving without noticing the scents or the harsh damp.

Every day his conscience tormented him over what had happened, though she didn't believe him. It had been happening for a long time and still nothing had been said about it. But he was certain of inevitable misfortune. Necrosis.

He was driving far too fast along a narrow dirt road that often ran alongside lakes sliced through by the wash behind divers and goldeneyes. The dark waters by the shores were as glossy as metal and there were reflections above the depths in the middle of the lakes, some pinkish like skin with blood running through it, others shimmering blue like the whites of children's eyes. Under the anesthetic of speed, he had emotions. But they were not pure.

Back in Byvången there was an unaccustomed east light over the village, illuminating the wrong houses. All was still. As he drove up the hill past the council offices, he noticed the curtains were drawn across in the police station, gray curtains with a pattern of blue-gray and yellowish-green leaves, and he thought he could see a light behind them. The curtains were quite thick but there were strip lights behind them.

I must, he thought. Now.

He knocked on the windowpane and the crack widened between the curtains. Then Vemdal came out and opened the door. He looked gray, patches of pigmentation from his sunburn uneven over his face, his blood retreating inward. A slightly sour smell came from him.

He said nothing, but went on ahead into his curtained office. Birger had expected piles of papers, files, and card indexes, but it was almost empty. A pad of paper lay on the green underlay; Vemdal had drawn spiral patterns with a ballpoint all over the top page and two words written and filled in over and over again: *Nasi Goreng*. Above the pad was the cage with the rat in it, sitting perfectly still, its eyes fixed on Birger as he sat down in the chair opposite.

"Thanks for phoning," said Åke.

That was just what he hadn't done. But then he remembered having phoned about Lill-Ola and the oddities in his freezer and boiler room. Vemdal sounded as if Birger had looked in on any ordinary afternoon, not at three o'clock on a Monday morning.

"We searched that boiler room."

"What did he say about it?"

"Made a hell of a fuss about human rights. Though nothing worse than they usually do north of Östersund. I'd got my papers from the prosecutor. Lill-Ola was up there on Midsummer Night. So we raked out the boiler and swept the floor. He had burned rubber boots and unplucked birds. Well, his wife did it for him, of course. Bojan."

"So they weren't sleeping-bag feathers?"

"Could have been both. They're being analyzed. He said he had told her to burn two capercaillie that had been in the freezer too long. That's a load of shit."

"I saw the capercaillie packets in the freezer. The first time I opened it."

"He had a pair of Three Towers boots standing on the porch. The footprint we found by the tent was from the toe of a new Three Towers boot. It looks as if he got his old lady to burn several pairs. But not the pair we think he was wearing."

The rat spun around, its rump sliding on the board that was the floor of the cage.

"You've still got it, then?"

"I can't just let it go."

They both looked at the rat, and it stared back.

"The girl's parents are coming," said Vemdal, as if he had found some kind of solution.

He had said her name was Sabine Vestdijk. Suddenly, Birger wished he didn't have to listen to this.

"Her father has a watchmaker's shop in Leiden."

Daughter of a watchmaker. Three days ago.

"Do they have to see her?"

"I don't know whether they're bringing anyone else with them. Otherwise they probably do have to."

Birger thought about the wound in her cheek, that gaping brown gash. They would be able to cover up everything else.

"Are you sleeping okay?" he said.

Vemdal shook his head. Should Birger offer him some sleeping pills? He was said to be too quick to prescribe sedatives. The pill doctor.

"I should have told you something else when I phoned."

Vemdal didn't look up.

"I know," he said.

"You know?"

"Yes. I suppose you mean about your wife. That she was with Dan Ulander."

"Yes, anyhow, it wasn't our boy with her," said Birger. "Saying Ulander was her son was supposed to be some kind of joke."

"She went with him up to Starhill to see how the commune lived. Then she stayed the night there. But he went to Nirsbuan. He wasn't sure when Annie Raft was coming, so he slept there."

Of course, decent people like Vemdal didn't smirk. They tried to smooth things over. That was almost worse. The rat was quite still, looking at Birger. The cage was small, so it could turn around in it, but no more, and it had arranged its exercise timetable accordingly. It regularly turned, a swift movement, its long, hairless tail curling outside the cage. There was a rustle, then its hindquarters and the smooth little head with fuzzy ears had changed places.

"What are you going to do with it?"

Vemdal didn't answer. He was staring at the rat, which was staring at Birger. But Vemdal's eyes were unseeing. Of course it would be disagreeable to kill it, a healthy animal. Its coat was brown, gleaming over its back and hindquarters, its rump heavy and dragging. It had survived.

"The cage is too small."

"She probably let it run loose," said Vemdal. "They hug them and fondle them. Have them lying around their necks."

"They shouldn't. Rats carry nasty parasites."

"The parents didn't know about it. Maybe it was a recent acquisition. We'll ask at a pet shop. Try to find out what they did once they'd arrived in Sweden."

He picked up a pencil and poked at the rat. It didn't move, but lowered its head and glared at him.

"There are three possibilities. That someone was after them. Someone who caught up with them here. Or that they knew someone up here."

"In Blackwater?"

"At the commune, perhaps. Or that fat Yvonne in Röbäck and her matadors. They deny it. But they'd do that in any circumstances."

"But it's the third possibility you believe in? A drunk. Some madman."

Vemdal shook his head.

"We shouldn't really believe anything. Not at this stage. That woman who found them, Annie Raft, she saw someone. A foreigner. That would indicate someone was after them. But it's difficult to get up there by car without anyone noticing."

Birger knew that was true. Every car on the forest tracks was seen by someone. It always was. You couldn't sneak in, couldn't escape those who saw and wondered what you were up to—putting out nets in someone else's waters, poaching, dumping something. But no one had seen a car driven by an Asian youth.

Indonesian? Nasi Goreng, it said on the pad.

Åke Vemdal ought to get some sleep. His mouth was dry, you could tell by the sound of his voice. He was sure to have a headache. The air was stale, though Birger no longer noticed it.

"He might have gone to Blackwater on a moped. Though how far can you go on a moped? It doesn't make sense. There were tracks of a moped on the path, almost all the way to the Strömgren homestead. And back. But we haven't found a moped with tires that match. Not yet. They've got one up at the Brandbergs'. But the boy has run away. He took the moped and went off the evening after the assault. He was afraid of his brothers and father. That was early evening, about seven o'clock, but all the same we'd like to take a look at the moped tires."

"Have you found him?"

"No, nor the moped."

Why is he here in his office? Birger wondered. There's something wrong. It's not just that he can't sleep.

"What sort of girl was this Sabine Vestdijk, do you know?"

"Enterprising. That man Ivo Maerterns hadn't particularly wanted to go with her, it seems, but she persuaded him. They lived in the same residential area. They hadn't been going out together or anything. I mean, they weren't in love. Though perhaps they became involved. Both lots of parents had had postcards from Gothenburg, but nothing after that. The peculiar thing is that his trousers are missing, and all his personal belongings. His parents knew roughly what he had with him—camera, bird books and that kind of thing, wallet, driver's license, and student card. But we don't think any of her things are missing. There were feathers in the tent zipper. If the man who did it opened the tent and stole the passport and the rest, then it's odd that he wasted time closing the zipper again. The knifing was done in a panic. Or rage, perhaps. Quickly, anyhow. She got the brunt of it. The doc counted eleven knife wounds on her and eight or so on him. That's just preliminary. Hard to count properly, for some of them were only scratches. He could see nothing. And they must have moved, thrashed around. So we don't know. And the man really hadn't any trousers, not anywhere."

He had started swallowing and licking his lips, as if he had only just realized his mouth was dry. Then, without looking at Birger, he said:

"When we were out at Blackreed River that night."

"Yes?"

"Did you see me all the time?"

"We were close to each other, weren't we? But I don't know whether I actually saw you. We were fishing."

The rat rustled and Birger felt a wave of nausea. He sat as still as he could, looking down at the gray-green linoleum and swallowing saliva.

"I must go," he said. He thought he smelled the rat then, probably his imagination, but he had to go. He had wanted to tell Vemdal to go home. He ought to offer him something to make him sleep. But he could say nothing.

When he entered the house, there had been a change. He could sense it as tangibly as if the furniture had been moved around, although everything looked much as usual. The framed watercolors in the hall gleamed, but he knew she had gone. The house was empty.

Tomas had gone on a railroad trip. That had been arranged long before. They had said good-bye that morning, but Barbro had said nothing about leaving.

He told himself he ought not to give in to forebodings and believe that he knew. So he went upstairs and opened the bedroom door, not bothering to be careful. The room was light and empty.

When he got back from his office that afternoon, the house greeted him with silence and light. At that time they would normally have had tea. He grabbed a beer and spread liver pâté on some bread. He was going to tackle the painting. It was quite light until eleven at night now. He thought she'd probably phone, but he wasn't exactly counting on it. When he finally heard the telephone, it took him some time to climb down off the trestle and go into the hall. But she didn't give up. The phone went on ringing until he picked up the receiver. She was calling from a public phone, but she didn't say where.

"I'll be away for a while," she said. "I must think this over. You can understand that."

Think *this* over, but she didn't say what. He was angry, though he had no right to be. That morning he had been woken by the alarm clock after a couple of hours' sleep. Then he had been furious and felt at the same time a deep, pure longing for her. But once he was properly awake and had gotten up, he no longer had any pure feelings. He felt shame more than anything else.

Their conversation had been brief. But she promised to keep in touch. She sounded friendly. No doubt she too had a sore conscience. On the Sunday evening he had asked her why she wasn't saying anything.

"What about?"

"You're packing but you won't talk to me."

"What is there to say?"

She had looked hostile. He hadn't dared go on, but he thought she was right; he knew what she meant. You never say anything yourself.

When the telephone call was over, he took another beer out of the fridge and went and sat down on the tall trestle. With his back to his handiwork, he gazed straight out into the pale green wreaths of birch leaves. I could go to Östersund now, he thought. Without having to lie. Park outside the Sulky. Straight there, no involved detours. Stay the night and drive to work at about five. It could be done.

You never say anything. No. What should he have said?

We've always lived like this. You've said what had to be said, Barbro. You've been articulate. Not in a facile way, either. You've really thought things through. Emotionally. Politically. Or near enough.

Meanwhile this had happened. But what the hell should I have said? What would I have called it?

Like this, Barbro. I'm in Östersund. It's January and stinking cold. Council meeting on the distribution of resources. But I'm sitting there thinking I'll never get the car started without an engine heater. And sure enough, I can't. By then it's late. We've been to Chez Adam and had dinner. So I phone home to tell you I'm staying. I phone from a hotel called the Sulky. Can't be bothered with a tow that late at night, and the car's horribly iced up.

It's a warm little hotel. The jockeys from the trotting races usually stay there. There are photographs of them and their harnesses on the walls. She's left up the Christmas decorations, too.

Barbro, my dear. You should have seen them. Red and green paper garlands. Turquoise, orange, red, silver, and gold glass balls. Gnomes. Nasty, malformed little monsters in red stocking caps all flopping in the same direction. German.

I liked them. They looked like the gnomes we always had on the table at Christmas when I was a child. And those were sure to have been German. The candy was German, too. Everything was fairly Germanic in those days.

Her name is Frances. I didn't think much about her to start with. Handsome woman, anyhow. Dark, with an American Indian profile. She had been married to a gambler. Sometimes he had owned horses, sometimes only shares in them. He lost and that was the end for them. I've heard she even had to take a job cleaning at the hospital. The house went, of course. He had cars most of the time and he was occasionally flush.

He died while he was on the way up. She knew it was temporary and he would soon have lost again. But then he went and had that coronary. A jockey once told me that when he was in the hospital, he stammered out slurred instructions to her on how to lay the bets for him. She nodded and wrote them all down. The jockey saw her doing it. But she never carried them out, for when he died, she still had the money. She bought the hotel —it was called the Three Lilies then. It was dreadfully shabby, but she restored it.

That was where I got a room. Sheer chance. Do you believe in chance? I suppose you do. Nowadays it's commonplace to believe in chance.

I go to bed in this nice warm little hotel. I am tired but not drunk or anything.

Perhaps it can be said like this. One thing at a time.

When I'm about to fall asleep, I see I've forgotten to pull down the blind. The streetlight is shining straight onto my face, but I can't be bothered to get up again. I let it be. I can hear cars going past all the time. There's a set of traffic lights outside. Sometimes a bus engine can be heard ticking over loudly.

So no peace. Nothing like that. No special atmosphere or premonition. Nothing.

I'm just lying there. I'm tired and can feel my blood pressure on a down. You know about my low blood pressure. But that doesn't explain anything. I've always had it. Even collapsed in the bathroom once. Remember, when I broke my glasses?

Hang on.

I'm lying there with my eyes closed, I think. Then it comes. Like a light from inside. Like, like . . . anyhow, like a feeling of light. Not in my eyes. In my body. As if it's expanding with light. It's all around me. There's nothing else but light. I am in the middle. I know everything. Not in words. Blissful.

Well, that's a word.

I don't know what words to use. Perhaps that's why I've said nothing. I'm lying in the middle of everything that exists and there is nothing to explain and nothing to achieve. Only this prolonged feeling of bliss. It lasted quite a long time. An orgasm, but more powerful. Like continuous waves, one after another in the light within me and around me.

It retreats. I begin to see the room again, the window and the street-light. I fall asleep like a child and sleep as soundly as you normally do only when you're small. Not until the next morning do I begin to marvel at it.

It's hard for me to leave that warm little overfurnished hotel. The explanation seems to be there, and I wonder whether to ask Frances. I would like to ask rather cautiously if anyone else had seen anything in that room, a light or something.

But I hadn't really seen anything. Not with my eyes. So it's pointless asking her. During the following weeks I read up about experiences of that kind, but that leads nowhere. I ought to have been hungry and exhausted, according to all the medical books. But I wasn't. I had eaten a substantial dinner and I was tired, nothing more. In the other kind of books, which I had trouble getting hold of at first, because it's an alien field to me, there's an abundance of words. Words like "bliss," for instance. There are too many. But I'll stick to bliss.

I get tired of reading. Haven't time, either. It's so self-referential. Like the jargon of politics or economics. Or medicine for that matter. It's the first time I notice the way writing is built up around feelings. Words are used as a kind of climbing frame to reach an emotional climax. At a pinch, writers fabricate feelings and force them to a climax. Even in expositions of council finances. I get sick of it.

I circle around the hotel, both in my mind and quite literally when I'm in Östersund. Sometime in March I stay the night there again and ask to have the same room. She sees nothing strange about that. Most of her customers are regulars and she thinks I want to be one of them. I sit watching television in the hall in the evening. You can get coffee out of a thermos jug and she has put out ginger cookies and crisp rolls.

I like it there. You would probably say it's tasteless because for you aesthetics are a matter of coordination. Those pale blue, mid-blue, and gray shades of our living room. The light-colored wood of the furniture. Bentwood. Metal rods. I think they're beautiful, too. The collection of glass in the window. The great tapestry you gave me for my fortieth birthday, showing a mountainside.

Frances never seems to have discovered any central perspective. She sees one thing at a time. Things lie about like islands. And when you see them, they are fun or great or whatever. Never actually indifferent. Not to her, anyway. She's been given lots of horses as presents, in china and wood, even stuffed ones with woolly manes. She puts bright orange winter cherry into a pottery vase flaring in every possible color and says that her grandmother always had it in that vase and on that very shelf below the mirror. Everything here means something to her.

Sometimes there's a rich, sweet smell in the stairwell and the hall. That means she's making a sponge cake for the jockeys sitting gloomily around. If things have gone well, they go out to celebrate. They're not allowed to drink in the hall.

I stay overnight there occasionally and I still think a lot about what happened. But I no longer think I'll ever understand what it was. It's enough for me to be allowed to go there occasionally, allowed to sleep in that room. I never pull down the blind. Perhaps I'm waiting, after all, but nothing further happens.

Of course, I've become a kind of house doctor. Frances is healthy, sleeps well, and needs only a little antihistamine in the spring when everything is in flower. But the jockeys have all kinds of needs. They're interested in amphetamines, but that's out of the question. I may give them the occasional diet pill, but only when testing out a drug. If I started prescribing it, heaven knows where I would end up. Sleeping drafts, of course, and a good deal of Librium and Valium. But in justifiable amounts. I'm certainly not the bloody pill doctor they say I am.

Then there was Christmas Day three years ago. We both had our mothers staying. Things were slightly tense, but still cordial. You took coffee and candles around on a tray and sang, "Good morning, good morning, both master and mistress," and then you all went off to church. The early service had been just too early. I set about fixing the mulled wine, spiking it a bit, planning to give the ladies some before lunch to keep things cordial a little longer. Then Frances phoned.

A guest had died. He was in bed in his room and he was dead, she said. She thought he had taken his own life. There were several empty medicine bottles on the bedside table, one of them prescribed by me.

I told her to keep calm and wait, and I would phone the police and the hospital for her. But she said no, she wanted me to come. I explained I couldn't do that. Maybe he could be saved. We must get hold of an ambulance quickly.

Not until I was in the car and heading for Östersund did it occur to me that Frances and I had become close. I had confidence in her. I was quite sure he was beyond saving. She's practical. I shouldn't have done this. But I had confidence in her judgment.

He had gone to his room on the twenty-third and hung up the PLEASE DO NOT DISTURB sign. When she found it still there on Christmas morning, she thought he had forgotten it, so she knocked on the door. She was going to take him early morning coffee. There were six guests at the hotel, of whom this one and two others were regulars. It was Frances's turn to keep the hotel open over Christmas. One hotel always stays open and the others refer guests to it.

The room was cold and smelled bad. He really was dead, and he had been dead a long time. A thin body. Fine pajamas. Everything appeared to have been carefully prepared. He had wished to do it tidily, but he had assembled drugs that guaranteed no pleasant sleep. He had vomited and in the end had not been capable of leaning out of bed to rid himself of his vomit. His skin was whitish-gray. The bedclothes and mattress were soaked with urine.

It was a long time since I had seen a corpse that had been around for a while. I remembered my first bodies at the School of Anatomy in Uppsala and was furious Frances had had to see this, as if she had been abused. Not by him, not by this pale, troubled little gambler—professional or semi— who had crept in here in his brand-new pajamas on the evening before Christmas Eve. He knew nothing about death.

On the table by the bed were jars that had contained various antidepressants. I felt uneasy when I saw the label with my prescription on one of them, but I was also glad it was only one.

Frances had a request. She had already had a plan when she phoned me. Racing people are superstitious, she said, worse than anyone else. I'll never get my regulars back after this. That'll be the end. The trainers, the owners, the big gamblers, and the nervous little semi-professionals. The jockeys—they're the worst. None of them will come and stay here again.

He was nice but he didn't know what he was doing when he did this here. I suppose people think mostly about themselves at such a time.

She simply wanted to get her other guests out of the way to some other hotel before calling the police and ambulance. Then there would be some chance that it wouldn't get out that it happened at the Sulky. She had also worked out how to do it.

We said she had called me in because she was in pain. I diagnosed a kidney-stone attack and phoned a hotel owner she knew. Fortunately, he wasn't away, though I think she knew that. Frances was pale and extremely determined.

He agreed to take in the guests, but we couldn't get them all to leave at the same time. We waited all of Christmas Day. I told you it was an attempted suicide and I had to stay until I knew which way it was going. I was terribly afraid you'd phone the hospital to ask for me. Frances stayed in her room and didn't show herself.

By the time the last guest had gone, it was eight in the evening. Then I stood outside that room, ready to go in. I was to pretend I had to disturb him to tell him he would have to change hotels, then pretend to find him. It was sickening. And it was even colder in there now.

Frances had to look as if she were in pain when the police came. It was complicated and unpleasant. I had never been involved in anything like this before. I felt as if we had murdered him. He was so helplessly cold, actually stone cold when they came. He had apparently turned off the radiator before lying down. Had he been afraid it would be a long time before anyone knocked?

We didn't know. In a way, he was probably being considerate. Well, then I was to go back home, but I simply couldn't. I don't think Frances could have coped with being alone in the empty hotel.

That was probably roughly what I told you, that I hadn't the energy. That I was affected by what happened. My patient had died. I would stay overnight.

I wonder whether you thought I was escaping from Christmas celebrations and the mothers.

We were overcome by hunger, quite literally. She got out marinated herring and carved some ham. We had a schnapps each. We ate thick slices of dark bread and I remember there was a crisp, sweet crust on it. We spread butter. Everything was good. The pilsner. The jellied veal. The liver sausage one of the guests had brought her.

She smelled strong. Not bad, but strong. That long, curly, dark auburn hair hung down over her shoulders. She dyes it with henna. Where it's grown out, you can see that it's streaked with gray. The bush down there is dark brown, a real bush. She was still in her bathrobe. This is not the kind of thing I can tell you, nor am I doing so. I'm only trying out words.

For our exhilaration. Our hunger.

She hadn't shaved her legs, probably because it was winter and she usually wore trousers or quite thick stockings. Her skin felt prickly to the touch, up to her knees. Then she was soft, white. Then prickly again. Curly. Smelled. It was like two hairy animal coats we had down there, chafing against each other, courteously, as animals do.

She has a long, pear-shaped ass. Long legs with clearly defined muscles and sinews. Her stomach arches. The furrow in her spine goes down to the dark slit between her buttocks. I wanted to be there and everywhere. Always, really.

But we go on living in that parsimonious way you have to live. Calculated. Usually with words. But for those hours there were no words.

In the end it ceased between you and me.

Presumably I have gone wrong. Or else right. I don't know.

The women didn't stay long. A day or so went by before he noticed they had gone. He was shut in with his aching foot. And all he could see through the window overlooking the river was the racing water and flickering leaves. The women's voices vanished, like the voices of birds. When?

The Silver Fox could sometimes just be seen on the other side of the river, and Johan occasionally heard the sound of a shotgun. Shooting grouse in the middle of the breeding season, was he? Like Pekka. Johan couldn't care less.

Pekka always laughed off Gudrun's lectures, and she didn't really bother all that much about closed seasons, either. She just wanted them all to be respectable, to be decent people, as she put it. Johan had recently begun to understand what that meant to her. She was waging a continual battle. Hunting seasons. Changing shirts. No dogs in the kitchen. Theirs was to be like a house in Byvången. Or preferably Östersund.

Väine had shot birds of prey, sometimes just for fun. And yet he had joined in when they beat up the German. That time they almost went too far. The brothers had caught the German by the Röbäck, and when they opened the trunk of his car they had found three frozen birds. Two buzzards and one short-eared owl. Someone must have gotten them for him, but they never found out who. They kept knocking the German down until he lay there on the ground.

The pastor found him in the covert down by the stream. The pastor, of all people. Väine laughed at that along with the others, though he was only fifteen when it happened and couldn't have had much to do with it. The angry little pastor, they called him. But of course, the German hadn't reported them. He had that much sense. He stayed at the parsonage for several days.

The previous pastor had never bothered about fishing. In his day, anyone could fish in the church's waters and put out nets where no one was looking. Then the new one came and started fishing and spending his time out of doors. He acquired a boat and kept it up at Whitewater. Pekka and Väine were fishing with a long line there one evening and the damned pastor had appeared and started gabbling away in his reedy voice.

He had begun something he called "forest services" and had invited guest speakers to talk about the company's spraying and clear-felling policies. No one had counted on his being out and about all the time. Everything that wasn't town or indoors he called "nature."

Him runs round t'marshes, the old men said. He had learned to make his way through the downy willow and leap between the beaver holes without breaking his leg.

But no one had predicted his beginning to make a fuss about fishing, and that's why the boat disappeared. He put signs up in three villages: BOAT STOLEN FROM WHITEWATER, COLOR GREEN. Then people knew, and they also realized who'd done it. Gudrun hemmed and hawed, but Torsten had no objection because the damned pastor had once come chugging up in that silly little car of his, walked straight into the kitchen, and told him that he knew the Brandbergs dumped waste oil into the Blackreed River. That made the shit hit the fan, but luckily for the pastor the kitchen had been full of people.

That was the kind of thing Johan told Ylja. He had not intended to at all, but once he was confined indoors with his foot, his thoughts kept going to Gudrun, Torsten, and the brothers.

He was miserable stuck indoors, peeing into a coffee can, the other, too, then having to heave it out the window into the river. He couldn't expect her to run around with a pot for him. But on the second day he went out. She gave him an old carved walking stick for support and it felt better peeing out of doors. He could wash in the river, too. She told him he needn't be afraid of being seen any longer. The Silver Fox had also left.

They were alone, yet there was no mention of Johan moving up to the house. She seemed to have grown tired of him, at any rate in the daytime.

She was doing something up there, writing and reading. He had been stupid to talk about Gudrun and Torsten. All that sounded so ordinary. He realized she liked his being a Sami. She said Lapp, of course. He had said he was a full-blooded Sami and told her about the man with the scooter. But now she appeared to have lost interest.

He found it very dull in the daytime and slept a great deal. He was tired, too. She liked to keep going at night. He was given as much food as he liked and he wondered just how much they had carried up there. She slept with him at night, but no longer told him about the great forests and the Traveler and the women. Maybe it was childish, but he wished she would have continued. It made her different. He found it easier to like her when she talked about the forests and the fires glowing in the clearings at night. Dark nights they were, warm. The women hid from the Traveler, the dark deciduous forest full of laughter like birdsong. Though the birds had long since gone to sleep in the dark summer night that was Europe, that was not yet called Europe, but was just greenery and fast streams and wooded mountains.

Instead, she got him to tell her about Torsten and Gudrun. She never really asked him anything, but she listened.

"You've got an Oedipus complex," she said one evening. "Do you know what that is?"

"It's when you don't like your dad."

"You want to kill Father Torsten and sleep with Mother Gudrun," she said. At that he hit her, slapped her in the face. He felt the palm of his hand against her soft face and her cheekbone.

Afterward he found it incomprehensible and had no idea what to do to have it undone. It was as if it hadn't happened, as if it had been nothing but a nightmare.

The atmosphere between them had been troubled. They had been tired and not sober. She was very pale, and then she had said that. It was too crude, as if she'd told a dirty joke. But as soon as he had hit out, a split second afterward, as she sat there with her head down and her cheek at first flared, then showing marks from the blow, he realized she had only been talking the way she usually did. Ironically. Outspokenly, but not seriously. She hadn't meant he wanted to sleep with Gudrun and fantasized about it. She had meant something else, something foolish which had no significance at all. And he had hit her. Like a machine. A piston firing. No—he was dreaming.

"You're that sort after all."

Her mouth was open, her eyes still fixed on him. She had the same expression as when she was astride him.

"Torsten's son," she said.

Then he knew that at all costs he had to get away.

On Tuesday morning, Vemdal phoned before eight to say he was sending a man to fetch Birger's boots. In fact, two police officers were already there, which Åke clearly didn't know. They wanted much more than boots. They rummaged in the laundry basket, holding up Barbro's white bra and examining panties and towels. When they had finished, they put the heap of clothes on the kitchen table. Birger considered that not only wrong but also disgusting. They included filthy fishing clothes he had thrown into the basket on Midsummer Day, the underpants stained from the accident that had almost happened to him at the approach to Blackwater. They went through the pockets of his green trousers and found a whole lot of mint-toffee papers. Violent rage raced through him, like congestion of blood in the head and a moment of severe pain. An attack of migraine that didn't come off.

One of the officers opened the washing machine and fumbled around inside the cylinder; the other hooked up the grid over the drain, using a small, pointed spade. Turning the spade over, he started scooping the sludge from the drain into a plastic box.

They wanted his knife, which was still hanging from his belt. It was a childish knife, the first one Barbro had ever had. But she had never been very keen on fishing. The knife had deep grooves along the top, perhaps for scaling perch.

They asked him if he had any more knives. He said, "What the hell do you think?" opened drawers, and took out knives: heavy Mora knives in black plastic sheaths, some with paint on them and ruined cutting edges; and Tomas's Japanese fishing knife encased in wood, which had swollen so they couldn't get the narrow blade out. There was a little lady's knife Tomas called the Lapp knife, a souvenir from the south with reindeer skin on the sheath.

"And then we need the boots."

"I haven't got any Three Towers boots," he said. "So there can hardly be any confusion."

They asked about other boots, and furiously, he fetched several pairs from the garage and the shed. Tattered, patched boots, plastic boots that had cracked in the cold, alternately Tomas's and his own, because they took the same size. The police made no comment, but simply took them and numbered them. He had to go upstairs for his hunting knives and they went with him, their eyes roaming, taking in the gun rack and the stand of old weapons. They took all his knives away with them.

He was forty minutes late getting to the office. Märta was not pleased. He didn't want to tell her the police had been to his home. He thought he would go out and buy some buns for coffee in the afternoon to appease her. If he had time.

Märta ran the office. Everyone knew she decided who would see the doctor before whom and who needed to go to emergency. When Birger had started his practice in Byvången, he had been afraid of her.

At three o'clock she came in and said he was to go to the police station, managing to make it sound as if she had decided that herself.

Åke wasn't there. A total stranger was sitting at his desk, older than Vemdal, his graying hair brushed forward. A uniformed policeman was in charge of the tape recorder at a side table.

Afterward, Birger could remember nothing of the questioning except odd sentences. He didn't get home until after six. It had lasted almost three hours.

He ate nothing that evening. He was too tired to prepare anything and he was feeling sick. They had gone on and on about Dan Ulander. About the staying overnight. About the tent. They knew perfectly well Barbro had not camped out.

"But you thought she had, didn't you?"

He didn't know what he had thought. It was hardly possible to camp that high up at midsummer when the spring floods were still under way.

He said he hadn't known and still didn't know who Dan Ulander was. The graying policeman said that wasn't true. They had met. And in a way he was right, since Ulander was one of those environmentalists.

Much had been made of the fact that Birger had gone to Blackwater, that he had been so near and yet had not sought out his wife. How the hell could I have done that? Gone haring up the high mountain?

Hadn't he been worried about her? He remembered the question but not what he had answered. During the whole interrogation he was thinking that Barbro was in a bad situation. She had lied and said that Ulander was her son. Birger had tried to explain that it was only a joke. She was so much older than Ulander.

How did he know that?

Well, how did he? It showed. Or had she said it? It was that kind of joke . . . between people who . . .

Made love together?

The bastard. What a way to put it. Like a soap opera. Fucking bastard.

Nor had the gray man taken it back. On the contrary—he had asked painful, intrusive, offensive questions. And Birger had replied, all courage and authority apparently drained out of him. From exhaustion. From weariness after all the repetitions and questions he had already heard before. Until the last round. He remembered that, for then it had been easy to answer.

Had he left the fishing place by the river at any time during Midsummer Night?

No, he hadn't. He'd been with Åke Vemdal all the time.

He woke in the middle of the night. The windowpanes were wet. He didn't give it a thought until later, after he had long since given up any attempt to go back to sleep—rain was coming at last.

B arbro had said she didn't want to take anything from the house as long as Tomas was living there. He had a right to live in his environment. She didn't say his home. Perhaps she sounded artificial only when she was talking to Birger, or perhaps it wasn't the words but the metallic reproduction—membranes vibrating, electrically charged materials. Since Midsummer, they had talked to each other only on the telephone.

He took on the responsibility of keeping Tomas's home as it had been before she left. Cleaning on Saturday mornings. Buying flowers. He wouldn't go out and pick any; it took up so much time and would have looked just too pathetic.

Only white flowers were supposed to be in the living room, or green leaves and grasses in glass vases. He bought a white cyclamen, but it died. Overwatering, said the cleaning lady who came in nowadays. In the long run, he hadn't time to clean the house and Tomas always found some excuse to get out of having to help. Birger had to try to get the painting of the woodwork finished before the autumn rains came, and he realized he couldn't run the house on his own. Though he resisted. He had resisted all the time, but had never mentioned it, nor even given it much thought when Barbro had found a cleaning lady.

It was really so simple. He wanted to be left in peace. He wanted a place where he could be absolutely on his own. Not have any comments. No one looking in. No talk about what it looked like at the doctor's.

But he had to accept the cleaning lady, though the result was not what he had hoped for. She changed something as she chased around with the vacuum cleaner and various cloths. Perhaps the smell? She drenched the cloths in chemicals, presumably not the same things Barbro had used. And some materials didn't like water, even he realized that. He looked at the delicate, silky surfaces of birchwood and wondered whether they had dulled. He wanted to keep the beauty of the rooms, at least the rare, pale, almost transparent beauty of the living room. The glass birds in the window, their slight hovering movements when he walked across the floorboards, now a hundred and fifty years old but fresh and polished to a dull sheen.

He found out that glass was difficult to keep clean. Water-spotted Finnish Iittala vases with yellowish chalky rings on them appeared. The cleaning lady broke one of the glasses with spiral stems. She had put the pieces on a newspaper together with an explanation, improbably spelled. She must have realized they were expensive, because the next time they met she said, "No one could drink out of them, anyhow."

It did not escape him that she sounded downright hostile. The seven glasses were twisted like flowers reaching out for the light.

"No, you can't drink out of them" was all he said, and he found he was afraid of her.

No one came to the house any longer. He didn't invite people home, nor did anyone drop in. He was pleased to be left in peace because he had become obsessed with the sandpapering and painting of the elaborate latticework he thought gave the big house its character.

Maybe he had thought someone would call and ask him out to dinner. But they were Barbro's friends, though he had never considered that before. He hadn't had time to acquire any of his own. None of them phoned to find out how he was. Had they taken sides? If so, why against him? He did feel some guilt, but they wouldn't know anything about that.

He was glad to be left in peace with his painting, but in the long run couldn't avoid noticing that his life was falling apart. He thought about flesh putrefying. Something grayish-white. Salt ling fish soaking. An absurd image he had long had.

At least he cooked his meals. He had promised himself that and kept to it.

He saw nothing of his neighbors. They shared a subscription to the *Östersund Post*, but he hadn't time to go across and fetch it. Barbro had always done that. He read it at the office, so quite a time went by before it occurred to him that the neighbors had not brought it over. In fact, they never had.

One evening he met Karl-Åke outside the newsstand. Without any preliminaries, he asked Birger to do something about the linseed. At first Birger didn't know what he was talking about, but then he remembered that Barbro had leased a patch of land and paid their neighbor to plow and harrow it. It had been sown with linseed. Birger trudged off in the evening and found the patch. It was in full flower, a lovely blue, a sight to take your breath away, as he said to Karl-Åke later. But neither Karl-Åke nor Birgit seemed to understand that he meant it was beautiful. They were sitting at their kitchen table and they wanted him to take the linseed away. He said he didn't know what to do with it. It had been Barbro's project, jointly with the local community council, he thought.

"Perhaps you could cut it?" he said. "Or plow it in."

Karl-Åke looked so peculiar, Birger added:

"I'll pay you, of course."

For some reason that aroused Karl-Åke's ire. Or was it only an excuse to be rid of some sour old rage he had long been accumulating?

"Pay! Do you think that settles the matter? Linseed's a bloody weed. You can't plow it in. It seeds itself and comes back again."

"Well, I don't know," said Birger vaguely.

"You should have thought of that before you sowed it."

He wanted to say he hadn't been involved. I know nothing about linseed. He left Karl-Åke and Birgit, nodding good-bye and pretending he was in a hurry. I must think this through, he thought. There's something odd. Hostile.

He remembered Barbro's outburst about the neighbors after her miscarriage. And then there was that time he had been in bed with the flu. It had snowed heavily all January.

She had half killed herself shoveling it away. Karl-Åke cleared the drive with the plow as usual. That had been agreed and he was paid to do it. But not once over those three weeks had he offered to help shovel by hand up to the steps. He joked with Barbro, teasing her, she said. "Now you'll have to set about it. Now you know what it feels like, eh?"

Suppose she was right? She had been here at home and presumably at the receiving end of their hostility, their envy of a life they believed was easy because it entailed no physical labor. The security of Birger's appointment. His salary. It struck him that they must know how much he earned, for that was a comment he had heard before, but it had passed him by. Now he remembered and thought they must have gotten it from the tax authorities. The sum had actually been correct.

"Some people have it all right," Karl-Åke's father had said as he was digging in the potato patch when Barbro happened to be passing. At the time she had been working on the council tapestry, the bilberry picture against the Agent Orange defoliant (though that didn't show directly on the huge dewy blue berries in the tapestry), and the hours she was putting in were absurd.

They must know how he drove like a maniac around his vast district, available at all hours of the day and night, his mouth dry with lack of sleep and worry that he might have made a misjudgment. Sleeping with one eye open. Never counting on any free time or a regular holiday. And yet this: Some people have it all right!

And he thought so himself. They had touched on a sore conscience with their clumsy joke, which was nothing more than an outburst of envy. They had touched on a conscience he did not want and had no reason to have.

He forgot the linseed. Having offered Karl-Åke money to take it away, he put it out of his mind. He was free of it and had really never had anything to do with it at all.

He decided to ask some people to dinner because he realized he was drifting into something he would have jokingly diagnosed as paranoia in anyone else. He phoned Vemdal. He ought to have done that long ago. The situation was strange, not knowing anything and hearing nothing from the police since that thorough questioning. For a while he had been so paranoid, he had thought they suspected him of having stabbed through that tent by the Lobber in the belief that Barbro was in there with Ulander. Since then he had calmed down. So he phoned Vemdal and said he was going to get a fillet of venison out of the freezer.

"Thanks very much," said Åke in a wooden voice. "But I can't possibly at the moment."

Birger had encouraged him to choose another day, but he didn't want to come.

Later, Birger was overcome with a self-pity that was so fierce, he couldn't even laugh at it. His thoughts were scattered, yet manic, circling around his neighbors, the cleaning lady (who had quit without explanation), and Åke Vemdal. He thought the only damned person who hadn't changed was Märta, but she had never been particularly friendly. He dwelt on all the calls he had made on neighbors without charging a fee, the medicines he had given them from his own supplies. He longed intensely for Barbro. A trip to Östersund to see Frances would make no difference. That was another world. She wouldn't understand the weight of what was happening all around him and it would sound so trivial. Fetching the newspaper. An overgrown field of linseed. A cleaning lady who had quit.

He telephoned Barbro's mother as well as her brothers, then finally got hold of her. As he was speaking to her, he found he had difficulty breathing. Her voice was low and intense, a dark voice, always had been. Dark like her hair, eyes, and the bluish-brown skin of her eyelids. Like the hollows that became visible deep down below when she parted her legs.

When the cramp in his chest let go, he started shuddering, sobbing. She called out over the phone, not realizing he had started crying. He hardly realized it himself. He asked her to come home. Afterward, he had no idea why he had done so, nor why he had been weeping. But she came.

That turned into three unreal days which he remembered afterward as if they had lasted only a few hours. The first evening he drank too much at dinner and particularly afterward. He woke alone in front of the television on the upper landing, and the bedroom door was shut.

They had still said nothing about what had happened. She cleaned and he tried to explain what had befallen the indoor plants. In the evening she wanted them to sit in the living room, and he recognized at once almost everything she said from those desperate early spring days. She kept talking about people with whom she had things in common, people who no longer wanted to live on these terms.

What terms? And why did she say people? His name was Ulander.

Birger helped himself to a whiskey and she said quite sharply that he had to listen to her. That meant, you mustn't fall asleep this evening. He was confused, but would do his best. When she had been talking for about an hour, the telephone rang. It was a mother whose son had an ear infection. They had been to the office that afternoon and now the child was spitting out the penicillin. He told her what she should do, but two more calls were necessary before she had gotten the dose into him.

Barbro said he ought not to let people phone him at home in the evenings. He replied that he didn't, but they phoned all the same. Then she went upstairs to bed.

The next evening she was decisive. She wanted them to talk it all through. He felt slightly scared and said she wasn't to be angry if the phone rang.

"It won't," she said.

He didn't understand what she meant. He was careful not to pour himself any whiskey and brewed coffee instead. She waited, strangely irritated, and didn't touch her coffee. Then she talked, and finally she cried. He felt totally helpless, not knowing what to say or do. His mind was quite blank.

She talked and wept until she got a cramp. But he didn't know if she meant any of what she was saying about loneliness and silence and his indifference.

She said that even his impotence was due to his indifference. He was almost relieved that she thought he was impotent. She said, "A kind of cold, sullen indifference which is really political." She used words like "bourgeois" and "cynical" and he didn't think he had to take such non-sense. So he started telling her about his working days, the long trips to patients, the road accidents, the suicides and cases of abuse, and all kinds of things about which she already knew perfectly well. He couldn't under-stand why he was degrading himself with this litany. Without his knowing how it happened, they were upstairs. She was lying on the bathroom floor, slapping her own face with both hands.

He leaned over the rigid, tense body and tried to lift her up. He could feel how cold she had become from lying on the floor. She resisted and went on hitting herself. He said he would give her something to calm her. The slapping and screaming ceased for a few seconds, as if an engine had stopped. In an almost normal voice, she said he had been trying to drug her for several years.

He went out of the bathroom, took his bedclothes, and decided to sleep on the sofa in the living room. But it did not go quiet upstairs. He could hear her sobs and screams and persuaded himself he could also hear the blows against her cheeks. He went out.

It was cold and damp outside. His breathing began to return to normal as he took in the night air, but his head started to ache, a flashing ache just above his eyes. He sat down on the steps with his head in his hands. He heard a car, then steps on the gravel, but was unaware someone had come into the garden until he felt a hand on his arm.

It was Märta in a raincoat over her nightgown, asking why he hadn't answered the phone. There had been a road accident on the border. The ambulance had left Östersund a quarter of an hour ago and Ivar Jönsson was on his way to it in his taxi with the injured man. But Birger must go to meet Ivar. He was afraid the man was bleeding to death, and he needed painkillers. She went in with him and already in the hall she heard the screams. She looked him straight in the eye and he didn't know what to say.

"You go," she said. "I'll see to this."

When he got back toward morning, Märta was in the living room doing the Friday crossword in an old copy of the *Post*. She had brewed some coffee and found a blanket to put around her legs. She said Barbro was asleep and the telephones were plugged in again.

"I didn't know they'd been unplugged," Birger said.

It was quite light now and he could clearly see the gray hairs in Märta's sandy, severely permed hair and the hair on her upper lip. He thought he ought to say something about Barbro, but he had no need to. Märta said several people had had breakdowns.

"These interrogations are driving people crazy. They ought to stop now. They serve no purpose, anyhow. It'd be best if they dropped it. It all drags on far too much."

He didn't know if she really meant it. He had found Märta to be a fairly stern moralist, but she always had her own opinion on things. She had medical intuition and a talent for organization on which he had become dependent. After she had left, he found himself thinking about what she had said, as if it were worth testing out.

If only you knew it wouldn't happen again—what would it be like then if they dropped it? Like a natural disaster. An accident. A landslide. Would it ever be explained even if they found whoever had wielded the knife?

He knew that killing often had little to do with the victim. And whoever had held that long, sharp hunting knife up there by the Lobber— did it have anything to do with him any longer? With the killer?

His thoughts dispersed and he felt very tired. He took the blanket Märta had had over her legs and lay down on the sofa. He soon fell asleep and when he woke he heard Barbro in the kitchen.

His thoughts, his emotions, were wide awake, clear, and unmuddied. He wanted her to leave and not return. But he didn't want to say it.

He longed for his solitude and the dull, regular days, for his office and the treatment room and morose Märta. Painting when he got back home. The can of beer. The TV documentary and the Goldberg Variations. The weather forecasts. I'll subscribe to the *Östersund Post,* he thought. Alone.

She left the same day, and they said little to each other before she drove off. She had made no comment on his having painted the veranda. He supposed she hadn't even noticed how far he had gotten.

You cannot live in the world without living off it.

The words rang a bell in her head that told her they had not originated there. So she went around asking. Petrus answered.

"If by 'the world' you mean nature, then that's right."

Annie said she didn't believe "the world" meant "nature" and she had only wanted to know where the line came from. He didn't know. He gave her a long look, clearly thinking she was being contrary.

She didn't know whether she was being contrary. She was feeling good. It was warm and the scents from the meadow flowers were sweet. The old leader ewe in the flock had become so trusting that she would put her nose into Annie's hand, standing still and spreading warmth over her palm. When she brought up the cud and started chewing, Annie felt a puff of her mild, saturated breath.

No, the world did not mean nature. Bert, who didn't know where the words came from, either, but thought he had heard them before, said at once:

"The world is society, do you mean?"

"I don't mean anything. I just wondered what it was."

"Don't do that," Dan said one evening, his voice low and pleading. She felt a stab of guilt.

Whatever it meant, the world was full of cuckoo calls. She saw the cuckoo. At first she thought it was a bird of prey landing in a low spruce.

A rich smell of decay came from the forest, blending with the delicate acidity of the reddish cones forming on the tips of the spruce branches. She squatted down on her heels in the moss. In the quiet, the bird called and revealed its presence.

In the old days, people had thought the cuckoo became a hawk when the summer was over. Then he struck with his claws extended, getting his beak bloody. He was calling like a bell in the forest. She was so close she could see the slate-gray throat feathers trembling at each call. He was perched with his wings folded and black tailfeathers outspread, spotted with white.

As soon as he had flown away again, she turned and went back toward the houses. The first time she had walked down from the pasture and followed the stream in among the lichen-festooned trees, she had suddenly been frightened right in the middle of a step. Not by any sound, but frightened from within, icily and inexorably warned by an instinct she had never before known existed within her. She immediately turned around and started running back. Once she reached the woodshed, she sat down by the wall so the children wouldn't see her and stayed there until her breathing had become calm and regular.

They never mentioned what had happened down by the river. Two police officers had walked all the way up from the Strömgren homestead and in Petrus and Brita's cottage questioned them all again. The children had been left outside in the hot sunshine.

Petrus said afterward that the fact that they wanted to hear it all over again meant the investigation had ground to a halt. But he had patiently told them the same things he had said when they had been questioned at the homestead. Then they had never mentioned it again.

So it seemed as if it would be possible to live there without thinking about what had happened by the Lobber. What had happened had been an anomaly. Something extraordinary. As if the cuckoo really had become a hawk, just once.

According to Petrus, that one time didn't even count. Only the tabloid papers blew up the atypical. But Annie wondered whether anomaly might not be the origin of much of what was included in the ordinary scheme of things—in nature, as Petrus called it. Mutations, for instance, she said when they stared at her. Reproached slightly for intellectualizing her problems, she cried out, "*My* problems!"

At that moment Dan leaned right over his down-at-heel Lapp shoes and she sensed he was struggling with laughter. Again she felt the mixture of cheerfulness and desire that made it almost impossible to sit still listening to the evening's rundown and criticism. As usual, Dan was sitting in the strong sunlight pouring in through the window, lighting up odd strands in his ash-blond hair. Now, when he was trying to hide his face, his long hair fell like a flood of light toward the floor. Annie had a wild yearning to take it into her mouth. Not later. Now. Now, at once.

But first she wrote something down. She took out her notebook as soon as they had gotten back to their room because she didn't want to forget it. The wildly and chaotically unpredictable that formed the basis of new creation in nature must also exist in the world. In civilization. Was the world really the predictable progression of cultural and economic order now being described? Was it so unlike nature, which could at any time spew or spit out anomalies, wild ones? Was it not also in a sense nature?

The moment passed. Dan gathered his hair up into a ponytail and fastened it with some elastic she had given him so that he wouldn't wear it out with ordinary rubber bands. She could sense his irritation like kinetic anxiety in the room, glass trembling, books falling down. Though not really, she said to herself, trying to be sober for Mia's sake, pretending not to notice the shifts of mood of which unfortunately she was all too often the cause.

It didn't worry her too much that her philosophizing irritated him. It implied a certain amount of respect, whereas when Petrus held forth, Dan clearly found it difficult not to laugh. When they were on their own, they couldn't discuss it. All the same, she didn't really know where she stood with Dan in relation to Petrus. Whatever happened, she was not going to stop thinking in this way, because it was new and gave her some pleasure. It was like swimming or running. Sometimes it occurred to her that this life was ideal: physical labor and reflection, a great deal of staring at clouds and mountainsides, at trees and birds. The smells of sheep and grass. Dan's warm skin. Water—pure, murmuring, running water. Children's voices.

Before her inner eye she could see the burnt skin on a child's back, a girl the same age as Mia. The girl was running along a bombed road, but she was really moving in a pattern, a suffocating order scorching the map of its pattern into her back and arms. Was it like that? Was she part of an order? Annie asked Bert.

He had no objection to talking about it, and he replied that she was.

"And in Cambodia? Is that a new order establishing itself there?"

Her voice had probably been shrill. She saw that in Bert's brown eyes —doggie brown—rather than hearing it herself. He replied that peasant war was grim. Their order was grim. But then a new order would emerge. A new world.

World? So he meant that there would be peasant wars all over the world and then—a new world?

One morning Ylja brought his tea and said she had to go up to the car and go and do some shopping. She had brought some extra sandwiches; it seemed she was taking it for granted he wouldn't go into the house while she was away. But as soon as she started rummaging for money in the center compartment of her handbag, she would discover he had already done so. After she had left, he would have to make his way up to the road and try to get a lift, however bad his foot.

The fact that he had hit her had not changed the atmosphere between them. She seemed to be neither afraid nor particularly angry. More contemptuous than anything else. But hadn't she been that all the time?

He lay still for half an hour, then waited no longer. He had to get up to the road and start hitching before she came back.

He took nothing with him except the old staff, the money, and his sweatshirt tied around his waist. The mosquitoes were troublesome because he had to go so slowly, he couldn't much put weight on his foot. The swelling had gone down and it didn't ache as long as he lay still. But his foot was useless, and he still had to get around the lake to fetch the eel. He wasn't going to let it starve to death in a rat cage.

He had planned to let it go, but once he had gotten hold of it, it didn't seem impossible to take the cage with him up to the road. The eel would be all right for a while out of water. He tied the cage around his waist and made his way laboriously along the far too soft path. His stick kept sinking in, he lost his balance so that he had to put his weight on his foot, and then it started to hurt. It took him an hour to get no farther than back to the main path. In an hour or two she would be on her way back down from the car again, so he would have to listen out for her on the path to give him time to hide before she saw him.

He went on for a few hundred meters. As he sank to his knees, he could still see the lake through the pines and small spruces in the marsh. He had to sit down although the ground was wet. The pain in his foot kept up a slow, steady throbbing. He thought it would pass after resting for a while, but it persisted. At first he could think of nothing except the pain. Gradually he realized he would never get up again. He grew cold from the wet ground, and mosquitoes attacked his face and wrists. He felt like a corpse in a sacrificial place of slaughter. But still in pain.

He didn't hear her coming. Suddenly she was standing there and it was the only time he had ever seen her surprised. He knew his face was swollen and bitten all around his eyes. She might think he had been crying. Perhaps he had, too. The last hour, or hours, had blurred in his mind. He had kept looking at his watch but had regarded time as something static. The lichen swung stiffly in the drought and every breeze had freed his face of insects for a few seconds. The pain in his foot, though, had not stopped, but was throbbing like clockwork, in its own time.

She hauled him to his feet and he was forced to lean on her. When she saw the cage with the eel, she snatched it from him and threw it into the lake. He shouted and swore. Somehow he must have made an impression on her, because she searched around for the line, now caught in the willows along the shore, and hauled the cage back in. But then she didn't do as he told her, but opened the hatch at the bottom and shook the eel out. Johan caught only a quick flash before the eel had disappeared into the deep, dark water. He considered her unworthy of all his regrets, all his shame over hitting her.

Neither of them said anything as they made their way back, he leaning heavily on her, sometimes thinking she was almost carrying him.

When they got to the grouse shed, he simply wanted to be left alone but he didn't dare say anything. He kept thinking about the money. She must have discovered it was gone. But she said nothing. She rummaged in the rucksack and fished out a bottle of colorless liquid with no label on it. He thought she must be very much at home here. People trusted her, otherwise she could never have bought home brew.

She poured out a drink each and undressed when they had finished it. He sat on the chair by the table, unwilling to look at her.

She took off only her jeans and pants, then got hold of his trousers. She got him to lift his rear and pulled. He did it so that things wouldn't be any sillier. But it was, all the same; she pulled down his trousers and he did nothing, said nothing at all. His foot ached, the pain sharp, again and again running up from his foot. He thought she ought to understand, but he simply couldn't say, Leave me alone, it hurts.

He remembered hitting her and wondered how that had happened. Now he didn't dare even open his mouth. He didn't really care what she said or thought of him. She had already shown that so many times, though he hadn't wanted to understand. He had thought he could play with her judgment of him just as he had played with those small reddish-brown lips in her pussy. But she looked at him just as she had when she'd opened the car door to let him in. If she said something scornful or smutty, something that hurt, he would start crying. That was because he was tired and in more pain than he had ever been in before.

Tears are only fluid, he thought. Nothing but secretion. Like snot, sperm, whatever. But they mustn't come now. They mustn't come pouring down his swollen cheeks, now covered with mosquito bites.

She said nothing when she found his prick limp. She ran her forefinger rapidly back and forth, making it strike like a clapper. She seemed absentminded—or thoughtful. Then, without warning, she leaned over and took it in her mouth. It promptly betrayed him. All the blood in his body seemed to rush there and start throbbing. He could feel the pain in his foot, naked but distant.

She snorted, as if laughing to herself, then she clambered up onto him. He felt cold all the time as she did so. Her movements were measured, her face slightly stiff, not looking at him, her gaze somewhere on the hollow of his neck.

His body refused to obey. He felt desire when she moved, but then he happened to put his foot down hard to accept her rocking thrusts and the pain immediately shot up from his ankle. He could feel nothing except the stabbing and throbbing, his face soon covered with fine sweat that ran down his neck. In the end he couldn't keep it up and of course she noticed and at once got up. She acted as if she had finished with him, though he was sure she hadn't gotten what she wanted.

She took her rucksack and left without saying anything. He curled up on the bunk and tried to sleep away the pain in his foot, but it was difficult, he was so thirsty. She had left nothing behind but a newspaper and a new pair of socks, which she had tipped out from the top of the rucksack when looking for the bottle. He realized he would have to go out to drink from the river, but he didn't know how he was going to manage it.

Morning came with the rain. He heard it in his dreams, the sound of running water growing louder. When he woke, there was no rustle of rain on the roof, but a powerful sound of river water that told him something had happened up on the mountain. Clouds had opened, the rains had come.

He limped out to find the leaves and grass covered with a veil of moisture. The river was singing, and he splashed water over his face and let it pour down over him. He managed to scramble down to the sweet-smelling, mossy ground where the buttercups were still flowering, and put his mouth to the water dancing and swirling around the skull-like stones. He drank and peed. His foot was stiff, but the pain didn't seem to have woken properly yet. When he got back, his jeans were wet at the bottom and so was his shirtfront. He hung them over the back of a chair and the top bunk and limped out again with the soap. He managed to find a small place on the riverbed free of stones, where he could put his feet, and made sure he was standing firmly in the racing water. Then he washed himself as he had never washed before. The chill of the water at first took his breath away, but he got used to it and started breathing less heavily. Rubbing with his hands, he lathered the soap time after time and washed himself all over, his crotch, under his scrotum, in the crack at the back, his armpits, scrubbing his neck and arms. He squatted down and splashed water over his head, rubbing soap into his scalp and his face until it stung.

The ache in his foot had started up again, aggravated by his movements, but the icy water numbed it. He rubbed himself over once, then a second time, then started all over again. He was really cold now and thought it wonderful.

It was drizzling. He became more and more mobile, apart from his foot, which was thrust down into the sand as if made of china or wood, and he managed to get his head down so far that he could let the water in the deep pool race through his hair.

As he got up again, a squall came and shook the birches along the river. It was a cold, harsh wind blowing down from the mountain, followed by one squall after another, which shook and swirled the treetops. Then the rain came. He cautiously got out of the river and stood on the moss, the cold from the raindrops striking his skin first like needles, then blows, then more and more diffuse, in the end like a kind of heat. He stood with his mouth open, letting the water run and run, for the wind had dropped now and the rain was falling straight down, heavy and strong. A curtain of rain was drawn through the trees, a cloak of water over all that was hot and mangled and ragged in the foliage above him, making the lichens swell and move and the moss raise its soft coat. He was clean now, as clean as a rinsed stone.

When she came with the tea basket, he was lying flat out on the bottom bunk, naked but with a towel over him. Not for a moment was he afraid of her. She was not to touch him. When she gave him tea with no milk, he remembered she had said he was spoiled. That had been true then.

She was looking gray and she was sober. She sat down at the table and started reading the paper she had left behind. He thought she looked old, bored, her complexion sallow.

Perhaps he would have to wait a day or two. But as soon as his foot was better, he would leave. He would accept any food she brought, but he had no intention of asking for anything. There was water in the river.

She sat there for a long time, reading without speaking to him. Then she suddenly closed the paper, folded it, and put it into the basket.

"Now, Jukka, my boy," she said. "The time's come. You're going home now."

She went off with the basket and was gone a couple of hours. He didn't know what she had meant. He had to wait for his foot to heal. Then he would leave whether she said anything or not.

When she returned she brought her rucksack, fully packed.

"Take this now."

She gave him a small folded paper packet. He didn't know what it was, so she unfolded it for him. It held a white, grainy powder.

"It's like tablets," she said. "You hold the paper like this and let it run into your mouth. Then rinse it down with water."

When she saw him hesitating, she said:

"Do you think I'm going to poison you? It's only an ordinary hangover powder. For headaches. Painkiller, Johan. You won't be able to walk on that foot otherwise."

He poured the powder into his mouth. It stuck between his teeth and to the insides of his cheeks, and he had to fill his mouth with water to loosen the grains.

"One more," she said.

She had a whole bag of packets of powder. He hoped they were strong. For he wanted to go now. He would go.

At first he hopped along with the staff, a short distance at a time, then resting, leaning on it. Gradually he found he had to sit down when he rested. His armpit began to hurt when the stick dug in.

They said nothing to each other. She walked ahead, frequently turning back to look at him. When he began to lag too far behind, staggering every time he hopped forward, she went back to him and he put his arm around her shoulders. They went on that way, her body close to his.

He could feel nothing, not even embarrassment. All he could think was, We'll soon be there now. In an hour or two. Perhaps three. It rained now and again, but not heavily. Sometimes he sat resting with his eyes closed, listening to the rain rustling in the grass and trees.

The rests grew longer and longer. They still said nothing to each other. He didn't even wonder whether she was getting rid of him because of the money. He had thought of leaving it on the seat when he got out of the car, but then changed his mind. He didn't have to go with her in the car. He would keep the money and stop up by the bridge to get a lift.

His foot was hurting really badly when they got there, but he said nothing. He didn't want her to know. She couldn't know how he had injured himself. Or had she realized when she'd seen the open window?

"I'll be all right now," he said once they were there and he was sitting on the bridge railing. "I'll soon get a lift."

He was wet, and so was she, her hair darker, flat in wet strands. She had mascara below her eyes, a blurred blue-black semi-circle.

"You're coming with me," she said.

He had no desire to argue, but he still thought he would keep the money. He had to find somewhere, get a room and lie down with his throbbing, exploding ankle.

He fell asleep in the car. It was good to doze off and he didn't want to talk. Nor did she. But they had been walking for so long, the silence between them had begun to be unreal.

She woke him an hour later and told him to get out and phone home. The car was standing by a building that looked like a community center in a village he didn't recognize. There was a phone booth beside it.

"Phone home now," she said. "They'll have to come and fetch you."

She gave him a handful of Norwegian coins and he took them, though he had no intention of telephoning.

"I'll go and buy some cigarettes," she said. Her voice sounded dry, almost rasping. She helped him out of the car, and once he was upright with his stick, she got back in and started the engine, then drove off. Quickly, he thought. He could see no store where she could buy anything.

He went into the telephone booth, but he didn't call. He didn't want to ask Gudrun for help, so he just stood there, propped against the shelf as he waited.

He soon realized he had waited far too long. He went out and sat down on the grass, unable to stand any longer. She didn't come.

He wondered what that last little scene had meant. Decency? Consideration? She would be far away now, smoking her damned cigarettes in the car. He was sure she hadn't run out of them. She never let things slip that far.

Anyhow, she was out of his life and that was what he had wanted. He was standing by a community center in a village he knew nothing about, his sweatshirt over his shoulders and the long walking stick with its brass knob and leather loop to lean on, but he knew he would not be able to go much farther.

Late in the afternoon he got a lift on a truck loaded with fiberglass. The driver did not get much joy out of him, because he soon fell asleep. He was woken in Namsos. He knew where he was there. It was horribly, ordinarily, and tangibly Namsos: the warehouses down by the harbor, the small side streets. He could just see Karoliussen's bookshop.

He limped across the street to where he had seen a sign for a guesthouse. It had a dining room and smelled of fish, a stale though not too greasy smell that also clung to the curtains and bedspread in the room the landlady gave him.

He tried to pull off his boot but couldn't, not just because it hurt, but it stuck over his ankle. He knew he would have to get the boot off and hopped out to the landlady again to ask for a pair of scissors. A large pair of kitchen scissors. She helped him cut through the thick rubber. His sock was soaked through and very tight.

When he at last got his foot out of it and saw the dark blue, distended skin, he knew he couldn't go on. He asked if he could use the telephone.

Gudrun was at home. She was nearly always at home. She spoke terribly quietly and he could make nothing of what she was thinking or feeling. She just said she would come.

"Stay where you are. What's it called?"

"Lucullus. In Havngatan."

"Stay where you are and wait. It'll probably take two or three hours. And don't phone anywhere."

She repeated that before hanging up.

"Don't phone anyone else. Just stay in your room and wait."

He couldn't do that because he had to get something to eat. It was too late for dinner and he couldn't go out. But the landlady took pity on him, heated up some fishcakes and fried large, floury pieces of potato in an overheated pan. He ate it all. While he was waiting for coffee, he limped over to a newspaper, a two-day-old copy. When she brought the coffee and saw it, she said she would fetch a more recent one.

"No," he said. He just wanted to be left in peace to read. At the bottom of the front page was a big photograph of two women and a man by a road sign saying Blackwater.

What the signpost actually said was BLA KW TER. He couldn't make out why on earth Blackwater should feature in this newspaper, an Oslo paper, and he was ashamed of the tatty signpost.

In a column on the center spread was a photograph of a rather pretty, dark girl. It said Mountain River, but they must mean the Lobber, because there was a crudely drawn map with the Strömgren homestead and Starhill on it. A small tent had been drawn by the river. There was something about a road to a summer pasture. And a moped.

It was stale news and he couldn't make it out at all—the big center spread with photographs of tourists by the general store, by the homestead and by the Lobber was a follow-up. TOURISTS IN DEATH VILLAGE.

He found it at last in the caption below the picture of the girl: A young girl and an unknown man had been knifed to death in a tent on Midsummer night.

By the Lobber.

He had had the newspaper all that last night in the grouse shed. It had been on the floor, folded over double. He remembered the photograph of fishing boats at the top of the front page. Ylja had read it.

She had read it that morning and then she hadn't wanted to have anything more to do with him.

Can you really live in the world without living off it? Unexpectedly enough, it was Brita who recognized the words.

"It's not a question," she said. "You've twisted the whole thing."

She had been walking around heavily in the last weeks of her pregnancy, apparently not listening to all their talk. But she was the only one who knew where the words came from.

"It's St. Paul, the First Epistle to the Corinthians. 'And they that live in this world, not living off it: for the fashion of this world passeth away.' "

Annie wanted to get hold of a Bible at once, but no one had one. Brita thought there had been one lying around in the trash they had taken over to the fishing-club loft when they moved into the old house. Annie got up there by putting a ladder against the end gable and crawling through a hatch. It was full of timber and just by the hatch, lying in the sawdust, she saw a whole lot of papers, damaged by the damp. She opened a book with a stiff gray cover. Enrollment book. Someone had signed up for military service, his name Arne Jonasson, in the year 1951. At first she thought she had mistaken the year. The few pages in the book had yellowed and looked as if they were beginning to be eaten away. Inserted in the book was a black and white photograph of cows on a slope and a house at the top; six people were standing in front of a fence at the bottom. It was an ordinary thin, shiny print, otherwise she would have guessed it was a photograph from the previous century. But the women's skirts were short.

Her first impression that it was a photo of cows was somehow right.

They hadn't just happened to be there. There were two children carrying long sticks up on the slope, and they were driving the cows on their way out of the photograph. The cows had no horns but curly foreheads and were spotted like a map of small islands.

There was a liquor ration book, the rations taken out regularly, a liter a month. In Östersund. Strange, if he had lived there. Perhaps the shopkeeper in Blackwater had done it for him. Had this man—Erik Jonasson was his name—gone once a month down to the village with his ration book? Why hadn't he taken it with him when he moved? Perhaps he had died? But then she remembered that liquor rationing had been abolished sometime in the 1950s. The book hadn't been stamped all the way through. Perhaps they had gone on living there in the fifties. Twenty years ago. The papers looked as if they had been there for a century. But I was at school then, she thought. I lived in Enskede and in Gärdet in Stockholm. With a fridge, telephone, and streetcars. Erik Jonasson and his family had been tucked away in a pocket of time.

Someone had cut photographs of cars out of magazines and stuck them onto squared paper. That could hardly be Arne, because the cars were bulging fifties models. They were on double pages that must have been taken out of a school arithmetic book. Had the teacher noticed it had become thinner and thinner?

A cut-out advertisement. "Technical articles. Private sender." The little cutting lay together with a doctor's prescription in a cigar box of thin wood. Technical articles. Dildos and leather items crossed her mind. He couldn't have trotted up to Starhill with such things.

They would have been condoms, of course. Why had people been so furtive about them? They weren't prohibited. Did people attract derision by sending off for contraceptives? She wasn't sure the cutting was only twenty years old. There were prescriptions going right back to the thirties in the box, some never used. No prescription had been used more than once, although most of them were valid for three doses. Had they recovered more quickly than the doctor had thought? Or had they been unable to afford more?

The thought dislodged the feeling she had had all the time she had looked at these moldering papers. Compassion, albeit a feeble compassion mixed with shame, as if she would have preferred not to see or know. Yet she went on looking through the papers and found a 1937 school report, from the third year in the village school in Blackwater. A report with many reservations, the marks all very modest, but the girl, Astrid Jonasson, had the top mark for conduct. She must have been ten years old then. Born 1927. If still alive, she wouldn't be fifty yet.

Why shouldn't she still be alive? She must have gone to school in Blackwater and spent most of her school years in lodgings. As I did, Annie thought. And not really much farther away from home than I was. Had she also had that feeling and still lived with it, a meager normal life above dark waters? Solitude. Devotion. Profound loneliness. One more wild attempt. Dry, cold loneliness. Like me. Until now.

The girl and her parents had left their private papers to the damp and the mice. It was impossible to say whether it had been sheer carelessness with the memories of their lives. They might have fallen ill and died. Or had Astrid and Arne thought of coming to retrieve their mother's and father's belongings one day, and then it had never happened? It was too far away? Perhaps they lived in Östersund or even farther south.

There were letters of condolence. White envelopes with black edges. She poked one out to see whether there was any Jonasson among the dead. Five printed letters of condolence with hymn verses and names of mourners. There was only one Jonasson. Arne, who had been drafted in 1951 and who according to his enrollment book had never returned for retraining in the reserve.

Had he died during his military service? Was it an accident? Or was his death connected with the big brown envelope from Österåsen Sanatorium? She couldn't make out the date of the postmark. Had people died of tuberculosis in the fifties? The envelope was empty, but something must have been inside it. Perhaps Arne's army book and the shiny little photos of girls and boys in their twenties. They must have sent back things like that. There were letters, too, not many, but some of them had Arne's name on the back of the envelope. She opened one and saw a few words: ". . . take them although they aren't mature . . ." Was he writing about trees? He was probably a forester. Perhaps he was in the sanatorium and worrying about the felling he could see from the window or the balcony?

It could be metaphorical. He himself was not mature. None of those twenty-year-olds in the photographs was. She didn't want to know what he meant. It could be cloudberries or spruce trees or people and she didn't want to read the letters. It was bad enough that they had been chucked in there in thin bundles, now falling apart.

She started gathering up the papers and shaking them clean of sawdust. Someone had drawn horses on school exercise-book paper, one horse after another carefully drawn with a much too hard pencil. Shaded to show the curve of the huge hindquarters, hooves filled in as darkly as possible with the faint pencil. Several of the horses had harness and bridles drawn in precise detail. She didn't know what the parts were called. They looked like small ears standing high up on the back, perhaps sticks. But whoever had drawn them knew what they were called. If still alive, he still knew every word for these complicated arrangements and knew the construction of the material of the straps and the harness down to the last detail.

There were several sheets of yellowish-brown tissue paper, apparently used, for they had once been folded in quite a different way. Creases had been smoothed out but not entirely eliminated. She had found no trace of the woman who had been the children's mother and the wife of Erik Jonasson. Perhaps the tissue paper was something she had saved. She could have made a pattern out of it by laying it over a dress, but who had a dress she wanted to copy? This wasn't the ghost of a dress but of a desire.

Annie found a notebook with songs in it. The first ones were written in very old-fashioned handwriting with an aniline pen the writer must have moistened now and again, for in some of the words the violet color was stronger. Verses about mountains and blue hills, about longing and all kinds of misery, among others that of the sanatorium. She felt an embarrassed compassion again, but also uncertainty. Had they laughed or cried as they had sung these songs?

Farther on in the notebook, another hand had written songs of the thirties and maybe the forties in pencil. "It's the Woman Behind It All," "Per Olsson, He Had a Goodly Farm," "The Old Bureau." She recognized her father's repertoire. They were all there, the older sentimental ones and the modern jolly ones, all of them very proper. She suddenly remembered the song she had heard while waiting for Dan outside the store. "Dad's Cock's in Front"! He had actually sung "cock." She noticed she had remembered it and decided to write it down. There must be an underworld treasure trove of songs that people did not write down but had no difficulty whatsoever in remembering.

There was indeed a Bible, and three bundles of diaries. They were tied together with string, ten to a bundle. She found six loose diaries down in the sawdust. She was now almost certain they had gone on living there until 1957. The series beginning in 1922 ended then, and all the slim volumes were bound and bore the subtitles "For the Year after the Birth of Our Savior Jesus Christ" and the name of the Luleå local paper.

Had the family come to live there in modern times when electricity and cars had already come to the villages? Had Erik Jonasson been a Luddite? A dour Jämtland man with a taste for the life of a loner, forcing his family to live in the wilderness and relinquish company, light, oranges, cars, and photographs of film stars? Or was the place inherited? Had Erik's family been the second and last generation up there?

The cellar dug out of the ground had been built in 1910. The date was carved on the crossbeam above the door. Had everything been over after two generations of frantic labor? They had carried up a grindstone and a sledgehammer, iron wheels, spades, and a chaff cutter. She had seen them in the sheds and lying in the grass. There was an old Singer sewing machine at the back of the woodshed. Wooden lasts they made shoes on, several small children's feet of darkened wood. Rusty flat irons. Medicine glasses and cake tins. A bottle of tincture called Universal.

She had hoped to find notes in the diaries about their lives, but she was disappointed. Very sporadically, first the aniline pen and then the pencil had been used to write abbreviated entries. They were impossible to make out: "HK. B Bt." Sometimes there were a few words about the weather. "Storm 3 days. Frost." That was July 3. She opened the diary of her own year of birth and leafed through it backward. On January 11 it said "−52°." That frightened her. Oh, but that was during the war, she told herself. Though what had war to do with the cold? It could drop to fifty-two degrees below zero here. War or no war.

So it had been fifty-two below zero when she was conceived. Not much less, anyhow. How and where could people make love when it was so cold? Perhaps they had to?

The soldiers had been billeted in barns and empty dwellings during the war. In Blackwater, her father had lived in a cottage they had named the Sun Hut. They put attractive names on all the houses: the Calm, the Bun House, Snowpeace, and Soria Moria. He can't have had sex with Henny in the billet. Had there been a guesthouse in those days? Was there a letter or any other record that would tell her where they had lived?

Henny was a great tidier and she would have thrown everything away if they hadn't stopped her. Perhaps you got like that if you had to keep a studio apartment in Gärdet in order? Before they moved house, Annie had also had to throw things away and she had lain in bed at night worrying about it and running her mind over the things she had left.

When Dan had told her that the commune lay above Blackwater, she had had a strong feeling of significance and destiny. She would be literally returning to her origins if she moved there. She wondered if the people who had left behind these tattered papers, incomprehensible in their in-completeness, had also suffered from a sense of destiny. Or had they looked on their lives, as the papers seemed to indicate, as something random and soon scattered?

Only a couple of hours before she had been sitting at the table by the window in their room, writing in her notebook, expounding on living in the world. Now her words seemed embarrassing. But she had found that dangerous ideas could come of thinking like that. In all likelihood she would never have noticed if it hadn't been written down.

However, she had never told Dan she had been conceived in Blackwater. That had been just as arbitrary as the fifty-two degrees below zero that winter of war. But why do we keep looking for meaning and connections? It's the way our minds work, seeking pattern and order. Yet we scatter our lives, helplessly and absently.

She gathered up the papers. When she first saw them, she had thought of showing them to the others, but now she decided to hide them. They should be preserved, not thumbed over, giggled at, or have compassion poured over them. The interval since they had been written was too short, and they held the secrets of living people. Somewhere there was a woman called Astrid occasionally thinking about Starhill and life there—as a sum-mer paradise with warm milk and freshly baked thin-bread, perhaps? As an awful dump where she was thrashed? Or, as Annie thought about Enskede, alternately wine and water? But well meant.

She had the few papers illuminating her identity and her past in her bag. Her mother was called Henny Raft and was born in 1905, a fact not recorded in the papers Annie had with her. Inquiries would have to be made to find that out. No one would even think of researching into Annie Raft's parents. Yes, if I had died, she thought. If it had been me. In the tent.

Mia? Did she know what her grandmother's name was? She had been an operetta singer, and Henny Raft was her stage name. Her real name was Helga, née Gustafsson, and Annie was sure Mia didn't know that. Henny's father, Annie's grandfather and Mia's great-grandfather, was dead. His name had been Ruben Gustafsson and Annie had gone to his funeral when she was about ten, but she could no longer remember where he was buried. He had owned a small publishing company, publishing among other things song books, collections of folk remedies, gardeners' almanacs, and books on the interpretation of dreams. Some of these could be found on the shelves at home, but no one else would be able to link them with the Raft family.

Henny, who for decades traveled up and down the country, had been born in a back-courtyard apartment house in Ostermalm in Stockholm. Annie had had it pointed out to her and they had gone into the courtyard to look up the steep stairway, but she could no longer remember whether it was in Skeppargatan or Grev Turegatan. Åke Raft, her father, had originally been a Pettersson. He had been born in 1908, the third son of a pastry cook. Annie didn't know why he became a musician. He was primarily a pianist and had worked in theater orchestras and as a *répétiteur*. He had married Henny Raft in 1939, when he was thirty-one and Henny thirty-four. Annie knew this by heart, because it formed part of the story of her birth, which Henny loved to tell. There had never been any talk of children. Henny's career as an operetta singer was at a sensitive stage.

They both legally took the name Raft when they married. Annie's grandfather had carted a large wedding cake by train all the way from Hudiksvall. The china bridal couple that had crowned it now lay in the top left-hand drawer of Henny's desk. The bride had a tiny veil of real tulle, and some caramel had remained on the plinth until Annie had sucked it all off.

Grandfather had died when she was small, but she couldn't remember the year. Grandmother had grown old enough for Annie to be able to sing at her funeral. Grandmother had wanted to have her favorite sentimental ditty in farewell, but naturally that had been impossible.

Annie felt ashamed when she thought about it. Why hadn't she done as Grandmother had wished? She had sat at Seraphina Hospital with that thin, yellowish hand in hers and promised. Now she could no longer remember her grandmother's maiden name and just hoped Henny had preserved it in some hiding place. Couldn't she have had her own way when her life was so soon to be scattered and forgotten?

Henny and Åke married at Whitsun. That September, the war came and Åke was called up, not into the forces' entertainment section as he had hoped, but into the infantry. He was sent to the Jämtland village of Blackwater on the Norwegian border. Henny went to see him there and became pregnant. Perhaps it was impossible to acquire condoms in Blackwater, something implicit in Erik Jonasson's papers. At that time, a lady presumably couldn't go into a drugstore even in Stockholm on such an errand. Annie was born in October. According to family legend, because of her pregnancy Henny lost the chance of playing the lead in *Annie Get Your Gun*, so instead she christened her baby girl Annie.

Annie was still quite young when she realized Henny would never have been given the lead. Dolly Tate was the best she could hope for. The aunt and uncle in Enskede had an old boxer called Dolly, so Annie had been quite content all her life with Henny's good-natured deception.

She ought to tell Mia that story. Thanks to the dog, it would probably register. She could tell her that the aunt and uncle she had lived with whenever her parents were touring the country were called Elna and Göte. But she realized she would never be able to show Mia their house, way out on Sockenvägen in Enskede, as it had looked then. And felt. It had been restored now and was presumably properly insulated. During the winters in the 1950s, it had been like living in a cardboard box.

She had shared a room with two cousins called Susanne and Vivianne, who were as soppy as their soppy names. She had felt guilty for even thinking like that. Mia was not yet much troubled by guilt. She wouldn't even speak to Pella because she found her name so hard to bear.

Two loud-voiced brothers called Nisse and Perra had occupied the former washhouse in the basement, which Uncle Göte had equipped. It struck her that it must have been cold and dark, but she hadn't thought about that at the time. She had just been pleased to have them at a distance. The whole family was noisy. But she hadn't been homesick, because their home in Gärdet was just a one-room apartment with a sleeping alcove.

It occurred to her that in the past people used to write down important family events on the flyleaf of the Bible. When she opened the Bible she had found in the sawdust, it seemed unread, the thin pages adhering to each other. Astrid Jonasson had received it from the congregation in 1942. "In Memory of Your Confirmation, Psalm 116:1–2." Had Astrid ever looked it up? Annie did not do so. But she hunted out St. Paul's First Epistle to the Corinthians and started reading it.

It was all about a small gathering of people exposed to contempt but in possession of something they called spiritual gifts. They were advised against sexual intercourse and eating meat, but if necessary could do both. They were seriously warned against doubting that people could live after death. As they believed, so it would be.

The passages on living in the world did not really sound the way Brita had quoted them, nor like the words that had preoccupied her. But she sensed the origins were right after all. It was clear St. Paul believed that a disaster was imminent and it would put an end to any possibility of an earthly life. So now people could—and ought to—give up worrying about their nearest as well as their own feelings and affairs and the world in general. This was obviously the opposite of her own fumbling but basically sensible thoughts.

She had sat for a long time inside that hatch into the loft. Gertrud and Sigrid had walked past a couple of times and looked up at her, but they had said nothing. Sigrid had a worried old face for her nine years. She would probably make her way up there and rummage in the papers. Annie had better hide them. But where? There was no cupboard she could lock and she hadn't even a box for her things. Everything was common property. She decided to put the whole lot under her bed for the time being and think up somewhere to keep them so that they wouldn't be spoiled by the damp or found and spread around. There were so many of them anyway, she had to make two trips down the ladder.

As she stood on the ladder fetching the last lot, she stirred up the sawdust and caught sight of a cardboard box in one corner. It had damp patches and must have been there much longer than the rest. It had once been a blue chocolate box bearing the name Freia, and the gold lettering was in Norwegian.

When she opened it, small paper clothes welled out. Cut out, beautifully painted, and quite undamaged, they rose out of the crush underneath the protective corrugated sheet of gold paper. Every flap to hook them on to the paper doll's body was intact. She couldn't see one that was ragged or had been torn off. They were all in the style of the forties—the yokes, straight shoulders, pleated skirts, belts, and hip draperies. There were clutch coats, topper coats, and blazers. She remembered the terms Henny had laughingly used when she showed her old photographs. A muff with flaps that had been folded over and over. The paper doll lying almost at the bottom resembled Ava Gardner or Joan Crawford and had her arms held away from her body. The muff had to be fixed to the sleeve of her coat—she was to make a gesture with it. As if meeting someone. In town. It was cold, the snow falling and perhaps Christmas Eve with bells ringing —as in an American film from the days of the coat.

The doll of hard cardboard was homemade, as all the clothes were. You could tell the bright red lips had been colored with a red crayon, the point of which had been moistened. The clothes were painted in paler watercolors, perhaps from a school paintbox. Flowers, squares, stripes, and dots. Lace edges to collars. Sequin embroidery. Sewn-down pleats. Stitching and smocking. Everything was reproduced with loving care. Yes— love. She felt it herself as she touched the paper clothes. Carefully she put them all back under the gold paper and put the lid back on the box.

Åke Vemdal phoned. It was so unexpected, Birger could find nothing to say. But Åke said:

"I can come now."

"Come?"

"You invited me to dinner."

Was he quite shameless? After all, he had refused the invitation without even thanking him. Birger was taken aback.

"Of course. Good to see you. When can you come?"

He was tense as he cut up the venison and prepared the casserole. Åke must have been feeling the same, because when he arrived he didn't seem interested in the food. He sat sipping his vodka as if it were some kind of liqueur, though it was ordinary Smirnoff. He was supposed to add caraway or St. John's wort to it, but he forgot.

"I hear Barbro's gone away."

Birger felt extreme annoyance. People talked, but no one said anything to him. No one had asked, not even Märta. Åke Vemdal was the first person to mention that Barbro had gone away, and on top of that he was clumsy enough to try to console Birger.

"You'll see, she'll be back when she's calmed down after the hearings. They've questioned her over and over again. They've got about seven hours of tape."

"They?" said Birger. "Why do you say 'they'? Haven't you been involved?"

Åke drank his vodka back in one swallow. These large glasses had never been used when Barbro was at home. Birger's father had been a qualified forester, employed at an estate in Gästrikland, and he had been presented with them on his fortieth birthday. They had flying ducks engraved on them and a huntsman and his dog on the decanter. Vemdal was now scrutinizing the decoration on his glass as Birger told him about them. But he didn't seem to be listening.

"I've been taken off the case," he said finally.

"Officially?"

Birger felt this was something similar to what Barbro's absence had been in the beginning. Something perhaps not definite or even quite real. But Åke said that was so. Official. Stated outright.

"Why?"

"I'm considered too involved in it."

"Was it because I spoke out of turn about that Three Towers bootprint?"

"I haven't even heard about that. We can talk freely now, because, as I told you, I'm out of the picture. But I don't think they've gotten much further. It's come to a halt."

"They were creating hell around here," said Birger. "Do you want some whortleberry with it? There's some pickled gherkin here."

But Åke ate practically nothing. The color in his face was unhealthy.

"I still get a hell of a lot of anonymous letters. Telling me to do something about it. Get the man who did it so people can go out. So the tourists won't be frightened away. Though it's the other way around. Tourists descend like flies. Busloads of them. I get letters to say I should stop snooping around, I should watch out, and some nasty, smelly things have been sent to me. A soiled sanitary napkin. I wanted to bring it into the investigation—that little Dutch girl had her period when she died, and I thought perhaps someone had found it, someone who didn't want to admit having been up there. That was when I found out I had been taken off the case. When it was stated outright, I mean. And they said the sanitary napkin was nothing but a comment on my involvement. Can you believe it? It's not impossible, for that matter."

"In what way are you supposed to be involved?"

"I'm not involved."

He sounded slightly irritable.

"Are you sleeping all right?"

"Oh, for Christ's sake, shut up! Don't you know what they call you?"

"Yes," said Birger. "I do. I think you should eat something. Then we'll go and listen to some music. Perhaps skip coffee. Nothing wrong with you taking a few sleeping tablets back with you. I'm no pill doctor. And nor are you what they say about you."

He didn't really know what music to put on. He didn't think Åke liked either Bach or Schubert. In among his first LPs, he had one called *Down South,* dance music of the very slow kind. He remembered that one of his sexually more enterprising medical friends had borrowed it whenever he hoped to bring a girl back home with him. When the dark, hoarse phrases came slowly welling out of the saxophones, filling the bright room, he felt like laughing and Åke noticed.

"What is it?"

"We're a couple of old bachelors, you and me. Irretrievably."

"Don't know about irretrievably. And you're married, after all."

"Have been."

"I've had so little time. Though sometimes I think this way takes up more time. All this bloody—what's it called?—courting. Unless you take the very simplest way out."

He wanted some coffee anyhow.

"You keep the place in order, I see," he said, out in the kitchen.

"I keep it in order and I cook dinner every day. I'm living kind of . . . under a glass dome. Palpating people's bellies and groins but not talking to them. I've given up reading about the case, too."

"No need to bother. There's nothing new. You've read about Ivo Maertens, have you?"

"No."

"He turned up at his home. His parents phoned. He came home on the first of July. It wasn't him. He'd had a tiff with the girl in Gothenburg and they'd parted. He had no idea who it was she had with her in the tent. Nor have we."

"What was the tiff about?"

"There was a major rock concert in Gothenburg. Ivo Maertens and Sabine Vestdijk were staying at the campsite in Långedrag and made contact with someone who wanted to sell them tickets. Black market, but at a reasonable price. Ivo didn't believe it. He was sure they'd be cheated, that the tickets weren't valid and they would never get in with them. So he didn't want to. So they fell out and he started sulking. I think he's pigheaded. She went to the concert. He doesn't know who she was with, whether it was the person selling the tickets or someone else. Ivo never saw who it was. But he thought it was a man. She didn't come back that night.

He got damned worried by the morning and thought of going to the police. He went and asked at the reception tent if they'd seen her and he asked in the tents next to theirs. However, she did come in the end. Out of another tent. That was the end between them. He was so furious, he packed up his things and left. He hitched home and that took a few days. He knew nothing about what had happened when he got back to Leiden. There they received him as if he had been resurrected from the dead. He doesn't know what plans she had when they parted in Långedrag. But there had been no talk about the mountains, ever. So it seems as if that was the other man's idea. Sagittarius's."

"Sagittarius? Had he shot someone?"

"Not as far as we know. The only thing of his we found in an old bag was a notebook. It had a sign of the zodiac on it: Sagittarius. That's really the only thing we think we know about him."

"Why?"

"The notebook was bought here, from the general store in Byvången. You can see that from the price tag. They had all the signs of the zodiac to choose from. So why should he have chosen one other than his own? They remember him. Though not that he bought a notebook. There were lots of people there on the day before Midsummer Eve. We've been able to trace Sabine Vestdijk and him all the way from Långedrag, because they stayed at campsites all the way up. In that big tent. There's been such a hullabaloo in the papers, people have phoned in. They arrived in Byvången the day before Midsummer Eve and rented a room there for the first time. That was at the Three Pines. In her name only. The landlady doesn't remember if they said he was her husband. Anyhow, Sabine went to bed in the middle of the afternoon and he went to the drugstore. The assistant there remembers him. She thought he was good-looking. Though unpleasant. She thought he was a druggie. He had a headband and looked a bit sloppy, she thought. Though you never know. That depends on her own standards, and in the store they said nothing about his appearance except that he had quite long hair. He kept on saying he wanted Saridon. He couldn't understand that all strong drugs are on prescription. I don't think the assistant spoke much English, either, and he spoke only English. 'Painkiller,' he kept saying over and over again. At first she didn't understand. She noted the word 'killer' and thought he was unpleasant. I think Sabine Vestdijk was feeling ill and needed a painkiller."

"Period pains."

"Yes, if they can be that bad. I don't know."

"Young women can have very severe period pains."

"Anyhow, he drifted around the place. It's not definite that he bought the notebook himself. The assistant in the store can't remember his doing so. She remembers him because he spoke English. She doesn't know any English, she's an older woman, so she had to go and get help. That's how she remembered what the man wanted—beer. Nothing else. The store manager who helped her remembers the same—he bought only beer. So who bought the notebook? There were crowds of people the day before Midsummer Eve, but no other customer spoke English. We don't even know if it was Sagittarius who wrote the telephone number in it. Norwegian. He was extremely careful with it anyhow, and hid the notebook under a plastic-covered piece of cardboard at the bottom of the bag. I got quite excited about that. But the number was to a small self-service store in a backwater on the coast above Brønnøysund. They know nothing about him there. And I think that's true. There were some Norwegians at the Three Pines that night and they've been questioned, too, of course, but they didn't even know where the place was. Hard to say whether they were lying. But they weren't people who'd normally have anything to do with long-haired youths in ragged, grubby jeans. They were a teacher couple from Namsos and a vet from Steinkjer. The poor girl never got any painkillers, but may have drunk some vodka, since there was an empty bottle in the room. Koskenkorva."

"What about the powder you showed me?"

Åke looked embarrassed.

"I had the same thought about him as the pharmacist's assistant had. But when they analyzed the powder, it turned out to be mostly acetylsalicylic acid. Caffeine, too, and cola seeds. Same as in Coca-Cola."

"*Semen colae,*" said Birger. "But I don't recognize that mixture."

"No stronger than aspirin, anyhow. That was all she had taken. They had gone in the morning—left without paying. Probably very early. No one knows what they got up to in the morning. Eventually she appeared at Lill-Ola Lennartsson's. The man went shopping at the store. He actually asked about a mountain. But I'm beginning to think they had simply driven the wrong way, for it wasn't a mountain anywhere around here."

"Which was it, then?"

"Starhill. That isn't here. Meanwhile she's at Lill-Ola's. So it's possible Lill-Ola thought she was alone. In that case, it wasn't all that strange that he fooled around and lent her a tent and so on. He's quite a one for the ladies. They say he's so bloody cheeky, he goes in to lone wives in rented cabins when their husbands are out fishing at night. I don't know."

"You've had to listen to an awful lot of shit."

"Yes, I've heard quite enough about Lill-Ola Lennartsson. He was the one who said he saw you crossing the road and going into the forest. Up by the Lobber."

"Then he's insane."

"He may have seen someone else, of course. And thought it was you. But I think he said it because I had his boiler room searched. He realized you had tipped me off."

"I find it hard to believe . . ."

"You're nice, Birger, that's what you are. But wait—that's not all. He said I began to persecute him afterward. Searching his cellar and house. That I was protecting you. He's lying, the bloody creep. But they believe him."

It had gone quiet, the turntable whirling around, but Birger couldn't bring himself to choose another record. He was so disgusted, he didn't want to hear any more, but nevertheless said:

"So they really do think I went up to the Lobber?"

"No, they don't. They don't think anything. They're trying to work without any presumptions. And I think they've gotten nowhere with your things, boots or whatever it was. You would have heard from them again. You mustn't take it so hard that there's been so much questioning. Lill-Ola. His wife. She may have been up there wanting to see what he was up to. She's not unaware of his little peccadilloes. They've questioned Dan Ulander and Annie Raft and the whole Starhill lot. Yvonne and her men. They've turned over every stone in the village. But they did believe one thing, and that was that he *had* mentioned seeing you. That he said it to me at the very first interrogation. They think I thought it absurd because I'd been with you, and that I thought we'd been in contact all the time. But they think I couldn't know that, not for sure, and that I ought to have included his statement in the records. Even if it wasn't believable."

"So that's why they've taken you off the case?"

"Yes. I've made a formal error, they say. However foolish I thought his statement was, I should have taken it down. But it doesn't exist! And they don't believe that. Recently I've been thinking I was going crazy. That shit! That shady bastard! He burned a whole load of Three Towers boots. He was afraid the police would come snooping into the house. They must have been stolen goods, for there's no such delivery in his account books. He has no delivery note, no invoice, nothing. And he sold them incredibly cheaply. Almost everyone in the village bought some. That doesn't exactly make the investigation any easier. And they believe him."

"What about the capercaillies? Why did he burn those? He's paid his dues and has shooting rights for small game. Surely there was nothing to be afraid of there?"

"I don't know. It's conceivable they've got somewhere with that, but I've heard nothing about it. They're looking for sleeping-bag feathers."

Åke wasn't looking at Birger as he spoke. He was gazing over in the direction of the big window facing the garden, but there was nothing to see except reflections in the glass. He was gazing at nothing, looking inward at winding marshland paths disappearing into the night mist. He could see people moving around the Area. He could see them appearing and disappearing from his gaze, which was no gaze, but grinding thoughts.

He was obsessed. He was following the paths in the marshlands and along the highways from the village as Birger each day followed the whorls in the latticework of the veranda. He had been taken off the case, but all his energy was still going into it. To no purpose.

Dan was lying on her bed as she came in. He was alone in the room and lay half turned to the wall, naked, the light from the window reflected on his brownish skin, which looked slightly moist. He was holding his penis and moving his wrist and lower arm. She started backing out, but he had already noticed she was there.

"What are you doing?" she said, hearing herself laughing what was not a real laugh.

"Masturbating," he said in a not entirely clear voice. Annie sank to her knees and slipped the papers and books to the floor, trying to do so as quietly as she could. Then she didn't know what to do. She picked up a bundle of papers and a few diaries, then put them under the bed. She could hear he was breathing faster. He made a movement and the bed creaked, then it was quite quiet.

Her mouth filled with saliva, making her swallow, but she went on pushing the diaries in toward the wall. He had gotten up off the bed. When she had finished and had to get up, he was standing in the doorway wiping himself on a towel. Confusedly, she thought that it belonged in the kitchen.

"You mustn't disturb me when I'm thinking about you," he said. She pretended to straighten the shawl she had used as a tablecloth as she tried to find something to say. All she could think of was He's more natural than I am. He would laugh if he knew how I feel. How dramatically I take everything. She hurriedly slapped shut the notebook lying on the table and when she turned around, he had gone.

In the last few days Dan and she had made love several times in the hayloft above the barn. The hay was dry and sharp and prickled through the material of her blouse. Afterward she had wanted to stay there in that scent of summer. She would have liked to fall asleep there, but the smell was not really all that pleasant. It was old hay.

He wanted them to do it in the room at night as well, but she didn't want to because of Mia. She couldn't rely on her being asleep. It rustled up there occasionally. Mia played with her dolls in the dark, whispering to them.

Annie had hidden in the hayloft when the journalists had come. She had heard them walking past with Petrus, and she heard him telling them about keeping goats and breeding sheep. She was the one they wanted to meet. They wanted her to tell them what the slashed tent by the Lobber had looked like and how much she had seen of the bodies. Instead, Petrus had told them all about how to make cheese when there is no electricity.

They stayed for a long time and now and again she heard their voices. To pass the time, she had taken the opportunity to look for the box for her diaphragm, which she had lost in the hay. Stirring up dust and chaff, she rummaged around, and soon felt a hard edge. It wasn't the box, but a white plastic medicine jar. A tranquilizer. Prescribed for Barbro Torbjörnsson, and almost empty.

She went on searching for her box and found it, as well as a nail file and a small hotel soap container. The contents of a toiletry bag must have fallen into the hay. She showed the things to Dan and he took them. She said she was feeling dispirited.

"Why?"

"I thought it was our hayloft. Our hay. Yours and mine."

He said she couldn't expect that they should have anyplace to themselves up there. Private bedroom. Individual hayloft.

She was having to make many changes. Stop listening to the radio. She was tied to the little plastic box, listening in bed, the round speaker pressed to her ear. Couldn't sleep if she hadn't heard the eleven o'clock news; Vietnam, Cambodia, Mozambique. She had to hear the words.

"Changes don't happen so quickly that you have to listen every hour," said Dan. "It's poison."

He might have been right, but that was the way she was. Dependent. On one thing or another. As he was on her body, she had thought before. But was he really?

Sometimes she thought he was weird. But she realized that was a word with which you disposed of anything that didn't really interest you. And yet it was the other way around—she was intensely aware of him. How thin he was, how slim his back and fine his hands and feet. The way the color of his hair changed in the lamplight from ash to gold. More than every fifth strand was golden. She often lay with a lock of it on her arm or breast, examining it hair by hair.

She had noticed him among a group of more than twenty new students standing outside the door of the classroom. He was unlike them with his slim, supple body, and he moved like a dancer. In the lecture room, in the dullness of a winter afternoon and the muffled atmosphere of wool and exhalations, he was a core of pure energy which she had to reach.

At first, before anything personal had passed between them, she had thought of him as that strange student. She started fantasizing about him. He might say something in a lesson that bewildered her or made her feel uncertain. Afterward she would think out a continuation. She found clever answers and it became a conversation. A kind of conversation.

In fact they were monologues she held, always silent. She had found a great deal clarified when she said it to herself, to him. But in reality she hadn't said much, not even when they had started sleeping together.

Her reserve still came from a kind of dependency. Poison—in his fierce words. Something she held on to with an atavistic, dark, and tangled part of herself. She thought it came from Enskede, and later from the Academy and Karlbergsvägen. From a life that would be utterly inexplicable to him.

Sometimes they had agonizing scenes, misunderstandings, conflicts—whatever it was called. It felt like knives in her stomach, and she didn't dare touch him because that cold point ruled. She could see it in his eyes, at the center of the pupil: mistrust.

Sometimes he mistrusted her, thought it was nothing but a game to her. An affair of a few weeks. A nice little game with political ideas and strong sexual attraction. Sometimes he actually said he was nothing but a body to her. Golden and fuzzy. Like an apricot. That he was too young.

There were nine years between them. Occasionally he had said she didn't take him seriously. He seemed to sense sometimes she had that feeling, the feeling that he was weird. Totally unknown. Like living tissue that is rejected. Alien, incompatible tissue of the soul.

Önis was standing in the doorway asking her if she had forgotten the evening milking. Yes, she had forgotten, and she was uneasy about the smell in the room. She picked up the towel and bundled it up under the blanket. Önis watched her, but said nothing. She had Sigrid at her heels and Sigrid said it wasn't really Annie's turn to do the milking. The rota had been drawn up wrongly.

Annie put on a large apron Brita had given her and went out with them to the goat shed. She didn't like the goats and she had never done any milking before she came to Starhill. She assumed that was why she was not allowed to do it with Dan, who was slow and clumsy. She was on Önis's team, on which Lotta should also be, but Lotta was nowhere to be seen.

They were variegated goats, brownish-gray, yellowish-white, streaky and spotted, no two alike, but she hadn't yet learned to tell them apart. They had bulging, slightly hairy udders with stiff teats. They leaped up on the milking table quite willingly, and it wasn't difficult to squeeze the milk out of them, though more so to remember all the stages. The udders had to be wiped clean, and the first splashes of milk were not to go into the bucket, because they were full of bacteria. Petrus had taught her that if she forgot to wipe them, no suckling reflex would be released.

The smell of goat was overwhelming. If she turned away and stopped the squeezing and pulling for a while, the goat was uneasy. The animals had strange, ruptured eyes with oblong pupils. They gleamed like crushed amber. Some had dangling growths on their necks, little clappers of flesh. She didn't want to know what they were. She would rather have worked with the gentle, lanolin-smelling sheep, but they needed nothing at this time of year.

Afterward, they had to deal with the milk. They cooled it by carrying down the churns and putting them into the stream. They had to boil the curds every day now because of the heat. When the milk had curdled she had to stir it with large forks they called riddles. It took forever and her arms ached. She wasn't trusted with squeezing the lumps and putting them into molds, but she was allowed to deal with the whey. That had to be boiled until it was brown and thick and could be ladled up into soft cheese.

Mia refused to have anything to do with it all. The first time she had held her nose, then she had disappeared with Mats and Gertrud. Sigrid always wanted to help and Annie noticed she was a good milker. She also kept a check on the milking rota and found it very difficult to admit she might have made a mistake.

"Dad did the milking on Midsummer Eve, not Önis. It's not Önis's team today. It's wrong."

Annie knew she oughtn't to start arguing with her. She was only nine, but she was obstinate. She followed Annie to the kitchen, going on and on about it. Annie's arms and back were aching and she could feel her irritation rising. She stopped in the doorway and held on to it to show she wanted to go in alone.

"I did the milking for the first time on Monday," she said. "And the second time was today, Thursday. There are two days in between, as there has to be when there are three teams. That's okay, isn't it?"

"But the rota's wrong."

"So you say. Let's drop it now. Your father can't have done the milking on Midsummer Eve, because he was in Röbäck then."

She went on in and closed the door, regretting it the moment she had done so, but it was good to be alone for a while. She could see Sigrid through the window, pacing back and forth, hitting at the grass with a stick, clearly furious. A future dogmatist?

"Just let her be right," Önis said as they heaved the milk churn across the threshold together. "She's fearfully upset. The pastor's coming to fetch her and Gertrud on Wednesday."

"The pastor in Röbäck?"

"No, their dad. Didn't you know?"

One clergyman had already come up to Starhill and Annie had kept out of the way that time as well. She thought he was the same one who had opened up the parish hall on Midsummer Day and invited people in for coffee and buns. For the shock. She'd heard about it while sitting in Oriana Strömgren's kitchen and the police were going in and out. But this was a pastor who had been married to Brita and was the father of Sigrid and Gertrud. Önis said they were in dispute over custody.

She couldn't take it in. There was something so primordial, so primeval about Petrus's little family. She had thought the girls looked like Petrus. They had his long goat face. If Brita had been a clergyman's wife, that at least explained why she knew her St. Paul. Annie wished Dan had told her something about all this.

"The pastor has the cheek to say that Starhill is an unsuitable place for the girls, but for their sake he was going to take it easy. Come up here and persuade them. I'm not sure that's needed, for that matter. His trump card was the school. That they had to live in Röbäck in the winter and be away from their mother. Yvonne isn't all that suitable, of course. I mean, from the authorities' point of view. But then they heard you were coming to be the teacher here. Then it looked as if Brita might have won. Until this happened. Down by the river. Now they'll come and fetch them. Will you see to the milk?"

Annie was left alone with the boiling. She stood with the thermometer in her hand, staring down into the milk still swirling around after Önis's stirring. So that was how they saw it. If Mia had had a father who'd known she was there, he would perhaps have arranged to have her taken away because it was dangerous for her to live there. It's as if there are two worlds, she thought. One out there. Where it happened. And another here.

"Would you write down how much milk, please?"

Önis had opened the door and called out. Her face was rosy and smooth. She wore no makeup and her lips were a touch blue. A lovely fat girl. She could have been one of Krishna's milkmaids whose lips had taken on some of their color from kissing his skin.

If there had been any danger there, deadly and nearby, she wouldn't be occupied with milk quantities and concentrated feed. Önis was a sensible person. She could milk. She was from Öhn in Jämtland and had been a social worker.

The milk records were pinned to the wall and a ballpoint hung on a string beside them. Annie wrote down "38 liters" and signed it. The others put abbreviations of their given names. Her AR looked rather officious, but she didn't want to change it because that was how she had started. Petrus wrote P-us. She saw his name in the column for Midsummer Eve. "36.5 l. P-us. 40 ls. P-us."

Her first thought was that Sigrid had been right. She ought to go out at once and tell her so. Then she remembered the work rota in Brita and Petrus's house which they went through every evening. According to that, Sigrid was wrong.

The girl was still walking around, slashing with a stick at the tall grass outside the cookhouse. She was slender and thin, and Annie could see her spine outlined under the T-shirt as she bent forward. Annie felt like asking her about the milk rota, but was ashamed of wanting to manipulate her. Several people had done that. She looked defenseless and miserable from behind, a row of small vertebrae, brittle as shells. A small stalk of a neck and heavy hair hanging forward in two greasy braids. She ought to wear pants, not a skirt. Her legs were swollen with insect bites.

Soon she would be taken away from Starhill. Or not. Regardless of what she wanted. Have her hair cut, or not. She probably didn't really know what she wanted. How could she? The voices around her were loud. One of them must have told her to go and fetch Annie and Mia from the bus on Midsummer Eve.

There had been only children at the bus in Röbäck; Sigrid, Gertrud, Mats, and Pella. The number was right. She had seen them. Mats's Inca cap and their Lapp shoes and birch-bark knapsacks. No adult had been with them. Sigrid was sure to have been in charge of the troop. She was dutiful. One of the adults had said, "Go and meet Dan's girlfriend and her little daughter. They're coming on the bus today." But the children had gone back and said that Annie and Mia hadn't come.

She had been in the churchyard, washed over for the first time by the chilly mountain air, and she had seen the children, but she hadn't realized they were looking for Mia and her. The bus driver hadn't known Mia and she were members of the commune. She had actually denied it.

Now she could call out to that disappointed, angry little creature and ask her where Petrus had been on Midsummer Eve. How easy it is to push little girls hither and thither, she thought. With emotions.

Then Sigrid stopped. She dropped the stick and looked over at the window as if expecting Annie to call out to her at last. But Annie moved away, letting her face fade into the dim light of the dairy. From Sigrid's shoulders and back it looked as if she had given up. Perhaps she already knew they were too many. That they were adults and would never admit she could be right.

Annie carefully took the thumbtacks off the four corners of the milk records, folded the paper up, and put it into her apron pocket.

After Åke Vemdal had left, the dishwashing was left to do and the brown gravy had dried and stuck.

Telephoning. Getting the meat out of the freezer. Doing the shopping. Cooling the vodka and letting the wine breathe. Cooking dinner. Altogether, it had taken hours. Sitting opposite each other and talking about their obsessions. Talk, talk. Apart from chewing, and some drinking sounds. Looking at the cut glass, explaining when his father had been given them.

Not the way it really was, but lightheartedly. He had not mentioned that they sang the "Horst Wessel Song" on Father's fortieth birthday in 1941. It would have been impossible to explain that that was just to annoy Mother.

Father said she was one-eighth Jewish, though he hadn't really cared about it. Nor about National Socialism. All he cared about was tormenting her for having been born rich and for having to put up with life on the estate, one housemaid, the coop, and once a year a trip to Stockholm. They had been very close, and that close tie was their only reality.

His hatred was hopeless. Once she had said, "Your father had a strong character." He had been dead for fifteen years then. But she remembered the rapes, of course. Sometimes Birger had heard them through the wall in his bedroom. Still she bothered with the euphemism so as not to humiliate herself. Father's silly National Socialism had also been a euphemism, perhaps for a hatred the strength of which he never understood.

Rinsing the dishes. Putting them in the dishwasher. Putting away the glasses and never taking them out again.

Having people to dinner.

Finishing off with a small whiskey. Two.

Never again talking with his lips to an ear, a warm ear.

When he had finished the dishes, he went out, cutting across the hay meadows. It was almost dark, but he could see the linseed field in all its degradation, rotting heaps of tough stalks soaked from the rain.

He realized that Karl-Åke and he now had a reason for their mutual enmity. It was one of those absurd, far-fetched reasons that lay behind every village hostility, manufactured according to a pattern as complicated as crochet work. Yes, absurd to the point of childishness, almost imaginary. But the hatred was real.

Gudrun Brandberg drove her son in the Audi up toward Steinkjer. She was looking angry. He glanced sideways at her, but he didn't get the sense that she was angry because he had run away. He himself was pretty angry, but as usual she scarcely noticed that.

She hadn't driven up to the guesthouse, but had phoned from the Statoil gas station on the outskirts and said he should come and meet her there. When he explained that he could hardly walk and had nothing to put on his feet, she'd told him to take a taxi.

Taxi!

He had paid the landlady with Ylja's money and got a lift to the gas station. He hadn't really wanted to touch the money. Gudrun didn't ask him how he had been able to pay, and not until after driving quite a while did she ask him what he had done to his foot.

The Audi was going much too fast along the hot strip of asphalt. Gudrun's profile remained the same, and it occurred to him that it wasn't anger. It was absence, an absence so total, he was grateful they were not heading for Grong. She might have driven off the road on a bend and aquaplaned straight out into the Namsen.

She hadn't come the previous evening. At about eleven, she had phoned to say there was a lot to do. He had gone to bed and tried to sleep despite the pain. She'll regret it when she sees my foot, he thought.

"Don't phone anyone," she had said in a small, sharp voice. "Do you hear? Don't talk to anyone."

At the Statoil station the Audi was there, the backseat full of stuff—bags, cardboard boxes, and loose objects. He saw to his astonishment that his ice hockey skates were there, and his club. She was drinking apple juice from a container, and he noticed that her lips were dry and she was very thirsty.

"Do you want some?" she said, handing him a fiver to go and buy some juice. He didn't take it. She had on the same floral dress she had been wearing on Midsummer Eve, and the same white cardigan was folded up on top of one of the bags in the back. It looked as if she hadn't been out of her clothes since, or as if time had stopped over there in Blackwater.

"I saw in the paper . . . there was a murder. By the Lobber."

"Get in," she said.

Once they were out of Namsos, he asked who had been murdered. At first she was silent for a long time, as if she didn't want to answer, but then she said they were tourists. Foreigners.

"Has it been solved?"

"It never will be."

He couldn't understand how she could say that. He said he didn't think it was right.

"What do you mean, right?"

Proper, he had thought of saying, but he didn't. She must have noticed how peculiar it sounded, because she tried to explain.

"I meant only that it's almost hopeless. An evening when there were so many tourists around. And foreigners."

"Aren't people scared?"

"I don't want to talk about it. We've had enough of that back home these last few days."

She sounded as if she were reproaching him for having gone off when things were at their worst.

"I went off because I was furious," he said. "Per-Ola and Pekka were shitty, and so were Väine and Björne. They went too far. They followed me up to Alda's."

"I don't want to know anything about that. And you're not to knock Björne. If it weren't for him, you'd really be in trouble now."

She was angry with him after all. And she didn't ask where he had been. Only whether he'd talked to anyone. What did she think—that he'd hidden in the forest?

"Why have you brought all my things?"

He could hear how whiny he sounded as he said it, but it was too late to make his voice any deeper. Her voice was at least kinder when she answered.

"We've got to arrange something else for you. The atmosphere at home isn't good."

"Was Torsten furious?"

She didn't answer directly and he felt sick inside at how unfair it all was. He wasn't allowed to tell her, either. She simply didn't want to know.

"It'll go to court," she said. "Vidart's been raving about a rake handle. But that'll all get straightened out. Anyhow, we'd better arrange something else for you. I thought of Langvasslien."

The name caused a soft jolt inside him. A wave of blood, throbbing all the way out into his ears, into his lips. And he waited. He even imagined what tone of voice she would use when she at long last told him. Low and confidential, a little embarrassed. Or half angry and defiant, as if to emphasize it was her business what she had done, not his.

Should he say he had had some idea all the time? Guessed that he was really Oula Laras's son. Not Torsten's. Or should he pretend not to know, to make it easier for her?

She didn't go on. Not just now, he thought. It'll come later. She's ashamed. It's as hard for her as it would be for me to tell her about Ylja. Impossible. But she must. Before we get to Langvasslien. Probably before Steinkjer, and that couldn't be more than ten kilometers now.

When they drove into Steinkjer, she said they were to stop and get something to eat.

"I've got to go to the hospital," Johan said, realizing she was never going to suggest it. She didn't seem to be interested in his foot.

"Is it that bad?" was all she said.

When they got to emergency, he took off his sock as they sat waiting, and she gasped.

She probably hadn't thought it would take half the day. They had agreed to meet at the cafeteria when he was ready, and there she was, looking exhausted. As usual, he felt guilty. Then he was angry. He couldn't help it that she had had to wait for so long. She could have asked the doctors. He told her that his shin bone was broken and the ligaments in his ankle torn. He was in plaster. He had been given some crutches so he could move, but they had to pay for them because they weren't Norwegian citizens. She went to the receptionist and told her he was to start senior high in Steinkjer in the fall and that he lived in Langvasslien and could bring the crutches back when he came for a checkup.

Saying he already lived in Langvasslien was a bit much, but the woman behind the counter accepted it without comment and asked for the address.

"He's living with Per and Sakka Dorj," said Gudrun. "Post Office Box 12, Langvasslien."

Sakka. His aunt. Gudrun's older sister. He didn't ask if what she had said was true until they got in the car.

"Am I going to stay with Sakka?"

"Yes, of course. What did you think? Who else lives in Langvasslien?"

That evening the rain came. To begin with, the wind brought clouds of thin, chilly vapor, which settled like a membrane on the grass and across their faces. It turned dark and the wind blew up. By the time they were all inside with Petrus and Brita, it was raining hard.

The kitchen was transformed. Once no sunlight fell on the slate slabs, the brick wall of the fireplace appeared to grow and the window framed the dark greenery behind the broad belts of rain.

Now she saw them for the first time without the strong sunlight. In the dim light, their faces looked worn and gray, except Dan's. His face was relaxed; he was calm, playing with a strand of hair. The skin on Bert's face was too loose. He must once have been much fatter. His cheeks were scarred and pitted. Perhaps it was the memory of his pimply youth that had made him so repulsive.

Enel's face was taut under her kerchief, her skin sunburned and tight over her cheekbones. Perhaps they had all grown thinner—except Önis. She had told Annie that walking up to Starhill had given her sores between her thighs, so she was reluctant to go down to the village. She was biting her sore, swollen fingertips. Mia had screwed up her face and was watching her.

Brown shadows flitted over Brita's face, and her eyes were hollow. She was very heavy despite her thinness, almost as if the fetus were on its way down. She held on to it with her hands, not listening while Petrus talked about cooling the milk. Lotta sat curled up on the floor below her, like a child, her face the color of well-worn linen.

Even Sigrid had this worn and weary air, and she was only nine. All of them had it, except Dan. Admittedly, they were dressed up. But with no electricity, no dissembling was possible. You can't just pretend; you bear it. An existence devoid of irony slowly twisted their joints, stretching their sinews thin and hard. Annie felt a fierce longing for town; for trying on clothes, people, and rooms the way you try out a quotation in your mouth. Starting. Driving fast. Touching on terror or desire. Turning and forgetting.

They had come to the time for criticism. Petrus avoided the word, but she recognized the setup. On the first evening he had used the word "problem." Now he just asked whether they had anything.

"I've got something."

His face was bearded; hairy, rather; soft gray-brown hair swirling down from his temples and untidily uniting with the stiff beard. His lower lip was red and full. But it was never easy to see his expression beneath all that hair. She thought his gaze had become fixed rather than attentive. He reckoned she was going to make a fuss.

"I'd like to apologize to Sigrid," Annie said.

The girl flushed scarlet. What a child she was—her skin so easily suffused with blood, her eyes defenseless against this, which would surely be of no joy to her. Annie had an impulse to drop it and just say, "I was mistaken when it came to the milking rota." But instead, she said:

"Sigrid has observed that the way the work rota has been written down is wrong as regards the milking. I wouldn't listen to her. But she's actually quite right."

Brita wasn't bothered, indeed didn't seem to be listening, her eyes following the runnels of water streaming down the window. Lotta was sunk into herself, and Önis kept biting and tearing at her already bleeding cuticles. Petrus and Dan were the attentive ones; Bert, too, to some extent. Difficult to say with Enel, her expression not easy to fathom.

"Perhaps we could look at it," said Annie.

"Is there something you object to?" said Petrus.

He was hostile. What had she expected? I'm making myself unpleasant, she thought. How stupid of me. And just like me, Dan would say. Nevertheless she went on. But she had to fetch the work rota herself. Petrus had put it on the sideboard when they had gone through the tasks for the following day and he made no move to fetch it back.

"According to the rota, Dan was to do the milking on Midsummer Eve and Midsummer Day because he was on his own here. But it must have been Petrus."

She handed the rota over to Petrus, who read it without touching it. She then handed it on to Enel and it went around without arousing any interest. Only Sigrid was eager, her cheeks still scarlet.

"Uh-huh," said Petrus. "It's possible. Not that I understand why you sound so sure. Mistakes happen. Does it matter?"

Annie took the milking record out of her pocket, unfolded it, and smoothed it out.

"I'm perfectly sure," she said. "Sigrid is, too. First, Dan can't milk, anyhow not well enough to be able to manage on his own."

"He wasn't on his own."

"Wasn't he?"

"He was here with Barbro Torbjörnsson."

She didn't want to look at Dan, but she could sense he was sitting absolutely still. Then Önis and Lotta both began talking at once.

"She wanted to see Starhill."

"She might move up here."

"It's a chance for us. She weaves and has sold lots of her stuff. So Dan had to show her."

He doesn't even have to defend himself, she thought. He was leaning back with his eyes closed.

"Maybe so," said Annie. "But it was Petrus who recorded the quantity of milk on Midsummer Eve."

He took the piece of paper and read.

"So," he said. "Good. Isn't it, Sigrid? Are you satisfied now?"

She was childishly triumphant and flushing.

"That's that, then."

"No."

Annie avoided Dan's eyes as she went on.

"It was wrong when the police were here. You referred to this erroneous work rota. They were given wrong information."

"I think we'll call it a day now," said Petrus, getting up. "Dan, explain to Annie what the situation is. Once and for all."

But Dan explained nothing. He went out ahead of her, and when she entered their room he was lying in silence on his bed. Annie thought that was because Lotta had come, too. She had been allowed to move back again with her cat pictures and the two bags containing all her possessions. Mia liked her and enjoyed her things. She used to sort out the faded T-shirts and cotton pants, then line the rest up on her bed while Lotta, in her slightly hoarse voice, told her the story of the things. She had an electric hair dryer and a radio that could not run on batteries, and three pairs of shoes with heels impossible for walking at Starhill. A hairpiece of dull, coarse, light brown hair and a chocolate box of photographs. A plastic bag containing a coral necklace and Indian jewelry of blackened silver with bloodstones and dull turquoises. A teddy bear made of synthetic plush. A wallet packed with snapshots, bus tickets and cards with addresses on them.

They were playing Pelmanism at the table with a pack of dirty cards from the days of the fishing club. Lotta seemed to realize that Annie and Dan wanted to be on their own. Annie lay down on her bed and waited. The room was full of the energy coming from the immobile body on the bunk above.

Annie couldn't talk to him, nor could she say anything to Lotta. Her strength was trickling away like the rain on the window. It was possible to be mute or immobile in dreams, but she was awake and presumably could move. If she gave way to this sense of powerlessness, she would never be able to go on. She took the radio off the chair beside the bed and switched it on. It crackled and the sound of a voice reading the news billowed back and forth with fading strength. The batteries were running out.

Mia got a card she didn't want and shouted angrily. Annie turned up the volume. In a capricious wave the power came back and a voice boomed that *The Reuter News Agency reports that sources from Hanoi* before she could turn down the volume. The bunk above swayed and creaked. Dan jumped down to the floor and momentarily she saw his torso cut off by the upper edge of the bed and his hands held out with the fingers splayed as he shouted, *"For Christ's sake, stop it!"*

He was out of the room before she had time to do anything. Nor was there anything to do. The volume was already turned right down. Mia sat without moving, a card in her hand. For a long while nothing could be heard except the abundant splashing of the rain out of the broken drainpipes.

"You know he doesn't like the news," Lotta said. "Dan's not interested in politics."

"He used to be," said Annie. "He was the only one involved at college."

"Not exactly politics. I mean the party. All that came to an end two years ago."

She talked about him with a confidential officiousness and sounded as if she were imitating someone. Dan had explained, "She doesn't know how we live. Not what an ordinary life is like. Everything has to be learned. She has lived in something you can't grasp."

"I'm going to Mats."

Mia flung down the cards she had been holding and went out. The door slammed and shook in its frame. Annie had wanted to remember herself as a quiet child, not submissive but brooding on the injustice of having to live as a lodger in Enskede with no right to yell and scream. But now and then there was something familiar about Mia's awkwardness and angry outbursts. She had left because she didn't want to hear anything said about Dan, Annie thought, and she turned cold, although she had really known that for a long time.

"I know he's left the party," she said to Lotta. She couldn't really remember which of the minor parties it was, but didn't want to reveal that. She realized how foolish it was, the two of them trying to outdo each other in their knowledge of Dan's life.

"He didn't leave it, he was thrown out," said Lotta. "They were a group that had broken away and he was the leader. But another guy came along and took over and then Dan had to do some self-criticism. They hung out in the Nacka woods, by Nyckelviken, on a hill."

It sounded as if Lotta thought Dan had been playing Tarzan, and although she didn't really want to ask about Dan, she said:

"What do you mean—hung out?"

"His self-criticism. They had a rope with them and had tied it to a pine tree and made a noose. He was to hang himself, because his life was, like, pointless. He was rotten. Poisoned from the start."

"What by?"

"By being bourgeois."

"How could he be that? He would never agree to anything so stupid."

"He didn't, either. Though it was a close thing. Then he ran off into town, and that was when I met him. He used to smoke hash and then started on junk. Well, guys of his background usually have a safety net, and he ended up in the bin. His dad fixed that. Then he went to college. And now he doesn't want to hear anything about politics. Nor about the general."

"What general?"

"His dad."

Lotta had been trapped for a whole night in a subway elevator with a heroin addict who had a razor in his hand. Dan had told her that. Now Lotta was telling her, turbulence in her head and stories arising from it. Annie had to remind herself that they were called cock-and-bull stories.

She went out without saying anything to Lotta about what she was going to do. She knew that she was leaving her to endlessly picking over the contents of those two blue canvas bags.

The house was on a slope covered with willows and birches. Above it stood Mount Langvass, but the birch woods rose so steeply that the peak couldn't be seen from the yard. The road wound its way up from Langvasslien village down by the lake.

One of the people who had owned the house before Per had covered it with asbestos sheeting the same color as watery milk. It was a two-story house and from the green-painted metal roof protruded a disproportionately large attic room, with a balcony with rusty iron railings.

Below the steps was a clothes dryer with broken plastic lines and two red plastic washbowls. Grass and wild chervil shot straight up through a scooter sled. There were empty beer crates at one end of the house and a piece of bent piping propped against the wall. Flakes of green had snowed down from the roof into the grass and the bowls. When they got right up to the house, Johan could see a rat-gnawed elk antler and a rolled-up plastic mat below the kitchen window.

Gudrun had changed her shoes and was making her way through the grass on narrow heels. Per had come out on the steps, Sakka behind him, her hands dripping wet. She was alternately greeting them and apologizing: She had been doing the dishes and couldn't shake hands. But she put her own hands together and shook them in front of her chest. Johan thought with astonishment that it was just as if she were delighted. Their son, the same age as Johan, also came out to greet them, but he was shyer and stayed on the porch. He was mostly called Pergutt or the Pergutt— Per's boy—and the Brandberg boys had always thought he was a twerp.

All three had round faces, and he recognized his own eyes, nose, and cheeks in them in a way he had never done before. Gudrun and he had been to see them only when they were slaughtering or marking the calves up in Tjørn Valley. Johan had never seen the Langvasslien house before. On Gudrun's behalf, he was embarrassed by the mess in the yard and in front of the steps. Gudrun was very particular. Sakka wasn't. Perhaps that had something to do with what Gudrun had said about Sakka's appearance and age: "She's letting herself go."

Per was small and rather bandy-legged. Johan thought about Oula Laras, whose legs were slim and unusually long for a Sami, and about how the Pergutt was the very image of Per.

He would be able to see Oula Laras now, might run into him any day. He thought it just like Gudrun to say nothing, but to let him live so close to him. Otherwise it would have been simply banishment to dump him in this mess, especially if you looked at it her way, he knew that. She couldn't stand disorder.

The Dorjs wanted to offer them food although they themselves had just eaten. They wanted to talk and have coffee, and Sakka took out thin pancakes, spread butter on them, and sprinkled them with sugar. They wanted to know how Johan had hurt his foot and what the doctor had said and when he had to go back for a checkup. They were so kind, it embarrassed him. Even Per was sympathetic about the foot. Yet Johan knew he was a tough man. Two winters ago, he had driven the scooter over a precipice up in Tjørnfjell and had gotten stuck on a ledge with a broken leg. He had slithered down to the scooter, but hadn't been able to get it started again, so he'd had to make his way down the slopes in deep snow, dragging his leg behind him. He had been away for two days and everyone had thought that was the end of him. But here he was, eating sweet pancakes with the Pergutt, Sakka, and Johan. Gudrun ate nothing, but she smoked another cigarette, which surprised Johan. He had never seen her smoke so much before.

They said nothing about what had happened by the Lobber. Johan had the impression Gudrun had banned the subject over the phone. Nor did they ask why he had left home. The fact that he was to stay with them and start school down in Steinkjer seemed to have already been agreed on. Gudrun must have had long telephone calls with Sakka the night before.

He thought the Pergutt would talk about the murder by the Lobber when they were alone together, but he didn't. He was rather shy and simply asked Johan if he'd like to see the pups. They went out to the dog run and the Pergutt tied up the bitch so that Johan could go in to the pups. There were three of them and they looked about a couple of months old.

"Them's one part Lajka and two parts Lapphound, then there's a bit of Siberian, too," he said. "Them's bitches. Then we've the dog she mated with, he's half Swedish hound. So there's five sorts. Aren't they great?"

One of them had light blue eyes and Johan liked that one in particular. He said it must be the Siberian that had come through.

"If you'd like a dog you can have it," said the Pergutt.

By then Johan was thinking everything had become so unreal he must be dreaming and that he had been dreaming for a long time. When he thought about Ylja, he could no longer see her face in front of him, only a blurred, shifting surface. And he thought about the well, and for a brief moment he thought he had injured his foot when he fell into it.

But that was not how it happened. He had jumped from a first-floor window of a house in roadless country. Where? He had told Gudrun a Finn had given him a lift. The Finn seemed almost real to him. Then he realized it was the Silver Fox. He stared at the Pergutt and tried to think what to say to sound natural, what to reply. Pergutt had asked him something and his round, open face was glowing with eagerness for a reply.

Sakka called out to them and when they went in, Gudrun was all ready to leave and Per was putting some money into his wallet. Johan flushed when he saw it. He hadn't considered that Gudrun and Torsten would have to pay for him. He was to board with them. It was amazing that Torsten had agreed to pay money for him, surely a lot of money. Gudrun had none of her own, he knew that. She was talking to Per about the money, but they were speaking the Sami language; Johan couldn't understand and realized he wasn't meant to.

He was feeling peculiar. His foot ached and he was feeling rather sick after the pancakes and weak coffee. Gudrun was in such a hurry to leave, he could hardly believe it. Wasn't she going to stay until evening, or even stop overnight, now that they wouldn't be seeing each other for several days? He wanted to ask her lots of things. About money, for one. Was he going to have any of his own?

But she thanked Per and Sakka, shook hands, and, as soon as she had painted her lips at the mirror in the hall, she was ready to go.

"Come out with me," she said quietly.

She changed her shoes by the car and then told him to get in the front.

"That person you got a lift with? What was his name?"

"I don't know," said Johan truthfully.

"You said he was a Finn. Does he otherwise live in Finland?"

"Yes."

"There are lots of interrogations going on," she said. "The police are questioning people about where they were that night when it happened. We told them you had already left in the evening. At roughly seven o'clock, on Midsummer Eve. We told them you were angry because Torsten thought you had reported him. That you took the moped and set off down to the village. We haven't let on that you went up to Alda's and the pathway there. So now you know that."

"Am I to say that, too?" he said.

"I think you should. If they come asking questions. Unless that Finn can put in an appearance and say otherwise, of course."

"I don't think that'll happen," said Johan.

"Good-bye, then."

He thought that that was the first time all day she had looked at him. But not for long. She started the car. He got out and reached for the crutches he had left leaning against the car, but she drove off too quickly. They fell into the grass as the car moved off.

He was eventually to share a room with the Pergutt, but as long as he found it difficult to get upstairs with his plastered leg, he was to sleep in the living room. Per and Sakka went to bed early. The sofa was already made up for him, but once he was alone in there, he was sure he wouldn't be able to sleep. It was too early, only half past ten, and the sun was pouring a reddish light over the hay meadows down toward the lake. They hadn't been cut for several years. There was no wind, but the tufted hair grass had gone to seed and looked like silvery-blue waves petrified in the sea of grass. Through the mosquito window he could hear a song thrush in the birch woods, its persuasive, yearning note reminding him of Trollvolden, where the song thrushes had gone on and on and on singing at night. But it had been meaningless singing. Or false. No yearning.

The television screen was gray and slightly dusty, the light falling on it so strong that there were no reflections in it. Nor were there any blinds. He recognized the table as having been his grandmother's. It was round and shiny with a pedestal base, and a lace cloth lay in the center. Gudrun had one just like it; his grandmother had made them. A fruit bowl made from a knot of wood stood on the cloth. He had always thought such knots looked diseased, and so they were—diseased, malformed birch. Tumors.

The sofa cushions were stacked up by the wall, including three ornamental cushions with cross-stitch pictures of dogs' heads on them. There was another dog in a picture, a kind of spitz, he supposed, large and yellowish-brown. Another picture showed a herd of reindeer on a slope of bluish, snow-covered mountain. A third depicted a lake with an old man in a boat, holding a fishing rod. The whole picture was done in silhouette and you could even see the fishing line outlined in black or dark purple. There was also an enlarged color photograph of Pergutt at his confirmation, in Sami costume, a hymnbook in his hand. Johan was reminded of his grandmother, Gudrun's mother, at her funeral. Someone had put a hymnbook between her dead hands. They were rigid, not holding on to it.

Gudrun hadn't wanted him to go with her to look at Grandmother, but he had insisted although he thought it horrible. Then he had told Väine what she had looked like, and he had had to tell all the brothers. He was the only one of them who had ever seen a dead person.

He wasn't feeling well. His foot was aching even more now that he was alone, although he had taken some of the painkillers he had been given in Steinkjer. He was feeling slightly sick and his hands were cold. He realized he had been as good as driven away from home, though of course it was he who had left initially.

And Torsten was prepared to pay to be rid of him, just like Ylja. She had wanted nothing to do with him after she had read that in the paper. She had seen him coming out on to the main road early that morning, in just that area. She must have seen that from the map in the paper. What had she thought?

Anyhow, Gudrun thought he would be in trouble if the police found out he had been up at Alda's with the moped. They said there were tracks of a moped that had gone all the way up the pathway. And then back. As if whoever had done it had gone on a moped.

They're trying to protect me. They want to help me so that I don't get into trouble.

Gudrun had said that Björne had already helped him. But how? Did they really want to help him or just be rid of him? The most unbelievable thing of all was that Torsten was willing to pay for his lodgings.

It struck him that perhaps it hadn't been Torsten. It could have been Oula Laras. Suppose Gudrun had phoned him in the end. Asking for help.

Torsten would probably have preferred to tell the police that Johan had gone up to Alda's and the pathway. In revenge. Why should he want to protect Johan, who wasn't even his son? Perhaps Torsten didn't even know for certain what the situation was. But he could guess.

He's only got to look at me, Johan thought. My eyes. My hair. The shape of my face. That's why he's never been able to stand me.

That was perhaps how Björne helped me. He was probably the one who said, "Let the boy go to Langvasslien, where he belongs."

It was like trying to run in a soggy, swaying marsh. He had to think quickly if he was not to sink. He felt sick and his foot hurt. The television screen was gray and the light outside sharp.

Someone knocked, or was fumbling at the door, loosely, as if the person standing there was afraid he was asleep. It was the Pergutt. When Johan opened the door, he said:

"Would you like to play Monopoly?"

Johan said nothing but the Pergutt must have thought he had nodded. He got the board and the box of notes and cards out of the sideboard. It was a Norwegian version and so he changed to speaking Norwegian. Johan said the Pergutt could be the banker, but then almost regretted it because it wasn't easy to know the value of streets and squares without seeing the cards in front of him.

"I've never been to Oslo," he said when things began to go badly, which they did almost at once.

"Nor have I," said the Pergutt. But he already had Parliament Square and Princes Street. It was horribly expensive to land on them and Johan soon did. He was unlucky, too, for his next turn he got the Go to Jail card.

"Hell," he said. "Lucky it's only a game."

The Pergutt agreed and they played another game, which he won easily. Then he fetched some Pepsi-Cola and potato chips, by which time it was half past one. He asked whether they should go on and Johan said yes. He took another painkiller and then it was his turn to be the banker. They both sat on the sofa so that whoever was waiting for his turn could lie back and rest. Johan was woken at about five by the Pergutt's snores. He was lying at the other end of the sofa with his head on a cross-stitch cushion, Ulleval Hageby, Princes Street, Parliament Square, and Trondheim Road spread out on his chest. The sun was falling dazzlingly in through the other window and the fieldfares were chattering away at the tops of their voices in the birch woods behind the house.

The rain was cold, drenching her head and shoulders. As she walked, she felt the material of her blouse soaking through and the hem of her skirt trailed wetly in the grass. The sheep were huddled together under a large birch, their backs a dark dirty gray in the wet.

She searched in the cookhouse and the goat shed, certain he was alone somewhere. In the little cowshed they couldn't use because the mangers were insufficient for all the goats, the light was a dim brown, apparently still full of breathing, as if the strong smell of cows now long dead had darkened and was hanging beneath the roof trusses. The layers of cobwebs were lifeless and fluffy with dust. She went over to the steep stairs and listened, but could hear nothing, though she thought she could sense his presence. He did not reply when she called.

When her head emerged at the top of the stairs, at first she could see nothing except the bright gray daylight trickling through the cracks. Then the shadow in the hay thickened into his body and she saw he was lying as before in the house, quite still on his back.

"What is it, Dan?"

She didn't expect an answer. She knew they had a ritual to come, silences, sorties, ripostes, paralysis; silence and a new start. Taking turns, she thought with a weariness she had never felt before. Fear was what she usually felt.

Then at last they got started, his voice grating at first and hers warm, only tepid really, like meat or pudding. He always heard false tones of voice, and he went for her.

"Can't you hear yourself?" he said. And she could.

"How the hell do you think you can come up here and sound like that? What sort of bloody kindness is that? Who do you really think you are? Do you think the rest of us are a school class you have to question and reprimand?"

She saw herself, heard herself distorted, but unfortunately not beyond recognition, and she lost all desire to defend herself. Soaking wet, she just sat glumly in the dry hay and for the first time during a quarrel—for she supposed it was a quarrel—thought about something else. She simply thought about the hay, how old it must be, how dry and ancient and quite without strength. Nineteen-fifties hay. Then, when he had finally gotten it off his chest, she said she was miserable because he hadn't met her and Mia when they had come on the bus to Blackwater, but had just sent the children.

"You didn't at all think I was coming on the old Midsummer Eve. You knew exactly when I was coming, and you had made sure I would be met in Röbäck. I was the one to say that about the old Midsummer Eve, and you agreed because that was easiest. But I don't mind that you let me think that, and I don't mind about her, Barbro what's-her-name. The name was on a jar here in the hay, by the way, you know that. I don't mind. Really."

He must have heard that her voice grated now, too, but this time he said nothing. She thought wearily. He knows we can't afford any amount of honesty. The rain had lightened, only rustling on the roof now, and she could hear the monotonous, harsh whistling of the bird she and Mia had not yet seen. She crawled over and lay down beside him in the hay. She saw that he still had his eyes closed.

"Is your father a general?" she said.

"No."

"What is he, then?"

"A lieutenant-colonel."

She had no need to ask any more. She could look him up in the telephone directory. Djursholm or Östermalm, or any expensive residential area. But it was a long way to the Stockholm directory.

"You said you had grown up in a poor home. Terribly poor."

"I did. Poorer than you could possibly imagine."

"Can't we be honest with each other?"

"Go ahead."

Yes, what had she herself led him to believe? Almost nothing about Mia's origin. He had once wanted to know who the man was, asked if he'd been at college with her. She had said yes. A lie in a way, but not in another way. Like that poor-home story.

We can't go on like this, she thought. We've been through the stage when lovers tell each other their life histories and it is self-illuminating and intense—when they summon it up for each other. What we have chosen to tell is now a kind of reality. It is the one we've got.

"Where was Petrus on Midsummer Eve?"

"Here. You must have bloody well worked that out by now. You don't like Petrus."

"I never said that. I just think it's strange that he lies about where he was on Midsummer Eve—and that night."

"All of us are lying. There's nothing strange about it."

"That's what I don't understand. Why do you help him lie?"

"We don't help Petrus. We were all here."

"Weren't you in Röbäck?"

"No, we were here. I drove the kids down, that's all. Then I came back with Barbro Torbjörnsson. I fetched her from Byvången. She was going to the demonstration at Björnstubacken and I had told her to come up to Starhill and spend the night with us. I thought I'd be able to persuade her to have a go at moving up here. It was so important to us, I thought you'd cope that evening. You could have stayed with Mia at Yvonne's. It was all arranged."

So he hadn't been alone with her! Although the idea was Annie's and she thought it had stayed inside her, it made Dan move violently in the hay and lie on top of her. He touched her face with the tips of his fingers. He wanted to see her and feel her. He knows what I'm thinking. He likes it. We are intimate again, intensely intimate. We charge the space around us for each other, we can feel each other as you can smell thunder, electricity.

"You're soaking wet!"

He was lively again, and before she could stop him, he had pulled off his shirt and spread it out on the hay. He started undressing her, exposing cold skin, which he licked and said it felt like reptile skin; she was a frog from a well, with wrinkled skin and warts, though only two, and he would make her human and hot in the rain and cold.

"The diaphragm," she said.

"I'll get it. I'll go and get some clothes for you. For Christ's sake, Annie, you never forget anything. You're a born teacher."

He was right. She had been on the verge of saying that frogs weren't reptiles. While he was gone, she lay naked on her back, his shirt under her, hugging herself with her arms against the cold. When he came back, he pulled a sweater over her head, but nothing below, and he put the blanket he had with him underneath her.

"Tell me how you could be here at Starhill on Midsummer Eve," she said. "Everyone except you and Barbro Torbjörnsson came up from Röbäck on Midsummer Day and stayed the night here. They were all questioned. Petrus, too."

He lay over her and told her; now it was his skin that was wet and grainy from the cold outside, so she had to rub him. He told her they had started walking down after the morning milking on Midsummer Day. She couldn't hear everything because occasionally his tongue was in her mouth, and it rustled when she rubbed his back dry with the shirt. She couldn't understand why they had not gone across the bridge. That was the quickest way to Björnstubacken. Had they really gone across the ford? In that case they would have seen the tent.

They had taken that way because Petrus considered that the other way belonged to the Enemy. The road was the timber company's and they shouldn't use it. He had principles they didn't always take into consideration when they had to carry up packs. But when he was with them, they had to walk on the proper, old path. Dan had gone ahead with Barbro Torbjörnsson and they were still quite high up when they saw something moving down by the river. They were on the exposed rock where the pine forest started and they had a clear view down toward the Lobber. He had seen through the binoculars that it was the police—coveralls, blue caps, shoulder harness—he could see it all and the stretchers they were carrying, two of them, covered.

"No faces. You see? When they cover the faces, they're dead. We stood up there and saw it all, though we didn't know what it meant, and we turned back. We hid a little farther up, where the view was blocked, and we waited for the others there. That took some time, since Brita is so heavy now and Önis has sores. But they came and we let them go up between the trees and look through the binoculars, so they all saw the police and the stretchers. We could watch them for a long way on the marshland, where it was open. Then we didn't know what to do—go back or take the route over the bridge to Björnstubacken. We didn't want to go down from Starhill and land up among the police."

But why not? She couldn't understand, and she held him off, grabbing his upper arms and forcing him up so that she could see his face.

"You're a teacher, so of course you would have gone up and asked what had happened and put yourself at the disposal of the authorities."

His mockery was now friendly. She remembered the interrogation down in the Strömgrens' kitchen and thought he was mistaken about her. But not entirely.

They had not wanted to get involved. He said Petrus and Brita were worried about the girls. If the Starhill commune were mentioned in the papers because they had been questioned by the police, that wouldn't be good for the custody dispute. Nor was it good that people had died close to Starhill, and it would be best not to know anything whatsoever about what had happened.

One of them had had the idea of going down to Röbäck and pretending they had been there all night. The children had slept there, hadn't they? It would seem credible that the adults had also done so. But Dan and Barbro had to go on to Björnstubacken because the VW Beetle was up there. Barbro couldn't have been in Röbäck. She didn't know Yvonne and had no good reason to be there.

So Dan and Barbro had set off eastward where the path divided and had continued down to the bridge and Björnstubacken. The others had left the path and gone down toward the Klöppen. It had been difficult for Önis and Brita to walk on unbeaten tracks, but then they had found the path along the lake and followed it to the outlet at the Röbäck and had turned up at Yvonne's. She had been in complete agreement that they had done the right thing.

His penis was between her thighs, trying to nudge its way in. She felt it as a round head, puppylike, with an innocent forehead. She had no desire to reject his playfulness, nor could she. But it was strange that while he moved inside her, she was thinking about that light night when she had been drifting around in the marshlands, looking for the paths.

He was not that big, but swelled inside her and her own desire also swelled for every soft thrust, her walls tightening and loosening again, assuaging the memory of her terror, diffusing it, melting it down into a blurred recollection of confusion.

If he had asked why she had walked across unfamiliar and treacherous ground instead of trying to find somewhere to stay in the village, she would not have had an answer. She had answered in a muddled way when the police had asked her, almost lied, in any case kept some things quiet.

We didn't want to expose our confusion, she thought, not even to each other, though we ought to have. He had not told the truth about Midsummer Eve because he was ashamed. He hadn't gone to Nirsbuan expecting me to go there at all. He thought I was staying in Röbäck with Yvonne.

He had had a guilty conscience because he had done nothing about the cottage. We were to live there, he had promised me that. So he went there to see if he could do something about it in a hurry.

Dan always has so many irons in the fire. He promises too much. Dan, so delicious, so intensely warm and delicious, moving inside me, slowly, who is inside me and as confused and ashamed as I am.

"It doesn't matter any longer about Nirsbuan," she whispered. "I wouldn't want to live there, anyhow. Not now, after what's happened. It's better here with the others."

"Are you frightened?"

"Sometimes."

He tickled her with his tongue in the cleft in her upper lip. It was a game she recognized. In the end he used to get her to put her legs around his back and make a violent movement toward him. But her desire was splintered, coming and going.

"Don't think, don't think," he whispered.

"Just one thing. When you were at Nirsbuan. I can't understand how you got into the cottage?"

"Not difficult. The Brandbergs always hang the key under the eaves."

Later, when summer was on its way out and the haymaking over, Mia wanted to sleep in the hay. They took blankets and pillows up with them to the loft in the barn. Annie herself had helped fill it with the fine meadow hay from the pastureland. They lay enjoying the scents, which might have been mint, white clover, and maiden pinks. The bright yellow of the buttercups faded in the darkness and the columbines grew brittle. She and Lotta and Mia rustled and giggled beside each other. Mia didn't want to go back to bed that night, but slept in the hay. As you and Dan did, she said.

But Annie hadn't slept that night when it was raining, though she said nothing about it now, just fell in with Mia. Not until toward four in the morning did Mia start complaining of the cold. Annie carried her down and put her into her own bed, and Lotta followed with the blankets and pillows and the moomin book, which they hadn't been able to read because it had been too dark up in the loft. The summer was drawing to an end and it was no longer so brilliantly light at night.

No, she hadn't slept at all that night with Dan, although they had stayed there until three in the morning. He had slept, his breathing calm as he lay curled up in the curve her body formed around his back. She had hardly dared move for fear of waking him.

She had lain there seeing Nirsbuan before her eyes. The door of the cottage. The metal bar and the padlock that no one had unlocked. There was no other way of remembering it. That was what it had been like.

The man looked like a satyr—the
goatee, the moist red lower lip. Was that why the villagers said he kept a
harem?

A herd of goats had faced Birger on his way up. He hadn't dared turn
his back on the big billy goat and had had to make grotesque twists and
turns to keep it ahead of him. The billy goat was a shaggy gray and yellow,
his horns coarse and curved, a dark-spotted scrotum weighing at least a
kilo dangling between his hind legs. The goats were inquisitive, staring
fixedly at him, pressing around him on the path so he didn't dare sit down
to rest. Once up there, he was exhausted, a stitch in his side and blisters
here and there.

Märta had told him they had already had a visit from the social services, and he wondered who had had the energy to get up there. Märta had
shown him the large headline in the local paper:

First Child Born at Starhill

Below it had been a photo of the parents. The man with the cloven beard
was holding the child. He was wearing a kind of bobble hat. The woman
sat beside him on a porch entwined with hops. Two women, a small boy,
and a dog were sitting in the grass below the steps. Annie Raft could not
be seen in the photo. Around the corner of the house peered a face which
he thought was a boy's. Then he realized it was the little girl he had

examined at the Strömgrens'. She had had her hair cut and he thought she looked thin.

The memory of the little face he had seen at Oriana and Henry's came back to him. The grayish light of a summer's night in the room had been deceptive and he'd thought she had been abused, but then he'd seen the swellings were caused by insect bites. Looking at the photo, he was uncertain. The small face was blurred, thin, resolute. How was she? Did she get enough to eat up there?

The social worker had told them the baby was healthy. But had they looked at the girl? Märta didn't know.

The goat-man had no cap on now. He received Birger with a friendliness that made him ashamed of having acquired papers from the company to say he was allowed to fish in the two small lakes below Starhill and spend the night at the club cottage. He had been afraid they would be suspicious if he came for no particular reason. He remembered Annie Raft, her remoteness during that first questioning.

The Starhill crofter really had four womenfolk, which must have been what the villagers meant. No man put in an appearance and the diabetic man and his woman seemed to have gone.

They had come to his office a week or two earlier, the man pale and complaining of headaches. His skin was cold and moist and he had begun to get small sores on his feet that refused to heal.

The woman had sat in the waiting room in her long woolen skirt, a kerchief on her head pulled right down over her forehead, hiding her hair. She had said nothing and had scarcely even looked up from her knitting, but she had spread a strange atmosphere in the room. Eight people were waiting and not one of them said a word, nor did they touch any of the tattered magazines.

Birger fetched her in to ask about their diet and way of life at Starhill and she told him that the man had had severe insulin troubles. One day during haymaking he had almost gone into an insulin coma. He seemed ashamed to mention it himself. She had had the presence of mind to put out a bowl of the soft goat's cheese for him and he had gobbled down the lot and recovered. Otherwise they ate mostly potatoes and goat's meat, milk, and cheese, just the things he ought to be very careful about. Besides, he was supposed to take light and regular exercise, not do heavy physical labor. Birger advised him to move back to Nynäshamn, his original hometown.

"And when it comes to hash and that sort of thing," he had said, "you must realize yourselves that it's just not on in this situation."

Thank heavens they hadn't gotten angry. They were probably too tired. She just said quietly that they had nothing to do with that kind of thing—that was those people down in Röbäck.

He knew Yvonne in Röbäck had been caught when she had crossed the border with a stash of marijuana. She and her two lodgers, a couple of strays considerably older than she, had been charged. She maintained that they had only been on their way to a party and she hadn't sold anything. The court had been inclined to believe her. For one thing, they were friendly with some Norwegian petty rogues in a village just over the border, and for another, the marijuana was of very poor quality, according to the police. In fact, hardly salable.

The police had found hemp plants flourishing in a mountain crevice below Starhill when they searched the terrain after the murders, by the Lobber. Then the customs people had begun checking on Yvonne whenever she crossed the border in her old Volkswagen bus. She maintained the commune had nothing to do with growing it, but the police suspected one of the men up there. Birger didn't believe it was the diabetic. He and his woman had seemed much too wretched. Their faces remained with him, hers thin and sunburned, his pale and flabby. Märta had arranged a draft in the office after they had gone, to rid it of the strong smell of goat they had brought with them.

He couldn't smell it up there. One of the women was conspicuously beautiful, with very fair hair but dark eyebrows and eyelashes, dark blue eyes, and a marked cupid's bow. She was severely overweight and must have found it as difficult as he had getting up to Starhill.

That might be a solution for me, he thought. A plump woman. Swayingly fat. A meeting between two lots of generous flesh, our angular cores embedded. She must have dark hair down there. And those beautiful eyes and thick eyelashes, her mouth, the contours of her upper lip, which seemed all the clearer and finer because the rest of her face had flowed out into the fat. Buttocks fitting tightly together, huge thighs and breasts weighed down and swinging toward the midpoint of the earth.

The man with the divided beard was talking eagerly about cheese mold. The billy goat is in me, Birger thought. The satyr. This man's interested only in goat's cheese.

He knew people as far away as Byvången were divided into two camps, one considering the commune should be eradicated like vermin, and the other thinking they ought to be allowed to stay. They were putting a derelict place in order and bringing some life into the area, letting animals into the forest, which the company could well have done, mowing the pasture where the wild *Silvaticum geranium* and the poisonous monkshood were taking over and the scrub creeping in.

Without thinking about it, he had joined the tolerant camp. He was used to doing that with Barbro. He reckoned they could stay as long as they didn't neglect the children.

Up there he couldn't take a stand, his attitude vacillating. He was angry when he saw the ramshackle clubhouse and wondered whether they knew it wasn't insulated. How would they cope with the winter? When the fat woman called Marianne leaned over and poured herb tea into his mug, he was uneasy. She didn't smell of goat, but of milk and cotton fabric and warm skin. The divide between her breasts was deep and narrow. In confusion, he raised his eyes and looked out over the pastureland. In three directions he could see the mountain ridges, the dark blue precipices, the patchy, still snow-covered peaks that looked like grouse breasts in the thaw, the shifting green and blue slopes of marshland down toward the forest. The sky was blue-white, sizzling in the hot air above the pasture.

He wondered what it would be like to live alone there with four women and have their quiet voices and gentle movements around him all day. The murmur of the stream and the wet, swaying tussocks in the marsh down toward the lakes. The feel of water.

He couldn't think of it in any other way: the feel of water running through the ground, flowing and trickling over it. The meadowsweet had firm whitish-pink buds in their panicles and he could smell that they were just beginning to come out. *Filipendula ulmaria*. Soon they would sweep sweetly over the fields. At night when he was out on call, he sometimes had to drive off the road and sleep for a while. When he woke and got out to relieve himself, that scent lay floating like bands of something ambiguous and intoxicating in the smell of the marsh. Elks would stand there munching in the mist, half-asleep perhaps in the fragrance. You lived in it there and walked every day on the oozing ground, inhaling the smell of the marsh and seeing it ferment and brew as the clouds of morning mist swirled above it.

That angular Annie Raft had become calmer. She had also had her hair cut short and was wearing a pair of incredibly ragged, faded jeans instead of that long skirt. Her pants and extremely short hair made her look modern among the others. She kept out of the way quite a lot, but didn't seem to have any objection to his talking to the little girl.

Mia told him that she didn't drink goat's milk, but her mother had had dried milk brought up for her. And Party Puffs. Birger didn't quite know what they were, but they sounded sweet. He was told that her mother had had her hair and her own cut short so that it was easier to wash. He felt relieved. Mia dragged kid goats around and showed him a dead shrew her kitten had caught. She was thin, but looked quite healthy and was sociable.

He had quailed slightly at asking the mother whether she would like him to prescribe vitamins for Mia and the boy who belonged to the beautiful Marianne, but his suggestion was not taken ungraciously.

He went fishing in the evening, and as he came out of the birch woods, he could see the long marshlands sloping down toward the lakes. The lakes were on different levels, and from this high point just north of Starhill, he could see two of them like steps of water, reflecting the sky and taking their light from it, but the dark yellow, metallic shade seemed to come from their own depths. The shores were already dark, the light receding rapidly now. He could see the frost-scorched sedge marshes shifting in red and brown and and a great many shades of yeilow, their scent so unique and bound to those colors that the open channels in the marsh really seemed to be fermenting and steaming in reddish and golden brown. On the nearest marsh were a few poles from some long-ago haymaking.

Even right up here, he thought. Wherever they could harvest the meager blades of grass. Everywhere inland farther north. The realm of the sedge.

Without the sedge, the inland areas would never have been settled. There were almost a hundred species and they used to be called alpine sedge, fingered sedge, bird's-foot sedge, and many more. Lapp sedge. Quaking-grass sedge. Now it wasn't called anything.

The marshes had sunk into oblivion. The water in the pools glinted against the sky, and the sky saw nothing. The pines twisted, even when dead, providing a silvery-gray but hardly ever read sign for storm. The marshes and their dark poles were now lying in the shadow of time. The poles had once been racks for drying the hay and had now slowly fallen apart, just as the barns had long since fallen apart, decrepit and greenish-gray where lichens grew over them. The water kept bubbling under the ground, seeping through it and flowing over it in the spring light, dissolving everything done by human beings.

He wondered again what it would be like to live there. To live right out on the edge of the shadow that lay over the land, over the country villages and small hamlets, over everything that was slowly falling apart. To live right out in complete oblivion, going through its motions and rhythms. Did they even know what they were doing?

As long as he went on walking, the insects kept away, but once he got down to the first pool and stopped, he had to set fire to some bark and sticks in a herring pail he had brought with him, putting grass on top and standing in the thick smoke as he started baiting his line.

He had a telescopic rod that reached a long way out, but the salmon trout nonetheless kept guardedly just beyond his reach, making circles like silver nooses in the turgid, gleaming water. The bunched stars of bogbean could be seen by the shores, their pinkish petals, hairy inside, as yet untouched by brown shadow. Here it was full summer, although the frost had already scorched off the tops of the grasses out on the marshland several times. But he noticed the absence of birdsong and thought how quickly the lightest weeks had gone, and that he had mostly been miserable, thinking the light painful and the birds raucous in the mornings as he had lain awake thinking about Barbro.

The salmon trout were now leaping high up over the water out there, but he couldn't reach them. Perhaps he had frightened them from the edge with the heavy tramp of his boots on the swaying ground. Or cast a dark shadow over their crystal-clear space. He decided to try the other pool, and made his way down there as quietly as he could, stopping two or three meters away from the shore. When he cast, the line landed right by the bank, which cut sharply down in the black marsh soil. He had a very light hook, neither float nor sinker on the line, and he could feel the worm wriggling. A bird of prey flew like an arrow straight past him above the darkening surface of the water, nothing but a black silhouette, front-heavy. An owl?

At that moment he got a bite. The line straightened and sang, the fish pulling on it and swimming in wild, wide curves. When he hauled it in, it danced down into the crowberry scrub, a large, almost black salmon trout, glimmering dully as if it had oxidized silver rivets in its neck. He had to get out his glasses. Fish lice. A cunning old devil with lice in its coat.

He was suddenly exhausted and started walking back as soon as he had gutted it, plodding along without thinking. Night birds cut through his field of vision. The tussocks were glowing. Millions of white tufts floated in the cold layer of air above the tops of the sedge grass. Thin sedge, scorched by the frost, washed out. The summer would soon be over, its frenzy and abundance.

He had been allocated a sleeping place in the room where the diabetic and his family had lived. Someone had put in a glass of small pale harebells and sparse lesser stitchwort. There was a pillowcase on the pillow and a blanket over the mattress. He hoped the beautiful woman had been the one to pull on the pillowcase and put the flowers on the chair by his bed.

It wasn't that late, but he was exhausted, mostly from the long walk up to Starhill. As he closed his eyes, he longed for the radio. A few minutes later he heard one from the other side of the wall. That must be Annie Raft listening to the weather forecast. Every word penetrated through the boarded wall next to him. He tensed in case she would turn it off once the mountain district of southern Norrland was covered. But she didn't. She left it on throughout the shipping forecast, and he could follow the light-houses from the Atlantic all the way up into the Gulf of Bothnia. Not until the journey was complete did she switch it off. He lay there in the silence, wondering whether that had been sheer chance. Or did she always follow them from Oxöy all the way up to Farstugrunden and Kemi just as he did himself?

No one mentioned the events of Midsummer night. On the way up, he had crossed the ford without looking at the place where the tent had been, with no particular feeling of unease. But he wanted to return while it was still daylight.

First he bought some cheese from Petrus Eliasson. It was yellowish-white, a very mild goat's cheese, and when Petrus realized that he valued mature cheese, he went to fetch two small brown ones wrapped in damp linen. He unwrapped them with greater ceremony than he had shown for the wrinkled little body of his infant. Brita Wigert (not yet his wife, Birger realized) stayed in the background, the babe in her arms. He saw that she was in the symbiotic state and it hurt him to look at her, remembering Barbro with Tomas held to her in the same way. Her breasts had become blue-veined, the skin shimmering, thin, and extended. Her areolae had flowed out, their dark brown color muted to pinkish-brown. She had nearly always had her lips against the child's scalp when she had him in her arms. She said he smelled of almonds there.

The child. Tomas. Tomas with his gruff voice and downy chin. Puppylike and kind. Could still come nudging and nuzzling when he was about to go to bed at night, as if wanting to be cuddled. Birger used to nudge him back or pat him on the back. Couldn't she have given him another year? Why had she suddenly been unable to stand it? And where was Ulander?

He stared at the cheeses. Petrus Eliasson cut a piece out of the brownest, the spotted, scabby crust like the underside of an old boat. It was almost brown inside, yellowish and creamy like the innards of a large insect. They ate, looking each other straight in the eye. Birger nodded several times.

"I don't sell that," said Petrus. "No doubt you understand why. It's priceless. But this isn't far behind. You can buy half of it. And I'll throw in a bit of the soft cheese. The hunting will be starting soon and I suppose you'd like a little in the venison casserole."

They were kind, but they were also unhappy. Brita was not only bound to the child in that impenetrable state of milk and the smell of almonds. She was also bound by sorrow for her girls, who had gone to their father. They wouldn't be allowed to come back until next summer. He wondered why she had chosen Petrus. But perhaps she hadn't chosen at all? She had had the child and she couldn't very well make the trip down to some parsonage in Blekinge with another man's child and demand that everything should be as before.

Annie Raft had said that she lived with Dan Ulander. Where was he now? She was going to teach the commune children, but now there were no schoolchildren left. Marianne Öhnberg's boy didn't look anywhere near school age.

They offered Birger porridge and he said he would like the yellow milk separately in a mug. Mia watched him and the glass, noticing that he didn't drink any. He winked at her. Annie Raft said little when the others were talking, but when she heard he had come down from the Strömgren homestead, she became interested.

"Are you going back that way?"

He said he had left his car up at Oriana and Henry's place.

"I wanted to look in on them. But to be honest, I wasn't at all sure I'd make it all the way up here. So I thought I could fish in the Lobber if I couldn't get this far. The water's fine and calm down there. It races along in Björnstubacken."

He wondered whether Annie was frightened of the Lobber. He would have liked to ask her whether she was sleeping well, but he didn't dare.

He didn't get away until about seven that evening. It was still very light and would stay that way until about ten. The path ran steadily downhill between very large, high spruces. He heard a great black woodpecker whirring and the fine whistling of bullfinches. A lovely strong scent came toward him on a breeze, the summer-warm air that had lain still all day and now smelled of almonds and infants. It hurt, and he wondered if he would always have to turn away from memories rising out of the slopes of tussocks of twinflower, out of a warm bed or a child's downy hair. Or would he become sentimental? Sucking and dwelling on it.

He was already tired and stopped to get his breath back. Then he heard footsteps on the dry ground. A twig snapped with a sharp little sound. He waited.

It came again and he felt a certain unease. They must have been footsteps he had heard and now they had stopped, as if someone were waiting. He had seen no one behind him. He pretended to stand looking up into the trees. He was sure someone was watching him. But he didn't want to turn around and look back up the path.

He started walking very quickly. As long as he was walking he could hear nothing. He came to a crest and half ran down the slope on the other side until he was sure he was well ahead and wouldn't be seen in the hollow. Then he turned straight in among the trees, aiming for a large stone covered with white moss, and hid behind it. He could see the path between some birch branches if he inclined his head slightly. And now he could hear the footsteps. At that moment he regretted hiding. He should have hurried on instead. Got away from there.

It occurred to him that he had been too trusting. The atmosphere had been friendly up at Starhill. Petrus Eliasson looked like a billy goat and had offered him cheese. Marianne Öhnberg had smelled of milk.

So that's the kind of judgments I make, he thought. Like a five-year-old, or a pet dog.

He could hear a light crackling on the path. He had been running on pine cones. There she was. It was Annie Raft. She stood still and listened, then hesitantly went on downward. Then, of course, he came out and called:

"Did you want me for anything?"

He regretted that, too, right away, but it was too late. She spun around and stared. She had nothing with her except binoculars on a strap around her neck. He went up to her, thinking he was crashing around like an elk. Her face was very like the little girl's—those watchful eyes, the mouth narrow, lips pressed together. Her hair was slightly auburn now that it was short, and her eyebrows were so dark, he believed she dyed them. But would she do that up here? She had a small, straight nose and was somehow rather good-looking. But dismissive, totally without warmth or openness. Besides, she had crept up on him.

"What do you want?"

"Nothing."

"But you're following me."

She stood there, biting her lower lip, almost ridiculously like her daughter.

"I was just going to watch you," she said finally.

Perhaps she's crazy, he thought. That peculiar tremor around her, the lack of contact. It's frightening and you daren't talk to her as you would to others. How the hell can she be a teacher?

Then she said, in such a sober and lightly persuasive voice that he could perfectly well imagine her as a teacher:

"I was only going to watch you through the binoculars as you crossed the river."

Was this some kind of consideration? He was uncertain, but then he remembered the way the path went.

"You can't see the river from here."

"A little farther down. There's a plateau—there's a view over the river and the marshes toward the homestead from there."

"No," he said. "Not here in the steep bit. It's thick forest all the way. In that case, it's probably over toward Björnstubacken. And you can't see the ford from there. It's several kilometers away. If that was where you planned to watch me."

"I'll find the place" was all she said. Then neither of them knew what to do. Sooner or later he had to go on down. Was she going to follow him at a distance? That would be ridiculous. She must have thought something similar, because she said:

"I can come with you for a while. Until we find the place. The viewpoint."

"It doesn't exist."

Of course, she didn't believe him, or she pretended not to. They went on, he ahead, she just behind. His head was completely empty. He couldn't for the life of him find anything to say to her, but that didn't seem to worry her. After they had been walking for five or perhaps ten minutes, she stopped.

"This is where the path divides," she said.

"Yes, the one to the right goes down to Björnstubacken."

She stood still, and he thought she was looking strange.

"I'm going back now," she said.

There was no point in asking her anything. Her face was closed in on itself, on some kind of sadness. Or fear.

"Bye, then."

She turned abruptly, and not until she had done so and gone a bit of the way up the path did the uneasy atmosphere release its hold on him. She looked comical from behind. Those jeans with the legs cut roughly off with scissors were so thin at the back that they looked like a grid of pale blue cotton threads. Between them he glimpsed her not altogether white panties, her buttocks swinging a little as she walked.

"Hey, you," he called. "What kind of weird trousers are those?"

He had meant it as a joke. But she swung around and stared at him. He could see her eyes in the dim light of the forest, wide open and dark.

"Lucky I've seen you from behind before," he said. "Otherwise I'd think you were hollow at the back like a witch of the forest."

But she didn't reply, presumably because she didn't think it funny. After a moment she turned around and started up toward Starhill again.

Her mood still had a hold on him when he got down to the river. He didn't look around. All he could think about was that in twenty minutes, at the most half an hour, he would be up at the Strömgrens'. It wasn't that late. He would go in to Oriana and Henry and talk about ordinary things. Fishing. The level of the water in the river. Offer them some cheese.

Now all he had to do was to cross the river, quickly. Up into the silence of the marshland, away from the water, from the sounds that were like small screams and mewings. From the splashing over the stones and the pull of the dark, racing water.

Henny had acquired a pale blue quilted jacket and white sailing boots. She was wearing a white beret with a silk pompom on top. After walking for two hours, she wasn't even out of breath. She had her famous singer's diaphragm to fall back on. Besides, Henry Strömgren was carrying her pack in a rucksack; she had arrived at his place in Ivar Jönsson's taxi. Whether she had paid Henry or whether he had agreed anyway was not certain. Henny didn't paralyze people as Annie had thought when she was younger, but people were always taken with her, even captivated. Henry had seen her in an old feature film.

"Just imagine! There he sits, watching me as some gangster's moll starring with Åke Söderblom, then two weeks later I'm outside his door right up in the mountains, saying, 'Help! Where is my daughter?' "

Not starring with Åke Söderblom. Sickan Carlsson or Anna-Lisa Ericsson starred with him. In the same film as. In a scene with.

Annie had started correcting Henny's statements when she was about fourteen, but always silently. (Don't mention puberty! It passed Annie by!) Since Henny had appeared in the hollow by the stream, they had all been staring at her and listening to what she had to say. Even Petrus. He was the one most affected. His mouth fell open.

She made her way through the grass without showing any signs of fatigue, her voluminous hips swinging. She had always had the most feminine figure, narrow-waisted, big-busted, and curved behind. Nowadays the kilos were visible. (If only I'd had Gaby Stenberg's *height* to my voice!) She was sixty-eight, her profile still clean but flowing out below her chin. She raised it against the wind.

"God, how beautiful it is here! Do you *know* how beautiful it is?"

Perhaps they thought she was stupid or didn't think before she spoke. She sat down with Mia on her knee and praised the slate wall of the fireplace.

"What exquisite stonework!"

Not for a moment had Annie expected her to be anything but exuberant. Henny had seen every grotty boardinghouse in the country, had acted on wooden stages put up in public parks for the evening, and tussled with the drunks. She had never complained and always got her own way.

I'm pregnant.

The moment that white pompom, that beret, that quilted jacket, had emerged from the hollow, realizing that it was *her* (her walk, her voice), Annie had had the thought. At that very moment, not a minute earlier. Missed three times. Been feeling rotten. And my breasts. Although I'm so thin.

I'm pregnant. I've been so since Midsummer Day in Aagot Fagerli's cottage. That time with no diaphragm, when I was so frightened, I forgot it. That's when it happened. I must have known it. But not known, after all. As if I were two people. And now knowing immediately. Just seeing her. Before she even gave me that look. Will Mia feel like this one day?

"My dear child, how sunburned you are, and how healthy you look! You don't usually get so brown."

Had the brown shadow come? The first signs? Or can she see it around my eyes? Is it like she used to say—it shows around the eyes?

Dan. She'll ask after Dan.

But she didn't. She unpacked the presents, a pink tracksuit for Mia, rabbit slippers with ears of fluffy material and large shiny eyes. Two bottles of red wine. For Annie a blouse which would show her breasts.

Henry Strömgren couldn't stay for the evening, although he wanted to. You could see he wanted to. They would drink red wine and try some of the maturest cheese in the store. Petrus wanted to show her the earth cellar and the well so that she would see some truly excellent old stonework. Henny arranged with Henry Strömgren to be fetched at Björnstubacken in twenty-four hours' time. Åke was still in the village, at the campsite. Walking in the woods was not for him. They had rented two cabins, one for Annie and Mia, another for themselves. Incredibly nice!

In the middle of all this, Annie thought of the campsite shower room. And the television set. Then she thought: I must be left in peace. For an hour. Or a moment, at least. I've never been so tired in all my life.

But she couldn't go away. The program accelerated. The stone cellar. The cookhouse. The goat shed. Mia fetched the young kids. The clubhouse with Annie and Mia's room. The beds. Mia's dolls. The rabbit slippers under the bed beside the box of paper dolls. Not a word about Dan, about Dan's bed. Not yet.

Tea drinking in the afternoon. Henny maintained you really always ought to drink herb tea because it was better for you. After that, the milking. She had a try herself, amid much laughter. The milking rota was suspended; they all milked. It was like a feature film. Starring Henny Raft, though not Åke Söderblom.

There was beet soup for dinner with bilberry pancakes afterward, plus red wine and the cheeses. Henry loved strong cheese. She also loved fermented Baltic herrings, spiced aquavit, griddled blood pancakes, marinated herring, and so on, none of which Annie could bear. They talked about it and it turned out that Petrus loved boiled ling fish that had been soaked in lye, and he was going to do the same with the dried pike nailed to the wall of the cookhouse. He had netted them in the Klöppen, and he explained that the lake was low. In that way, they came to the Lobber and, without a moment's hesitation, Henny asked them whether they weren't *frightened?*

"Yes," said Brita. "Sometimes I think it's all so horrible."

She had never said that before. None of them had ever admitted that it had concerned them. In the end, Annie had begun to think she alone had that desolate feeling on the edge of the pastureland, and the fear of the forest as soon as she went a little farther in.

That was where they had found the earthstar. Mia had spotted it between the spruces, its dark tips splayed out in the moss. Mia hadn't realized it was a fungus. She thought it was a rare animal, the same kind as a starfish, and that it would move when she touched it. It had smelled like Dan. But Mia didn't know that.

Henny had gotten Brita to say what it was like—that she was sometimes frightened. She had said it in a quiet, sorrowful voice, and Henny clearly felt this was something you only touched on lightly, for she hugged Mia and suggested they sing "The Maiden to the Well Did Go." Mia was to be the maiden and Grandma the hazel branch. As they had no accompaniment, Annie was to sing harmony. She didn't know it; Henny said, "Oh, give it a try," but Annie didn't want to. So Henny asked Mia to go and get the melodica. Then Mia sang with Grandma and it was lovely:

> *"I feed on sugar and drink wine*
> *that's why I'm so very fine!"*

Annie thought the melodica was a dreadful instrument, but everything livened up when she played it. Petrus changed the words on his own initiative and sang, "I feed on cheese and drink wine." He was given an ovation.

Suddenly Henny was standing by the fireplace, leaning lightly against the stonework and about to sing. I'll go out, Annie thought. But she knew she would stay. If they laughed, she would look straight into Henny's eyes and hold her gaze. She had tried to do that in Mälarvåg. Åke and Henny had come to a social evening. They had listened to the obscenities in the student revue without batting an eyelid and with expressions of cheerful appreciation and mild absentmindedness. Afterward, persuaded by the principal's wife, they had gone up to the rostrum. Henny had sung, Åke accompanying her on the battered piano. At first the students had just fidgeted and scraped their chairs. But when Henny sang "Turn to me, turn from me, like a fire, let me burn," throwing dark looks at Åke, who had closed his eyes behind his thick glasses, some had begun to yell, and then there were various ill-suppressed sounds. Many of them had been drinking beer and needed to belch. The sounds caused a few laughs and finally general laughter and the crash of chairs tipping over. Henny threw back her head and sang on loudly right to the very end.

> *"You and only you follow me*
> *for love of my glowing youth!"*

When the dancing began, they had vanished. Annie had found them back at her home, sitting at the kitchen table, the light out, with a glass of brandy each from Åke's pocket flask.

But now Henny was singing, and although Annie felt she must be dreaming, she accompanied her on the melodica. Henny's voice was full and rich:

> *"Maybe he's lazy*
> *maybe he's slow*

> *maybe I'm crazy*
> *maybe I know . . .*
> *Can't help loving that man of mine."*

She had appeared in *Show Boat* in the 1940s, bubbling around in the part of Nolie's sharp-tongued mother. But it was the part of the disreputable Julie she had dreamed of. She sang it now and they all stared at her, Annie prepared to slap the face of anyone who thought her ridiculous. But no one did. She had touched them with her dark voice.

Next, Mia was to sing again. She sang "When Little Mouse Goes for a Walk," and they applauded and said she had inherited her grandmother's voice. According to the program fixed fifteen years earlier, Henny should now have said, "Voice! No, my dears, the voice is *there*." And they would have looked at Annie. But Henny said nothing.

It's over, thought Annie as the merrymaking continued. She's expecting nothing more. I'm too old. She'll never torment me again.

Desolation was what she felt, not relief. What was Henny feeling? How would she survive now—with no hopes even for her daughter? Annie had always been convinced that Henny would go mad when her engagements ceased. Åke had gone on playing in restaurants and at rehearsals until the day he qualified for an old-age pension. He stopped on that day and had never said anything about missing it.

By the time Annie had graduated from school and gone to music college and the Academy, Henny's engagements were already few and far between. Still, Annie had inherited her voice and was to become a trained singer. (Training! Just think if I'd had a proper training!) But Annie suffered from stage fright. Just standing there made her feel sick and break out in a cold sweat. She thought she would faint and could never get her breathing right. However, Henny said that would pass with training.

But Annie hadn't gotten what Henny still had, whatever that was. Her way of moving her hips, among other things. Church music had gone better for Annie. She didn't have to be seen. She could stand on the platforms in churches and sing at simpler funerals. The court singers sang at the grander and more lucrative ones.

Henny enjoyed hearing her in church and always appeared clad dramatically in black. Annie was afraid they would think she was one of those persistent attenders of funerals. She herself was troubled by the words. She found that the most beautiful music in the world had been created to put across words that at best were stupid but more often senselessly cruel. She hunted out their origins in the Bible and found something she had never known before because she had never been interested in religion: a compost of superstition, war frenzy, and mysticism about rotting corpses.

She sang nonetheless. *"Bist Du bei mir,"* she sang, seeing a man with dark, curly hair above a warm, swelling penis and a wrinkled blue-brown scrotum. To produce the notes, she had to put everything she found warm and sensually appealing against that repugnant shattered head, dripping saliva and blood, the stinking bandages and the gust from the opened grave. With her images, she drove away the staring head of the prophet on the dish, the raging swineherds and soldiers slaughtering children. If for once she found something in these insane and cruel litanies that reflected earthly desire or beauty, it filled her with warmth. One simple act of friendship toward another human being or anything that wasn't solemn and lethal.

Like Aaron's staff sprouting on the bloodstained altar in the preacher's tent, greening with buds and flowers and ripe almonds.

It didn't work in the long run. She felt guilty, and she tried, but it didn't work. Åke had found her a studio apartment in Karlbergsvägen and Annie knew it had cost him his life savings. You must stay out of debt, Henny said. Annie took on all the work she could get to be able to live free of debt—funerals, singing classes, school choirs.

She was capable. That was what she was. She played the piano or the bass at assembly room gigs and at student unions. But she couldn't sing solo before an audience. When she tried, there was a sour smell of sweat in her clothes afterward. Henny went on saying it would pass, but Åke no longer said anything.

He was an imperturbably dignified man, well dressed and courteous. She had always admired him. But she began to understand that he wasn't driven by any high ambitions. Gradually she realized that his elegance was also questionable. Co-respondent shoes, brown and white, still lay in the attic, and spats, the kind called dog jackets, to wear over pumps. An excessively loud striped jacket.

Henny's life was a drama. She wept and stormed when she was cheated of an engagement or got criticized in a review. But things had mostly gone well with her. She had found her slot, the amusing, bold female supporting role. She drove out vapidity by bandying words and putting a spin on the romance in operettas. This was written into the parts;

it was the way it should be. But the amazing thing was that there always seemed to be a role and a stage in the world specifically for Henny. On the other hand, none for Annie.

Åke was a fine musician and he had a good ear. But he was remarkably uninterested. Or had he become so over the years? Annie couldn't remember his ever playing at home, except when Henny had wanted him to accompany her. He used to read.

He was nearsighted and wore glasses with thick lenses, behind which he lived like a goldfish in a round bowl. He read his way through decades of bus trips and life in a one-room apartment with Henny ceaselessly talking, practicing, and vacuuming. He had a leather briefcase with large metal catches which Annie used to play with. He carried it, crammed full, to and from the library. Annie had taken this for granted, just as it was taken for granted that Uncle Göte had read one book in his whole life, the memoirs of a great liar called Kalle Möller.

Without giving it a thought, she herself had become a reader. Once she had left school and escaped from the ramshackle wooden house in Enskede, she wanted just one thing, a room of her own. To be left in peace. To read. But since she had gotten a position at college, she agreed to start studying singing, and Henny had said how tremendous and fantastic it was simply to have been accepted.

After two years she realized she was not doing well at the Academy and she really ought to change to the music teacher course. That meant failure, and she wouldn't be able to bear it. She was at a total standstill, incapable of leaving, incapable of singing. That was when Sverker Gemlin became one of her teachers.

He taught harmony and counterpoint. He was a quiet, sensitive man; Mia got her brown eyes from him. They would look into each other's eyes and quietly talk about commonplace things. She would lie on her bed for hours, analyzing the meaning of what had been said. Once they held hands, in a taxi after a party, hiding their hands under her coat.

She had lived a cautious and parched life Sexually she was not inexperienced; she had had lighthearted relationships, though when she thought about it, they hadn't been much fun. But with Sverker, a grass fire started.

One morning, he came and stood behind her at the photocopier and pressed his crotch up against her behind. He didn't kiss her, only held his lips pressed against the nape of her neck, parting the hair first to reach it. His hands were on the photocopier. She could see them on either side of her, the tips of his fingers whitening. He had a strong erection and she could feel it through their clothing. He stood like that for a little while, not quite still, and she almost fainted.

Two evenings later, she stayed behind on the premises when she knew he was teaching. They met in the corridor and stood still for a long spell at quite a distance from each other. A few minutes later they were locked in his office. She had just had a bath and had bought a lace bra, making all these preparations without really thinking about their significance.

Beside themselves with desire, they tried to make do with the narrow blue couch in his room. The main difficulty was trying to avoid the wooden armrest. Either she had the back of her head pressed against it, making the angle of her neck lethal, or her head hung right off the sofa.

From then on they met at Annie's place. It couldn't be very often, because he had My. Presumably that wasn't her name, but it was what he called her. It was even in the telephone directory. Annie stared at the Ängby address and the number, but she never phoned.

He spoke of his marriage in graceful circumlocutions such as, we must cherish what we have. What he had, of course, was My, the children Jesper and Jannika, the house in North Ängby, and a summer place in Kullen together with My's parents. Annie had her small apartment in Karlbergsgatan and her precious freedom. He talked about that a lot. But it was Annie who had brought up the subject.

When summer came, he went with his family to Kullen, where she couldn't contact him. They didn't write. "That's impossible because down there we all live on top of one another," he had explained. She turned over his words again and again. Sometimes she pictured the whole household with in-laws and children and the cocker spaniel as a great snake pit of lecherous writhings.

She sang at a summer wedding and was choir leader at an adult education course that summer. In July, she spent a few days at home and took the opportunity to go to the college to photocopy notes. She ran into Sverker in the entrance. He knew her times. She had written them down in case he was able to make himself free during the summer.

He said the trip from Kullen had been unplanned and he had forgotten which days she would be in town. At that, she realized what the situation was.

A raging woman took over the stage. It was not Annie; it was Brangäne or Medea. Her performance lasted scarcely an hour, but long enough for him to retreat forever. Temporarily he calmed her down on the blue couch. She had no contraception with her, since she hadn't known they would meet. She left the Academy. The time before she knew she was pregnant was very difficult to remember. She had been in the eye of the storm, unbudging grief and hatred, but she couldn't remember what it was like.

As soon as she realized she was expecting, she had decided to apply for teacher training. She told Åke and Henny she was going to have a child. When they were alone, Henny had said:

"But what are you going to do?"

She had meant an abortion, though she would never have taken that word into her mouth. For the first time in her life, Annie had known what she wanted to do. As she was to have a child, she had to have a job. To support herself and the child. Not dither around. Not sing at funerals. Not have an affair with a married teacher. Nothing of what had gone before. Just herself and the child.

At first she had considered registering the father as unknown. That would be revenge, but he wouldn't notice. She realized it would be an injustice to the child. At the time, she imagined it was a boy. A boy couldn't grow up without having at least a name for his father.

All this was unpleasant and she thought about it during endless walks across the city. It was a wet autumn. She felt disintegrated, whipped through by water and wind. Brooding led to nothing. She wanted to hurt him but couldn't. There was no way to do that except by writing to My and she didn't want to be mean. Without being mean, she couldn't get at him.

Gradually she extracted from herself the germ of revulsion from which all this had grown: She was afraid he would question his paternity. It was like the fear of reviews. Someone would write that she had a thin, sharp, hopeless little voice and an affected manner.

She hadn't slept with anyone else, with one exception right at the beginning, when she was confused and hadn't known whether the affair would continue. But what did he think?

He became paralyzed and thought nothing and said just as Henny had:

"What are you going to do?"

She explained she wasn't going to do anything except get herself training as a teacher, and he dropped a piece of his almond cake into his cup of coffee. It was sodden and he had held it in the air too long. They were at Tösse's and it was very warm inside. Both of them had kept on their outdoor clothing and he had beads of sweat along his hairline. She thought, What if he wants to bring Christmas presents? Or come on the child's birthday? What shall I say?

"Have you thought about it carefully?" he said. "I mean, it's a big decision. There are other ways of thinking. If that's how you put it."

He didn't want to say the word, either. Then they parted. He knew what Mia's name was and her date of birth, but not where she was. He had no idea that at the moment his maintenance payment was essential for the existence of the Starhill commune, because Pastor Wigert had stopped his payments.

She could never think calmly about Sverker, nor with indifference. All the same, seven years had passed since he had silenced her outburst on the blue couch.

"Where's the ephebe?"

Henny went on talking to Petrus, but Annie was sure she had caught that aside.

This had happened before. Henny's outpourings of friendliness were always under control. They were not questioned as long as feelings ran warm. Then a lightning attack. Pure surgery.

Ephebe? Something from an operetta. A youth with sparse down. Now Annie felt a greater weariness than ever. But it was not possible to get away yet.

Clear, cold scorn. Because she knew, sensed, sniffed the scent of— what? Something more than bickering. Sadness and fatigue.

Fear. No, she could not guess that.

Henny had very properly written in advance and said they were coming and Annie had written back to say it was no good. They couldn't be fetched from Blackwater because Dan had the car—he was away on behalf of the commune. But naturally Henny was not to be stopped and Annie should have known that. The moment when she appeared by the stream had been illuminating in any case. Although this kind of thing would inevitably become clear sooner or later. Worse had been the moment when that chubby doctor had turned around and called out: "What kind of weird trousers are those?" She had ripped the pants off as soon as she got home. That had been really disgusting.

Yet she regarded it as an illuminating moment. Though not decisive. She couldn't decide anything. That had happened time and time again in her life. Standstill.

"As if it had nothing to do with you," Henny had said at the time Annie was messing around at the Academy. And later in Mälarvåg. All had gone well at first. She had liked it in a dull way. Gradually it had come to a standstill, though she had never noticed until Dan came and started asking about her life.

She had thought of burning the jeans, but couldn't think where. She wanted no one to see her doing it and the thick denim probably wouldn't burn well. She realized that was why she still had them. They had been wet way up the legs when she saw them hanging outside the tent. Over a spruce branch.

She must have recognized them all along. The grid of threads at the back. The label. It was as if she were two people. One who knew. And one who happily pulled on the jeans when she had grown tired of wearing skirts. Cut off the legs, which were too long. Too long for Dan, too. She ought at least to have thought about that.

But she hadn't. Not until that doctor had called out—he had no idea, of course, she realized that afterward—"What kind of weird trousers are those?" Then she knew.

She had wanted to rip them off there and then. Thought she would vomit on the path. But she just ran and it kept thumping in her head: he lied he lied he lied.

She had suspected that there was no viewpoint from which you could see the tent. And it was just as she had thought. He must have been right down by the tent. Or else they had all been down there. He had gone on lying, although he'd said he would tell her exactly what they'd done. He had never slept at Nirsbuan.

But that night she had dreamed that he was back and lying in her arms. He smelled strongly; out of his newly washed body rose a smell of earthstar, autumnal and brown, and she recognized it. In her dream they exchanged fluids and they were still pouring out of her when she woke; she wept and she was wet.

Henny poked and pried. She sensed something, perhaps not the worst. She thought Annie had begun to tire, that she was ripe for a minor attack.

Ephebe.

She loathed making a fool of herself and Henny knew it. In that respect Annie was like her father, and Henny knew them both. It was the lesson of her life and one she had had to learn properly.

She meant well, of course. Annie tried to imagine Mia as a grown-up. Mia mindlessly, perhaps fatally in love.

Mia unhinged.

Evening came and she withdrew. The ewes were grazing by the stream, the grass rustling as they tugged at it. After a while they gathered around the stone she was sitting on. The leader ewe lay down first to ruminate, and as she chewed, she blew through her nostrils. A sigh. The air was chilly, the insects no longer daring to emerge. The ewe's udder had shrunk and the sores from insect bites had healed. But she was in lamb again. She laid her long, slightly curved nose in Annie's hand. Annie could feel the hard jawbone and the soft tissues between. She was pressing hard.

A weariness was visible in the very grass and leaves. They had paled and bent over, the turning inward had begun. Toward the root. Toward the placenta. That had nothing to do with knowing. It could elude all light. It happened. Throbbing like water in the flooded moss by the stone, the pulse beats, gently touching the lobes of flat fungus.

Oh, to be carried along! To move with the slowly pulsating water and yet be quite still. Like the water weeds in the stream, rigid hornwort and water lobelia.

She felt a strong desire to test out her voice and see whether those diaphragm muscles were still there. Whether her voice had any volume and she could open up for the keynote. She moved a little farther away. The ewes didn't follow her across the stream, but they got to their feet and stood watching her as they chewed the cud, their jawbones working. It made them look absentminded.

She climbed a bit up the shale slope and tried seated at first, but was unable to produce a note worth mentioning. Then she did some exercises and could feel it beginning to swell. She sang. It was a strong feeling and just the same as before. The note hadn't shriveled, nor the feeling. She sang:

"I feed on earth and drink water
that is why I'm so fine!"

Again and again she sang it, filled by the tone and the feeling, which was the strongest she would ever experience.

"I feed on earth and drink water
that is why I'm so fine . . ."

But she knew that if there had been people down there, rather than sheep, her feelings would have been of anguish and fear, and her clothing would have smelled sour with sweat. She had been given a gift. But only one half of it.

The ewes raised their heads as she passed them on her way back. The pasture was still. No smoke from the chimneys dissolved into the sky. September dusk. She opened the door very quietly as she went in, hoping they were all asleep.

He had to take Galm out of the reindeer enclosure and scold him. But actually he was glad to be able to get away for a while. He was supposed to be one of Tuoma Balte's laborers and look for his markings, but he couldn't distinguish many in that maelstrom of bodies, hooves, and horns. Stamping and grunting and clicking. The largest antlers hovered above the herd. Most of them were speckled gray, but white animals gleamed here and there, trembling in his field of vision as long as he could keep track of the body in the whirling, creaking, hawking wheel of beasts. The click of hooves sounded like the ticking of a huge clock.

Galm was totally wild. He didn't herd like the Lapp dogs—he hunted. Someone came toward Johan as he was struggling with Galm.

"Dov biene dan nihkoe!"

Johan didn't understand, though he thought he knew a little by then. When he looked up it was Oula Laras. At first he hardly recognized him because he was so much smaller than he remembered. What little of his black hair was showing under the cap was streaked with white, like a badger.

"What kind of wild thing you got there? Is't a Siberian?"

In his haste, he said yes, then immediately regretted it. The first thing he had ever said to Oula Laras was not entirely true. Only in part. But it was too late now, for Laras took hold of Galm by the scruff of the neck and said:

"You should have a team of these. And compete."

"Yes, I'd thought of that," said Johan, though that wasn't strictly true, either. But it became so that very moment.

"Who are you, then?"

He was just about to say the Pergutt's cousin, but at that moment the Pergutt himself came toward them and Johan remembered what they had agreed on at school. He didn't want to be called just Per's boy any longer. So Johan said:

"I'm cousin to him—Lars Dorj."

"He's Torsten Brandberg's youngest," the Pergutt said.

"And Gudrun's," said Johan.

He didn't see how Oula Laras reacted when he was told, because he hadn't dared look up. His face burned and he knew he had flushed scarlet. But Laras said something to the Pergutt that Johan didn't understand, though he heard him calling him Pergutt. Then Laras ran his tongue under his lip, caught the wedge of snuff, and spat it out. He rubbed his front teeth with a curved forefinger, then smiled a whiter smile and said:

"Now, lads, time for some bloody work!"

Galm barked, hearing from the tone of voice that something was going to happen, and he went on barking at Laras for a long time after he had gone back to the enclosure and disappeared behind the seething stream of creatures rushing clockwise inside the fencing.

"What did he say to you?" said Johan.

"Nothing, just 'So you're to go to school, eh?' "

Pergutt also went back inside the enclosure and Johan could occasionally see him close to Laras, sometimes far away. His lasso swirled around in the air and shortly after, with the help of his father, Pergutt was dragging out a bull reindeer. The creature was rolling its eyes and tossing its antlers. When they got to the slaughtering shed, it thrust its four hooves into the ground and tried to get away from the smell of blood and the sound of the saw. A diesel engine was rumbling evenly, and water was spurting out of the hose from the pump down by the stream. He could see the ravens sailing above the stack of heads and antlers, but he couldn't hear them. Oula Laras cried out as he was almost dragged down by a bull. His knife dangled at his belt as he ran, a long, curved knife. Must be the same one. Johan tried to remember it all again. It had gone too quickly this time as well.

That time, it had been late winter—April—the light strong and the silence like a glass bell around the mountain. Now all the dogs were barking, the generator rumbling and the bone saw whistling. He could just see the peaked cap. It was orange with white lettering on the front and easily spotted.

"Christ almighty!" Oula Laras yelled. "Calm down a bit, can't you, you old devil!"

W e walk in a dark forest, thin strings of light between the branches of the trees. There is a strong smell of lichens, as if from the coat of an animal. Not much foliage inside the dimness scarcely penetrated by the light. The birches are shaggy with black lichen.

The scent of almonds comes welling up out of all the acidity and decay. Strong and sweet. Do you want us to follow it?

I don't know who you are. Sometimes I catch a glimpse of an un-shaven cheek, a pair of round glasses of the kind we used to laugh at. A long overcoat of stiff woolen fabric. We won't imagine each other. That's not good for us. You walk with me.

There's a wolf in here. A she-wolf. She's roaming around the edge of our field of vision.

What shall we do with the wolf? Have you got a scooter? If it were winter and you had a scooter, you could harry her to death. Now it's summer and there's a strong smell of almonds over this sun-spotted, mossy ground. The air is very still and when it moves, the breeze brings with it the scent of predators. What can you do with a wolf except kill it? We must go now. We must leave the forest and we are already far away from that other smell, the familiar smell that was so strong, it was almost bitter. We never found out where it came from.

Shuffling. The day always began with the shuffling or the squeak of the stove door. Petrus put a log inside. Then his sheepskin slippers shuffled

across the floor again. He was over by the window, reading the thermometer. If there was a scraping sound, the window was covered with a jungle
of ice crystals. He made a peephole with the nail of his forefinger among
white ferns and starwort.

Then she remembered the forest in her dream. It was painful.

The bed was a nest of body heat, but the tip of Mia's nose was cold.
She was lying with her back and bottom against Annie's stomach and
chest, curled up like the child inside. The fetus. She usually straightened
out. She sometimes fetched a log, too.

Petrus was peeing now, splashing into the pot. It made her angry,
hearing it. As early as November, they had had to move into the old
cottage. Annie had hung blankets as a curtain around the bed in which she
and Mia slept. She always washed and dressed behind the blankets and
when she used the pot at night, she tried to be restrained. Petrus just
splashed. Sometimes he farted, too. She wished he would wait until he had
dressed and could go out. He probably didn't sleep much. He kept the fire
going all night.

She tried to remember that he was kind and also deeply miserable,
though he never said anything. Brita was in Röbäck for the winter, with
the baby, and he hadn't been able to go down there for almost two weeks.
First there had been storms, and then it had been too cold. They had
received no mail. There might be a letter from Dan in the box.

Cold is standstill. Her own was over. It had lasted ever since that
doctor had called after her in the forest. The ragged jeans had long since
been burned, but she hadn't been able to decide anything else. She was
considering abortion. An abortion in Östersund?

It was Dan's child as well, though still only a fetus, a shoot of herself. A small tumor she had to have the right to remove. He didn't
even have to know, so she said nothing about it in her letters. She had
thought she would wait until he came back, and now she hadn't even
an address.

When did it become a child? And when did it become his?

Petrus disposed of the kids. People disposed of dogs that had turned
fierce or were no good for hunting. The expression was repugnant.

There were mornings when she woke feeling blissful without knowing why. She had dreamed, but what? That they had slept together, of
course. But there was something else.

She had dreamed that he explained. She couldn't even laugh at it in
the daytime, but at night when she was asleep, it was vivid. All his lies had

been explained and he wanted the child and to live with them. What she had felt when they exchanged their gentle flow with each other was true.

In his letters he never said that he was going to come back. All he said was that he had been in Alved again, sleeping in a tent for the second time. For a whole month he had been running off stencils on a duplicator in a basement in Högbergsgatan. He thought he might be able to find a couple to replace Bert and Enel. He wrote that he was working on it.

He still knew nothing about the child. It was a child now. Mia put her ear to Annie's stomach and listened. She could feel it in there. It was like the birds in the timber wall at night. Heartbeats and small movements.

Annie believed Dan had taken the car away from them. They became dependent on Yvonne and her old bus, and she thought it inconsiderate, but assumed he hadn't meant to be away so long. Sometimes they got a lift with Henry Strömgren down to the store and the post office in Blackwater, and one day he had asked whether it wasn't Annie's car that was parked below Aagot's barn.

"A pink Beetle?"

She asked him to look at the license plate next time he went down there. When they met again he said that was right. It was her car. It had been there all the time.

That night she lay awake. At about one in the morning she heard footsteps on the floor. She lay waiting for the stove door to screech. As soon as Petrus had put two logs inside, he usually shuffled back to bed. But there was no shuffle. Pattering. She thought it was Önis getting up for a pee. There were whispers, then a bed creaking. She was just about to fall asleep, when she heard a suppressed noise, as if someone were whimpering.

A few nights later she heard the pattering steps again. Then the bedsprings squealed and after a while there was no doubt whatsoever about what she was hearing.

She thought they were betraying everything. Brita. The commune. She remembered Ola Lennartsson's sly grin, his dirty innuendo. They were living down to the expectations of the village. Stoking up the prejudices.

Though that wasn't logical. The village knew nothing. Only Annie knew and she felt like a voyeur. Or an auditeur, if there was such a thing. It was considered normal to be a voyeur in front of a television or movie screen. But how many would stand the reality? That light moan. Broken-off gasps. The rhythmical creak of the bed.

They did it almost every night, at about one in the morning. Petrus was never the one to take the initiative. Marianne went across to his bed. Sometimes Annie thought she understood them—anything for a little warmth and closeness in this cold. But she never longed for Dan when they were moving over there. She was sickened and thought they were preventing her from dreaming about him.

She often dreamed. Awake, she was frightened and bitter.

Her old antipathy to Petrus had returned. For a while she had quite liked him. He was an oddball. He thought mostly about cheese, talked like the Bible, and did everything very slowly. But he did it well. Now she was remembering repellent things.

When Brita had given birth to her child and the journalists had come, Petrus had taken over. It was he who had told them what it was like to have a child at Starhill. At the time, she hadn't wanted to read the article. Now she hunted for it while he was out. She found a whole heap of newspaper clippings. He had been collecting clippings on the murders.

In the interview on giving birth, he had said he had buried the afterbirth below the kitchen window. It made good manure.

He wanted to do what they used to do before, in the olden days, as he always said. But he didn't understand that the afterbirth was sacrificed so that the earth would be fertile like the woman. Petrus thought it was about manure. That was not only stupid, but vile.

She wanted to leave, a vague but persistent desire. But then the cold had come. It had grown much too cold to ski down, though she had tried once. It was twenty-seven degrees below freezing, the first morning in almost two weeks that the temperature had not dropped to thirty. But when she got up a little speed down the first slope, the fluid from her tear glands had frozen. She thought her eyes might break like glass, so she had turned back.

She put out her hand and grabbed her sweater, longjohns, and thick woolen socks. Mia didn't wake as she dressed under the covers, which she then pulled over Mia so that nothing showed but a tuft of reddish hair.

It was hot next to the stove. They had put blankets and sheepskins against the windowpanes to keep out the draft. She peered through the hole Petrus had scraped in the icy armor of the pane. Eighteen below.

It was over. The cold was evaporating, the water moving, at least on the windowpanes. Her breath made the ice melt as she blew on it slowly.

It's over.

I am not the place, immovable, to which you will return. I am not marked and demarcated. I happen. Mobility.

When Önis handed her the mug of milky tea, Annie said:

"I'm going down today."

The snow was dry, a crystalline powder swirling up around the tips of her skis. There were no tracks over the pasture after the night of cold. The fox had lain still, the capercaillie burrowed down in the powder.

In the afternoon, as the light faded, a procession of titmice had crept in under the wind shields and into the holes left by the dowels in the cottage wall. They had heard them rustling. Twenty-gram bodies pressed against each other during the night, hearts beating as one. Now they were clinging to the lumps of tallow in the sun.

Bear Mountain was so white from the sun that she found it hard to keep her eyes on it; the sun's glowing core would follow and dazzle her for two and a half hours. The sky was thin and a brilliant blue, but at the zenith it blackened before her eyes. All the mountains were white with sides of sharp dark blue shadow, the ice glistening on the peaks.

There were bird tracks down by the stream. The grouse had been embroidering neatly with their feet, taking birch buds, spilling a little and leaving dry little droppings.

By now she knew this ground better than any floor. She knew what the moss beneath the snow was like, infiltrated with lichens and glossy scrub. She remembered the moist, acidic smell of earth. When it emerged from the snow her own life would begin to smell like sex, like wet hair.

She made her way ahead high above the ground. The birches' height had been reduced by the one-and-a-half-meter layer of snow. Deep down there were tiny remains of warmth, torpor prevailing, downturning, the precise economy of dearth.

She skied into the forest where the new snow had not reached, her skis scraping against the crust under a spruce. God knows what that sounded like to the voles. She was on her way down to the sound that carried all the way up to Starhill. Sometimes distantly, depending on the wind. On calm days they could hear it all the time. Rumbling day after day. They no longer talked about it.

She was afraid of the cold. The child weighed her down and the weight was growing in her belly. Every week that went by, she grew more afraid.

" 'Now bitter death doth bear upon us.' "

That was something she had once sung in church, though she hadn't understood what "bear upon" meant.

Approach. In reality.

Cold is standstill. The weather forecasts had said that the high pressure was at a standstill. "Death doth bear upon us." Petrus thought she was morbid. It was stupid to talk so much.

There were five of them now at Starhill. And three cats, a Norwegian elk hound, and nineteen goats. The billy goat. Eight hens. And rats. Not only the cottage mice that rustled across the floor at night; large rats had gnawed their way into the wooden chests of grain and feedstuff.

Lotta had left in September. She had sent several postcards, all with cats on them, assuring them she would come back in the spring. Suddenly the cards stopped coming.

Was she dead? A syringe in some lavatory. A madman. What thoughts. "Now bitter death doth bear upon us." It's morbid, Petrus would say.

The cold is death, is life curled down low. Wax-covered. With no fluid. No pulse. But inside me blood is throbbing, the waters in the fetal sac shifting with the movements of the ski sticks and skis.

Now she could hear the water. The mountain river. The river Lobber. The same sound that had been heard before the water was given a name. She had gotten right down to the river but could no longer hear the rumble she had gone to find. The noise of the water was louder, the current rapid there. The stones wore caps of snow, threads and fringes of ice. The waves caught reflections from the sun and threw a mobile net across the riverbed. It looked as if the great black stones down there were moving, gliding silently beneath the golden net.

She had been fearful of the calm part of the river closest to the Klöppen and had gone too far north. Now she was almost up by the rapids. When she set off downhill, she saw that the wooden bridge had been replaced by an iron structure.

She skied about a kilometer back along the uneven terrain by the river before she heard the noise again, growing louder and louder. Up at Starhill they could hear the rumble for hour after hour throughout the short days and long after darkness fell. Petrus had crossed the river at the ford and had seen it. He said it was a processor and the company was going to clear-fell the forest right up to Starhill.

When it suddenly became lighter, she was unprepared. She saw the machine, yellow and as big as a bus. A felled spruce was being edged down to a transport track, branches and twigs flying all around it. The machine nudged the trunk ahead, grabbed it, and swung, roaring at every movement. She had to ski away, as the sound was unbearable for any length of time.

She couldn't quite figure out where she was. The space the forest had formed down toward the river had gone, and there were inexplicable waves and hollows in the snow. She could see a long way over the marshlands on the other side. It was all far more violent than she had thought.

She could see the man right up there in the driver's cabin. He was wearing a helmet and large ear protectors. He hadn't spotted her, and she didn't dare go any closer, afraid a tree might fall on her.

It had seemed so simple to go down and speak to him, but now she didn't know how to approach the processor. When she saw the destruction down toward the river, she became frightened of the driver, although that was not sensible. He was only a man in a yellow helmet.

She hadn't realized how quickly it all went. The machine would soon have crept toward Starhill.

When they can't get the hemp they won't stay long, someone had said, getting a laugh. In some places, people were pleased the company was clear-felling below Starhill. But many others thought it a pity that the whole mountainside down to the Lobber was to be scraped bare. Would it ever grow again after replanting? It was so high up. Frost and sun would scorch it. What would happen to the pastures when the forest no longer protected them?

Dan had written that the company had asked the police to help evict them from Starhill. He would come then, he said. Annie had imagined dogs, Alsatians, police in coveralls with harnesses and guns in holsters, Mia terrified. She could picture them marching off with the goats behind them and the children crying. But Petrus had said they were only warning shots. The company didn't want things written about them in the papers.

Now they had begun clear-felling instead. It went quickly and the change was so violent, it was incomprehensible, although it was happening right in front of her nose. At close quarters the sound was terrifying. Perhaps elk were standing there, just as she was. Bears. Perhaps creatures were standing listening between the spruces farther up. She hadn't imagined the felling to be like this. She had thought it would be all right to go up and speak to someone and that there would be more than one of them. Now she had to keep moving on the edge of the forest and wait for the driver. Her face began to grow stiff with cold.

Suppose she got frostbite? Suppose the only result of this trip was frostbite? Perhaps he wouldn't even speak to her. She hadn't even considered that he might feel solidarity with the company. She hadn't said a word to Petrus and Önis about what she planned to do. She couldn't cope with discussions. There was nothing to discuss. There was only the weight in her belly, growing greater every day.

She skied around and around the felling area, clambering on the uneven ground between the spruces, often pausing to rub her mouth and cheeks.

He finally stopped the machine, and the silence was like a collapse. Some time went by before she noticed she could hear the water again. The driver was climbing down, clumsy in his padded jacket, tough working trousers, and steel-capped boots. When he got down to the ground, he lowered his head and stood looking at her.

She skied over to him, but when she tried to speak, her lips were so stiff, she had to rub them first.

"I'd like to ask you something."

He said nothing, but stood unhooking his chin strap and taking off his helmet, revealing a lined leather hood underneath it. He was a large man with small, close-set eyes. He was probably dark and presumably quite strong, perhaps fat. But it was hard to see. He nodded and headed off toward the bridge. She didn't know whether he meant she should follow him and made a few hesitant movements with her ski sticks. He turned around and looked at her. No doubt he thought she would follow him.

She skied behind him across the bridge. It looked like some military arrangement. The old bridge lay tipped over on the side of the road. There was a car parked there, and a blue trailer with the company logo on it.

"Come on into the hut," he said. "Looks as if you've frozen your face."

She went in after him and cautiously rubbed her cheeks. It was warm in the trailer. A gas heater was alight and there was a bunk, two chairs, and a hardboard table with a newspaper and a coffee cup on it. He took out an aluminum lunch box and lit a gas ring. Annie sat down on one of the chairs and unzipped her jacket.

When he took off his leather hood, she recognized him. She didn't know what his name was, but he was one of the men who had come into

Lennartsson's fishing store on Midsummer Eve. He had snapped off Ola Lennartsson's flagpole. His brown hair was sweaty and curly. He made coffee, scarcely looking up as he did so.

"I'm from Starhill," she said, but she could see that the information was superfluous. She was wearing the pale blue quilted jacket Henny had left behind for her, thinking it made her look like a tourist. But there were no tourists in early January. And there was no other car parked by the bridge apart from his.

"I was going to ask you if you would take me and my daughter down to the village," she said. "And our belongings."

He said nothing, just went on pouring measures of coffee into the pot.

"Though I didn't realize you had only a car here. I thought there was a tractor. We can hear the sound all the way up there."

"Be all right with t'scooter," he said. "And t'sled. I could bring that up. On Saturday. When I'm free."

"I'll pay you, of course."

"No need," he said.

He poured out the coffee and gave her a slice of brown bread and liver pâté. There was a pickled gherkin pressed into the pâté. She wondered who had packed his lunch box for him. It contained meatballs and macaroni.

"Do you think you could phone Aagot Fagerli for me?" she said. "Ask her if I may rent her cottage by the road."

"Then she'd better put the electric heating on this evening," he said.

He didn't ask her about anything, but nonetheless she thought she ought to explain.

"I'm going to have a child," she said.

That only embarrassed him. He bent over his lunch box, eating rapidly.

"I daren't have a child up there. If anything should happen. I thought I'd wait at Aagot Fagerli's until the time is nearer, then go to Östersund."

It was getting darker. She had no great desire to go out into the cold again, but she had to hurry away before it grew too dark. She thanked him for the coffee. He said nothing.

"See you on Saturday, then?"

What if he doesn't come? she thought. What if I'm standing there with everything packed and Petrus and Önis are miserable and angry?

"You're sure you can come?" she said.

Yes, he would come. And before he left on Saturday morning, he would go and light the stove in the cottage.

And we thought he was the Enemy, she reflected as she made her way back up toward Starhill in the failing light. The company lackeys, Dan called people like him. I've gone over to the Enemy. She snorted. It wasn't often she laughed at herself; perhaps hardly anyone ever did. It was as if a lid of cold and ill temper had been lifted that day, a winter's day like any other. But it was the Day. She realized that; the standstill was over.

TWO

He hadn't woken properly and was feeling no unease, only desire. It came over him as he lay half asleep and turned into a dream. He was trying to nudge his way into her, cautiously nosing his way in. They were lying in front of a hot, crackling stove. From the base of his swollen, stubby member, desire radiated like the current from a small battery. But he knew he must go carefully and take it easy. The concentrated and at the same time delimited pleasure woke him.

He must have been dreaming about the first time, when there had been fear in her, as if those thin membranes and tensed muscles contained a memory. What had happened to her? He had never been given any answer, and it was all so long ago now.

He wished she would call back but did not want to hear the phone ringing. It was her voice he wanted, her voice close to his ear. Her lips, really. Those warm lips and her warm breath.

The leaves of the birches were glowing now in the sun outside her window. In his room the light was penetrating between the slats of the venetian blind. He slid back down into sleep, and it didn't seem to him that he slept long. But when he woke up it was half past seven.

She had phoned early in the morning and almost whispered that she had seen the boy who one Midsummer night long ago ran past her on the path to the Lobber. And perhaps toward that tent.

Birger didn't believe it. Not for a moment. Time must have changed the boy, and besides, he was a foreigner. Why would he turn up in Blackwater almost two decades later? She had seen a face, a face reminding her of the boy's. Maybe not even that. A feeling had come over her, like dreams or visions in a half-awake state. Déjà vu?

A dream and a delusion. He wished she were there with him. Now.

It struck him that she had called before five. Whom could she have seen at that hour? Had she been out? He had talked to her last thing before he fell asleep. They had said good night. That had been past eleven. It had been her term end, she had been tired and was going straight to sleep.

As he reached out for the telephone, it rang. He was so convinced it was her that he cried:

"Annie!"

"Hurry, please come! She's bleeding! She's bleeding!"

An avalanche of words, in the local dialect intermingled with guttural Arabic *schsch* sounds. It took him a while to make any sense of it. At first he thought the man was talking about Annie. Then he remembered there had been a fight in the refugee camp on Friday night and he thought it had started up again. But it was only Ahmed from the food takeaway. He had nothing to do with the camp and would never go there. He minded his own business.

"Leila's bleeding! You must come."

"Phone the health center," Birger said, trying to sound decisive, but of course the man took no notice. Birger had to set off for the apartment above the kebab takeaway to make sure she went. Ahmed's wife was four months pregnant.

"Nothing to worry about," he said to calm him down, though he wasn't sure.

Another torrent of words. They had made Ahmed stop offering his Dish of the Day. He had been fined. Leila had been scared and had had a miscarriage.

"You won't get a miscarriage from fines," said Birger. "But you might get paranoia. You should have stuck to kebabs."

"They talk about me like a dirty pig and Leila cries all day, all night. About our kitchen."

"No, they don't. You need to have permission. You have to have showers for the staff and this and that. Fans and things. I don't think Leila will have a miscarriage. She'll be given injections and will have to lie still for a while. It'll be all right."

That was his message. Always. Did he believe it?

The asphalt was already hot as he walked across the square in

Byvången from the kebab takeaway, once a haberdasher's, to his own place. It had taken some time to get Leila away, and now he had to shave and change, because he was due at Life Core to sit through a seminar on health care. If he hadn't been billed as a speaker himself, he would have chucked the whole thing in and gotten into his car. The Blackreed road took an hour. Now he would have to wait until the afternoon.

He showered, and while the coffee was brewing he thought about phoning her, when he remembered she had said she couldn't talk.

She had someone there. That was why she hadn't phoned. Or wasn't she at home? But where would she have gone? Or driven? There was something odd about it all, something that didn't fit, was inexplicable. Most of all, it was quite unlike her.

At first he listened to the councillor, who was a Social Democrat but wearing Levi jeans and a white Lacoste polo shirt. As usual, he was promising to sell the community. But he didn't mean for good. He wasn't thinking of disposing of it to Germany or the Cellulose Company. He was going to sell it the way you sell a beautiful girl.

He went on to talk about health and lifestyle. He didn't say "the EC" or "Europe" quite so often as he had a year before, nor did he use the expression "quality of life." He implied that the lifestyle in their district was health-promoting. He talked about water and snow and air, about forests and mountains and streams. He didn't mention diabetes, back trouble, or coronaries, nor had he brought any suicide statistics.

Later came a lecture on the mucus membranes of the mouth. In a nutshell, people were as healthy as their mouths looked. Birger was irritated by the speaker's using the word "diagnostics," which was inappropriate. After the inside of the mouth, they were given coffee, tea, or herbal tea. Life Core was no longer as orthodox as it had been when it was called Byvången Health Home. It was a modern conference hotel and had gone bankrupt in April, but they continued their activities. Birger had cheesecake and coffee.

He spoke after coffee, looking over the audience's already tired faces and ice cream colored clothes. Many of them were wearing Life Core T-shirts with the halved red apple on the chest. He could feel expectation in the air. Ah, here's the doctor who's usually so amusing.

But he wasn't. As soon as he got up on the rostrum, he felt he was falling. His ears closed and for a moment he thought he had gone deaf. But they must have heard him through the microphone, because no one complained, the faces gleaming like empty bulletin boards at him. He had no idea what he said.

At first he only slowly recognized the feeling—faintness, nausea, paralysis, and mechanical behavior. He talked and talked, unable to remember when he had felt like this before or how he could know what it was. It was fear, great fear.

Again and again he had to sip the mineral water. His mouth was dry and he thought his voice was disappearing. Thirty minutes. Then there was to be a discussion. He postponed it, saying he had to go and phone about a patient, cunning even in the midst of panic. He stood with his mobile phone in an empty studio and let it ring ten, fifteen, twenty times. Tried again. But she didn't answer.

He couldn't understand why he hadn't realized something was wrong before. She ought to have answered. She wasn't going anywhere because she was expecting him. He had promised to come the moment the seminar was over.

He ran out to the car, shouting to the receptionist that he had to go out on call and wouldn't be back in time.

The Blackreed road. What if he had never gone that winter evening? Would there have been another time? He didn't think so, though he couldn't explain why.

It was called chance. If it hadn't been for that abdominal case. He had forgotten what the patient's name was, but he had lived in Tangen and was a suspected case of peritonitis.

If he had gone back with the ambulance, would they ever have become close?

The phone had rung while they were having a meal. He had invited the chief education officer with his wife and two others, he couldn't remember who. And that was only six years ago. So how could she, after almost twenty years, recognize a face she had seen for only a few moments? In bad light.

He did remember the chocolates they had brought with them, whoever they had been. He could still see a blue box with gold edging and the queen's face on it, lying on the coffee table by the vase of pink carnations. He had been called to the phone just as they were about to sit down, and when he went back, he said:

"An abdominal case."

There had been no time to warm up the car. He had cooked a Chinese meal. They had remained seated around the table with lighted candles and the carnations he had bought at the supermarket, lonely guests, as the Blackreed road swallowed up the car and the first house in Tuvallen glimmered. They had eaten and chatted while he raced on.

Houses, people, and villages lay curled up and dying in the dark. Pink nylon curtains against rotting cottage timbers, rubbish heaps, and wrecks of cars. And the darkness. One of the Finns clearing the Tingnäs stretch had said it was called Kaamos, the winter days of no light.

Kaamos takes us.

An abdomen. Mustn't take any risks. Just drive there and feel it.

An abdomen in Blackwater—an hour's drive in both directions. The lake had the same name as the village, or was it the other way around, and it was as black as ink on winter evenings. He raced on in the Volvo. The lake would keep its name after the last cottage had rotted away, and then it would exist without a name. Not very pleasant thoughts; sometimes he had them, sometimes not, as he drove by in the dark. The forest was grayish-black and even the snow seemed dark, swirling like a broom into the headlights. The outside light in individual farms shone white, a small crescent in the deathly dark.

Occasionally he wondered how depressed he had really been on evenings like that. Perhaps he ought to have taken something. He had prescribed for Barbro, but that hadn't helped.

It was the miscarriage. No, it was the felling. She caught fire. There are people like that. In hell. He had often been too tired, from chasing around palpating abdomens and listening to hearts. He was too tired; he had no energy for anything when he got home, and he had an underbite and a nerdy pair of sandals.

It was Frances. Barbro had thought he was impotent, and that was just as well. With Monica it was another matter. You couldn't even call that a failure. Something unreal, that's all, something that hardly happened, although they drove to Ikea and bought a whole trailer full of stuff. And turned the workshop into a doctor's office for small animals.

In Barbro's day he used to talk about the district and say that the solitary houses were full of warmth and secret life, that they held their own and people were courageous and civilized inside their cottages with their shimmering blue screens and illuminated indoor plants. But that was long ago now. The darkness had begun to bloody devour him after Barbro had gone. Well, he had had the car radio.

After an hour he could see the first lights of Blackwater. He stopped outside the store and let Bonnie out, though some people were annoyed with him for letting a dog pee there. Then he drove up to the nearest house and asked, because he wasn't quite sure where the people who had phoned lived. He had stopped relying on telephoned instructions.

This time he had to go out to Tangen. Dogs started barking as soon as he got out of the car. The whole of Tangen was barking. A woman came out on the steps and stood waiting with her arms folded. The snow was thinning out a bit. When he got inside, there was a smell of animals, dog and cat and unwashed human beings. The abdominal case lay at the very back of a room at the end of a passage lined with overloaded shelves. It was like going into a cave. He lifted the striped flannel nightshirt. The abdomen was taut and the whites of the man's eyes were showing.

Birger went out with Bonnie and trudged around in the fresh snow waiting for the ambulance. The sky had blown itself clean and stars had come out.

He went back in to check on the patient and then sat down at the kitchen table to read the local paper. He kept refusing coffee. He knew it would be pale and acid, and coffee that had boiled always made him feel sick. But he gave in in the end, accepted some and a piece of bread with slices of sausage on it. He was given a plastic box of cloudberry preserve. She said he should take it home and put it in the freezer.

Then the ambulance came and got stuck in the snowdrift down the drive, so he went out to help shovel. When it finally got away, he was soaked with sweat, but by the time he got his own car started again, he was frozen stiff.

Now he would be seeing it all backward. Röbäck, Offerberg, Lersjövik, Laxkroken, Tuvallen, and finally Byvången. His guests, of course, would still be sitting around the low table. He hoped they had helped themselves to brandy as he had told them.

As he drove past the Blackwater school, he saw a light in the basement and realized the sauna was on. He thought how good it would be to wash off all that icy sweat and get really warm, to relax on the wooden slats and have a chat with one of the old men and perhaps be offered a beer.

His guests would know nothing except that he was very late. They would go home. They would probably do the dishes for him and the chocolates they had brought with them would still be on the coffee table when he got back. He was so damned tired.

There was a pile of clothes on a bench, but no one in the washroom. He had neither soap nor towel, but he borrowed some shampoo out of a bottle on the floor and washed himself from top to toe. When the heat from the little sauna struck him, he closed his eyes with pleasure and later realized he must have grunted. He climbed up as high as he could, so high he could feel his bottom scorching. Then he saw who was sitting there. Rosy and naked.

"Oh, sorry!" he cried, and was about to rush out, but she just laughed. She was sitting on a towel and she picked up a corner of it and placed it across the very modest pale red tuft of hair in her groin. The teacher. Annie Raft. That person. He hadn't seen her since Aagot Fagerli's funeral. On that occasion she had been wearing a black coat and even a little hat. There had been a kind of old-fashioned dignity about her which he couldn't quite reconcile with all the crap he'd heard about her over the years.

He held his hands crossed over his penis, which in any case lay nice and wrinkled, just where it should. He must have looked very foolish, but her laughter was not malicious. As he made his way sideways toward the door, explaining he thought it was the men's day, she said he could stay.

"They've changed the times. The men hardly ever use it. Only people from the south, during the shooting season. I don't think anyone'll come. I'm usually on my own at this late hour."

He could see rosy patches all over her skin, and her breasts were pink around the brownish-pink nipples, smooth from the heat. He wondered if they would contract when she went out into the cold. He confessed to having borrowed some of her shampoo, and she said:

"So we both smell the same now."

Then she got up and went out, which he thought was a bloody great stroke of luck because he could feel he was getting a hardon. It came on so violently, it must have been preparing itself while he had been looking at her sideways, but he had felt nothing then. But when she said that about their smell and at the same time turned her back to him, that finished him. He closed his eyes and breathed out. At that moment she came back in again with a scoop in her hand and flung some water on the sauna stones. Hot steam billowed up and for a moment they couldn't see each other. But then it was obvious. He tried to hide it all behind his hands and said:

"Sorry, sorry . . ."

She gave a little laugh, a teasing look, then went out again, only to return just as rapidly.

"Quick," she said, flinging a towel at him. "Out you go."

He thought he would have a heart attack as he tumbled into the relative cool of the washroom. She pushed him over to the lavatory door and shoved him inside. His clothes followed, and finally his shoes.

"Lock the door!"

He did so without understanding. Then he heard women's voices. They must be undressing in the room outside. He rinsed himself down with water from the basin and thrust his fingers through his hair for lack of a comb. He wanted to look good. He knew he would go back with her now. He didn't know how he could have known that, but he did actually know.

He could hear the women showering and chatting away to each other as he dried himself with his undershirt and put on the rest of his clothes. Once the women had gone into the sauna, Annie had drummed lightly on the door. He opened up and they slipped out, she close behind him.

It turned out just as he had known and realized. She left the kick-sled at the school. Some of the embers in the fire were still glowing back at her house. She had a large Lapp-hound cross that barked at him. Bonnie had to stay in the car.

She gave him tea and sandwiches at first and everything went very calmly. He felt it was right that this should be so, and they had a lot to talk about. He wanted to ask her a great many things. About Aagot. About the school. And why she had come back to Blackwater. She laughed a little at his eagerness and said they would have to take one thing at a time. When she got up and cleared the dishes away, he followed her, grabbed her from behind, and steered her over toward the warmth of the fire. Her hair was short and it was easy to find the nape of her neck. The first place he kissed her was the back of the neck. He could feel the knob on her top vertebrum very clearly and he was overcome with a tenderness for her so great that tears came to his eyes.

"So much has happened," he murmured. "So many years."

So much loneliness, he thought. He knew she had been living with that gutless worm Göran Dubois for a couple of years. And that she had been some kind of almost official fiancée to Roland Fjellström. But he also knew, and could feel it in the tension of her deltoid muscle, how lonely it had been. How long the winters. How light the sleepless summer nights. How she had sat reading for hours in the little room that had now been extended with a bedroom section. In Aagot's sister's day they had done the baking in there.

"If you put a couple of decent logs on now, it'll burn for a while," he said. She had electric heat, but confessed she didn't want to be without the fire.

"How do you manage for wood?"

"I buy it. I get help with the chopping, too. Björne Brandberg is my household gnome."

"Is that since that time?"

She nodded. Then he saw she was crying quietly and he was sure she had not cried over the dead child for a very long time. Perhaps not for years. It's thawing inside us, he thought. In me, too. A whole lot of longing.

She insisted on changing the sheets. It was almost solemn. Then he undressed before she did. She had already seen him naked, but he asked all the same.

"Do you think I'm too fat?"

"I think you're nice and plump."

Because of that they fell into bed laughing, she dressed and he naked. It was much less long-winded than his peculiar turns with the Östersund ladies whom he had had to give expensive perfumes or—even worse—take out to starchy dinners at the Winn Hotel.

He was fascinated by the red hair on the mound between her thighs, not stiff and curly but as soft as silk. She was worried it was thinning out. He examined her everywhere with fingers she maintained were short and stubby. He asked her about a scar on her shin and looked carefully at the white streaks on her belly. He wanted to know whether she had had an easy delivery when she gave birth to Mia, and he confessed there were a whole lot of questions he had wanted to ask her at the time, when she had come to see him. But he hadn't dared, for they were things that had nothing to do with him. Not at that time.

"Now we're going to do this," he said, very gently parting her legs. "In a moment, you'll be as good as engaged to me."

He realized she hadn't done it for a very long time and that she was slightly scared, physically scared that he would go too far in and be too rough. But he had no desire to be rough. She was small inside and only slowly became moist.

Yes, there was fear in her. A flash of furious rage went through him as he thought about Dubois and Fjellström and that incredible shit Ulander. But he realized he should put aside all such thoughts, all thinking, for that matter, to make it good for them both.

Then she seemed to melt inside and start flowing. They kissed hazily and moistly and he forgot to be careful, forgot everything he had thought out for her sake. He stopped thinking, and so did she. She whimpered occasionally and he turned her quickly, pleased that he was strong, and it was all so intensely wonderful, he was just about to come. But then he heard their breathing, out of step, and thought about his haunches going up and down, and she noticed he was thinking about something and asked what it was. All he said was what a peculiar activity it really was.

"I'm chief medical officer of the District Health Authority, did you know that? Here's you, lying whimpering under me, and I'm doing everything I can to make you whimper and gasp and the best I can do about it is this . . . and this . . . and this . . ."

Then it was all over, but she just laughed.

"I think I'm dreaming," he said as he lay on his back.

"Never mind. You'll still be chief medical officer of the District Health Authority when you wake up."

There was a space between the bed and the wall, and he was lying with his arm out, wondering why she had arranged the furniture so oddly. He felt with his hand and found something cold and metallic. Then wood. Fine, dense wood. A butt. He had to look.

"Do you keep a shotgun here?"

"Always," she said.

"A fine ol' gun," he said when he hauled it out. "Real nice, little ol' lady's gun. What do you shoot with it? Hares?"

They fell asleep, forgetting to put more wood on the fire. When they woke he said "Hell!" because he had only just remembered Bonnie. The car would be cold by now, so he had to bring Bonnie in and they both hoped it would be all right. But the two dogs immediately started fighting. He tried to separate them by pulling Bonnie's hind legs, but almost got bitten by the other dog. Annie filled a pan with water to pour over them, but he took it away from her. In the turmoil of growls, sharp barks, and threatening snarls, he pulled her back into the bedroom again and closed the door.

"To hell with them," he said. "They can't kill each other. Bonnie's stronger, but the other one's more aggressive. They'll give up when they find that out."

"I think Saddie would fight to the death," said Annie. But it was already calmer beyond the closed door and they lay down on the bed again. It was just as he had said; the dogs would have to get used to this.

He liked remembering that evening, the whole of that winter evening and night, and when he recounted it to himself in his mind, he browsed through it in images. Images of chocolates on the coffee table, the roses of warmth on her breasts, the ambulance jammed in the snowdrift as if trying to hide, the tense abdomen under a gray-striped nightshirt, the stars, the bulletin board beside the general store with its schedule of evening classes and advertisements for bingo in Norway. But he realized he had amalgamated images from a great many journeys in the winter darkness on the Blackreed road, the abdomen one of dozens, perhaps one of hundreds of sore and distended abdomens he had palpated in musty bedrooms. He couldn't be sure he remembered correctly even when it came to the house and the woman and the cloudberry preserve. It had all happened. But it had happened all too many times. Image had been superimposed upon image; the memories of that evening were precious, and he had amalgamated them with care. Perhaps he had taken some of them from elsewhere, from other long journeys and other dark, glimmering, somnolent, and dying villages beside ice-covered or jet-black water.

And what did she remember? A face she had only glimpsed before it vanished in the uncertain night light. A boy. A dark head of hair and an expression. Of What? Agitation perhaps. Or excitement? Birger couldn't remember exactly what she had said. And she could see nothing but a blurred patch in her memory where that face was supposed to be. Someone had filled it in for her. Wishful thinking?

The summer day was hot now, the light drab as he drove along the gravelly, frost-damaged Blackreed road. He was driving too fast, not a habit of his. He was annoyed with health freaks who disapproved of plaque and obesity, but tolerated twenty dead in the weekend war on the roads. At Offerberg a pothole made him hit the roof and there was a bang from the chassis. Again and again he dialed Annie's number. Still no reply.

When he got to Blackwater, there were a lot of cars and people by the store, which was just closing. Norwegians had been shopping for the weekend and were coming out with sausage rings, cartons of cigarettes, and boxes of snuff. He drove through the village looking straight ahead to escape being stopped. He could see the little white house on its ledge below the ridge. As usual, nothing was moving up there. That was normal.

He drove up to the house and sat waiting for a few seconds. The kitchen window gleamed. From the door handle hung a plastic bag with something inside it. He saw a thermos and a plastic box as he went up the steps. The door was locked.

He knocked a few times. Although she was rather deaf, Saddie ought to have heard him by then, and he was somehow cheered by the fact that she had Saddie with her. That seemed normal. He realized he must have gone over the top when he rushed away from Life Core like that. He had also acquired a headache.

He had no keys with him. They were still at his apartment, but he knew she kept a key hanging in the woodshed. He fetched it and went in.

There was a strong smell of flowers in the kitchen, mostly lily-of-the-valley. Fat little bunches of them from the end-of-term ceremonies stood on the table, the worktop, and in both windows.

There were two used mugs on the table, a sugar bowl, and a bread basket. No jam. The cheese was in its plastic bag on the worktop. There were crumbs on the tablecloth. It looked as if she had just been clearing away.

She had had tea with someone, then gone out. He felt the teapot. It was cold, no tea in it, only a thick layer of used tea leaves at the bottom.

In the living room he saw that Saddie had rucked up the rug under the coffee table and lain on it. There were more flowers in there. Annie's bed had been made. For a moment, he sensed her loneliness just as strongly as when he had gone there for the first time.

We damn well ought to be married!

That suddenly broke through, and it was true. Though he had always agreed with her that things were best this way.

But he hadn't wanted it like this. Perhaps it was right for her, but he wanted to be married to her, to live with her, and he had wanted that all the time. To have her. He oughtn't to have left her alone in a house with no neighbors. With that damned Sabela she maintained she could load in twenty-two seconds.

It was panic. He recognized it. He suddenly remembered squatting down above Westlund's and shitting his guts out. Out of pure terror.

That was long ago now, almost twenty years. That affair up by the Lobber, although half forgotten and wiped out of their conscious minds, still had power over them. Annie's whispering voice had sounded frightened. And now she had infected him.

He felt calmer once he had realized that. He went out into the shower room and found some Alka-Seltzer. As it fizzed in the bathroom glass, he put water for coffee on the electric plate. It was too hot to light the stove. It looked as if it had rained on her newly sown bit of land, but the moisture had long since evaporated from the grass. No midges yet, no stingers, and hardly any mosquitoes. She was spending her first free day doing what she had longed to do. She was walking. Not far, presumably, because Saddie was with her. The dog had bad hip joints and could no longer go uphill. Annie had taken the car and perhaps driven up. But she had forgotten the thermos of coffee she had prepared.

She wasn't far away and he would wait for her. It looked like a fine, warm evening. He opened a window in the living room. The smell of decaying lilies-of-the-valley bothered him.

man and a woman were skiing
east down the mountainside and it was raining. The snow was transparent
and crackled around their skis; the rain was light, whipping in squalls on
the wind. Their faces were wet, the rain not pouring down but flying
toward them.

The snow was shrinking. The streams, silent all winter, were now
rippling loudly. They had to walk long stretches over the mountain heath,
carrying their skis on their shoulders. They came down to the river and
crossed it on an arched bridge of ice and packed snow. He held his breath
as he heard the water rushing below.

She was pregnant and he was so delighted he had shouted aloud as
they raced downhill. They had been moving with the patches of sun all
morning, chasing them over the mountain but never really catching up
with them. He had shown her an old place of sacrifice. He wanted to show
her everything. That was why they were back home. When she had un-
hesitatingly taken a steep downhill run, he had sounded like his grandfather:

"Now, now . . ."

He was careful with her. All kinds of things he had never thought of
before now occurred to him, as well as a great deal he had only heard
talked about. The darkness of Sami tents, warning yelps from dogs, and
bear spears. He wanted to protect her with dog, spear, and bearskins, and
he laughed out loud at himself from sheer exhilaration.

To him, this was home. He realized that it always had been. It was a place he could describe only in this way. It had no name and roamed like a patch of sun between shadows of clouds when he started thinking about it. But they were racing around in it now. He wanted her to be in it.

He thought about the baby that was not yet a baby. She didn't even want him to say "the baby." Not yet. "The fetus" sounded too clinical, but he hadn't had to say that either. She had understood his half-question and assured him it wasn't harmful to move, to go skiing. Despite obvious discomforts, she was secure in her early motherhood. But as she skied across the bridge of hard-packed snow and hollowed ice, she had no inkling of the power of the water beneath her, the cold, or the savage force of the current below.

Naturally the water had a name. The river was called something it hadn't always been called. He didn't feel like saying it. It had its name in the other language, too, older but not as old as the water.

The sound of the water between the stones had existed and still existed, with not a single night's interruption, as long as could be imagined: always. The cold could force it down to a noise under the ice, the cold that felled birds in flight, that killed an old man and his old dog in a badly insulated cottage down by the river's mouth. He had told her about it, a story so old that the cold was the central character, not the old man. Even beavers had probably died then. That was long ago, so far away. New ones had come shuffling along, burying their noses into the muddy tussocks and beginning to dig. But their territory was still as much as half a meter beneath the two of them. Across the snow they traversed the animals' passages and holes.

"This place really belongs to the beavers," he said.

But it wasn't a place. It was events. She had been part of some of them as a child. He would tell her others. There were things to keep silent about, too. They were not going to pass the spot where the Dutch had had their tent. Did she know about it?

They had fastened their skis to their boots, Johan's own old wooden ones, and Väine's. He had found them in the cookhouse and managed to round up three ski poles for them. They had made their way up, but for long stretches they had slithered on the scrub and moss. The night was light and there was snow up toward Bear Mountain. The river waters roared beneath the bridge of ice.

They came back to Nirsbuan. At first he had thought of stopping overnight there and getting up in the morning blinded by the light as green buds on the birches burst out. But a musty puff of air had hit them as the door opened and they realized it wasn't possible. A blanket on the bed lay entangled with some grubby sheets. He ripped them off so that Mia shouldn't see them, revealing a foam-rubber mattress yellowish-brown with age and full of peculiar holes. Maybe mice had taken bits of it down into their nests. A filthy towel hung on a nail by the stove, the name Hotel Winn unfortunately still visible. What kind of people will she think we are? he thought. That was the first time in eighteen years he had thought of the Brandbergs as "we."

He had gotten the stove going but realized they couldn't lie on that damp, evil-smelling mattress. But someone had. Someone had been living there, he could tell from the food in the cupboard, the new battery radio, the dates on the newspapers. Someone who wasn't there at the moment but who had recently fried pork in the cast iron pan and left a layer of fat on the bottom.

The raw cold had driven Mia out of the cottage. She was sitting on the steps, her legs apart, her face raised to the sun and the moist wind. Sounds began to rise from the marshland below, an exhilarated babble rising and falling. Maybe it was the last of the late night and early morning delirium; the sound rose now as if trying to stop the light putting an end to the intoxication of the spring night.

She said she had been six when she had heard it for the first time. She hadn't understood what it was at the time. She still thought it sounded feverish, inhuman. And yet like singing or cries.

"The marsh is rutting," he said.

They listened for a while over their coffee and then walked across the river and the marshes toward the place where they slaughtered reindeer, their faces turned up to the mild drizzle. They could still hear the black-cocks when they got to the parking lot.

He had tried once before. That attempt had also been unpremeditated. He had been in Östersund, had three days free and was going to go home to Langvasslien. In the evening he had felt like driving across the border to Blackwater. It was a long way around, and he might have had the notion of staying the night.

He regretted it as soon as he got to Tuvallen, but by then it was too late. The road was deserted, it was January and very cold. The forest was nothing but white wall with black streaks on either side, the road a tunnel in the beam of his headlights. He had met no one since leaving Laxkroken. If his engine packed in, he would freeze to death.

It didn't, of course. He got to Blackwater and parked the car a little way away from the store, leaving the engine running as he went to look at the bulletin board. These days it was illuminated, otherwise just the same. The thermometer on the wall by the mailbox said almost thirty degrees below zero. It was half past eleven at night, not a light in a single window and nothing moving on the road. Of course not.

As he got back into the car, he noticed a light on the other side of the lake. Not still. An uneasy light up on the Brandberg slope. Must be a strong light to be visible across the lake. It seemed to him to be crawling.

Then he remembered Gudrun had told him that Torsten and Per-Ola had bought processors and together they had formed a company. She had been defiantly proud of that development and things had gone well for them. Per-Ola was go-ahead and not afraid of large loans, and Väine was to work for them as well. But he wasn't a partner in the company.

"Don't you go thinking I won't make sure of your rights," she had said, touching in her determined eagerness. She always insured his rights. She explained that he would inherit from Torsten and with that a share in the company. He needn't be afraid of losing anything by the formation of the company.

No, he wasn't afraid. He didn't think he had any right to inherit from Torsten. But he didn't say so. The processor hadn't become real to him until he found himself sitting in the car watching the play of that crawling light far up on the mountainside.

That must be it. Per-Ola and Väine working despite the cold night, presumably working in shifts. If they let it stand still, they couldn't pay the interest.

Twenty-seven degrees below zero. The white light crept along the mountain slope, playing jerkily across the falling trees. The machine up there must be roaring and creaking, but nothing could be heard across the silent white lake.

Crawling light. Crawling over all that sleeping life. All that shitty life that didn't deserve the warmth. Didn't deserve the song, the playing, and the water. Not even leaves.

It's the hatred in me that crawls in the forest, he thought. I am a part owner of a processor. It has to be worked day and night, winter and summer. It costs money, it costs lives. The hero in the driver's seat with his head beneath the stars is working harder than I have ever worked. I'm nothing but a part owner. It's the hatred in me crawling along up there.

He had driven away from the streetlights that had appeared since he was a boy, and on into the darkness on the Norwegian side. He had been afraid of the cold, afraid of his engine failing. But he got away from there.

This time he had made another attempt and it had gone well. Quite well, for he had avoided the house. It worried him that Gudrun might hear on the grapevine that he had been in the village with Mia Raft. He thought of phoning and explaining as soon as he got back to Östersund. That it was an experiment, and had been done on an impulse. More or less.

Two or three times a year, Gudrun traveled to Trondheim to see him, usually dressed in her best and fairly wrought up. Each time he saw her, she had aged a little. She had some kind of trembling in her hands. She was fifty-six now and dyed her hair black. Johan no longer knew much about her troubles and nothing at all about her everyday life. He had to assume that much was the same as before, though things had gone well for Torsten. He had several diggers now, a crusher on the other side of the lake, and a new gravel pit up by Torsberget. Gudrun's clothes were not cheap, and she still drove an Audi. It was new and it was obvious it was her own.

As Johan was sitting in the car waiting for Mia, he looked up toward the house. He could see the kitchen window, the curtains drawn so far across, it must have been almost impossible to look out. Or look in, so perhaps that was the intention. He presumed she was in there moving between stove, refrigerator, and sink. The treadmill. Though he knew she had a dishwasher.

He was waiting for Mia. It had gone well. If it hadn't been so filthy and cold at Nirsbuan, and there been so little wood, he could have stayed another day. Mia had suggested he should go on up to Gudrun and Torsten to get a few hours' sleep. But he drew the line at that. He had driven her up to her mother's cottage, which he still thought of as Aagot Fagerli's, and he had slept in the car.

She was asleep, her cheek rounded and shiny with cream, her eyelashes faintly reddish without mascara. He thought his own thoughts when she was asleep.

She was very sleepy in the evenings now that she was pregnant. It didn't matter to her if he kept the light on and lay reading. She slept like a child. When she was awake she was very sensible. He reckoned she felt very much at home in the world, that she understood it.

Alone with the lamp lighting up her slightly curly, auburn hair, he felt for the threads that bound her so profoundly to him. Previously he had been turned on like lightning and lived in a state of mild intoxication for a few weeks, particularly in the summer. But since he had grown up, his relations with women had been sensible, at heart perhaps amused. Both ways.

Mia was sensible, and they took it lightheartedly even when desire made them dizzy. She rapidly sobered up again. It amused him that she was always planning—outings, maternity leave, work projects. But he liked it. He liked her strong will, as fresh as a clean nut in a young, green but already hardening shell.

There were other things. Finer threads down among the feelings he found difficult to put into words. Then again, it could be expressed brutally simply: When he met Mia it had seemed to him that she had come to take him home.

That was an unattractive thought, but it was there and it worked. Telling her about it, even implying it, would be injudicious. He didn't want Mia to feel like a tool. Nor was she. She was a prerequisite.

When she was asleep, the room turned slightly alien. She had a poster on the wall above the bed with a face and a name on it he didn't recognize, a black singer in mirrored sunglasses. A hat hung over the reading lamp as an extra shade, black and decorated with large cloth poppies. He had never seen her in a hat and couldn't imagine it on her head. He wondered why she had bought it.

She had been disappointed when he had wanted to drive straight back to Östersund. Eventually she would like to visit Torsten and Gudrun. He could foresee it and knew it would happen. But not yet.

She was disappointed but not cross as they drove away. Mia never sulked. Usually she got her own way, and instinctively knew when she should give in. It had been a lovely day despite the rain in the morning, and naturally it was not tempting to go back to Östersund. He tried to compensate by taking her out to dinner. She said the salmon tasted musty.

It wasn't off, he would have noticed that. When they got home to her place she vomited. She came out of the bathroom looking determined. She was having some troubles but said they would pass.

She fell asleep early, presumably because she hadn't felt well. At about nine he went out and phoned Gudrun. He didn't want Mia to wake and listen to their conversation.

He felt miserable afterward. Gudrun had never suggested he should come home to Blackwater to see them. This time she had made no comment on their visit. He hadn't thought much about these things before. He looked on the Dorjs as his nearest kin. But since he had met Mia he had started thinking that unnatural.

Basically he knew this had nothing to do with naturalness or nature, but with conventions. But it was all part of Mia's worldly wisdom that she had some respect for them. Reasonable respect.

Several of the humorous, sensible, and unconventional women he had taken back home to Langvasslien and given a ride behind his sled dogs had balanced along very narrow planks over rushing water. Over pure chaos.

When he got back, he went to bed and read, but lay there for long spells, looking at her. She was sleeping soundly when the telephone rang. When he woke her and handed her the receiver, she found it difficult to understand what it was all about. It was almost one in the morning. He went out and put on water for tea and made some toast. She usually felt sick when she woke and her stomach was empty. When he brought the tea in, she was still talking, not really saying much, but calming someone. Perhaps succeeding, because in the end she put back the receiver and curled up again.

"Mom's bloke," she said. "Torbjörnsson. She's gone off somewhere without telling him. Now he's half crazy."

She fell asleep again without touching the tea. He lay there wondering how he could get her to move in with him in Trondheim. Strong feelings make us mobile. But he still hadn't dared ask her.

In the middle of the night Birger discovered the shotgun had gone. It was light indoors and he was lying on his back on her bed, still dressed, his head aching fiercely. He had talked to Mia. It was she who had had tea with Annie in the morning. She hadn't been worried. All she said was that her mother had probably taken it into her head to go somewhere.

Mia didn't know what the situation between them was. She had no idea about the telephone calls that morning and evening. She probably thought what was between them was quite practical, an arrangement that secured company for them at weekends and sex without either of them becoming too involved. He had never considered that it might seem like that. It was an unpleasant thought.

For a moment he had considered phoning the police. Then he had stopped thinking about anything for a long time and just waited. He hadn't really been able to eat anything all day. But he kept spreading butter on pieces of thin crispbread and eating them one after the other. The hours went by slowly. Outside, the birds had gone insane. He couldn't understand how she ever got any sleep at all at that time of year.

The kitchen and the living room were still full of fat bunches of flowers the schoolchildren had brought; cowslips, globe flowers and red campion, forget-me-nots with tiny flowers, lilies-of-the-valley, their bells turning brown at the edges. They had plundered the flowerbeds. Even the boys used to bring flowers. They had found wood anemones that had been grotesquely enlarged but still hadn't faded, and they had picked them as if they had a price per kilo on them. And they'd sung to her, sure to have.

They are small religious creatures with no theology, she had once said. They repeat actions without asking themselves what they mean.

But reluctantly, she had been moved and had taken the flowers home. He wanted to throw them out but was afraid that would upset her. They had handed over these fragrances as if apologizing for all the musty odors from their clothes, hair, and mouths throughout a whole winter.

We are releasing you. Be someone else now. Alone and free.

Her happiness, if it existed, was perhaps linked with solitude. He didn't want to know that. But she had never been inconsiderate toward him. Never gone out without telling him where.

Why had he reached down into the space between the bed and the wall? He had had no suspicion, because the discovery sent a physical spasm through him, as if he had walked into an electric fence.

Then he leaped up and started searching everywhere for the gun.

The search party for Mia's mother started up at the Strömgren homestead, where she had left her car. They had found out that her mother really was missing when Birger had phoned in the morning.

They got into the car as soon as they had had some coffee, and when they got to Blackwater several cars were already on their way up. Then everything became slightly more real for Johan. Nonetheless, it mostly seemed very strange to be walking with twenty-meter gaps between them from the road across this half-forgotten but familiar territory, his legs apparently remembering on their own all its hollows and mounds. Advancing inward and upward, calling out the name of a person he had never met and who was going to be his mother-in-law. Grandmother to his child.

"Ann-iiee!" he called out with the others. "Ann-iiee!"

She must be sitting or lying somewhere up toward Fjellström's clearing, perhaps with a broken leg. Per-Ola was organizing them. He was leader of the shoot these days, and the search party consisted largely of the shooting team. Torsten had not joined them. Gudrun said his back was too stiff.

Per-Ola instructed them to call out at long intervals. They had to be able to hear if she replied and had to count on any answering call being faint. But it was difficult to listen for faint sounds, what with people calling and dogs barking. Despite everything, it was all slightly festive, a foretaste of the autumn and the shoot.

Per-Ola had greeted Johan with a nod. His small, light blue eyes had paled slightly and sunk even farther in. His body was stronger. He showed no surprise. Gudrun must have told him about Johan and Mia. She was walking some distance away from them. He had also caught a glimpse of Väine, but not Björne or Pekka. He presumed Pekka was working farther south somewhere. He was a crane driver.

The grass was gleaming as if it were painted. This was the time of year when everything was drawn up to a light that scarcely dulled even at night; the fern spires with their hairy shepherd's crooks, the cornets of may lilies, and the speckly buds of petty spurge. The shoots of the rosebay willowherb tasted like asparagus and were faintly pink.

She had gone to look for morels. Once Birger Torbjörnsson had taken that in, he had started phoning around. She had arranged with a friend to go up toward Fjellström's clearing, now two years old so just right for morels. But when her friend came to pick her up, she had already gone. There must have been some misunderstanding.

Johan called out the unknown woman's name and trudged on. The friend was Gudrun. It was strange for him to find out a little bit of Gudrun's everyday life in this way. All those meetings over the years, stiff conversations in restaurants in Trondheim or by his own coffee table, had not resulted in anything so simple. Gudrun and the teacher out picking morels. Though this time nothing had come of it. The teacher had gone off on her own. "I suppose it was never quite clear which car we were going to take," Gudrun said.

They walked on until the clearing came to an end, and there Per-Ola sent a message down the line that they should veer west and take the rest of the clearing on the way down. Twenty-meter gaps as before.

The ground was rough going, with deep tracks left by the forestry tractors. Up there the birch leaves were still sticky, grooved, and pleated. The brushwood rose in yellowish-green and reddish clouds over the piles of stones and collapsing heaps of scrub.

They were all faintly dispirited when they got down again. No one had any idea where to look next. Per-Ola had inserted a great wedge of snuff and was standing there in silence.

Johan had disturbed a sitting sandpiper and had caught sight of her blue-spotted eggs. He had also found a couple of unusually large morels which he put in his pocket. But he hadn't yet shown them to Mia. It seemed hardly decent to be picking morels and looking at bird's eggs at such a time.

Finally, Per-Ola spat out the snuff and said they should all go back home and get something to eat. Those who were willing could assemble again in two hours' time. Johan stayed by the car with Mia, watching Gudrun leaving in Per-Ola's Ford. She didn't look in their direction. Mia clearly never gave it a thought. Johan was glad he didn't have to explain, but he knew he would have to sooner or later.

There wasn't really anything else to say except what he had told her from the beginning: Relations with his father and brothers had never been good. It had always been like that. Anyhow, he couldn't remember anything different. And it'll always be like that, he thought. Would Mia be able to understand this? Or did she think that everything could be put right as long as you were sensible and looked on the positive side of things? He never really knew how deep her bright matter-of-factness went.

He wondered what her mother was like. Birger Torbjörnsson was standing farther up the road, staring down at the gravel. A woman in a pink jacket was talking eagerly to him, but he looked as if he weren't listening.

In the end, all the cars had driven off except Johan's and Birger Torbjörnsson's. The big, heavy man came slowly over to them.

"Johan?"

"Mia and I are together."

Johan thought it best to get that over with as soon as possible. But Birger made no comment. It might not have sunk in. He was staring down at the ground and looked tired, his hair clammy with sweat.

"I have to talk to you," he said to Mia. "I don't think she went up to the clearing."

It was a peculiar thing to say, because it was he who had given instructions for the search party. Mia also pointed that out. He sat down on the verge and stared down into the gravel, his heavy face closed.

"I don't know," he said. "I haven't slept. I found the bag on the steps. Gudrun had hung it on the door handle when she came. Annie had already left by then. Gudrun thought she had just nipped out on an errand or something. So she hung the bag there."

"What bag?"

"It was a thermos of coffee and buns and so on. And she wrote a note to ask Annie to phone her when she got back. But Annie never did. She seems to have found something else to do."

"But you said Gudrun Brandberg had already gone off in her own car and Annie had followed."

"Yes, I did say that. But I don't know if I think so any longer."

"What *do* you think?"

"I don't know."

They waited for him to go on, but he said nothing more. In the end Mia went and sat in the car.

"Let's go down and get something to eat," she said. "Then we'll have to see."

As Johan was getting into the car, Birger Torbjörnsson took hold of his arm.

"She has a shotgun with her," he said. "I know that, because normally it's always behind her bed."

"Why?"

He didn't reply and Johan didn't know what to say, either.

"Was she depressed?" he asked.

"No, for Christ's sake, there was nothing wrong with her!" Birger burst out. "She was expecting me. I was to go there yesterday afternoon. There was nothing wrong with her!"

"What's the matter?" said Mia from inside the car. But Birger was already on his way over to his own car.

"He didn't sleep at all last night," said Johan.

They drove on down and he said nothing about the shotgun to Mia. Nor did he think he could ask anything. But he would have liked to know what Annie Raft was like and why she kept a gun by her bed when she slept.

On one of the first occasions they had been together, Birger had told Annie what had happened to him at the Sulky. He described the experience as best he could, although he had no name for it. He also told her what the consequences had been, that he had begun to be with Frances afterward and in that way had wrecked his marriage. She had listened without interrupting. After he had finished, she said:

"I don't want to get near the other reality. Even if I could, I wouldn't want to provoke visions and altered states."

He was very surprised. He had expected objections, but of another kind. She accepted his story and that almost disconcerted him. How could she keep a balance between incompatibilities in such an untroubled way?

"I like this reality," she said. "Or the unreality. But I can't dismiss the other. The weave of reality is often loose—I can see through it. I've done that ever since I was a child, and it isn't a frightening experience, though perhaps it ought to be.

"I don't belong here. The surroundings I have ended up in haven't been chosen. Anyhow, not by me. They make me feel affection for what is all around me. Even for human beings sometimes. But mostly for the landscape—and houses."

"A little house like this," she had said as they lay beside each other in the bed in that winter-night dark room. "It can fill me with great affection. It is so fragile and temporary. It might burn down in a couple of hours one night when thunder rumbles over the mountain. But it keeps the fiercest cold out. Did you know we had thirty-six degrees of frost last winter? And it keeps out the rain rattling on its metal roof, furiously on autumn nights. Wait till you hear it."

Wait till you hear it.

That was how he found out that she also thought they would go on being together. He listened carefully in the dark, sensing that the opportunity would not come again so soon. She was seldom as serious as she was now. Ordinarily she wasn't particularly open at all, although she talked a lot.

"We're not alone here," she said. "This place houses a whole lot of creatures. They live here with us. Wasps, flies, beetles, silverfish, and mice. The hawk on the telephone wires by the wall belongs, too, and the stoat living in the foundations. So do the great tits under the eaves. On the coldest of winter nights, they creep in between the weather-boarding and the beams. The house had been here almost a hundred and sixty years when I first came, and it will still be here after me if it doesn't burn down."

When they got down to the house, Mia, Johan Brandberg, and Birger, it was empty. It made no difference what she had said about mice and silverfish and he was not in the slightest consoled by the thought of her words on unreality and reality. The house was terrifyingly empty and smelled stuffy.

Mia started gathering up the flowers and throwing them into the garbage bag. She had to get another bag to clear them all. She's got a sturdy rear, he thought. She's not really like Annie. But there was something about her hands. When she took a carton of eggs and a pack of butter out of the refrigerator, her hands looked like Annie's. Johan was sitting at the table, his eyes resting on her, those narrow brown eyes, usually so quick. Both the irises and the brown-black hair had paled considerably. Birger hadn't seen him for several years. Previously he had often come to their house with Tomas, but that had stopped when Tomas had moved to Stockholm. He wondered how Mia and Johan had met. As far as he knew, Johan never came back to Blackwater.

He was a meteorologist at the airport in Trondheim. Once, largely in jest, Birger had said he had chosen a profession in line with his origins after all, and Johan had been annoyed. He could be hot-tempered, anyhow had been when he was younger. "Do you think we go up into the mountains and stare at the clouds?" he had said. Then he had rather longwind-edly explained how he worked with tables and graphs.

Mia fried eggs and sliced some smoked lamb. Birger couldn't eat. He had some coffee with them and nibbled again at bits of granary bread. His thoughts wandered and he wasn't really listening to what they were saying, so Mia had to repeat the question she had put to him.

"Are there no morel places on the other side of the road?"

"There's only marshland down to the river there," Johan answered in his place. But she persisted that they should search on that side.

Annie hadn't gone out to look for morels. Birger had also hoped that. Now he would have to pull himself together and tell them what the situation was.

"She phoned me early this morning," he said. "Before five." They waited for him to go on but he couldn't. He couldn't think anymore. He got up from the table.

"We can't very well go on sitting here," he said. "Come on, let's go on up and start looking again."

They made their way down, across the road toward the Strömgren home-stead. The search party had set off uphill again, and their shouts could be heard right down at the old homestead. "Ann-iiee! Ann-iiee!" Birger saw a sharp expression, almost of disgust, forming around Mia's mouth. They started walking a little faster.

The old house was empty, the curtains in the windows dirty. The pasture had begun to grow again. Later in the summer it would be diffi-cult to get through all the sowthistle, monkshood, and meadowsweet. When they got down to the marsh, they saw the print of a boot in the wet path. Later, Birger remembered that he had wanted to suggest they should walk on the side of the path so as not to destroy the tracks. But he thought it a weird, almost distasteful thing to say. Especially as Mia was with them.

He never did get his thoughts straight that long Sunday. Revolting ideas about where Annie might be kept flickering through his head, then were gone. Suddenly, he found himself thinking about what they would have for dinner and wondering whether Annie had had time to do any shopping before she left. When they got down to the ford across the Lobber, he noticed Mia was now very uneasy. Hitherto she had been quite composed, although she had begun to see the situation was serious. Now she stopped and didn't want to go any farther.

"I don't like this place," she said quietly.

"No one does," said Birger.

"Those damn birds."

A couple of birds of prey were circling above them, making long-drawn-out cries.

"Are they kestrels?" said Johan.

"Peregrine falcons."

She sounded dead certain. One of the birds swerved away and flew out of sight. The other went on watching over them.

"So you know about birds?" said Birger. "I didn't think you were all that interested otherwise."

"Nature," she said with mocking emphasis. Birger had a feeling she was being ironic about one of Annie's doctrines; there's nothing that is not nature. We are all nature. Even the big cities will be broken down into quarries where eagles nest and lizards sun themselves on the walls. Into jungles or secretive formations of spruce forest.

He wondered how Mia saw Annie. With some criticism, presumably, unnatural otherwise. Or did she just laugh at Annie's faith in the cleared forests coming back? With affection, anyhow. He had heard her saying, "Mommy, Mommy." She used to say that when she was small and wanted to protect me, Annie had told him. He remembered the thin, sunburned child with her red hair cut like a boy's. And Annie at that time. She had had long, fair hair and timid—no, irritable, eyes. Narrow mouth. Always on her guard.

"I'll go down to the river," said Johan. "You two stay here. We can go on up toward Norbuan afterward."

"Aagot Fagerli taught me," said Mia. "She had those big bird books. I really only learned that one bird. The peregrine falcon. I thought it was called pere*grim* because it was very grim."

They had found one of the small islands of firm, mossy ground scattered over the marsh, and they sat down beside each other on a rotting birch, watching Johan making his way down. The marsh was full of pools of water like mirrors. Between them beds of sedge bubbled as if all the melting snow had absorbed water. They squelched when stepped on. Sky and earth met in those mirrors, and where the river ran they could see the grayish borders of the downy willow in the greenery. The sound of currents and small rapids was unclear at a distance, sometimes as if crowds of people were talking or even shouting at each other, sometimes like the sound of distant traffic, rising and falling, a totally mechanical mumble.

"I almost think I can recognize the place," said Mia. "And the birds are still here. I suppose they're the great-great-grandchildren of that bird."

"Surely you can't remember that Midsummer Eve?"

"I was six. I remember two peculiar spruces. My mother sat me on a fallen birch. There was bracket fungus just like on this one. They frightened me. I thought they were some kind of animals sticking to it. Mom was going to go down to the river to look for the tent because she thought we would be able to get some help there. But I went after her. I was terrified of losing her. There was that bird all the time. It dived down over the tent when we went there for the first time. Like a spool. You should see what force there is in them when they dive to kill. Strike, it's called. I got quite close and saw the tent. It was all bloody and ragged and I could see someone was lying there. A foot and all that. Mom was lying beside it, then she scrambled up and made her way down to the river and splashed and splashed in the water with her hands."

"Do you mean you really saw the tent and what had happened?"

"Yes."

"Annie doesn't realize that."

"No, of course not. She wouldn't be able to cope with that. Though she must have seen I was much farther down the path when she came back. I thought she'd be angry. But she never even noticed."

"Angry?"

The picture she had drawn for him was a strange one. Her voice was light, almost shrill, scarcely the voice of a grown woman any longer.

"Then everyone talked about it all."

"Did they talk to you about it?"

"Yes, of course. Though I was the only one who knew how it had happened."

"How did it happen, then?" Birger whispered.

"The bird dived down and stabbed them to death with its sharp beak."

She laughed at his expression. He had always thought Mia a splendid girl. Happy and jolly. Or, if he were to be truthful, a bit simple. Not particularly like Annie outwardly or inwardly. Now he wondered how much of that had been genuine.

"That was what I believed," she said. "For several years. I don't know when I went over to the general opinion."

She had sounded totally adult for a moment, but then suddenly the little-girl voice came back.

"I was frightened but didn't dare say anything. Mom and I were shit-scared that night afterward. She bailed out and ran up to Aagot's. I took my blanket and followed her. It was so cold outside at night and quite light. I wasn't used to that. I thought something was wrong. That it'd never be dark again. She couldn't cope with me. She was too frightened herself. I've thought about that. Did you know I'm going to have a baby?"

"No, I didn't. Annie hasn't said anything."

"She doesn't know yet. I thought perhaps you'd noticed, as you're a doctor."

"It doesn't show yet."

"No, but it's true anyhow."

She sounded slightly aggressive and added:

"Johan and I are tremendously pleased."

"I'm sure you are," said Birger.

"Aagot put Mom to bed in the other room. She was cold and shaking and said she could hear a strange whining sound. Though there wasn't any sound. Neither the old lady nor I could hear anything. You met Aagot, didn't you?"

"Many times," said Birger.

"Sweater over nightgown and no teeth. Well, she put them in later. There was a smacking noise when she clamped them down. She fixed a bed for me on the kitchen sofa, but I didn't dare sleep alone. I'll sit here, she said. All night. I won't leave you. I thought it was so odd that she said night when the sun was already shining outside. You could see all the way down to Tangen, the sun on the first houses there. I didn't dare go to bed. I stayed at the kitchen table and got cold. She lit the stove. I had never seen a stove like that before. It crackled and banged. She heated up milk and of course it boiled over and burned. Then she started swearing. Do you remember how Aagot used to swear? In a mixture of Norwegian and American. And Jämtland dialect. "T'hell with t'saucepan," she said. "Niver git thissun clean again. Dammit. Hell and damnation." She went on and on like that. She got out another pan. Everything became so ordinary, although there was that awful light in there. Then I said I'd seen that bird. I didn't say what it'd done, because I don't think I'd really understood that yet. That came later, when people talked. It was only the bird. And those bloodstained rags of tent. Pale blue. When I told Aagot where I'd seen the bird, that it was just by the river, just before the lake, and she said it was the peregrine falcon, I thought a very grim falcon was right. That it really was scary, like a cruel spear. I'd seen it swooping down. Then she took out a big book, awfully heavy, by one of the von Wright brothers, of course.

Mom's got them at home. She bid for them at the auction when Aagot died. We sat there at the kitchen table and leafed through it till we got to the peregrine falcon. Its beak and yellow eyes. It was the most horrible thing I've ever seen, not just grim, but terrifying. She read about it to me. I suppose she thought she could distract me from all that horrid business. Then I read it myself, many many times. I was a wizard at finding the place. Daylight Birds of Prey. Subheading Falcons. Falco peregrinus."

Johan came walking along the path. They got up and went to meet him. The marsh was squelching and swaying under his boots as he came unsteadily toward them.

"Shall we go up toward Norbuan now?" said Birger.

"No, we'll go to the road. We've got to talk to them."

Mia went ahead and Birger soon noticed Johan was dropping behind, waiting for Birger to catch up, then Johan grabbed his arm so fiercely that it hurt.

He had seen the face first. The water pouring over it was so clear, he thought she was lying there watching him approaching. Her eyes were open and the hair streaming out in the direction of the current couldn't hide her gaze. Then he realized she wasn't looking and the white skin couldn't feel the cold of the water. It took on the colors of the riverbed and the stones as ripples in the current and sunspots moved over it; for a moment or two her hand looked as if it were gold and then it darkened to brown. And yet the skin was always mostly white, the whiteness apparently a quality independent of the shifts of light and water.

Johan stepped backward because he had no desire to see any more. Not for a moment had he considered going down among the stones into the racing water to touch her or try to lift her out. She was bloodless and as cold as the thaw water from the high mountain now rushing over her. He didn't have to touch her to know.

As he made his way back up to the marsh, all he could think of was how to tell Mia. When he got there, he lost courage, so it was Birger he told, and the large solid man bent right forward as if he had received a blow in the solar plexus. A sound came out of him as well. Mia came running up.

"What is it?" she cried. He had never heard her voice so shrill. Birger seemed unable to get his breath back and Johan could no longer think at all.

"Where is she?"

"Under the water" was all he could get out. She began running toward the river, talking shrilly all the time. Or was she screaming? He couldn't distinguish the words, but it sounded as if she was quarreling. Perhaps she was, with her mother. Then Birger woke up. He started stumbling after her and caught up with her just as she fell. Johan stayed where he was and heard her crying, her mouth wide open, her head swinging from side to side. Birger held her and pressed her face to his shoulder so the sound was muffled. Johan stood looking at them, thinking it was like looking at two strangers.

Annie had once said that the only thing about her death that she was quite sure of was that she would leave a sizable amount of rubbish behind. She hadn't meant it literally—or had she? She must have been talking about modern Western people, or something of the kind. Birger couldn't remember. He was feeling great irritation and was aware that always preceded an attack of pain.

It often happened. He grew angry. He thought she had talked a lot of nonsense and said unnecessary things. Her joking—or was it joking?—then turned into irony. If it could be called that. It? *What* was it that was ironical? Anyhow, he couldn't stand it. It was impersonal. Came out of nowhere. He wanted to scream, which, of course, he didn't. But he often stood there with his mouth open.

Mia was clearing up. Her face was sweaty, and she had gardening gloves on her hands. She was hurling rubbish from the shed into a black sack. In a clumsy way, he was prepared to help her, but nothing came of it.

He hadn't been to Blackwater since the funeral. It was July now, the air heavy with moisture and scents. Mia had hugged him when he came. That was nice of her. Then she had gone back to clearing up.

Johan was going back and forth with cardboard boxes and bags. Birger sat down on a box inside the shed and looked at the mess. He tried to look at one thing at a time: boules, electric cables, skewers, chisels, nails. Bundles of used stamps in plastic bags, ball-point pens, clothes hangers, an iron spit, a pickax with no handle, curtain rings. A round grid. He worked out that it was meant to be fixed in front of a headlight to protect the glass from stones thrown up, but as far as he knew, she had never had it put on. A dog leash with knots in it, wire lampshade frames, a dirty sheepskin, bits of polystyrene.

In some places the accumulation was untouched. He recognized it the way you know the pattern of an old carpet. In the places as yet untouched by Mia and still recognizable to him, there should have been no muddle. There hadn't been before. Only a compact and intricate accumulation. But now the pattern had been destroyed by *that*. That totally impersonal— inhuman?—atmosphere he took as irony, as bitterness, though it couldn't have either taste or smell.

Wire in lumpy coils, fuses, brushes full of dog hairs—Saddie's and those of a lighter-colored dog. Nuts and bolts, charcoal, putty knife, clogs, an empty glue container, plastic sheeting, flowerpots, tattered boots. Tins, cups with no handles. Two lovely great Höganäs jars. Bundles of newspapers. They were from Aagot's day. Pieces of hardboard, emery paper, a sledgehammer, a whole lot of calendars tied up with string, curtain poles, sheets of birch bark. There were paper sacks full of roofing shingles, but he knew of no shingle roof there. Hexagonal screwdrivers from Ikea, shoehorns, fishing floats, ski poles, spinners with rusty hooks, wine bottles, drainpipes, sockets, fishing spoons, a torn sunhat, a curry comb. A tea strainer. Medicine bottles, sunglasses, radio valves. Earplugs. Yes, there were earplugs there, where the silence at night was profound. The dirty yellow material looked like foam rubber. A bench for carding flax. He had seen one like it at the Folklore Museum. Stools, mosquito windows, a pedestal, a wooden club, an awl, tacks, shoelaces, lids of preserving jars.

"What are you looking for?" said Mia. He shook his head. He hadn't known it before she asked, but he was looking for a box of cartridges.

"Nothing," he said.

"Don't sit here, then," she said, affection in her voice.

He went out into the heavy air. The roses in the hedge were flowering in abundance. Their scent was strong and sweet, scarcely fresh. Annie had said they smelled of incense and myrrh, another time that they smelled like the armpits of the goddess of love, and during a heat wave she had complained that they smelled like a North African brothel. The way she talked! Presumably just to breathe life into words that would otherwise not be used. Now they came back to him robbed of the note of careless and good-natured raillery. A voice was speaking them inside him. It couldn't be his own and was too mechanical to be human. Nonetheless it was bitter. Caustic.

Johan had cut the grass. Three large sacks of rubbish stood at the back of his car. He came out with two cans of beer and gave one to Birger. They sat down on the carding bench Mia had carried out on the grass.

"Oh, so you brought the car right up," said Birger. Johan had no need to answer. Of course they didn't want to lug the garbage sacks all the way down to the road. But Annie hadn't liked people driving up to the house, though Johan couldn't have known that. Cars made ugly tracks in the grass when the ground was damp. Over all those years, she had carried her shopping and parcels of books up the slope, referring to Aagot and to Jonetta before her.

"Edit, up above Westlund's, do you remember her?" said Birger. Johan nodded.

"She broke her leg in March last year and had to go to the hospital, then to a long-term ward. In the summer her family came up to straighten everything out, for Edit wouldn't be coming home again. A large heap of rubbish lay just where we usually park when we go up on the shoot. Old cake pans and stacks of magazines, tattered galoshes and preserving jars. They had even thrown away Edit's cloth strips she had cut up to make rag rugs."

He fell silent and thought there had been at least twenty skeins of strips of cloth on that rubbish heap. It wouldn't have been possible to rescue them because it had rained a lot and by the autumn they were half rotten. Anna Starr had been there and felt them. "You wonder what kind of people do things like that, throwing away ready-cut rags," she had said, although she had known perfectly well it was the sons and daughters-in-law.

"Anyhow, there was Edit's hat on the very top of the rubbish mound. The one she used to wear when she was out chopping wood or taking up potatoes. It was a brown felt hat that looked like a pot and had two flowers made of the same felt material on the front. Do you remember it?"

Johan looked at him sideways but said nothing.

"I was up with a beagle I had borrowed. It was November and I thought I'd see if there were any hares up there. On my way down the path, I heard someone chopping wood. It was dusk. I walked past Edit's woodshed, the one that has HUT 3 on it, because she got it from the company. That's when I saw her. She was inside and the flowers on that old hat bobbed every time she split the logs."

He fell silent.

"She was back then," said Johan.

Why did I tell him that? Birger thought. It had just come out. Almost as if it had to. He had at least stopped himself before finishing the story as he usually did: that when he had seen the grayish-brown figure in the autumn twilight he had thought it a premonition of Edit's death. The point was that she was alive. She had come back from the long-term ward, found her felt hat, and presumably quite a lot of other things on the rubbish heap, then had set about chopping wood for the winter. The way he had told the story to Johan, it was pointless.

He did talk away like that sometimes, without really knowing where it would lead. Then he saw that grin. With no face. In recent weeks he had mostly been silent. That was better.

Annie had left him alone with a cold, scornful smile. It wasn't hers. It was a cold smile with no face.

Mia came out carrying a dirty coat of black cloth and opened it. It was lined with stoat pelts, the thick summer pelt in shifting brown colors. White streaks from the belly and neck patches. The seams joining them together had begun to give way. It looked as if the pelts were about to crawl out of the coat.

"Do you think it was Aagot's?"

"No, when Aagot came back after the war, she was dressed like an American," said Birger. "That's Jonetta's coat. Her sister's. She got it from Antaris. She was married to him. He was a Lapp."

Antaris must have caught the stoats in traps over many years. She had probably been given the coat because he never bothered to fill in the cracks in the chimney breast or tried to insulate the walls. The cold swirled in and she was freezing cold. Antaris had been laborer to the reindeer herdsmen when they married, but then they meant to keep cows and goats. Jonetta came from a peasant farming family across the border, but Antaris never liked farmwork. Annie had shown Birger the stonecrop growing between the stones on the slope. There was also angelica from up on the mountain. That's the kind of thing Antaris brought home to Jonetta. And he had the coat made. But she must have been cold. When Antaris and Jonetta had gone and Aagot moved in, she had put in electric radiators.

But not right away, he thought. He remembered one January storm, the first time he had ever been to Blackwater. In the late evening the snow was swirling in a gray storm and the roads were slowly being snowed up. He didn't know where he was. Then he suddenly saw a light glowing in a window high up above the road. It was an electric light, but the squalls of snow seemed to suppress it. He had realized the electricity might go off at any moment, plunging the village into darkness, so he got out of the car and trudged up to the cottage while he could still see something. He wanted to ask where he was. Snow had already drifted up in front of the steps. When he peered through the kitchen window, he saw a woman sitting on a chair, reading in front of the wood stove. She had her feet at the oven door, halfway inside the oven. She was calmly reading, and he stood there for so long looking at her that he saw her turning a page of the book.

Then he had knocked on the window, but it was some time before she heard him. That must have been the storm. Through an open door into the other room, he could see the television was on, but he could hear nothing. It was a flashing black and white picture—a sandstorm or a cosmic blizzard. The woman in front of the stove went on reading without looking up.

"What are you thinking about?" said Mia.

He shook his head. That was nothing to talk about just then. But he had been thinking that Annie had taken over Aagot Fagerli's life. It had been there all ready, a style to step into. Of course she had modified it. But it was a lifestyle she had taken over with the house. Though Aagot hadn't needed to sleep with a shotgun beside her.

"I was thinking about that snowstorm the first time I came here," he said. "It was about fifteen below zero and certainly even colder in the squalls."

"It was thirty-one below when I was here a few years ago," said Johan. "Black as ink, and white. Not a soul."

"I thought you'd not been back here since you moved to Langvasslien," said Birger.

"Yes, I came and took a look one winter evening. Then I went back home across the border. That's all. And that time recently when we went to Nirsbuan and I drove Mia here."

"Did you drive Mia here?"

"Yes, we got here at about four. I slept in the car afterward. Parked down in Tangen."

"But you drove her all the way up here?"

"Yes, he did," said Mia. "I'll make some coffee. Get the cake out of the freezer, would you, Johan?"

Saddie had displayed discreet delight when Birger had arrived and was now lying at his feet. He tried to talk to her, but when she looked up with her dim eyes and gave a subdued wag of her tail, he started to weep. Her nose was gray and white. He couldn't remember how old she was.

Johan came up from the cellar with a Black Forest cake and put it in the sun to thaw. When they started eating it, it occurred to Birger that it might be a cake left over from the funeral. Just how practical was Mia really?

At the funeral gathering at the hotel, he had sat beside Annie's mother, old Henny. He had picked her up at the airport and she had leaned very heavily on his arm, making her way with great difficulty on her bad legs. Not once had she given in to tears or any outburst over the senseless and cruel thing that had happened to her only child. She had acted a part. There had been no falseness or dissembling at all in the way she had played her role. She coped with what had happened to her in the same way as she had coped with and borne a great deal in her long life; she took it on herself as if it had been a part written for her and no one else.

She had given him strength. He remembered little of the three weeks that had passed before they were allowed to bury Annie. In the end, he had been forced to take sick leave. When he saw the tiny, compact little lady in black with swollen ankles coming down the airport stairs, he had felt compassion and tenderness. That was the first time since the event that he had felt anything but a confusion that sometimes seemed like drunkenness or numbness, released momentarily by a sharp pain localized just above his diaphragm. Between the attacks, it came again, leaving him somehow helpless. Or disabled, he now thought.

What he had felt for Henny Raft had been fierce and unexpected, and it had helped him through the funeral. Only when the thin voices of the church choir sang did the pain come back again and cause him to double up, pressing out of him a sound that was grotesque. He heard it himself and was ashamed. Then Henny put her hand with all those rings, the most prominent a huge bloodstone set in marcasites, over his hand and kept it there until he could breathe normally again.

"Have you found a box of cartridges?" he said to Mia. He saw her turn pale, the freckles standing out. She was dirty from clearing out the shed.

"Why do you ask that?"

"There must be one somewhere."

A charge of shot had hit Annie in the lower part of her chest and her diaphragm. The shot had severely injured her, but had not killed her.

According to the investigation, she had probably tripped as she had been wading across the river carrying a gun without the safety catch on. It had gone off. During the spring floods, the water level had been so high, she had ended up under the water and drowned.

"She kept two cartridges behind the clock radio," said Birger. "They were still there. The police took them. I saw them that night I was looking for the gun. But I saw no box of cartridges."

"We haven't found any."

"You ought to have, if the police are right."

"Why are you talking like this?" said Mia, and tears began to pour down her cheeks, smearing the dirt.

"There was no box," said Birger. "She had only those two cartridges."

Mia was crying, no longer listening to what he was saying, but Johan was attentive.

"I don't think she had the gun with her," said Birger. "I think someone else took it and went after her. Someone who didn't know about the cartridges behind the clock radio. I'm sure that those were the only cartridges she had. I've never seen a box of them here. She never went shooting. She had learned to load the gun. No more than that. It wasn't even her own. Yes, she had paid for it. But it was Roland Fjellström who helped her buy it. The license was his. He gave her two cartridges. He still remembers that."

"Have you told the police?" said Johan.

"Of course."

"Stop it, now," said Mia. "I don't want to hear any more. It's all horrible. Everyone talking a whole load of shit. Do you know what old Enoksson said in the store? That his father also did away with himself. That's what they think!"

"But we don't," said Birger.

"He said that Magna Wilhelmsson in Byvången had told him that people who do themselves in have to be reborn for twenty-six thousand years as poverty-stricken Indians."

"Magna's crazy," said Birger. "She ought to be shut up in the Folklore Museum."

"But Mom had accumulated an awful lot of bad karma."

Birger didn't know whether she was being serious or whether that was modern jargon he didn't understand. He saw that Johan hadn't understood, either. He had put his arm around Mia.

"I've been to see the police again," said Birger. "They know she phoned me and was frightened. They think that may explain why she had the gun with her when she went out. She really was frightened. But they think she may have imagined seeing someone. Or dreamed it. It's not possible to confirm that she really did see anyone that night. If nothing new comes up, they say."

"And nothing has," said Johan.

"Yes. Something did just now."

"What?"

"She may have seen you," said Birger.

He disliked Mia's tears. A moment ago he had wept himself when he saw that Saddie couldn't grieve, only wait. Mia was crying loudly and rushed back into the house. She makes herself out to be more childish than she is, he thought as the door slammed shut.

"I presume that may have occurred to her," he said. "Has she said anything about it to you?"

"No."

"What about you? Have you thought about it?"

"Yes, of course."

Johan seemed older now. Mia's presence made him young. Perhaps that was what he wanted. For a moment the idea of an aging man doing sit-ups and trying to keep his stomach in floated through Birger's head. Johan was the same age as Tomas, and that must mean he was eleven or twelve years older than Mia.

Johan got up and went in to her, Birger following. They could hear thumps in the kitchen, and when they went in he saw she was clearing out there as well, sniveling and taking half-full bags of flour, sugar, and oat flakes out of the larder. Johan had gone over to stand by the cold stove, his hands thrust into the narrow pockets of his jeans, an unnatural or at any rate awkward posture. He was biting his top lip and looking at Birger. He seemed to be waiting for him to go on.

"Do you think it was you she saw?"

"She probably saw me from the kitchen window. We stood out here for a while. I think she must have heard the car."

"Why don't the police know all this?"

"There was probably some misunderstanding."

"Had you realized all the time that she'd seen you and thought you looked like that boy?"

He didn't reply, but lowered his head.

"But you've said nothing about it."

"No. But it's not as you think."

"What do you mean, as I think?" said Birger.

Johan again said nothing.

"We must tell the police," said Birger.

"Yes, I can see that you think that."

"Don't you?"

"No."

"Mia?"

She was dirty and very pale, the freckles almost dark brown against the gray skin. She was looking at Johan, strange sharp lines at the corners of her mouth that did not seem to go with the smooth young face. Birger recollected that she had been a fussy little miss about food as a child, those lines appearing around her mouth whenever she saw goat's milk or fish guts.

When she was a teenager and he had gotten to know her again, she had always been restless and impatient during the weekends she was at home. She had gone to junior high and on to senior high in Byvången, and she had been furious when Annie moved away from there and took the job in Blackwater. But in recent years she had found a strength or balance—or whatever the hell it was—of a kind Annie had never had. Mia knew what she wanted and mostly got what she wanted. After leaving school, she had read cultural geography and some other subjects that had not seemed particularly useful for making a living. But up to then she had never been unemployed, though she had been hired only for short-term projects, either with the local authority or the college. Her pregnancy is planned, he thought. That's more than her mother ever succeeded in achieving. She's got a well-educated and also good-looking man, getting on a bit, of course, but maybe that was what she wanted. Maybe it held an attraction for her. He couldn't see Mia getting entangled with the kind of young men that had been called nonvalid during his student days. Freedom neurotics moving in together on trial and gliding apart on trial like amoebae. Like that damned Göran Dubois, he thought.

"What are we going to do about it, then?" said Birger.

"Why did you come here?" said Mia quite sharply.

"You know why. I promised to look after Saddie."

She had started sieving flour into a bowl.

"Are you going to do some baking?" he said stupidly.

"I'm sieving this to see if there are any weevils."

He was suddenly unreasonably angry with her. Out with it all, he thought. Everything you've thought, all the criticism you've had to hold back—for you did respect her, after all—you can release by doing things now, cleaning and tidying up. Eliminating. You say it's going to be a summer place. But it won't be for long. I think you'll sell it, he said silently behind her back. And once you've sold it, you'll soon have forgotten.

Christ, how unpleasant the young can be! Christ, how unpleasant and vile everything is! Living and struggling and then falling apart because of an anomaly in cell formation, or a bunch of bacteria, or shotgun pellets— or water!

Enjoined through water. Why had she said that? "I am enjoined through water."

Living and talking—including a whole lot of quasi-religious crap— and trying to hold on although all the time you know you're going under —no, being dissolved. Truly enjoined. That's loathsome. That's unendurably loathsome. But all the same, the worst of all is the vile way young people pretend not to notice. No, they simply don't know anything about it. They have everything in their grasp. They plan! And some never grow up.

Johan was looking at him and Birger sensed he had noticed his anger. He turned around and went out. Saddie stayed where she was under the table. The cake was thawing and there were flies on it. Unplanned, he thought maliciously. Something not going the way it was supposed to after all.

"I'm a useless person," Annie used to say. Her words were as clear in his head as if he had just heard her voice. In this warm air, heavy with scents, in the rustle of the aspens. Those sober words: "I'm a useless person.

"I can't see any particular point in my life. I read a lot and I like being alone. I like being with you, too. And I like the birds and the sound of rain."

The rustle of the aspens, he thought. And the dry clicks in the autumn when their leaves fell to the frosty ground. She used to stand there on the steps and listen to them.

Slowly his anger and loathing dispersed, but he was very tired now, almost exhausted. He took the cake with him and went back into the kitchen.

"I'll take Saddie and go home," he said. "That's best. But you two must think this over."

"There's nothing to think over," said Mia.

Birger didn't reply. He went over to the cupboard under the sink and opened it.

"What do you want?"

She sounded sharp.

"Saddie's food bowl. I want her leash, too. And that old sheepskin. Then I'll go."

Johan was the one to go out with him, his hands still thrust into his pockets. He was looking rather stiff. He delayed their leavetaking down by the car, as if afraid of returning to the kitchen and Mia. Things are degenerating for them, thought Birger. Perhaps quite unnecessarily. He had that helpless feeling he had had ever since they had started looking for Annie. The feeling of complicity and impotence.

The village had never had so many cows as during the war, and very rich milk could be bought well into the 1950s. Later the hay meadows had grown meager and matted, the grazing lands were overgrown, and the birch shoots had moved in, as did the ineradicable willow.

Then finally the tourists came. They wanted to see the river Lobber. A society that absorbs its life force out of fatal violence has to pay tribute to the village and its mystery—because it is unsolved. There the force is unfettered.

That had been Annie's belief. That was the way she used to talk.

If you solve the mystery, the force runs out and the village becomes a dying village among many others. A place no one sees and no one knows about. The force goes over to the man who did it and you never solve his mystery. Yet it is just as attractive as the smell of well-hung meat. His dark destiny is transferred to you in swift electronic flashes. But the village dies.

And she had been consistent, he thought bitterly. Never a single contribution toward weakening the enigmatic force of the village.

After saying good-bye to Birger, Johan Brandberg walked back up the steep slope to the house and found he was out of breath. That annoyed him, since he considered himself fit and athletic, but the air was very heavy and humid, a spicy, cloyingly sweet scent coming from the roses. They were an old-fashioned kind that could be found in several places in the village, a multipetaled, deep purple rose. It flowered in abundance and the heavy heads hung over the stone wall terracing the slope in front of the shed. Many of the blooms had faded now, displaying interiors of decay and dissolution. They looked shameless at this stage, and those still flowering were full of hover flies and bumblebees. Such an abundant species should be checked before it got to the obscene stage. He wondered whether Annie used to deadhead them. He didn't know much about her. Anyhow, Mia hadn't done it.

He was annoyed with Mia. And worse. But he had said nothing until his thoughts had turned to the odd demand that she ought to have thought about deadheading the roses.

She had been clearing out and cleaning for three days now. It was hard, dirty work, and painful for her. She was trying to keep the shock and the draining grief at bay. Maybe she was just postponing them, but he couldn't reproach her for trying to do so by hard work and an effort of will. She was pregnant and wanted to be happy. She had used that word. He sensed that she meant something more modest, simply a state that was good for the baby. She was using the word baby now.

He had realized she was protecting him and had expected her to talk to him about it. But she hadn't. He had never imagined living with Mia in an atmosphere in which it was so difficult to breathe. Nor did he understand how he had accepted it for over a month. Maybe that was because he wasn't sure what she meant by protecting him. Whether she really meant to.

It was all very confusing and burdensome. He sat down at the garden table, knowing she could see him from the kitchen. The police had asked her whether she knew who it was Annie might have seen. Had Annie said anything when they were having tea together that morning? No, she hadn't. What about when Mia had come that night? No, she hadn't woken then.

"Then your fiancé didn't drive the car right up?"

"No, he didn't."

Just as simply and clearly as when she had replied to Birger.

"Yes, he did."

He had probably pushed it aside, but he could no longer do that. If she was protecting him, then that was because she thought there was something from which he needed protecting. Didn't she realize that it made it worse? That was what made breathing so difficult.

He got up and went inside. She had her back to him, still busy taking things out of the larder.

"Has he gone?"

"Yes. He was miserable."

"I couldn't stand him any longer," she said. "I'm sorry. He's like a wet old sponge."

"You don't want him to tell the police that I was the person your mother saw?"

"That's unimportant. Nothing but unpleasantness would come of it. The fact that she saw you and you look like that guy means he's right. She saw someone. She was frightened. That's why she took the gun with her."

"I was that guy."

It looked extremely peculiar, but she actually went on pouring rice out of one carton into another which wasn't quite full.

"It was me running up the path that night," said Johan. "I was on my way to Nirsbuan. I don't even know if I was on my way there. I just ran. But then I got there and slept for an hour or two. In the morning I paddled down to the Röbäck and got a lift. Your mother meant me when she phoned Birger."

"A foreigner?"

"A Lapp."

He said the word with an unpleasant sting that he himself thought sounded childish.

"She'd only just come here. I probably looked like a foreigner to her. Asian, she thought. Mongoloid, some would say. I had long hair at the time. It was darker than it is now."

"So what?" said Mia.

What he was afraid of had already occurred.

"Mia, you didn't tell the police the truth. You told them I didn't drive you right up to the house."

"Did I?"

That made him angry.

"You're not being honest now," he said. "What are you afraid of? At least admit it to yourself. I did not stab two people to death in a tent later on that night. I did not go after her with her own shotgun and shoot her. You know that perfectly well. I was with you in Östersund."

"When I woke up in the night you weren't there."

"I'd gone out to phone Gudrun."

"You went *out* to phone?"

This should never have been said. It should never have been thought. It was only some kind of delirium of words.

"Mia, you wouldn't even dream of protecting me if you really thought so badly of me. But if you go on being devious, you'll get into a bad mood and start thinking ill of me."

"Being devious? Am I the one being devious?"

She had said so much that afternoon. Once he found himself on his own—on a forest road just north of Lersjövik—he realized he had gone straight into the kitchen and caused the row himself. He had intended to be open with her and force her to be open—and to stop deceiving herself. He wanted to live in clarity with Mia. In dry air. He still found it difficult to see what was wrong with such a project. He had told her he had grown up in an atmosphere of silences and concealment, but had managed to get out of it.

"I ran away from it. I know quite a lot about the hatred generated in that kind of sludge of silences and suspicions. When my mother was twenty-one, she became pregnant. I've no idea what her hopes or plans were. I know only that the father of the child—my father, I mean—was married. He was a Sami like her. She started housekeeping for Torsten

Brandberg, who had lost his wife and had been left on his own with three boys and a baby. I don't know whether Gudrun decided to acquire a father for her child or whether it just happened. Anyhow, Torsten probably thought he was the father when he married her. But he must have gradually realized he had been deceived. Look at me. I don't look particularly Swedish. I looked even less so when I was a child. I don't think anything has ever been said. I'm convinced they just went on and on saying nothing. But I grew up in that mess of suspicion and humiliation and minor racist outbursts, protected by a powerful force. Mother love, Mia! Watch out for that."

"You're mad," she said quietly and bitingly.

"Yes! Mother love has thick, thick blood. It has substances you find in mares and female rats. It's good for eighteen months. Fitting and necessary. After twenty-four months it has to become human. Humanistic. Even dry and matter-of-fact. It has to acquire an element of indifference. Of consideration for other things. I ran away from it. I don't want my child to grow up in that thick, murky soup. I want you and I to know exactly where we stand."

"Then why didn't you say you were the person Mom saw?"

"I'm saying it now."

"You never said a word about it until you had to. I could have lived my whole life with you without knowing you were by the Lobber that night."

"But it had nothing to do with you. It was long before your time."

"I was there."

"You were six."

"Is everything that happened to you before I grew up to be discounted? Is that not part of you?"

He remembered the conversation, or the quarrel, or the confessions, as nothing but retakes. Sometimes an outburst became something to hold on to in the flood of repetitions, in the increasing disintegration.

"I think you're horrible!"

He tried to remember that soberly as well. That meant, You frighten me. Everything you've been involved in frightens me. But it made no difference. He remembered the feeling even better, the fierce jab that had caught him unawares. Yes, he was also frightened, though he had expressed it more soberly than she had.

"Now you're being illogical, Mia."

They were both on vacation and had been going to put Annie's house in order, then go home to Langvasslien to fish and walk in the mountains. Now she said she was going to Stockholm, because she was feeling sorry for her grandmother and would like to go and look after her. She could go to Åland with her.

He couldn't imagine Henny Raft wanting to leave her little apartment and walk on her swollen feet up the Åland ferry gangway. She would rather stay at home and feed her gulls and crows and squabble with the neighbors and the public health authority about the matter. She was considered a character (by those who did not consider her a dotty old bat who let crows and gulls shit all over the balconies) and she lived up to the image with determined dignity.

He ought to have pretended that it was good, or at least reasonable, for Mia and her grandmother to go to Åland. But he was caught in the process of grinding disintegration, and tried to convince her it was something else she wanted, not just to look after her grandmother.

It was all fairly simple, he realized that afterward. She wanted to be left in peace for a while. But he couldn't leave her in peace. He wanted everything to be all right. They would sleep together, talk about the child, walk in the mountains, go fishing, take photographs—he wanted it all to be normal again now, once and for all.

Just because of that, he made her say things that should never have been said. He wanted to talk about the baby and she didn't. She said it wasn't certain there would be a baby. He ought to have left it at that, but he was scared and blurted out:

"You won't have a miscarriage now, that's not likely, so what do you mean?"

She never said it. But her tone of voice was cold and conclusive when she told him that she had no intention of making the same mistake her mother had made.

"I know what I'm doing. I wanted to be pregnant and I became pregnant. But I've no intention of raising a child on my own. That's a wretched existence."

That could have been an assurance that they would stay together. But he wasn't sure. She packed her belongings and emptied the fridge. They hadn't eaten and she did not ask him whether he wanted anything. They had arrived in separate cars, meaning to take a whole lot of Annie's things to Östersund. Now Mia left the cardboard boxes in the kitchen and maintained that she was going to see her grandmother.

He drove ahead of her toward town. He thought they had agreed to stop and rest at her usual places, but as he turned off into a forest track north of Lersjövik, she drove past him and disappeared around the bend. It was absurd, so childish, he found it hard to grasp that it was also serious and alarming. That his only hope now was that thick, thick blood. The mother substances. A soup that eventually would be sufficiently strong and murky to stop her putting a clinical end to everything.

He had seen a great many dead people over the years. And he had also seen relatives beside their dead. Some caressed them, but most observed a rigid decorum, sitting upright on a chair, waiting out the minutes—seldom a matter of more than minutes. A wake was just as unthinkable as breastfeeding a child for years.

Someone collapsing and weeping or screaming was unusual. Most people knew themselves, and if they sensed that they would not be able to bear it, they declined.

Annie had sat with two fingers on the dead baby's cold skin. She had put the tips of her fingers where the chest sloped down toward the armpit. He had not understood why.

She had driven in her own car from Blackwater. Mia had had to stay behind with Aagot. Annie's suitcase had been packed and ready for a week or two, and she had inteneded to go to Östersund maternity hospital. At Offerberg she was taken by surprise when the waters broke. She had had no idea the course of events could be so much swifter the second time she gave birth.

She drove from Offerberg to Byvången, stopping each time a pain overcame her. In Tuvallen she had to take a taxi. She arrived in Byvången pale, angry, and already becoming exhausted. It was a quick delivery. After all these years, Birger could still remember his encouraging cries to her. But memory had distorted them, at first they had been hearty, then gradually cynical and inappropriate. The ironic twist had of course been totally impersonal—inhuman. He was not cynical. He had wished her well and had thought everything would be all right.

The baby was not born, it came out. The umbilical cord had twisted tightly around its throat and strangled it.

He couldn't remember if he had tried to comfort her at the delivery table. He must have. However wretched he had felt, there were words and sentences he always used. On the other hand, he remembered going in to see her an hour or so later. That was when she had asked to see the baby.

He had been very uneasy, not least because she had shown no emotion. She was pale and not really communicating, just making sure she had her own way. He hadn't been able to think of any way of refusing.

The baby was female, a large, well-formed fetus. She had never opened her eyes. Her skin was bluish and covered with glistening fetal fat. He had wiped her as clean as he could and wrapped her in a large white towel without covering her. He left the door of the treatment room open and in person went to fetch Annie Raft, maneuvering the bed with some difficulty; he was not used to the task. But he hadn't wanted the assistants to have anything to do with it and had waited until the evening, when only the receptionist on duty and the night nurse were in the building.

His idea had been that she could glimpse the child through the door and decline in time if she felt she couldn't bear it. But she had him push the bed right in and asked him to move it closer. Finally, she had put the forefinger and middle finger of her right hand on the cold blue skin and held them there for a long spell. It looked like when two fingers are laid on the Bible to take an oath. In his mind he always thought about this incident, which he didn't understand, as the time when he saw her swearing on the child.

He himself could not have borne to see Annie. But he had had to. And, he thought afterward, "bear" is an empty word. Just a kind of exclamation. You bear it. You put two fingers on what has happened and feel it.

Birger Torbjörnsson lived in a yellow brick building in the square in Byvången. The police station and the drugstore were next door—with the venetian blinds down. It was Sunday and the supermarket across the square was closed. Birger was so pleased to see him when he arrived, Johan was ashamed.

The apartment had three rooms. The living room was overfurnished. Johan recognized the pale gray-blue sofa from the old house, and the tapestries on the wall behind it. But there were bizarre elements in the subdued decor. He remembered Birger had lived with a woman who was a vet. She had probably rebelled. But Barbro Lund's sobriety still dominated, although transferred to a rented apartment, dusty and broken up by colorful cretonne. He had a feeling Birger seldom used the living room. It smelled unaired.

A half-open door in the hall led into a room where he kept his skis, hunting rifle, boots, and fishing rods, as well as the winter tires for his car. Presumably anything of value got stolen from the basement storerooms. He had a desk in his bedroom, overflowing with papers and files, a locked medicine cabinet on the wall and his medical bag jammed on the bookshelf. Johan wondered why he kept a stethoscope and stainless steel bowls on the shelves. Did he have private patients? The room was rather grubby for a doctor's office, but the medical utensils and the carelessly made bed reminded Johan of the vets' office in the community center in Langvasslien. Saddie was lying on her sheepskin in the middle of the floor. She raised her head and wagged her tail a couple of times.

They ended up in the bedroom-cum-workroom because that was where Birger finally found the whiskey. Johan thought it a good sign that he didn't seem to know where to find it, or possibly a bad sign that he kept it by his bed.

He was easy to talk to. His questions were straight to the point—much as if he were noting down medical symptoms—and he didn't rush to draw conclusions from what he was told. But when he did, he saw no reason to discuss them.

"Girls who are pregnant," he said, "young women having their first baby, often have these sudden attacks. It's no more peculiar than the fact that they often have gas or throw up. At first it's nice to expect a sweet little baby doll. They fuss around and arrange things and everything seems all right. But then the backlash comes. Presumably more often than they say. Most of them just probably seem a bit sulky for a while. But Mia is lashing out now. She's under great strain. They wonder what the hell they've done. What they've let themselves in for. Mostly they say nothing. But those who manage to spit it out say ugly things. They may also be frightened. But it'll work out."

"It doesn't always. Sometimes things don't go the way you expect. They get disorganized. And it hurts."

"Yes," said Birger. "Sometimes it hurts."

He was tilting his glass backward and forward and looking down at the grubby rag rug. He was over sixty and looked as if a long life had wound him up. He worked like a clock. Occasionally a stab of pain would double him over, his eyes closing and his mouth opening. Then he went on, saying what he usually said. Even changing his shirt. And eating. His familiarity with solitude and loneliness and a disciplined, dull, industrious life helped him plod on.

"You look scared," he said.

"Yes, though I'm not usually," said Johan. "That night many years ago, that Midsummer, I was then. Though I haven't thought about it all that much since. But now it's come back and I recognize it. Sort of like remembering an accident or some injury when the same thing nearly happens again. Though you'd forgotten."

"What were you afraid of that night?"

"I don't know. That it would all go wrong. It was just this feeling that things weren't working out as expected, or as they usually do. But badly. Really badly."

"What were you up to that evening?"

"I went fishing."

"The police thought you'd run away to Norway."

"I took the moped up to Alda's first, to get some bait. But my brothers caught up with me."

"And beat you up?"

"No. Pekka's rather complex and he'd thought up something better. They let me down Alda's well. It wasn't all that bad, because there was very little water in it. But I was down there several hours before I figured out how to get out. Then I didn't want to go back home. I hadn't decided anything, but just ran. I never saw Annie Raft on the path. I didn't hear about her seeing someone until long after, but then I realized it was me she had seen. So did Gudrun and the brothers, and Torsten. They lied and said I'd already gone off in the evening, and that I had taken the moped. But I walked to Nirsbuan and slept an hour or two there. Then I paddled down to the Röbäck and got a lift. That was about five in the morning."

"It's odd that the man who gave you a lift said nothing to the police."

"It was a woman. A Finn. No, a woman from Finland. She was damned fussy about that."

"Fancy you remembering that."

"I spent several days with her."

Birger looked up.

"Having a bit of hanky-panky, were you?"

Johan laughed. That was unexpected, and he needed it, he thought, with everything so damned awful at the moment.

"You could say so," he said. "Though not exactly idyllic. She was quite a tough nut. I hurt myself, actually broke something in my foot and she gave me quinine powder and some vodka and made me walk on it. A long way."

"That was an odd mixture."

He had gotten up and put his glass down on the desk. For a long while he stayed there with his back to Johan, almost as if looking out over the asphalted square below. But there was nothing there to see.

"Are you sure it was that? Quinine powder?"

"Yes, I thought it sounded horrible. There was a Red Indian on the bag."

"And Koskenkorva?"

"Yes."

"Quinine powder and Koskenkorva. That's what Sabine Vestdijk was given for her period pains."

"Who's that?"

"That was her name. The young Dutch girl who was killed in the tent together with a man with no trousers. A man whom no one has identified and no one has missed. He tried to buy painkillers for her at the pharmacy in Byvången, but couldn't. Then she was given that quinine powder and Koskenkorva vodka. By someone. The bottle was found there, and the packet of powders. Where did your tough Finnish woman come from?"

"I thought she came off the Finland ferry."

"At five in the morning?"

"I never asked. But she'd also been to the pharmacy in Byvången."

"Did she tell you that?"

"No."

He was suddenly horribly embarrassed, as if he were sixteen again and having to confess to rummaging in her handbag.

"She had a paper bag from the pharmacy," he said. "With the receipt still in it. She'd bought some condoms."

"Sounds as if she'd hoped she would meet you."

"We never used them. She never said we should be careful or anything like that. I thought she was on the pill. So I couldn't make out why she bought those condoms."

"You were an innocent lamb."

"Yeah, you could say so."

"I guess she had had someone else in mind. Someone she thought she needed to protect herself from."

"You mean from infection?"

Was it that simple? He was a doctor and naturally thought along those lines.

"Who, then? There was a man up there, but she wasn't together with him. The packet of condoms was unopened. Who was she thinking of?"

"Sagittarius," said Birger.

Johan didn't know what her name was, but she had called the hunting lodge Trollevolden. There was a cave nearby and a river ran alongside the cottage he had stayed in. He remembered the murmur of it all day and night.

"Anyhow, the house belonged to her family."

"Although she was a Finn?"

"From Finland."

"This trouserless man had a telephone number hidden at the bottom of his bag. It was to someplace on the coast, to the north. A shop. Was there a telephone in the house?"

"There was nothing. Not even electricity. No road, either."

"Did you see a shop anywhere near?"

"I didn't see anything. Only a large, dark house. A dog run and an icehouse. They were derelict, but the main house wasn't. Just rather shabby. I think it must have been a big family, because there were an awful lot of beds. Bunk beds."

"We'll find it," said Birger. "That can't be difficult. Then we can get hold of the Finnish woman's name."

His way of finding it was the way almost everything was accomplished in the villages. You turned to someone you knew. Or to someone who was the son of, or acquainted with, or only a son-in-law of someone you knew. In this case it was an insurance official in Stockholm who had been head of the police in Byvången. He had been removed from the river Lobber case and had taken that so badly, he had resigned. But he had a large cardboard box full of photocopied material from the case, an arrangement greatly approved of by Birger, though it was totally against all regulations, of course. Åke Vemdal had hoped to be able to puzzle out the answer at his kitchen table and triumph over all those who had snubbed him. He hadn't done so.

He usually went shooting up in Blackwater in the autumn, with the same team as Birger. He used to have a spell of fishing in June as well, and they occasionally met in Stockholm. Vemdal would book a table in the restaurant at Solvalla racecourse and they would spend a fortune on the meal—damned cheap at the price since you get such a good view from there—and laid bets on the horses. At first they had talked about the case every time they met, but now they hadn't spoken of it for a long time.

Vemdal didn't want to give them the telephone number Sagittarius had hidden at the bottom of his bag. He was going to phone himself.

"I'm surprised he was home," said Johan. "It's the holidays."

"He's a loss adjuster. There are lots of burglaries these days. And he's his own boss in the evenings. A bachelor. But not like me. He's a confirmed one. You can have ladies anywhere, he says. In sailing boats. In politics. But not in kitchens and plumbed areas. They regress there."

He fell silent.

"Though not Annie," he said seriously after a while. "She didn't spend much time in the kitchen, for that matter. Would you like some food?

Have you had anything to eat? You must phone Mia. You two mustn't mess things up."

A tourist hostel. They found out on Monday morning. It was still called Trollevolden, but was owned by the Norwegian Tourist Association. People who went to the mountains or went fishing could stay the night there. It had been a simple unstaffed establishment eighteen years earlier and the tourist association had in fact owned it since the end of the war. Before that it had been a hunting lodge and had belonged to a businessman from Trondheim.

Johan felt as if he were still the gullible sixteen-year-old who had hidden away in what she had called the grouse shed. She had made it all up. Or, as Birger expressed it, "she talked a lot of bullshit, the lying cow."

The number—it had been changed but Vemdal tracked it down—was to a village shop on the coast north of Brønnøysund. They knew all about Trollevolden there.

But that didn't produce a name. It was unlikely there would be lists of names—if they had kept records at all. If there were, that that would be police business. Vemdal advised them to go to the police.

"Nothing's happened over all these years," said Birger. "But then you come. Annie saw you and recognized you, amazingly enough. She was so frightened she rang me up although it was not yet five in the morning. According to the investigation, she took the gun with her because she had had a fright and was scared of meeting that—man. You, that is. But she didn't say anything to Mia about it. Does that sound reasonable?"

"It sounds as if she wasn't really sure."

"I've already told you the cartridges were still there. If she had a box of cartridges, then what happened to it? She did quite a lot that morning. She was up at Gudrun Brandberg's and agreed with her that they should go and look for morels. Then she went down to Anna Starr's in Tangen. Anna's place is quite isolated, so Annie would've had the gun with her if she was that scared. But she didn't."

"What did she do at Anna Starr's?"

"It's rather odd. Hardly serious. I mean, if she was frightened, then it was a peculiar enterprise. She was asking about a UFO. Or some phenomenon in the sky they had thought was a UFO. She wanted to know exactly where it had come down. Something bright and dazzling crashed out of the sky outside Tangen a few years ago. You can see the place from the exercise track, halfway between the far headland and the little island with spruces on it. The next day, six old biddies, members of the sewing bee, went around the village asking who else had seen it. They had all seen it together. They'd been standing in the Neanders' window, looking out like snow-white angels—Westlund saw them. Whatever was dazzling and flashing hurtled through the night down into the water and vanished. They even dragged the place later on. The women got a couple of men to do it from a boat, but they found only the usual scrap iron that people had dumped. Actually a whole lot of people in the village had seen it and everyone gave roughly the same description: that it was like a firework display and hurtled straight down into the water, which was as black as ink that evening. That was late autumn. There was ice below the store, though it was thin. But farther out where the lake is rougher, the water was open and that's where it disappeared.

"She talked to Anna about it and then appears to have forgotten about Gudrun and the morel picking. Anyhow, she drove on up on her own, first to Aron and Lisa Kronlund. She used to leave Saddie with them when she was going somewhere and couldn't take her along. So that means she was going to be away from the car for quite a while, as otherwise Saddie just used to stay in the car when she was walking in terrain that was too difficult for the old dog with her bad hips."

"Did she say where she was going?"

"Not to Lisa and Aron. But she met their granddaughter—she was there for the weekend. She told her she was going down memory lane."

"That sounds rather solemn."

"She went toward the Lobber. Her memories from there were not particularly pleasant. As far as I know, she had never been there since it happened. Then we don't know any more."

Then he leaned over the table and at first Johan thought he was sneezing. But it was a sob. He had started weeping, snuffling loudly. A moment before he had sounded quite matter-of-fact. He had come into the dusty living room where Johan was sleeping, with a cup of coffee for him. He was sitting on the bed, so close that Johan now thought he ought to put his arm around him. But he didn't know how to go about it. The deep, shuddering sobs were the only sound in the room, and Birger's face was red and swollen. He pushed away his cup, dropped forward over the table, and wept even more violently, his bowed, powerful back shaking, strings of what looked like snot trickling down on the table.

Saddie struggled up from her place under the coffee table and padded out of the room, cowering as she went. He had frightened her.

Finally Birger managed to get up and go out into the hall, fumbling as if he couldn't see. Johan clumsily followed him and made sure he found the bathroom. Then he went back and sat at the low table, listening to him pulling at the toilet paper and blowing his nose over and over again. At last it was quiet, but almost ten minutes passed before he came out.

"You must go to the police," he said. "They can get further with that Finnish woman."

But Johan didn't want to, though he found it difficult to explain why. Birger might think he was afraid they would suspect him, but it was nothing as concrete as that. He thought if he did something now, then anything could happen. Just think what he had released merely by letting himself be seen through a window.

Or would it have happened anyhow? There was something ambiguous about Annie Raft's actions that morning. He didn't know what sort of person she was and didn't dare ask Birger for fear he would start weeping again. Had she acted rationally or had she been acting on obscure impulses she was unable to explain even to herself?

Mia, who was so sensible, had shown him sides of herself he hadn't known about. She had behaved erratically, almost maliciously. Late the previous night, Birger had said that women sometimes showed faces that were difficult to keep your eyes on. Which women?

"They don't look you in the eye," said Birger, whiskey-blurred. "If they turn their backs on you, you may see nothing but air. *Niente.*"

Now it was morning and once again Birger thought Mia had behaved normally and predictably. In her condition, it meant nothing more than gas and morning sickness.

But what if it were fatal?

Johan had phoned and talked to her. Her voice had been dull. She was sulking. Grandmother did not want to go to Åland. But Mia was going to Stockholm to see her all the same. Then she would come to Langvasslien.

It sounded normal. She had calmed down just as Birger had predicted. But Birger hadn't considered that the decision rested with her. What part of her was it that decided? Scarcely a year earlier she had met a man she had taken to be a Norwegian driver in a dogsled race in Duved. She thought his Siberians were beautiful with their light blue eyes and intelligent faces and she also found him personally appetizing—that was what she said. As good as strawberry ice cream to lick—and God knows, she had licked. But what was it within her that had decided he should be the father of her child? Or that he would not be allowed to?

He busied himself with forecasts. He was tracking the movements of water-laden clouds driven by the winds. They usually came from the west out of the misty or surging and sunny Atlantic and moved on an easterly course. But they could swing at an angle of ninety degrees. That kind of thing happened. Usually he knew if they were going to be difficult to judge, but there were some he got wrong from the very beginning. They made him feel superfluous. Not powerless or inadequate with all his assembled data. But superfluous. Unnecessary. Then it rained on his face and he wondered about it in a way that could not in any way be called scientific.

W hen it came to choosing where
Annie was to be buried, anywhere but the Röbäck churchyard had been
out of the question. Even old Henny said, in her deep, cultivated voice,
that that was where Annie belonged.

In his funeral oration, the minister evoked a picture of Annie in the
forest. He meant well; his intention was that they should see Annie walking in a fresh spring forest, a younger and healthier Saddie at her heels.
She belonged there, said the minister. Annie would not have agreed with
him.

She had once said to Birger, "You're not the only one who has walked
with me here in the forest or up to the mountain and said this is where I
belong. They all think I move quickly here and find my way. I appear to
be at home where they themselves feel lost or even terrified.

"It's true I walk in the forest every day and I am the only woman here
who goes walking outside the berry-picking season. And who dares to
walk alone. But that doesn't make me feel at home in the forest. I think
the timber company's men or the Brandberg men on their road-making
machines feel much more at home."

I walk here as Rousseau did in the woods of St. Germain, dazed by
fantasies, scents, and visions of beauty. The point is, my visions are the
opposite of the civilization I live in. I'm seeking an alternative. Per-Ola
Brandberg isn't doing that as he drives his tractor. His visions are not in

opposition to the society he lives in. Not even when he disturbs a hare or notices the cloudberries have started to ripen.

Naturally, in time I feel more and more at home in what is alien, just as Per-Ola feels at home in the resources he is abusing. But it is my fantasies that make me feel at home, and they are reinforced by the wildness and scents of the forest. Per-Ola benefits from roughly the same things. But he wouldn't call them wild.

We are two children of our time and dependent on each other, at least I am on him. Without the felling, the village would be uninhabited and I wouldn't be able to live alone here to have my visions and fantasies. That would be going native and is something quite different. That's what Björne Brandberg has done and he seems to be lost. He doesn't even drink any longer.

You know, quite a few bachelors and lumberjacks have ended up like him in a cabin or a surplus company hut. They begin to find people difficult and listen more and more in toward the forest. The solitude has a powerful influence on them. They become dependent. I don't really know what kind of experiences they have. What they tell you is often about the wee folk who help them when they're exhausted, and ferns that cure their backaches and allow them to sleep, sometimes too soundly. Nowadays all that's told knowingly, not really naïvely. But it must be a matter of words put to experiences—which they are.

Björne has simply done an about-face in time and gone backward into the olden days, as he calls it. In the olden days people did such and such. In the olden days they thought, saw, understood.

But what they understood was how to live in their own time and the loner in the cabin doesn't understand that.

Afore things was better'n they is now
now you's worser off than you was then.

They rattle off that jingle at country fairs. Not Björne, of course, because he never goes to them. But he too denies tuberculosis and incest and abuse and near-starvation and ignorance—he even denies aching joints, although the damp of his cabin gives them to him.

The difference between the loner in his cabin and me is that I always go back to school on Monday morning. I know my attempts at finding an alternative are imperfect, and that my job is to teach schoolchildren to think.

It was the dog days, in the compost, in the newspapers. Something swelled and ran. The flies became intrusive. The newspapers reported murders and perverted sadists. The arts pages stank of rotting flesh, as if from the fridge of a mass murderer.

Birger didn't read about it, but he dreamed of it at night. He was being chased, he saw someone cut to pieces before his eyes, and he was acting mentally ill to escape the same fate.

He woke, got up, and drank some milk. He spread some crispbread and heard it crackling and crunching between his teeth in the silent gray morning. He thought about that time, about the tent and the bodies. He didn't usually do that.

Nor had Annie. At any rate, she hadn't talked about it. He remembered once when they had been watching the news on television, a report from some republic that had recently been part of the Soviet Union. Two men lay on the back of a truck, dead, their throats cut, one with his mouth wide open so you could see all his top teeth. Birger and Annie had been eating when the report started. After the two corpses on the truck, a young man came on and said other men had cut his father's arms and legs off and slit open his belly, letting the intestines well out, and all this had happened while his father was still alive, the son looking on. Another report eventually came on and Birger started eating again. Annie had long since gone.

That was quite usual. All she said about it was that she had seen the effects of murderous violence once only and that was quite enough.

No one believed any longer that Annie's death was accidental or self-inflicted. They wanted to arrange an exhibition in the community center in her memory. It was also to be a statement against mindless violence.

"I'm not sure it was all that mindless," said Birger when the minister had telephoned. They were thinking of moving the summer church's coffee room from Röbäck to Blackwater. That was where the tourists stopped off, ever since the police had held a press conference and retreated from the accident theory. On the Sunday, the exhibition was to be opened and the minister was to say a memorial prayer for her. Birger thought that was mad. She hadn't been indifferent to religion as most people were, but utterly hostile to his Christianity.

All concepts of a god had begun as belief in ghosts, she had said. A power-drunk gangster keeps his tribe in terror and awe. When he dies, they are so terrified and dominated by his will, they hallucinate his voice and his steps and his mad laughter at night. And they claim they can still hear them, or that was her understanding of it, though they've covered it all with sugar icing. She was extremely grateful that neither Henny nor Åke nor her uncle and aunt had taken her to any church or made her go to Sunday school. She sensed that if you imbibed those confused outpourings early on, you would always to some extent be susceptible to them.

It would have been tactless to tell the minister that, and anyway he wouldn't have believed it. Annie had led the church choir and she had sung a solo every year from the gallery at funerals and weddings. None of that tallied. Nor had she ever claimed that it did.

The minister was to contact Mia for contributions to the exhibition—pictures and drawings from Annie's school material, her nature screens and all that kind of thing. Birger phoned Langvasslien and Mia came down with Johan and six Siberian huskies in a dog van. She was pleased about the exhibition. As long as Annie's death was said to have been self-inflicted, there seemed to be something shameful about it. Now Lisa Kronlund patted Mia on the cheek and said:

"You poor thing, you, losing your mother."

Mia came down in the dog van with Annie's most beautiful drawings. The chairs in the community center had been taken out and stacked in the little coffee room. The minister was up a ladder in his wine-red shirt and discreet little dog collar, fastening a nylon fishing line to the head of a white paper dove and trying to find the right place to fix it so that the dove didn't tip over when hung up.

Screens had been put around the walls in the assembly room. MEMORY

LANE it said on the first one and underneath was a childlike drawing of a house, diagrammatical and at the same time very complicated. In each room one object had been drawn in detail. In the first basement room was an ax on a chopping block beside an amputated foot; in the other two, broken jars out of which something red was pouring. The rooms were numbered and their contents macabre, possibly a little more gruesome with each floor.

Mia stood there with her cardboard box in her arms, breathing fast. The five people in the hall were working by the screens, busy with paper and drawing pins. Clumsily they put down their utensils and came over to greet her, their faces expressing compassion and embarrassment. The minister, alone familiar with grief, came quickly over. But he couldn't catch up with Mia, who was striding swiftly from screen to screen. At the fifth or sixth she started saying something between clenched teeth. It sounded like "hell." In the intervals her mouth was moving as if she were chewing something between her front teeth. Suddenly she caught sight of a thin man in a crocheted skullcap.

"Petrus! You bloody creep!"

Petrus Eliasson's goatee was quite white nowadays. He was wearing a shirt of heavy cream-colored material that fell beautifully over the cuffs around his wrists. The Tree of Life was embroidered on the back of his crocheted vest. He had been at the funeral, but either Mia hadn't seen him there, or he hadn't succeeded in annoying her. Birger had thought it quite touching that he had come all the way down from the Gädde district, where he lived with his women and his cheesemaking. His women were new. One of them worked, just as Annie had, as a teacher. One came every weekend from Östersund and her job in a builder's office. The third was a textile artist, a younger version of Barbro Lund.

"You've arranged this," Mia hissed at Petrus. Then her voice rose in volume. "Take it down! Take it all away!"

Petrus stood there, blinking. Anna Starr and the members of the church choir were breathing heavily through their open mouths.

"Are you involved in this? Don't you understand anything? Take it down. There'll be no exhibition. *Are you deaf?*" Mia shouted. "Take it all down! Help me, Birger! Johan! All this has got to come down. Out you go, all of you! Don't imagine you can do things like this."

The minister approached with all the assurance gained from a professional attitude to crises in life. Mia flung down her box and made whisking movements with her hands right in his face, as if trying to wave away an apparition. And she succeeded. As the women retreated into the coffee room, the minister followed them, but he stopped in the doorway.

Petrus approached Mia from behind, his head on one side and constantly licking his moist lips. When he addressed her in his soft singsong voice, she spun around and slapped him across the face.

"Out! Go away! You've no business in this village. Stay at home with your bloody stinking goats and your intellectual witches."

He stumbled toward the door. The pastor had gotten the hiccups and was trying to keep his mouth shut, but kept forgetting. Birger itched to intervene with some good advice, but then saw Anna Starr holding a glass of water to the pastor's mouth. She carefully closed the door behind her.

Mia didn't start crying until they were left on their own. She wept with her mouth wide open and went on ripping the drawings off the screens.

"Johan, get a garbage bag out of the car!"

Petrus opened the door, leaned forward, and said that the material had not belonged to Annie. It had been her schoolchildren's. They had collected it from pupils who were now adult and they had to return it. He had to keep on talking for some time, since Mia was at the other end of the hall. But when she strode across the floorboards and hit him with a piece of cardboard, he retreated.

Birger thought Johan was looking rather pale, but he was working efficiently, asking no questions. They filled two bags. Mia kicked them into the coffee room, where the banished ones were lying low.

"Do what the hell you like with them. But don't exhibit them. Not anywhere. Leave my mother in peace! Do you hear! *Leave her in peace.*"

When they got up to the house, Mia was exhausted and went to lie down on Annie's bed. Birger made coffee and Johan sat at the kitchen table.

"What was all that about?" he asked in a low voice.

Well, what was it all about? Shame, partly. Shame and affection.

"Annie had rather original educational ideas," said Birger. "Mia will probably tell you about them later."

At first Annie had spoken of it only flippantly and in passing. When there was no longer any risk of his thinking consolation was what she wanted, she told him. Corny or not, she had said, but I loved my work and was fulfilled by it all those years in Byvången. Otherwise I would have probably lived like most people and kept looking at my watch during working hours.

At first, of course, it was the usual mild boredom. I had little encounters that brightened the day. I read a lot and longed for bed and my book. Moved in with Göran Dubois. That didn't last long enough to be serious. His mother put an end to it. But that was nothing important. I realize that now. I was sleeping spasmodically and eating too much.

The tedium of school has a particular flavor. Knobbly sweaters and unwashed bodies. And that lethargy. They did as I told them. Snorted sometimes, giving me shifty looks. That meant some internal joke I hadn't heard. Occasional shoving, chairs scraping, bursts of laughter, and suppressed swearing. But never a protest.

They were prepared to spend six years in this half-light. And they obeyed me. They never asked why they had to learn this or that. They just tried, most of them absently. The girls were more ambitious, but their efforts were also swallowed by the winter darkness. Toward the end of the autumn term we were like fish in a lake that has almost frozen solid.

Then Police Day came. The police chief and his assistant came to the school in their black-and-white car. They were in uniform and carrying briefcases. For a whole day they went from classroom to classroom to talk about their work.

At the time there was considerable contempt for the police in radical circles. The idea of a PR drive had originated higher up and down south. Demonstrations or the formation of terrorist groups were unlikely up here. In my classroom there were only future drunk drivers and workers in the black economy who might occasionally bash the wife or a neighbor. They would add an amplifier or an electric typewriter when reporting a burglary, but they would never think of protesting against anything. In what the police chief called the present scenario, the children were not interested in hearing how he and his assistant served the community and made life safe for people. They wanted to hear how they chased robbers.

The police chief came to my classroom late in the afternoon. Maybe he was exhausted, because when they asked him, he told them without any evasions how he had chased a robber.

This was two years ago, he said, when he was working in Sveg. There was a nationwide alert out for a bank robber. He had escaped while on a hospital visit, stolen a car, picked up his girlfriend in Borlänge, and driven north. In Mora, he had abandoned the first car and stolen a red Cortina.

At about two o'clock in the afternoon someone had phoned from the main supermarket in Hede asking the police to go after a couple who had left without paying for two shopping bags full of beer and food from the deli counter. They were in a red Cortina.

The red car got away, but the road was blocked farther north. Our police chief, an assistant at the time, was one of those who found the car up in Vemdalsskalet. They had run out of gas. That night there had been a blizzard that lasted until toward noon. The car was buried in the snow and all tracks obliterated. The police searched through a whole holiday village for the runaway and his girl and found them finally in the only real building up there. They were dead, frozen to death. The wood stove was stuffed with logs and newspaper. They had used up several boxes of matches. But they had never opened the damper. It had smoked in, but they hadn't died from inhaling smoke. They had died of cold.

"They went out like a light."

All eyes were on the police chief. Behind him, the green blackboard was blank.

"They died because they didn't know how to light a wood stove," he said. There were questions and cries, objections and assertions, but he stuck to it: They had died because they couldn't get the stove going.

When the bell went, he had to go to the next classroom. But the children carried on. I saw them in the playground. In the deepening dusk they were gesticulating. I had never seen them do that before. They usually stood with their hands thrust into their jacket pockets, their shoulders hunched in the cold. The bus from town went past and the beam from its headlights swept over them. Some children ran over to the shelter to catch the bus back to Blackwater.

Why should I learn this? The police chief had managed to arouse this question in them. Not me. To survive, was the harsh answer his story gave. That was how we got on to what you needed to survive. Without even a cottage. Lighting a fire. Filing a hook out of a barb. Out of what? What do you use? And have you any fishing line on you? Do you go around carrying a fishing line?

Tying on a fly. Making a cooking vessel out of a beer can. Looking for Norrland lichen. What about when the matches run out?

A girl pointed out that you could avoid going out in mist and blizzards. If you behaved yourself, you wouldn't have to escape from prison, either. Then Stefan with the brown eyes said:

"But what if everything runs out?"

"What do you mean, everything?"

"The electricity. If the cables fall down. If there's a war and a nuclear bomb."

In that way, I had access one winter afternoon to their fears. That was a room they very seldom opened to adults. They had all seen a girl running along the road with her burning skin crackling into a white map pattern. They had seen her several times. She was running underneath the thick curved glass of the television screen. She was naked and the same age as they were, so she was real. They learned to read that map of cracked skin.

One bright spark said they ought to learn to light a wood stove at school. In case. Then suggestions fell thick and fast. Now it was a question of what you needed to survive the collapse of civilization. Not in reeking, radioactive ruins, nor on contaminated shores. No, they would retreat into the forest. Up to the mountain. The long slopes below Bear Mountain would still be there. They ran over unstable marshlands. Their skin wasn't burned away. They ran in cold, fresh air and I hadn't the heart to spoil their picture. Someone said they ought to learn to weave. And to build a log house. That should be taught at school. In case.

One of them who had mostly said nothing asked who decided what they should learn. I promised I would bring the curriculum to show them.

I was in a state of great tension, my skin prickling. I was full of laughter and had tears in my eyes. They had started asking the questions: Why should I learn this? Isn't it unnecessary? They balanced this against that *in case.*

I was feverish with eagerness that evening and simply couldn't sleep. I kept having one idea after another, my mind exploding and brilliant.

A red file. A green file. Two workbooks. One for continuity. One for *in case.* I had found my teaching method.

It started that simply. Every element of knowledge from the basic curriculum we put into the red book for a start, then weighed it against that *in case.* Computer knowledge against mental arithmetic. Social studies? What if no society existed any longer? Political parties? The capitals of Europe?

They figured out that things that weren't directly necessary for a settler life could be forgotten, and that was a pity. One girl wanted to transfer a crochet pattern of stars to the green book. That gave rise to several questions. Songs? Tunes? Notes even? The names of the stars and planets?

I watched out for inflationary tendencies in their new way of thinking. All by themselves—or thanks to a tired police officer—they had found out that they lived in a civilization. Now they were finding out that there were the remains of a culture in it and that both were fundamentally based on knowledge. If all conceivable knowledge began to swirl like fireworks around their heads, they would soon give up. Faced with complications, we bow down and go on jogging along. Better to be bored than insane.

So with no discussion I decided that everything they wanted to have with them *in case* should be written down in detail. No abstract generalizations, but recipes. Formulas. Construction drawings. Words and notes of songs. Thus the recorder, the loom, the sourdough loaf, and the composition of mortar all went into the green workbook.

Winter came and we tussled with the cirriculum, but relaxed with definitions of edible plants and a careful copy of "My Pony Has Gone." We discussed the manufacture of steel for knives and the tanning of elk hide. We got twice as much done and we felt no fatigue. We were playing, I suppose.

The fact that a teacher let the children have two workbooks, "one more concrete," as I expressed it, was nothing remarkable. Teachers of music, art, and sewing helped us with various projects. I didn't involve the woodworking teacher. Something told me that would be dangerous.

I was electrified from within by my ideas. They never seemed to come to an end. The children were excited or thoughtful, each according to his or her temperament. Many of them were ingenious, some sharp. Some were very imaginative, two or three rebellious. Perhaps, perhaps, I thought occasionally. But I was always on the watch for prophetic tendencies from within. I had quite simply found a way of teaching and that was it.

I lived for three years with those first children of the double files, and when they had moved up to middle school, I knew that my teaching had had an effect. I had echoes back through their new teachers. My experiment did not appear extreme. I blurred things whenever I was asked. It was not all that well thought out, I said. Just two workbooks. One for older and rather more concrete knowledge.

I was careful with my secret. It must not seem political. Anything political—that was the red rag that made the bulls snort and stamp at their kitchen tables.

For two more years I followed this double line in my teaching. With the new third grade, I had to do the police officer's exploit all over again, but this time as a trick. It didn't work. They had already heard the story of the couple who had died of cold because they couldn't light a wood stove. I had to make up other stories and the start was sluggish. To my sorrow, I noticed that the majority accepted the green workbook in the same dull and compliant way as they would have accepted any idea at all if coming from above. Of three rebels in this class, two were really grumblers.

There was one buffoon, of course. He was unusually unfortunate, an overweight boy, foul-mouthed and slow-witted. His genre was malice. With sleepy intuition he found weak points and squeezed. It was like being bitten in the thigh by a horse.

He was the one to suggest that first and foremost you had to have beer to survive. Roars of laughter and belches. Indignant girls. Hopeful light in the expressions of the grumblers.

But I went into it, and thanks to the brewing of beer, we actually got going. When they discovered its considerable complications—the bundle of straw in the vat, the mash that must not be over sixty-five degrees Celsius if the enzymes are to survive, and has to be quickly cooled so as not to be attacked by microorganisms—they sat in silence for a long time. They had to invent the thermometer. They had no fingertip feel for the temperature of a liquid. We established that in the physics lab. Several of the girls could distinguish between body heat and hotter. Some of them used the skin on their upper lips as thermometers. But for the difference between sixty-five degrees and seventy, they could find no way to react.

The beer never went into the workbook. It stopped at drainage, when one genius found you couldn't grow grain without it. They were used to marshlands. So their own catastrophe, too, was blown through by the wind from the Norwegian mountains and driving rain and snow from the North Atlantic.

We had been working for almost two years when a girl called Unni patted her green workbook and said:

"So us must jist have'n wi'us then."

That was how we started on ways of memorizing knowledge. I showed them *The Iliad* and the Gilgamesh epic and told them that mnemonic professionals had had all that in their heads. Thanks to them it had survived. They had to start ransacking themselves. What would they remember without the green workbook?

We started working out techniques. I have to admit that looms and making nails were shoved into the background in this class. They had found their sport. Even the most skillful soon noticed that there wasn't much they could take in and repeat, not in comparison with the orators of the past. I told them they had had their tricks, that the techniques of memorizing had even been a special science at the time.

They had pictured the memory store equipped as a large, handsome, and complicated building—usually a temple. It had halls, apses, corridors, and porticos. In the halls were altars and tables and pillars. In every room was an object they could connect with an element in the mass of knowledge they wished to remember. They organized it quite concretely, with imagery that was often startling, even macabre. I told them about the bloodstained, decapitated heads and the flayed deer, about the ram testicles and poisonous snakes that had lain in these echoing halls and to which people of the past had linked their knowledge.

The children had none of the adult demand for a meaningful connection between what they wanted to remember and the symbol that would remind them of it. Without difficulty they all thought up elements as they walked through the halls. The girls put five cute kittens in a memory room. Two boys found it more effective to use five drowned kittens.

The kittens lay on a flowery sofa, because we had to use the Ikea store in Sundsvall as a memory temple and their sofas were floral. We had recently been on a school trip and knew of no other large premises we could use. Then they had to construct their own memory house. But they lived in places where there were no large or remarkable buildings, so I gave them permission to go down memory lane out of doors if they liked.

But they were not to put too great a distance between the places, because then the memory became blurred. Many of the boys put their lane between the elk passes in the hunting areas.

One girl asked if memory lanes could be secret. I said yes, as long as they worked, they could be secret. After that concession, I know I lost control over two or three of them as they went down their memory lanes. I had no idea which halls they were going through or what they saw. But I had no regrets.

Everything had been quite calm, but in the spring of the fourth year, one thing happened after another. First, I was invited to dinner at the principal's house. I didn't feel very comfortable there. They were equipped with kitchen gadgets, a stereo, and inherited wineglasses. We had curried fillet of pork au gratin, bananas and cream, and the principal wanted to talk about my relations with the children. I thought his interest seemed unwholesome.

The second event occurred in the empty staff room. I met the principal and he talked about nothing in particular at first. All I remember was that he asked if I was depressed and found it hard to sleep. That was disagreeable. I said I was in fine form, but fell asleep late when my mind was full of ideas.

"Have you always had periods of depression alternating with periods of a great desire for activity?"

What do you say to that kind of thing? Of course, I said:

"Yes, haven't you?"

The third event: I was summoned to his office. He was more formal this time and I could see he was nervous. Without too much preamble, he asked me why I had given up my job at the college. He knows, I thought.

"You were teaching up at the Starhill commune, weren't you?"

Then the next incredible question: How had I taken that double murder? Taken. Double murder. They were words I simply couldn't fit into my way of thinking. They were so hopelessly inadequate.

I should have given the matter more thought. But I did as I usually do when people get too complicated. I thought, He's crazy. And left it at that. I went on working and reading.

The fifth event took place in the staff room. One of the teachers had a share in a racehorse. He used to arrange the bets. The stakes were collected up when you were paying your dues into the coffee pool. This time he had thought up something more piquant. The woman he was living with, a gym teacher at the school, was going to have a baby and she was quite far gone. Now we could sign a list and leave ten kronar, then bet on when the baby would arrive. Nearly every day for fourteen days ahead had already been filled in when I came into the room.

I was furious. I knew that five of the younger male teachers got together to watch porn films on Tuesday evenings when their wives were attending a batik course. That was silly. But this was indecent.

"Who wins if the baby's dead?" I said.

At first there was a silence, then a terrific hullabaloo because I refused to give way. I demanded an answer from him. The principal came past in the middle of it all. He took me to his office and I told him what they were doing. The racehorses, the pregnant partner, the lot. You can imagine how many friends I had on the staff after that. The principal said that of course no betting of any kind should take place in school. He asked me if I had taken it very hard when my own pregnancy had had such an unfortunate ending.

"That has nothing to do with this!" I shouted. "This isn't about my psychology. It's about decency!"

Then I went out and slammed the door so the glass rattled. The only thing I regretted was that I had said "decency." I really thought it was about dignity. But that word was too bizarre for this school, where senior pupils rubbed pea soup into each other's hair and men of fertile age got together to watch others screwing.

Things calmed down, though that was dull. Several teachers refused to speak to me in the staff room, but that didn't matter. I went on working. We were to have a parents' meeting.

I met the mothers of my class an hour or so beforehand, and we set the tables and decorated them. I thought they had put out far too many cups, but in fact a great many people did come. We had never had so many come to a class meeting before. Most came in couples. I wasn't used to seeing fathers there. The principal came down from his office and slipped in. Like an eel. The atmosphere was tense and I thought perhaps they were uneasy because he was there. Even a plumber I knew looked worried.

I began my little lecture, bade them welcome, and told them how far we had gotten and what plans we had. I was interrupted.

"Can we ask questions instead?"

I noticed they turned to the principal. He nodded, giving them permission to interrupt me just like that. But when they were to start asking questions, there was dead silence. That pleased me. I did nothing to help them out of their dilemma. The principal seemed about to intervene, when the first question—which wasn't a question at all—came. A woman's shrill voice said:

"I doesn't think it's right to frighten children with the end of the world!"

Then the questions started:

"Why do they have to learn the Ikea sofas!"

"Backward, for Christ's sake. Backward!"

"What's all this damn nonsense about the electricity being cut off?"

"Mats says he's got a room with five baby rats in a place and he's put the Bessemer process in there. Are you mad? How the hell can you teach kids that kind of thing? Rats! And the Bessemer process."

"Why do you say they've got a house inside their heads and that they have to learn all the rooms in the right order?"

I held up my hands and tried to quiet them.

"May I answer?"

"An amputated foot!" a woman cried out.

"Mats was to give a talk on the refining of iron," I said. "The house is an important part of the technique of memorizing. That there are five baby rats in a place means that is the fifth place. So there he will presumably remember the Bessemer process."

"Don't you know yourself what you're teaching?"

"They build their houses on their own. No one has any right to ask them what the buildings look like inside if they don't want to talk about it or draw it."

"Skeletons! Rats! Blood on the floor. A white lady with no head. 'Tis pure madness. And palaces. Anna-Karin has had to learn a whole palace."

"Sounds complicated," said the plumber quietly. "Isn't it easier to learn the ordinary way?"

That was a question I would have liked to answer, but I wasn't allowed to. And I had wanted to explain about the Ikea sofas. But now they started on about the Starhill commune, the smell of goat in skirts, about marijuana and maté, about a dead fetus Petrus was supposed to have buried.

"Afterbirth," I said. "And I don't live like them nowadays. I have a flat here in Byvången."

"Though what sort of furniture d'you have?" cried a woman who had never been to my place. "Cloths and wooden boxes! And a trestle table."

The principal had gotten up and kept opening his mouth without getting a word in, but his attempts were not really serious. They were doing his dirty work for him.

"D'you think everything's coming to an end?" cried a fat little woman whose whole figure I had rarely seen because she worked at the newsstand.

"Are you frightening the kids with that!"

"There's no need," I replied. "They're frightened enough already."

They didn't want me as a teacher of their children. Some thought I was mad, and most thought I was a leftie, which was the same thing, though self-inflicted. They demanded that the class should have another teacher.

The principal came into the firing line now that it was serious, so he had to get to his feet and take the abuse. He stood there in a blazer with huge lapels, tight flared trousers, and an open-necked shirt, the points of the collar spread out over his jacket, a silver pendant shaped like a fish dangling at his throat. His hair was brushed forward and grew just below the lobes of his ears, and the shoes he was wearing made him quite a bit taller than he was. I had been wrong to think they were afraid of him. He was one of them. Even though he'd been bright enough to become a principal, he still had to remember that his salary was paid by the taxpayers.

No one had had any coffee yet. The thermoses stood untouched on the red paper tablecloths and the pastries still lay there under the plastic wrap. Occasionally someone nudged a cup with an elbow or banged the table so hard, the china rattled.

"This has got to stop!"

That meant: Annie Raft has to go.

"Otherwise we'll have to go further up."

That meant the education authority.

Finally we were left alone, he and I. He said he at least partly understood that there was an educational idea behind my exercises with the pupils. But it was all far too original. And as the plumber had said, it seemed simpler to learn things the ordinary way.

"Cicero had that objection to this memorizing technique," I said. "But he hadn't even a whiff of what frightened them here."

"Yes, yes," said the principal. "You're full of ideas and there's nothing wrong with that. But one mustn't frighten the children."

"I haven't," I said. "I've frightened the parents."

"We've talked enough now. You sleep badly and are rather wrought up. You behaved in a very unbalanced way in the staff room. You'd better take some sick leave and then we'll see."

I really did feel ill. I was ready to throw up and I had a dreadful headache. It wasn't difficult to stay at home the next day. I had forty-five pastries in the larder.

Going back was more difficult. I decided to leave. After all, I had never meant to end up in Byvången. I went to Stockholm, thinking of substitute teaching until the autumn and seeing what cropped up.

But it didn't work. The city had changed. I remembered it as composed of artefacts, but it was becoming organic, with a substratum of sustenance. A green clump I had never seen before protruded out of the cliff above Slussen. Bad smells were coming from basement windows. The ventilation systems were crawling. The city hadn't stayed in place. It was growing, and smelled of procreation.

In August the air became difficult to breathe, heavy with humidity and invisible gases. Rats scuttled around in the creeper on the house in Strindbergsgatan, where I was staying with Henny. I went back to Blackwater and moved into Aagot's little red cottage by the road. Mia was lodging in Byvången and came back on the bus on weekends.

I had no idea what I was going to do. But then the teacher who lived in Lersjövik drove off the road on one of the first icy days and broke her arm. She became so scared of the daily drive to Blackwater that she resigned.

My principal was also the principal there. But he didn't turn me down. It was probably just as difficult to get teachers to come to this village as it was to get a pastor to stay in Röbäck. He gave me some fatherly advice. Stick to the curriculum. They'll keep their eye on you. That kind of thing gets around. And one mustn't frighten the children.

No, we mustn't frighten each other with the situation we already live in, which struggles and labors toward its fulfillment. It has neither invention nor direction, and yet it takes on innumerable forms, many of them so complex that some kind of fantasy seems to be indicated. And we mustn't try to predict the bizarre and cruel things that the end will produce before it reaches its own end.

I should have taken it more calmly. And yet the talk about radiation sickness and life without electricity was not that upsetting. For the parents it was the memory lane that was the real stumbling block. The fact that the children had an inner room that was empty except for fear, they had already sensed. They had one themselves. What frightened them more than anything was that the children might gain access to a large and strange building with many rooms, the contents of which they didn't have to tell anyone at all.

"Mia's mother was a proud creature. She would never have tolerated this defense. No affection that was mixed with shame. And most of all no compassion."

"But Mia was magnificent," said Johan.

She's taken the lead, Birger thought. All his life he'll plod along behind her, looking like this.

"What are you two saying about me?"

Mia had gotten up.

"We're saying you were magnificent," said Birger. "Petrus has an inspiring effect on women. But now I'll have to give the minister some venison."

"They were just going to use her for their own ends," Mia said.

"When Annie created memory lane, she was surrounded by very pronounced opponents," Birger explained to Johan. "Dark blue, true blue members of the Center Party. Cautious bourgeoisie in Byvången who looked on involvement as a sign of mental imbalance—I was one of them —and irresolute, politically ignorant women. Village women who one day want to live like their forefathers and the next day want to learn English and go to Rhodes with a woman friend. Away from their menfolk. But they leave food ready in the freezer: day 1, day 2, day 3 . . . That was their revolution, and it mostly didn't come off. Sometimes they come to life again. You saw them at the community center. Their aims aren't really dubious."

"But it was Petrus who took over," said Mia.

361

"He has a strong personality."

"He's an animal. And now he's become trendy as well. A café in a red and white cottage. Hand-painted signs. And money from the local authority for courses in ethics. But his breath still smells bad. And he's interested in only one thing: cheese and screwing."

"That's two," said Birger.

"He was already a dirty old man up at Starhill. We kids thought he was disgusting. He climbed on the ladies. At any time of the day. Well, not on Mom. Don't go thinking that."

Preferably not, Birger thought.

"Did you find it difficult up there?" Johan asked in a troubled voice.

"No, we had fun. Everyone was kind. To be fair, so was Petrus. They didn't squabble with each other."

"Was Dan kind to you?"

Birger found it difficult to say the name and felt he had moved closer to the morass within him. He didn't want to start crying. He was ashamed of these attacks, which came without warning and which Mia regarded with rigid dislike.

"Dan was great. He was so lovely somehow. Though I went crazy when he was with Mom. I wanted him to be with me. She thought I was angry with him. Dan never fought about anything. He sat there with his long, golden hair and laughed at Petrus and the women. Yes—he was angry once. Then he went quite crazy. That was all my fault."

She fell silent.

"What happened?" said Birger.

"I'd found a pair of jeans in that old barn they didn't use. We were always looking everywhere for fun things and there were lots. People had lived there once. We were always digging around and searching, and I found those jeans stuffed under the feedstuffs table. I gave them to Mom because they were too big for me. They were too big for her, too, the legs miles too long. But she was awfully pleased. She always wore them. Then Dan came home and they had an argument about them. He yelled and shouted and I was frightened. That was the only time. But that was because it was my fault. Though he didn't know that."

"Did Dan know anything about that business down by the Lobber?"

"He knew who the guy in the tent was. They all knew."

"Annie too?"

"I think so."

"She never said anything about it."

"No, they didn't want to talk about it. I've no idea how it all hung together. Though I do know one thing. I had a Barbie boy doll called Ken originally. But we rechristened him, the other kids and I. He was called John Larue. I knew how it was spelled and how it was pronounced. I was six. And in some way I have always known that it was the name of the guy in the tent. Us kids knew that."

J ohan hadn't often thought of Ylja. That memory was silent and cut off. A blind alley.

But he had thought about those forests. After almost two decades, he still remembered his dream of flying, without wings of any kind, above a sweet-smelling forest of deciduous trees: late-flowering limes, dark-leaved guelder-rose trees, oaks, and chestnuts, each treetop a world of its own. Gigantic ashes, elms with stiff leaves, silvery-gray willows by reflecting water. Hazel bushes in airy thickets, washed through with light.

He had thought out the names of the species of trees later. He had liked thinking about that twilight forest and the way he had slowly moved above its treetops in a gliding flight that hadn't surprised him in the slightest.

Gradually he had found out the truth about that roof of foliage, which had looked to him like a billowing floor. Ylja had been right. Europe really had been covered with forests. There had been huge marshland areas and morasses. Mountain ranges and wide rivers. But most of all forest. Far away beneath the Caucasus, trees had soughed, far out by the shores of the Atlantic.

He regarded his thoughts on forests as respectable, the kind you can dwell on occasionally. But her tall story about the Traveler and the women was not so good. He had never reflected much on it.

One winter afternoon, he had been in the county library in Östersund. He was waiting for Mia, who was out shopping, and he took the opportunity to look through what they had on Sami culture and religion. On a shelf labeled RELIGIOUS KNOWLEDGE, GENERAL, his eye fell on a spine with the title *The Myth of the Traveler.*

He could feel a movement in his chest. It was powerful and resembled the swift change of pressure in a bow when the arrow is released. He thought what he regarded as his ego was forever changing, though the process was slow and with a great many retakes. The idea of an arrow that had been in the firing position for almost two decades amazed him.

The book had been rebound by the library; the paper was shiny and heavy. It had been printed in Åbo and had a very involved subtitle inside. The author was a lecturer in folklore and religious knowledge called Doris Hofstaedter. It was impossible to get anything out of it by just leafing through and reading at random. When Mia arrived, he took it out on her library card. Laughing, she asked what he wanted that offputting tome for. For the very first time, he lied to her. He said it dealt with a Sami fairy tale he had heard as a child.

It had happened so quickly that not until afterward had he realized it was a double lie. He had never heard any Sami fairy tales as a child.

It was a terribly dull book and he never got right through it. It had a footnote system in small print that was the most comprehensive he had ever seen. He gathered that the myth of the Traveler was well known all over Europe. The author accounted for its spread and all the different variations in a thoroughly scholarly manner. There were no modern complications. The women who preserved the myth and who were spread all over the world had been invented by Ylja. He dismissed it as feminist blather, though that was not the way he ordinarily thought. He substituted it with fantasies of the kind he had at puberty. Ylja had known how to get the blood racing through his head and elsewhere.

She had not been a blatherer. More fervent and stern. Images came to him of her regular features, too boyish to be beautiful, of the coarse blond hair and her body, smelling of sun and dry forest slopes, stretched out on a foam mattress with a yellow-and-green-striped cover. Suddenly they changed. He saw Ylja walking toward the dark house in the dusky night, unsteadily and swerving toward the river. All the time she was singing:

> *"Below the belly*
> *hangs his prick*
> *like a little*
> *yellow tulip."*

"What are you thinking about?" said Mia.

Well, what was he thinking about? He wasn't thinking at all, just staring at images. One of them ought to have disappeared in the shedding of shells and emptying of content he had thought was the process that constituted his ego. And the other was one he had never known he had. He was feeling like a very old person. He had heard that old people could haul up fresh memories from the well of the past.

At first he thought Ylja must have read the book. Then he saw that it had come out two years after their stay in Trollevolden. But what does a lecturer absorbed in a major work of learning on the myths of wandering do? Lectures about them, of course, runs seminars. Ylja must have been one of a group of young students at a seminar in Åbo. Future scholars of religion.

No—that was too ridiculous. She had been studying another subject and had gone to the lectures out of curiosity. Only someone who approached the subject as pure entertainment could twist the myth of the Traveler around in the way she had done.

It then struck him that if Ylja had belonged to a seminar group, the lecturer would know her. If he described the fair, boyish, perhaps rather caustic girl student, it was possible her teacher might remember her.

He wasn't keen on the idea. He didn't want to go to the police. That was like putting your hand down into dark waters and fishing up God knows what kind of trash. He wanted to know what would be brought to light before he went to the police with it.

Things were all right between him and Mia now. But fragile. It had been that way ever since he had understood she could make unpredictable decisions.

He telephoned Åbo Academy and asked for Doris Hofstaedter. She turned out to have become a professor and had moved to the University of Helsinki. The receptionist was willing to give him the university number, but he asked for her home number. She didn't have it, and anyhow she wouldn't have given it to him just like that, she said ungraciously. She probably thought he was going to trouble the professor with rude words and heavy breathing.

It wasn't difficult to find her number and address through directory inquiries. Professor Hofstaedter did not suffer from female paranoia. He dialed the number, not expecting her to answer herself. It was summer and hot. Helsinki must be a desert. But Doris Hofstaedter was there and picked up the phone and answered absently and only barely politely.

He regretted it immediately, but had the presence of mind to speak in Norwegian. He asked her whether she was going to be at home over the next few days and would she be prepared to accept a large package of books from Oslo University. She was. What books were they?

"I can't say," he said. "They're all wrapped up."

He noticed with some excitement that he was able to lie swiftly and not without ingenuity.

He had imagined flying to Helsinki, a quick interview with the professor, then a trip to Åbo in a rented car to check seminar lists of eighteen years ago. After that, the tracking down would be trickier, he realized that. But he felt luck was on his side.

Birger Torbjörnsson wanted to come along. That was inconvenient, but hard to refuse, considering the sorry state he was in, pacing around his untidy apartment like a large, sick bear.

He wanted to go to the police with the name John Larue. Mia didn't think they would attach any importance to the name of a doll. Only if a John Larue were missing would there be any action. And no missing person had been reported at the time of the event by the Lobber.

Johan did not tell Mia much about the woman who had given him a lift and might be presumed to have met Larue. It wasn't just because he felt sorry for him that Johan took Birger with him. He was afraid he might talk too much. Not without shame, Johan remembered that he had preached openness to Mia. But he drew the line at Ylja. He had no wish to appear as an ardent and gullible adolescent.

Birger turned their trip into a long-winded affair. He found out that a package including boat fare and hotel room would be cheapest. Johan had heard that Birger seldom went anywhere except Blackwater for his holidays. Now he turned up lugging a heavy old leather suitcase. He found it difficult to adapt to the rules of mass tourism. He tried to buy some liquor without lining up, and to joke with the exhausted Finnish cleaners. When they went into the dining room, he was drawn to the laden buffet table. He described how during his training he had cultivated bacteria in a nutrient jelly that looked exactly like the aspic from which the salmon now stared at them with white eyeballs. He recounted this without lowering his voice, and aroused animosity.

They had shrimps, drank Finnish vodka and juice, and largely did what was expected on board ship. After coffee, Johan worked a one-armed bandit a few times and lost. Birger put some coins in and gave it a go. The apparatus rattled and spewed a flood of silver coins into the cup. It kept spitting them out, squealing and flashing its lights. The cup overflowed and the coins streamed all over the carpet at their feet. People stopped and watched. Birger stood quite still while Johan tried to gather up the abundance.

Then Birger started to weep. He remained upright, but otherwise he wept in the same way as he had when he had brought coffee to Johan in bed in his living room, his mouth gaping open, nose and eyes streaming. His regular snuffling gasps for breath soon left him in a state of cramp that made his chest and gradually also his capacious stomach tremble and bounce.

People laughed and he was given encouraging cries. They thought he was weeping for joy. Johan wanted to take him away, but, unable to leave all those gapers the money, he knelt down and collected up every single coin, while Birger stood there exposed, sobbing loudly, and dribbling mucus and tears.

When Johan piloted him into their cabin and was trying to get him into bed, Birger struck his head on the top bunk. The pain stopped the convulsive crying. Exhausted, he sat on the bunk, leaning forward. Johan put a wet towel across his forehead and placed Birger's hand on it to hold it there. Then Johan opened the whiskey bottle he had bought and drank almost half a bathroom glass. He was not sure it was good for Birger to drink whiskey after his attack of weeping, but compromised by giving him just a splash.

He knew Birger was weeping because Annie was dead, but couldn't work out why the cataclysm of the gaming machine had released the attack. Birger was talking indistinctly about an unbearable, mocking smile. At first Johan thought he was referring to his fellow passengers, but Birger said it was no one's, just a smile of derision. Then he said: It was chance, sheer chance. He kept saying the word over and over again, and it lost all meaning.

"Hardly chance," Johan said, interrupting him to put an end to it. "If so, in a very narrow sense. Those machines are programmed to give out money now and again. You could tell that this one was ready because there were staff standing around waiting to have a try. They keep an eye on the machines and know when they're getting close."

Johan went on talking about generating chance. He told Birger about how you could randomize in a computer, and to his extreme relief Birger fell asleep without any more weeping. He had an ugly red mark on his forehead.

In the morning, after they had handed in Birger's huge suitcase and Johan's bag at the hotel, they at once took a taxi to the address of Professor Hofstaedter. She lived in a late eighteenth-century building, weighty and impressive, untouched by the light and sea-blown classicism that had greeted them as they disembarked. Late summer prevailed in the market down by the harbor; big bunches of dill and beet, rudbeckia and snapdragons in the flower stalls, crayfish, lampreys, herrings, onions, and knobbly gherkins—an abundance of scents dispersing in the cool air and floating out to sea as lightly as violets. Inside this stony city there was no season at all. Hofstaedter's building was guarded by limestone gnomes holding up the entrance archway on their bowed backs. Johan pressed the bell on the entry phone and they stood listening to the clatter of trams from the street as they waited. But no one answered.

The building turned out to be not all that far from the Marski Hotel. The taxi had been unnecessary. They went into Fazer's café and had coffee. Johan ordered a sandwich with his, but Birger, untroubled, gorged himself on cream cakes.

All day they roamed between the apartment building and the inner-city attractions of Helsinki. Johan began to think they had come in vain. Birger didn't seem to care much about the outcome of their trip. He said he was glad to be able to get away for a while. He stood for a long time in front of Iittala's shop window, staring at the glassware. He also attempted to pat the statue of Havis Amanda on the backside, but Johan stopped him and suggested they should take a tram on the circle line and take a look at Finlandia House. Birger seemed to be enjoying himself and it was hard to imagine that at any moment he might have one of his heartbreaking attacks of weeping. Johan suspected that he was wound up like a clock. He knew what he was going to do and say, even when faced with a female behind.

At five in the afternoon they heard Doris Hofstaedter's voice over the entry phone. It silenced Johan, but Birger introduced them both and said they were looking for the professor on an urgent mission. She wanted to know what mission.

"We're looking for someone we think you know. A student of yours. From your Åbo days."

The sound quality was poor and she repeated her question several times, but in the end she let them in. They went up to the third floor in a creaking elevator with iron gates. She gave them the once-over through the peephole, then opened the door.

Everything in the place was old and impressive. Johan figured it was not the professor's parents who had furnished the apartment, but more likely her grandparents. They squeezed their way past a vast baroque cupboard in the hall, sabers and pistols hanging on the wall, paintings in heavy carved gilt frames of dark green landscapes in which only a silvery-white streak of a river or a foaming waterfall was distinguishable.

The professor herself was a gruff woman with short dark hair, streaked with white like a badger's. She wore glasses apparently designed for reading; idly she had pushed them down her nose instead of taking them off. She was wearing a black and white cotton dress of modernistic design with a zipper down the front, a kind of tent, the body underneath shapeless. Her face was puffy, particularly below the eyes where the glasses pressed. She had pads of fat below the skin that pulled down her cheeks and blurred her jawline. Johan thought she looked rather frightening and he felt awkward in this magnificent, gloomy apartment. But Birger plowed on without embarrassment, obviously used to going into people's homes and breathing in the odors they lived in. He looked as if he were quite genially about to lift up the cotton tent and put his fingers into the professor's abundant yellow flesh.

She took them into a room that appeared to be a library, the walls lined with shelves of leatherbound books. There was a sagging sofa with greenish-gray cushions covered with dog hair. Johan didn't find that out until later, on his trousers. There was no sign of a dog. The room grew dark. She had drawn the brown velvet curtains, then switched on a lamp. Johan found himself sitting right in the lamplight.

He told her that many years ago he had gotten to know a girl who was probably one of the professor's students.

"Why do you think that?"

"She talked about your research," said Johan.

"What did she talk about?"

"About the Traveler."

He had expected her to want to know more about what the girl had told him, perhaps out of professional vanity or quite simply because she was skeptical. But she said:

"What do you want of her?"

He was not quite sure whether she was being hostile or not. Her intonation was Finnish and not easy to interpret. In any case, she was certainly not forthcoming.

"She knew someone I want to find out more about."

"Who?"

"His name was John Larue," said Birger helpfully.

"I don't know what girl you're talking about. Describe her."

She had been standing with her back to the window and the drawn curtains. Now she sat down in a leather armchair with large brass-studded wings and Johan saw she was wearing sandals. Coarse leather sandals consisting of nothing but a couple of straps over a sole and a crude fastener. She had small, well-formed feet and seemed to have worn sandals a lot, for she had no bunions and her toes were classically straight and close together. Johan fell silent.

"Well?"

"She was fair," he said. But nothing more came. He stared past the feet down at the rug, which was a dark brownish-red, Oriental, worn but with a still-distinguishable pattern of stylized ornamental flowers. From somewhere behind him, perhaps from the blue and white jar on the floor by the tiled stove, came a strong scent of lemony spices and dried petals.

"Well, I must have had a lot of students with fair hair," she said. "What did she look like?"

He couldn't get it out. He could see her before him but couldn't describe her. No other words except "fair" and "dry" came to him. He could hear Birger's anxious, labored breathing.

"Well," she said. "It doesn't matter."

She got up. They had to rise from the sofa. Johan made another attempt, but got stuck with something worse than a lack of words. His throat closed. He couldn't get a word out and made a hissing sound when he tried to speak, as if he were very hoarse. Professor Hofstaedter laughed.

"Don't take it so hard," she said. "It wouldn't have helped however eloquently you had described her. I don't hand out names of female students to a couple of unknown gentlemen from Sweden and Norway."

"Why did she say Norway?" said Birger once they were down in the street.

"Because she recognized my voice. I phoned a few days ago and pretended to be Norwegian. I wanted to know if she was at home."

"Christ" was all Birger said.

The professor seemed to have shaken him more than their failure.

They couldn't think of anything else to do but have a meal to pass the time until they could go to bed. They found a little Russian restaurant down a side street in the city center, the interior all gold, black, and red with a heavy smell of perfume and food. Birger wanted to try bear ham, but simply seeing the words on the menu disgusted Johan. They agreed on borscht, blini, and chopped salt herring with onion and sour cream. It was all very rich and filling and Johan found it hard to swallow. They took a sweet brown vodka and Birger grew tipsy. Johan drank modestly, afraid of feeling sick. When they got back to their double room at the hotel, they went to bed with no more argument about their failed visit to Doris Hofstaedter. Birger slept heavily. Johan lay awake listening to the trams.

After an hour, he got up and dressed. He walked along the Arctic night-empty streets, and when he got to the entrance with the gnomes, he pressed the button and after a brief pause heard that harsh voice. She hadn't been asleep. He hadn't thought she would be, either.

"It's Johan Brandberg."

She received him in the same tent dress, but barefoot and smoking a thin cigarette that smelled foreign.

"Jukka dear," she said. "I thought you'd come back."

"**H**ow the hell did you find me?"

She threw the question over her shoulder as she went ahead of him into the apartment. Not a single light was on, and he could see reflections from the streetlights shining on a large dining table. No sign of the library; they were going in another direction. The apartment seemed to stretch in all directions from the dining room, which had four doors. He could hear someone singing, almost unaccompanied, a bass voice that grew louder the farther in they went. *"In diesen heil'gen Hallen,"* he was singing, his voice sinking through loose layers of darkness. They ended up in a room smelling of cigarette smoke and containing an overloaded desk. A green light indicated an amplifier on the far wall and the singer sang his aria to the end. Then Doris Hofstaedter leaned back and pressed a button. The green eye went out.

"Well?"

She hadn't forgotten her question. She sat down at the desk, which left him nowhere to sit except the leather armchair opposite. He sat down like a examination candidate.

"I found your book," he said. *"The Myth of the Traveler."*

"Oh, Christ, you've changed social class and got yourself academic qualifications and instincts."

Intimacy, he thought. Here it is. In this dusty room. Had he tried to tell himself it was possible to approach another person by being nice? Here she was, eighteen years later, not beautiful even then, making demands on his membranes and exposed skin. He had no desire at all to lie to her, and said:

"I found the book by sheer chance. But I have got a university degree, that's true. I'm a meteorologist."

"What do you really want?"

"I didn't know it was you. I was looking for the girl."

"Here she is. She's fifty-nine now."

He calculated in his head and saw her noticing.

"I was forty-one," she said, smiling broadly. He disliked the discoloration of her teeth by tobacco, and they were longer than he remembered. The gums had receded upward, and her eyelids sagged heavily into deep yellow folds. She wants to frighten, he thought. He went on counting in his head, for he felt he had been swept into a labyrinthine game in which he was confronted with stereotyped figures demanding passwords. There sat the Witch with the lovely feet. A few days ago he had met the Dirty Old Man. At the time when he was most enthusiastically climbing on to the women at Starhill, he had been no older than I am now, Johan thought. Had Mia also calculated in her head?

"You took a sixteen-year-old with you to your Trollevolden."

"Don't act innocent and seduced, Johan. You rubbed me raw inside."

She leaned back in her chair and peered at him. The chair rocked slightly.

"Jukka, Jukka," she said. "You were as keen as a hunting hound. No childish flesh between us, oh, no. Brutal, you were. A truly fine, clean animal." Her Finnish accent was still marked.

"Then you no doubt returned to a regular life?"

He found that difficult to deny, and she laughed.

"Swedish youth fed on soft cheese and social benefits have their excesses in the playground. Howling at rock concerts when the game leaders shout fuck fuck fuck and asshole. But twenty years ago you really did drive a thumb with Norwegian margarine up my asshole, and you had learned that at the movies, my friend."

"Trollevolden, by the way, belonged to the Tourist Association," he said.

"That's right."

"You said it belonged to your family."

"My grandfather was a merchant in Trondheim. Timber, fish, shipping—anything that could be traded. Every autumn he went north to shoot. He built the hunting lodge in 1905. Life on a grand scale, really.

Five hundred grouse was nothing unusual. Whole drifts of hares. Salmon. Bears. You could call it excess. Not like twenty thousand orienteerers subjecting game to days of death struggle without even noticing it. But right in it—with blood on your boots and gun smoke and skins turned inside out."

She got up and left the room. Johan didn't know what to expect. Was she going to come back with photographs? He vaguely remembered some photos of shoots. When he heard her returning, he could also hear a clinking.

"Whiskey or vodka?"

"Whiskey, please."

"His daughter, who was of a less flamboyant kind, met a Finn, an engineer." She went straight on with her story. "That was in a seaside resort on the island of Sylt. She moved to Finland when they married, and had two children. Me and my brother. When the Winter War started, we were evacuated to Grandfather. They hadn't counted on the Germans attacking Norway a few months later. I went to Amalie Clink's School for Girls in Trondheim, a very fine private school. Her name was really Lock, but we called her Amalie Clink. She had a little briefcase that used to clink inside. Port.

"Just imagine," she said. "Amalie Clink even had a port-wine nose. A real old-fashioned, coarse-pored, reddish-blue number. In that friendly little face."

She raised her glass of transparent vodka to him.

"But you've been careful," he said. "Only clear spirits."

"Johan, you don't like it that things have gone well for me although I've drunk vodka and smoked cigarettes."

"Have things gone well for you?"

"I've got a professorship. I'm a member of learned societies. I'm fit and never find life dull. Does that annoy you?"

When he didn't answer, she went on:

"During the war, the whole school went on an outing to Trollevolden. On the day after the semester's end. First by train, then horse and cart up to the house. It wasn't so overgrown in those days, you see, and you could get there by horse and cart. Grandfather was magnificent. Right in the middle of the gray old war, we had cream cakes and strawberries and eggnog and charlotte russe, if you know what that is. There were maids and enameled jugs of thick yellow cream. Pale veal steak with cream sauce. You don't know what veal is, Johan, the kind you could get before the war. Fattened calf, box calf, fed on cow's milk and tender as your sweet little prick. It was unforgettable—a childishly bright and easily digested extravagance. But it was Grandfather's last gesture; his business was failing, partly because he refused to cooperate with the Germans and partly because shipping was at low ebb. When he died, his fortune had gone. Trollevolden remained, but wasn't worth much. My mother was dead. She died of pneumonia during the last month of the Winter War. My brother and I gave Trollevolden to the Tourist Association so that at least the house would be more or less maintained. In the 1950s, the preservation of unique interiors was not a priority. But it was forgotten, fortunately. It was so remote. Anyone walking and wanting to stay the night was given the key at the store in the village. People were decent in those days. It got shabby, but never ruined inside. There's a warden there now. Lockable shutters. Tourist Association fittings. My brother and I have stopped going there."

"Was that your brother, the streaky man?"

"Yes. I wasn't keen on him seeing you close up. I was slightly embarrassed by your youth. I hadn't counted on his being there. Only the girls. And they were to leave after a day or two."

"Were they tourists?"

"Goodness, no. They were Amalie Clink's former pupils. Aged about forty, all of them. They were celebrating their thirtieth anniversary up there. In memory of that party in the middle of the war. We even made charlotte russe, but I don't think you got any of that."

"I haven't come here to listen to all this," said Johan.

"No, but it really does interest you, doesn't it?"

"I want to know more about John Larue."

"That's someone I don't know."

"You met him at the drugstore or in the store in a small village called Byvången. You gave him the telephone number to the store in the village near Trollevolden. I think you'd thought he was going there."

"Oh, dear me. A pickup, do you mean?"

"Yes, you bought condoms as well."

She really did look surprised then and had to take another cigarette. She extracted one out of a black lacquered box decorated in old-fashioned Russian red and gold.

"How did you recognize me today, Johan?"

"Your feet," he said, then thought that was tactless of him. But did she mind?

"Ah, yes, we've always got something unspoiled, haven't we? I've actually always looked after my feet. They appear in a novel. A romanticized autobiography by an elderly Finnish writer."

She went on talking away, her speech academically articulate. Not for a moment was she going to let him get any closer to her, and yet there was an intimacy between them. It wasn't—I know what you think. But—I feel what you feel. Like one flayed body hot against another.

"I want to talk about John Larue," said Johan. "You had no use for those condoms. Not one. I've been wondering about it, and this is what I think happened. You met Larue in the drugstore and heard about his troubles with his girlfriend and her period pains. He was good-looking. You wanted to take him with you. But you realized you would have to protect yourself if you were going to be with him."

"Oh, dear."

"Birger Torbjörnsson thought that one up. I think you wanted to lure Larue with you at once. But he was too decent. True, he didn't know the girl he was traveling with very well. He had only recently met her in Gothenburg. They had been to a rock concert together. You gave him Finnish vodka and quinine powder for the girl. You bought a notebook and wrote down the number of the shop in it. They had taken a room at the guesthouse in Byvången. I think you did, too. You counted on the girl falling asleep once she had dulled the pain. Then John Larue was to come into your room and have a little foretaste of the delights awaiting him in Trollevolden."

"The way you put it, Johan. Foretaste of delights. Oh, my goodness."

"But I don't think he came. Perhaps she was suspicious and surprised him on his way to you."

"Why not in flagrante?" said the woman he still thought of as Ylja.

"Because the condom pack was unopened. I think you stayed in that dismal guesthouse for a whole day in the hope that he would come back and go with you. He must have left that possibility open. But he didn't come. He went to Blackwater and then on up toward the mountain. You lay in your bed at the guesthouse and realized he wasn't coming in to you that night, either. I think you were really fed up by then."

"What happened next?"

"Then John Larue and his girl were stabbed to death in a tent."

"That's got nothing to do with it," she said.

"Tell me what has, then."

"I was exhausted and had a murderous headache. Couldn't sleep. That's what happened. I got up, dumped some money on the counter, and left. It wasn't even four in the morning. An hour or so later I spotted you."

"You must tell the Swedish police."

She laughed, but without smiling. She had dropped ash on her chest and brushed it off the black and white dress with a hand that was unchanged. But the fingers were swollen and the engraved doctorate ring was sunk deep into the flesh.

"I shan't be telling the police or anyone else anything. I have a good life and a respectable position. I have no intention of making a fool of myself either as a pining spinster or a randy old woman."

"Then I'll tell them."

"No, you won't," she said. "You'll tell them nothing. For then they'll come here and question me, and I'll tell them that I met that boy Johan Brandberg as I was driving from Byvången early on Midsummer morning. He was standing at the roadside, his thumb out and blood on his shirt."

Although he shook his head, she poured him out some more whiskey.

"Have a drink," she said, almost with affection. "The night is long."

Annie had said there was something about the Brandberg sons, something lumpish and rank. No woman failed to notice it, she said, even when just passing them in the post office.

She had never known the fifth son. He was fine-limbed and tall. When he was younger, he had been very slender. He didn't look well now. Dehydrated, Birger thought. He needs fluids. What the hell has he been up to?

Those lumpish sons had all been there when Torsten Brandberg was questioned about the assault on Harry Vidart. He remembered them as pretty drunk and grinning. A drunk and confused state. It was not inconceivable that things had gone really wrong for one of them later on that night. The police had questioned them many times. Birger had asked Vemdal again, and he had dug the old information about them out of that cardboard box.

Pekka was the most likely, judging by the way he had behaved after that event by the water. He had spent an incredible amount on drink—money he had earned on the oil rigs. He had badly beaten up a rival. That was in Sollentuna, but talk about it had reached Blackwater. He had once managed to scrape together a home with leather furniture and a stereo and had moved in with a very beautiful woman. She had thrown him out and he got none of the contents of the house. The reason was that he had been out sick and had been drinking heavily after an accident with a crane. A man had fallen from the platform and had been killed. Pekka couldn't work after that. He turned dizzy up there. During the last shoot he had been so drunk, they had had to take his rifle away. He was still working as a laborer down south but never on a crane. He was signing on now.

Per-Ola had been the one to take his rifle away from him, the new leader, the one who had so stubbornly stayed in Blackwater and had now built a house in Tangen. The square plot was a replica of any in a residential area in Frösö or in the suburbs of Östersund. He had grown heavier and middle-aged, but he still had his strength and swiftness. He was fair, or, rather, colorless, nowadays, his eyes small and close-set, his scalp clearly visible. Birger remembered one of the old men on the team shaking his head when they heard that Per-Ola had been chosen as Torsten's successor. Nothing except that shake of the head. Birger didn't know what that meant.

Väine was the one who most resembled Per-Ola. He was fair and had the hard, gnarled body of a forestry worker. He had married young, a Norwegian woman who became pregnant. That hadn't lasted long. Now he had a boy who used to come some weekends; Gudrun looked after him. Väine was often away working. He had a trailer which he lived in when felling. He was said to be a demon for work.

Björne was on a disability pension. Annie had liked him. He helped her with firewood and some other things. She had said he was amusing to talk to. He had started living by himself after he had cleared a parcel of forest, rather like Väine. But he stayed. Annie had thought it was some kind of protest against modern times.

For his part, Birger had never regarded these cabin loners as rebels. He thought they really belonged in the past and that their deprivation was primarily sexual. There were no women for them any longer, since they couldn't bring themselves to change their way of life. They didn't shower. They got too drunk and snuff juice dribbled out of the corners of their mouths. Their shirts were stiff with elk blood and engine oil. They always carried knives and their sexual signaling system was so primitive, it was taken as a joke. Birger had prescribed far too much Antabuse for Björne over the years, which was why he no longer drank so much. Birger was at a loss as to what to do about his prescriptions.

More often than might be imagined, it was possible for these loners and leftovers to put their misery into words. But as therapy, that was worthless. It never changed anything. Antidepressant drugs were just as useless in the long run. Cabin life sometimes ended with a shotgun in an open mouth. Björne at least had been caught by the social services in time and had spells in the Frösö clinic, where they thought electroshock treatment had a positive effect on him.

From the beginning, Birger had thought of warning Annie that Björne was not quite so teddy-bear nice as he might seem when he came lumbering with carriers of birch bark and resin-soaked sticks to light her stove. As an eighteen-year-old, he had tried to rape a girl of his own age. She had been in quite a bad way. It was never reported, but it came out all the same. Torsten had settled the matter with the girl's father. It was said that he had helped out with a sum when the father was exchanging his old car for another one, thus enabling him to buy a heavy four-wheel-drive American vehicle.

No one believed Björne had meant to rape the girl. He no doubt thought that was how it was done. Afterward he found himself isolated. The girls kept their distance and he was never again alone with any of them.

When Birger heard how Annie had made his acquaintance, that she had gone with him into the company trailer, he understood why Björne had become her knight errant. She had rehabilitated him. She became his link with the village long after his parents had ceased to be so. The fact that she approved of his romantic explanation for his lone existence bound him even more strongly to her.

No, Birger had never warned Annie. He realized there was no need to. The bad talk about Björne must have eventually reached her and she had ignored it. She knew he would never do her any harm. Birger was convinced she had been right.

The activities of the Brandbergs that Midsummer night had been banal and were preserved in Vemdal's cardboard box. Pekka had gotten hold of some woman. There had been no intention of continuing the acquaintance, and she had been embarrassed when she had had to tell the police that he had gone back home with her. She was Norwegian and lived in a hamlet seventy kilometers across the border.

But what was her statement worth? Or that of Per-Ola's girl? Väine and a friend had gone fishing that night. They had probably not had any success at the community center, nor even managed to get hold of any Norwegian liquor. There was a trailer by Röbäck waters and they broke into it, whether out of mischief or to steal something was not stated. The owner of the trailer appeared with a mate and caught them. They got beaten up—and what might be called an alibi. But everything said about the Brandberg boys' Midsummer night and their father's seemed fragile and transparent now, so many years later. It was as if the threads had slid apart so that the fabric was on the verge of disintegrating. Who could swear to anything now?

Johan lay fully dressed on his hotel bed. His face was gray and stiff and there were lines around the corners of his mouth. The balance of fluids in him was awry. Birger brought him some mineral water and cautiously woke him.

"Try to drink a little," he said. "What the hell have you been up to? Did you go out again last night?"

"Yes, I went and had a glass or two," said Johan. He closed his eyes as he drank.

Ylja, Ylja? She couldn't remember how the name had arisen.

"It was something you said, another name. It sounded Finnish," said Johan. But they couldn't pin it down.

He knew she was staying in the shadows, the darkness of the heavy drapes and furniture, just out of reach. She was not only bold, she was also cautious. She could never stand making a fool of herself.

He drank. He felt gutted, cleaned out, and now he was rinsing himself out inwardly. No headache, no dangers, and no ridicule. Just pure liquor.

"Did you know John Larue was handsome?" she said.

She was no longer bothering to have secrets. There was a bloodstained shirt between them. It was a lie, but it was powerful and would work. In a way, it was a pity that was needed, he thought. We might have come to some agreement anyway. But she was probably not a person to make agreements with.

"Not difficult to imagine the sacrificial knife in his body. He never became a spring god. But no doubt he wanted to."

Johan suddenly remembered the yellowing paper in her academic tome, the acrid smell from it.

"Christ, how I suffered in that guesthouse with its knotted rugs and wood carvings all around me. When I realized they'd gone after all. The streams running wildly up there, flowing over the marshlands. On Starhill. And she had him there. You like to think lust is just chemical whims and itching, Jukka dear. But you know it's worse than that. She was as infatuated with him as I was. Though fatally. She had him and had him. How many times do you think they managed it? And all I had was a pillow that tasted synthetic and drab daylight in the room all night. So I left. And met you. The night had been stingy but the morning was bountiful."

"What do you think happened up there?" said Johan.

She grimaced.

"I don't know. I think it's another story. Not theirs."

"But they were actually butchered—to put it bluntly."

"I'm glad it wasn't you. But you should watch out. I think your difficulties are still to come."

He tittered in the semi-darkness and drank deeply. The liquor no longer burned; it was as tasteless and cool as stream water.

"Are you clairvoyant?"

"You reminded me of the deer hunter who saw Artemis naked. He saw her in the middle of the day, in bright sunlight. She turned him into a deer. But he was still a human being inside, with a memory and guilt. Though mute."

"How did he manage to turn himself back again?"

"He didn't manage."

She emphasized the word as she repeated it, and with those broad vowels and her strong irony, it was pure scorn.

"He was butchered by his fellow huntsmen. All they saw was a deer. In those damp Germanic forest sagas we were brought up with, the hunter sees the appealing eyes. But in the dazzling white sunlight down there, they saw nothing. Only prey."

"You like your stories," he said. "You play with them."

"So do you."

That was true. He sometimes thought that he was under the rule of Njord in the mists and dragging rain. Or that Tjas Olmai sent him a flood in answer to his officious forecasting.

He had slept on the sofa with its dog hair. She was not in the room, or else was occasionally. Looking at him. He could sense her smile, which might just as well have been Gudrun's, and he slept raggedly and dreamed. The early morning was gray. He saw that the table by the window with its faded green velvet curtains was an altar. A cloth with wide lace was spread over it and between two candelabra stood a photograph. A young man in uniform. Fighting against the Russians had meant fighting for the Germans in the Continuation War, Johan thought. That was what obligation looked like. Or duty or honor, or whatever the upright young officer might have called it. Her grandfather had lost his money because he refused to cooperate with the Germans. Or was that a lie? Was Trollevolden on the contrary confiscated in the settlement after the war? Had he perhaps been a collaborator?

Why were these rooms almost untouched? Was she being faithful to something beneath all that mockery? But he didn't really want to know.

He met her on his way to find a lavatory. She now looked as she had when Birger and he had first seen her. Sallow and gray, absentminded. He splashed for a long time in the lavatory, which had a seat of lovely dark wood and was flushed by pulling a china handle on a chain. It solemnly roared and hurt his head. Light and sound made him feel sick.

She had put out ham and eggs in the kitchen. There was dark bread cut into slices, butter, and coarse-grained cheese. She was making coffee in an old-fashioned percolator as she talked about Artemis, though not in the way she had during the gray night. Now she was lecturing him.

"For a long time it was thought the famous statue of Artemis of Ephesus had a huge burden of breasts. That she bore her attribute of motherliness to excess. Round, bunlike, and fruitful. Then the archaeologists started looking a bit closer at them. Two Austrians, they were. They saw the buns didn't really look at all like breasts."

Off she skips, it hurts her tits, raced through Johan's head. Please God, keep my mouth shut. This isn't a hangover. I'm still not sober, though grayer. I'm fifteen. She has never met me.

"Have you seen a picture of Artemis of Ephesus?"

How would he know? He had perhaps seen it in some art book. A staring face. Bunches of breasts. Ylja put a plate in front of him. On it lay a slice of ham at least five millimeters thick. It was moist and pink and interspersed with white fat. There were segments of meat with something translucent in between. Water? Aspic? She had fried an egg so carefully that it had hardly solidified, the yolk shimmering like oil.

"Do you know what it was?"

He closed his eyes to avoid looking at the egg.

"The feast of Artemis of Ephesus was celebrated by the priests castrating young bulls before her altar. They tied the scrotums together into a wreath. That's what she wears around her neck and on her chest, Jukka. The virgin mother. Not a pleasant acquaintance."

He turned his head and slowly pushed the plate away.

"Can't you eat it?"

Then she broke an egg into a glass and poured in some vodka. She twisted the peppermill twice over the liquor and handed him the glass. He closed his eyes. The contents slid down like an oyster.

"I must go," he said. "I want to be back before Birger wakes."

"Be careful, Jukka," she said.

"Do you know something, or are you just talking?"

He had thought of saying, "talking shit." He was sick of her stories. And yet he felt like telling her she was right. Profound desire is not chemical. The soul is not a transformation of the ego. But he couldn't collect his wits enough to say anything. Well, he said good-bye. Quite politely, although he was pale and the palm of the hand he held out was moist.

He had to rest on his way back to the hotel. There was a park, the place where Birger had wanted to pat someone on the behind. A goddess. She was standing there on her plinth in the morning chill. He didn't want her to turn around and reveal a garland of bull's testicles and bloody shreds of scrotum around her neck. Otherwise everything was as usual, a gray late-summer morning. Fat tree sparrows. Ice cream wrappers.

J ohan and Birger were at the Mc-
Donald's near the crossroads in Odengatan in Stockholm, watching a door
on the other side of Sveavägen. Teenagers in red peaked caps were collecting trays, but on their table the greasy cartons and plasic litter were accumulating. Birger thought you had to keep fetching more if you sat there
for so long. They had taken a table on the sidewalk. The traffic was
roaring by and sometimes they couldn't see the door. A bus stopped in
their line of vision, the stench gaseous in the humid air. It was difficult.
That made Birger feel they were being useful. But the coffee was good.

"The Foundation," said Birger. "Funny name for a second-hand bookshop."

"Must be second-hand SF," said Johan.

Birger didn't understand what he meant, but it didn't matter. They
would soon find him there. Vemdal had tracked him down for them.
Birger thought they ought to ask Vemdal out to dinner, but Johan didn't
want to. He was afraid of him.

He said quite honestly that he didn't know why he was afraid. But
Vemdal must still have some of his police instincts. Suddenly it might be
too much for his conscience or his vanity and then he'd pick up the phone,
Johan had said. We might just as well lie low.

It was a narrow brown door with a grid-covered glass window in the
upper part and a brass letter box in the brown wood, a newspaper stuck in
it. They had looked closely at the door. There was no sign stating business
hours, only two locks, one of which looked like a new double lock. There

was only one shop window. They hadn't bothered about the books, but Birger now regretted not taking a look at them. He went in to fetch two more cardboard containers of coffee, and when he came back with the tray, Johan said:

"Something's happened."

"Has he come?"

"No. Look at the letter box and you'll see."

"Has someone stolen the paper?" said Birger.

"It was pulled into the shop from inside. There's someone there, although it's locked."

"Hell, then we'll bang on the door until he opens up."

"Wait."

The door opened and he came out. As he turned around to lock both locks, they looked at him. He was wearing a dark brown jacket with narrow cream-colored stripes. His jeans looked new and his boots were black. His long hair was tied at the back with a ribbon or a rubber band. It was no longer golden but dark blond, though it still came far down his back. There were some lighter streaks in it, but it was impossible to see whether they were silvery.

Birger wanted to leap up and rush across the street, but he couldn't move. He saw the slim figure setting off toward Odengatan, his back very straight. Then he swung around the corner by the bank and disappeared.

"Hell's bells!"

Johan looked at Birger in the way you look at a sick man but can't do much for him.

"It doesn't matter," he said. "He'll probably be back soon. I think he lives there."

"It'll soon be half past ten," said Birger. "Christ!"

Johan pried the lid off one of the containers and practically inserted it into Birger's hand. He's afraid I'll start crying. Birger thought. What an old wreck I am! He thought of himself as full of garbage, like the table. The garbage of time. And there, on the other side of the street, Dan Ulander was walking quite unmoved through time.

Less than ten minutes later he was back, a paper bag in his hand.

"Fresh white rolls," said Birger, so bitterly that Johan laughed. They left their coffee and made their way across Sveavägen.

The second-hand bookstore was small, but deepened and darkened as they went farther in. In the first section there was a dump of colorful pamphlets and books, rather like comics, Birger thought, but then he saw they were all science fiction.

Farther in were bookshelves, all with neatly handwritten labels. Asimov. Lem. Clarke. The names meant nothing to Birger. Dan Ulander was standing by an old-fashioned desk made of dark wood. He had switched on a tape recorder and the cramped space was filled with music. Birger felt shut in, a phobic feeling, his palms sweaty.

"Could you switch that off? We'd like to talk to you."

"You don't like it? It's Richard Strauss. Stanley Kubrick used it when he made 2001 ."

Birger repeated the only thing he could comprehend in the harangue. "Strauss?"

"Well, not the king of Viennese waltzes," said Ulander, smiling slightly.

In some incomprehensible way, he had maneuvered himself into a position of superiority. He hadn't recognized Birger. Of course not. He had probably never even looked at him.

"We've come in connection with the death of Annie Raft," said Johan. Occasionally Birger was reminded that Johan was a grown man, capable of taking over. But neither of them could interpret the vacant expression on Ulander's face as he said, hesitantly:

"Annie Raft . . . ?"

"From Blackwater," said Johan.

"Oh, Annie—the one with the little girl. Is Annie dead?"

"Don't you read the papers?"

"Yes—the small ads. For business purposes."

He gestured with both hands, holding them away from his body like a dancer. Birger saw how the shape of his head was enhanced by the long, austerely drawn-back hair. At close quarters he could see that he had aged. His skin was very pale. Perhaps he hardly ever left his bookshop. But that slender body, didn't it need exercise?

He didn't ask them anything and Birger found that strange, even suspect. Then he realized that Ulander thought Johan had meant he would have seen the death notice.

"This is Annie's partner," said Johan. "Birger Torbjörnsson. I was to be his son-in-law. We want to know what the situation was with John Larue."

"The situation?"

Was he trying to gain time? It didn't seem so. He looked genuinely confused.

"Some tea?" he said.

There were fresh white rolls in the bag, as they'd thought.

"No, thank you," said Johan. "Tell us about John Larue."

"Well, I don't know what Annie has said. To be honest, I didn't think she knew his name. Why do you want to know? Isn't all that over and done with?"

He stood there with his opened bag of rolls, apparently appealing to them. Something had happened, but Birger couldn't make out what, even less so when Ulander started talking. He didn't seem at all afraid of talking about John Larue. He was afraid of something else.

"Where did he come from?"

"Well, from Denmark most recently. Though I met him in Stockholm. He was a Vietnam deserter. Troublesome."

What a word to use, Birger thought. What a precious vocabulary this little dancer has. He looks like a queer. I wish to God that he had been one.

"He hadn't any papers. No passport. I promised him he could live with us."

"At Starhill."

"That's right."

"You called it Star Mountain," said Birger, "when you translated it for him."

"I don't remember. Why do you want to know all this?"

"Why did they put up the tent? Why didn't they walk on up to Starhill?"

"I don't know. Maybe they thought it was farther than it was. I'd sketched a map for them, but it had no scale. We had a postcard from Gothenburg. He was to come with a Dutch girl. The one who . . . you know. Well, him, too."

Touch on it lightly. Go on dancing, you little bugger, thought Birger.

"No."

"Was she going to live at Starhill, too?"

"No, I think he just persuaded her she wanted to see the Swedish mountains. That probably suited him."

He tittered.

"Tell us everything now," said Johan. "How you swiped the jeans and everything."

"I'll make some tea, anyhow," said Ulander. He sounded ingratiating. Something really had changed since they had gone into the shop and been flooded by his Strauss music. He opened a door and they could see an inner room like a ship's cabin, with a neatly made bed. Was it possible that he lived there? Alone? That he never read anything but ads for science fiction books in the newspapers, slept till ten or half past, and started the day with fresh rolls? When he came back with an electric kettle, Johan said:

"You remember all this very well although it's so long ago. Yet you could hardly remember Annie Raft."

"Oh, yes, I remember Annie, too. Of course I do. It was just the name —I'm not sure that I ever heard her last name."

"What a load of crap!" said Birger. "You were a student of hers."

"That doesn't matter," said Johan. "Tell us about when you took his jeans. What were you doing out so early in the morning?"

"We were all out. We were looking for Larue."

He had put out Chinese tea mugs. He put the rolls on a dish. When the water began to bubble in the kettle, he warmed a teapot, going about it all with great thoroughness. To empty the teapot, he had to go out to a lavatory alongside the sleeping cabin. He spooned out some tea leaves and poured the water over them.

"Sugar?"

"Oh, lay off," said Birger.

Ulander wanted them to sit down, but they stayed standing. So he sat down on the chair behind the desk and spread butter on the halved roll. He ate a few small mouthfuls before starting to tell them.

"I went to Röbäck on Midsummer Eve to leave the children with Yvonne. You know who she was? They were supposed to go with her. There was to be a demonstration against something. My God, there was a lot going on in those days."

He smiled at them.

"The children couldn't walk all the way from Starhill and up to Bear Mountain on Midsummer Day."

"We know all that."

"Well, then I fetched Barbro Lund, a textile artist who was to move up. Eventually. She lived in Byvången."

Birger said nothing, but he could hear himself breathing heavily through his nose.

"When we got up to an old farm just before the road comes to an end—"

"The Strömgren homestead," said Johan.

"Yes. We saw a Dutch car there. A small red thing. I thought that must be Larue because he had written on the postcard that he was coming with a Dutch girl. Then we went to Björnstubacken and left Barbro Lund's car there and continued on foot up to Starhill. We thought Larue would be there. But he wasn't. He and the girl never came. We waited all evening. In the end, we began to think they'd gotten lost. So we set off to look for them toward morning. We thought they would be wandering around in the marshes. Barbro Lund and I were almost down by the river when I saw the tent. I went down on my own."

"Did she see what had happened?" said Birger.

"I'm not sure. We didn't speak to each other much afterward. I saw that . . . well. But I had no idea it might be Larue and his girl. You couldn't see them. Only an arm and a foot. Then I spotted a pair of jeans. They were hanging over a spruce branch. They were Larue's."

"For Christ's sake, you couldn't have recognized a pair of jeans!"

"Oh, yes, in those days jeans were like works of art. Every tear, every patch, was a sign. An autograph. They were John Larue's jeans. I took them."

"Why?"

"To take a closer look at them, I think. I ran back up to Barbro Lund and we found the others on the path down toward Björnstubacken. We held a kind of council of war up there in the forest. We decided to pretend we didn't know John Larue. It would have been the end of the commune if we'd gotten involved in anything like that. There was a girl called Enel. She was actually quite a tough nut. She went with Petrus down to the tent and they fished out John's bag and emptied it. He had my map and everything in it. We went back up to Starhill and burned his things. The jeans were wet. That was why he'd hung them up. I hid them because the thick material wouldn't burn until it had dried. Then Barbro and I went down to Björnstubacken. We had to get the car. The others took the path along the lake to Röbäck. Later we said they'd been there all the time."

"You told Annie you'd slept at Nirsbuan."

"Maybe I did. Yes, I did. I phoned Barbro Lund, too. We agreed that that's what we would say. Annie thought I had been at Nirsbuan."

"Was it really necessary to lie to Annie? She wouldn't have said anything."

"Annie was a bit . . . how shall I put it? She had misunderstood the whole thing."

"What thing?"

"She was jealous," Birger said. "She had left everything—her whole life. She thought you two would be together forever. But it was as a teacher you wanted her to come up to Starhill. And you were going to have Barbro Lund as a weaver and designer up there. Your assignment was to get hold of useful people for the commune."

Ulander shifted a little in his chair.

"You recruited with your prick. But they misunderstood that. Annie did, anyway."

He was aware that Johan was keeping an eye on him and he fell silent. For some reason, Johan was in charge. Now he said:

"You remember all this amazingly well."

"Well, we rehearsed it over and over and over again," said Ulander. "All of us had to say the same thing."

"Memory lane," said Birger.

"What?"

"You went down memory lane. Over and over and over again."

"Let's go," said Johan.

Ulander had had no opportunity to pour out his tea. He followed them uncertainly to the door.

"Why do you want to know all this? You can't go to the police. Because of Annie, I mean. After all, she was involved. And it's all so long ago now. It would change nothing."

When they came out into the street, Birger was so tired he could have sat down on the sidewalk. More customers had come to McDonald's. More containers and cartons poured out and were collected up. They trudged over to the park by the city library and he sank down on a bench.

"How he talked!" said Birger. "I can't understand why he said anything at all."

"Can't you?"

"But he wasn't afraid of the police. Not any longer. If he or any of the others at Starhill had had anything to do with John Larue's death, he wouldn't have talked like that. But I can't make out why everything just poured out of him."

"He was afraid of you."

"Me?"

"When we went into the inner room and started talking about Annie, you looked as if you were directly threatening him."

"I did?"

"Didn't you know?"

"No."

He had never threatened anyone. He couldn't even imagine raising his hand against another person. But neither Dan Ulander nor he had been thinking.

A large body. Secreting anger. None of it was left now, only sticky sweat and weariness. The traffic roared by, squealing and juddering. He was as exhausted as if he really had tried to break all the bones in that light, dancing body.

He thought about time, moment added to moment in a line that pushed Annie and her shattered chest and diaphragm farther and farther back, inward. The image flickered as if under a mesh. Not even shock and pain were immutable. They moved.

He had had one experience of total stillness in his life. At the Sulky Hotel, time had stopped. But there was no more than an image left of that, the memory a changeable and moving image, and it was turning gray as if from dirt.

Then it occurred to him that the dead were in absolute stillness.

That thought turned his life over. He was in the dirt. The silent ticking of moments threw a veil over every sharp image. She was where he wanted to be.

It's that simple, he thought.

These were not thoughts of suicide. On the contrary, they helped him to get going again. He trudged off to the health center. Annie was where he wanted to be. He didn't have to avoid thinking about her. She was not in the water, shot to pieces. Not in bed with him. Nowhere where the inexorable ticking was going on.

She was in stillness.

He thought about there being places—or moments—that are as good as still. Where the ticking is as good as imperceptible. He liked standing by the open window at night, feeling the air against his face. Quite a few of the things he remembered Annie had done seemed to be confronting stillness. She had known about it.

She stood on the steps listening to the rain in the aspens.

He had given up trying to find out how she had died. He was ashamed of that, but it was true. An enterprise lacking all sharpness and fire. There was war in Europe, the event by the Lobber being repeated every hour. He would not be going shooting that autumn. The ravages. Twisted metal. Dung pouring out of intestines. That was what he saw.

But very little was needed for him to change his mind. Just Mia sending the key, with a short letter as well. A sweet letter. He hadn't expected it, for he'd thought she didn't really like him. She wrote that he was to keep the key and use Annie's cottage during the shoot, and in the future whenever he wanted to. She herself hadn't been there since they had cleaned up in the holidays. "I probably won't be there all that much," she wrote. The words evoked the abandoned state of the cottage for him. The rain in July and August. What did it look like? Had Mia asked anyone to go there and cut the grass?

He went on the Friday evening. The shoot was to start on Monday morning and it seemed quite natural to put his rifle into the car. It had long been decided that he would take his vacation during the shoot. What would he do in Byvången? He didn't want to go away anywhere. He wanted to go to Blackwater to cut Annie's grass.

It was almost dark when he got there, but he could still make out the great drifts of wet grass and frosted roses rotting in the hedges. He had wanted to start at once, but there was a lot to do inside, too. The air was musty and cold. He lit the stove. There was still some birch bark and kindling Björne Brandberg had put ready. He went out with a torch and searched for some flowers. She had always had flowers indoors and he thought they improved the air. He found nothing but yarrow. Although it had begun to turn gray, it still smelled strong and spicy.

He thought about how often he would have to go there in the future to keep back the ravages of time: the grass, the snow, trees felled by storms, the undergrowth creeping in, and mice gnawing. He would have to keep time at bay so that her house could remain untouched and still.

There was a point where stillness and the busy restlessness of life merged together. He didn't think much more about it. But he realized that he had a lot to do if the house was to be able to hold its own against time.

In the morning he saw that it was all much worse outside than he could have imagined. He tried attacking the tough grass from all directions with the scythe, exhausting himself. He took a trip down to the store to buy pilsner and sausage, and on his way back he went in to Per-Ola Brandberg to pay his shooting dues. He was given a drink at the smoked-glass coffee table and he answered questions about the investigation. Nothing new. He realized the village very much wanted to return to the belief that it had been an accident, that Annie had tripped on the slippery stones at the ford. But it couldn't.

After leaving, he met Anna Starr. She had two shopping bags from the store with her and he stopped to offer her a lift up to Tangen. When they got to the uneven little road that was really nothing more than two wheel tracks and a hump of grass in between, he felt the pain again. But it was less sharp than before, and he was able to say to Anna:

"Just think, this is the way Annie came on her way to see you. Wasn't it strange that she wanted to find out exactly where that UFO landed?"

He could feel her looking at him.

"That wasn't what she wanted to find out," she said. "She wanted to know where they'd put all the scrap they brought up when they dragged the lake."

"Come right away," Birger had said. "I've got something to show you."

He hadn't told him what it was, but Johan got ready to go at once. Mia thought it odd that he simply obeyed. He couldn't explain it himself, but he could tell from Birger's voice that it was serious. Mia couldn't accept it. She thought Birger was being unnecessarily secretive and she phoned him back, but all he said was:

"It's important that Johan sees this without knowing what I think."

When they said good-bye, Mia was standing with Lars Dorj in front of the dog run, and everything they said to each other was drowned out by howling. The dogs used to howl for twenty minutes or half an hour every afternoon. Mia was pulling at a ragged sleeve. One of the dogs had been playing with her and had torn it. She was wearing a thin, washed-out T-shirt and he knew the fly of her jeans was open underneath it. Her stomach was bulging and she had put elastic between the buttons.

He had been given no assurances, and yet he knew she believed him. She did so because she needed him. He felt no bitterness about this. She was tired and pale. She believed what was necessary for her to believe. She had no strength left for anything else.

Unemployed now. The project over. She had sold the car. He would look after her, but how could things be like this? Or, rather, how could what she had longed for and wanted so much be like this? Mia had rejected Annie's dry, frozen life, her flexible solitude. But what did she want now?

Pregnant, unemployed. No alternative. Calling out, trying to make herself heard over twenty-two dogs companionably howling. He could see her mouth opening. Suppose she was saying:

YOU CAN'T LEAVE ME HERE!

But she was probably saying only, don't forget to fill up the car, and check the oil, too. She was always so prudent.

He drove through the damp, dark but still-green river valley, then up to the mountain, where the colors were turning brown and yellow. Here and there a thin layer of snow lay on the shifting surfaces of the sedge. When he started going downhill again, the colors flared. There had been frost on the long slopes down to the lakes and the birches had tongues of fire. The water was harder and bluer than the sky.

The sign with the village name on it on the Norwegian side had lost a few more letters. If you didn't know where you were, what it said was incomprehensible.

BL   KW   E

Birger saw him coming and came down the slope to meet him. He must have been sitting waiting in the kitchen window. He was out of breath when he got into the car. Saddie had followed him halfway down the slope, then sat down.

"It's down in Tangen," he said. "Farthest out."

The village was quiet, people presumably at their evening meal. It would soon be dusk and Birger was eager to get out there before it got dark. They drove past Anna Starr's cottage and the road shrank to a couple of bumpy tractor tracks. With the four-wheel drive, Johan would make it all the way there, Birger thought. Parallel with the tractor path ran the road to the campsite.

The tractor road ended at a loading point. Tangen had been clear-felled, but the birch wood had grown and become impenetrable. They could make out pine plants with split and deformed tops. Elk lived out on the headland.

"The path's ruined," said Birger. "We'll have to get down to the shore as best we can, and I'll probably find the way from there."

The sky darkened, but it looked as if light were coming out of the lake. When they were finally facing the place—a steep, stony slope littered with scrap metal—they could make out only each other's faces if they turned to the water. A wheel glinted, a gas tank, a broken headlight. Johan went closer. The gas tank was shaped like a small body. He had often thought that when it had been between his knees in front of him. He had bought the enamel in tiny little cans. Such good quality! He could still distinguish the colors in the science-fiction landscape painted on the tank. Orange, violet, black, and yellow.

"My moped," he said.

"Are you sure?"

"Yes. Look at the enamel on the picture. Most of it's still there. Everything else is just rust."

"Yes, that's what I thought," said Birger. "Actually, I was almost certain."

They sat at Annie's kitchen table. It was dark out now, the wind tearing through the aspens. Birger had put out sausage and bread.

"Lumberman's food," he said. "You'll have to excuse it. But it'll get better. I'll start cooking proper food again."

He sounded as if he were making a promise to himself.

"I thought I'd fill the freezer after the disbursement. Mia wouldn't mind, would she?"

Birger didn't start talking about Annie until they had finished eating and were sitting on the sofa in the almost-dark room.

"She had so many whims. She talked such a lot. But we should have kept in mind how sensible she was. She really was tremendously sensible. Of course she hadn't run off to look for any UFO after she had seen you and recognized you. She didn't go up to Gudrun to suggest they should go and pick morels. That was probably just an excuse. I think she asked Gudrun about you. But she probably confused the issue, so Gudrun never thought anymore about it except as talk. Annie wasn't going picking morels at all. She went straight down to Anna Starr to ask where the scrap they had fished out of the lake was. She'd heard about it, of course. She made her way out there and looked at it. That confirmed it for her."

"They sank my moped?"

"They?"

Johan fell silent. Birger still hadn't switched on the lamp by the sofa. That made it easier. It was like looking into the dark and getting used to it. You began to distinguish faces. *The face.*

"There's a moment that I've occasionally thought about," said Birger.

"You remember what you were doing when you heard Kennedy had been shot. Or it's probably Palme for you. I remember what it was like when I found out what had happened up by the Lobber. Åke Vemdal had gone to the office on the campsite. He was talking to Henry Strömgren on the phone. Then he came back. I was standing at the window, looking out over the lake. I have always thought of it as serenity. Then everything became different, for me as well. Barbro and everything. Nothing was ever the same again after that moment. I saw Björne Brandberg rowing toward me. He was using an otter board. He must have been holding the long line between his teeth. When everyone else was sleeping off a hangover, Björne Brandberg was taking the opportunity to fish with the otter board. That was serenity."

He fell silent for a while. Johan couldn't see his face because Birger was sitting with his back to the window and it was growing dark very quickly now.

"It was only today I realized what it was I had seen. Björne had the otter board with him for the sake of appearance. He had been out on the lake to sink your moped. I don't know how he got it down to Tangen without anyone seeing it. After all, it's impossible to move around here without being observed. Never mind whether it's day or night. And the moped would have made a god-awful row."

"The Duett," said Johan. "I don't know if I remember it, or whether I just think I remember it. We were driving through the village, that woman from Finland and I. I saw Henry Vidart's Duett on its way out to Tangen. I crouched down because I didn't want anyone to see me."

"It's true that someone had moved it. It was by the road up to Vidart's later."

"The Duett had been parked up by the barn at our place. He could put the moped in the back without anyone seeing it."

He could hear Birger breathing heavily through his open mouth and Saddie snoring under the table.

"If only they had sunk the moped again, then nothing would have happened to Annie. That's the sort of thoughts you have," said Birger. "But they must have been afraid the nets would get caught on it. The fishing's good outside Tangen. They usually put out lines from the point and outward."

"Do you think he sank the moped to help me?"

"No. But Annie may have thought that. She decided to go down memory lane and ask him."

"Do you mean she was on her way to Starhill?"

"No, memory lane doesn't go that way. All the paths have been obliterated. There aren't any fixed points for the memory. It's a clear-felled area that became tundra. Hardly anything grows there. It's too exposed to frosts. No, all memory has been wiped out there. If Annie created her own memory lane with all the stations as she taught the children, I think it led to Nirsbuan."

"What would she go there for? Was that sensible?"

"Don't you know he lives there?"

"Björne?"

"He started living in a company hut by the bridge across the Lobber. That was when he was working on the clear-felling. It was a large area and took a long time. In the end he had to move to Nirsbuan. There's a narrow strip left there that belongs to your lot. Didn't you know that Björne has become the sort who can't live among other people any longer?"

"Gudrun told me he keeps himself very much to himself."

"He lives up there when he is not admitted to Frösön. I think Annie was on her way to him. We must go there tomorrow."

When they got up, Johan saw that the streetlights were on, a bluish-white light in the foliage along the edge of the road. He wondered what they were supposed to illuminate.

T hey walked over what had first been called the Starhill area, but now, after almost twenty years, was never called anything but the Area. The other clear-felled areas had gradually filled in. First with birch and rowan scrub. Then the pine plants came out of their tubes and fought their way up to the light.

But the Area had not become forest. It was mossy and even had patches of berry scrub. In among the low birch thicket, here and there a spruce plant had survived, deformed by the snow, elk, and storms.

They had had difficulty getting away. It was already Sunday afternoon when they left the car at Björnstubacken. Birger didn't want to cross the ford at the Lobber. Johan was also glad not to have to see that cold, racing water.

A path had once run there. The path began to run when the grass bent over. Summer after summer. Soles and hooves and the weight they carried repeated the action. The bilberry scrub finally learned and retreated.

A network of paths, walking veins, memory vessels—finer and finer out into the headlands of spruce forest toward the marshes and mountain heaths.

Remembering right out into the stony scree. Not getting lost. Remembering with your feet. Not with a sick tumor called longing that reproduces images wildly and crudely and crookedly. No, foot memories, leg memories. The capercaillie's coarse droppings—of pine needles, on pine needles—below a large pinetop he had ripped at with his beak.

The Anton Jonssa path. He herded horses for the village. And the horses thundered out the path, thumping it so that it came into existence and stayed firm. Everyone knew it.

The morels: Their white threads found themselves in a fresh pile of soil kicked up by a horse. They remembered year after year with their brown bodies in the Whitsun damp.

In the olden days the Lapp took timber for his reindeer enclosure here. Barking dogs and soft calls. There, there. Peaked Lapp shoes pointing out the path. It was steeper then, up toward the stream. Later the sowthistle grew into it. Lynx tracks in the mud of the stream. The lynx makes no path. She is present but outside. Hunger holes where the soul of the lynx should be.

The memory must also have time to lose itself slowly. Grass to rise. Grow again. New path. Behind the Lapp path, working backward. Another new path, taking another winding curve. Strange to call it new when it is older, but memory renews. All the way back to the youth of the forest.

Imagine a time when the ground responded to the foot. That is how young the earth was.

Leafy treetops. Birds. Fires.

The path had gone. There were the remains of a tractor track, but that led upward. They had to follow the river to find it. johan had Birger ahead of him and saw his great body taking the steep falls and plodding on up the rises. He had strong thigh muscles, visible under the material of his trousers, his buttocks small, his weight all in front, arching him forward at a sluggish but steady gait. He had walked trackless ground a great deal when out shooting.

Johan couldn't figure out what they were going to say to Björne. They had seen his car, an old wine-red Saab, at the Strömgren homestead. He must have taken the path and avoided the Area where he had driven the processor.

Birger showed no fear once they had gotten going. He had taken some packs of dressings out of his doctor's bag and put them into a rucksack. Johan carried it for him.

They came to the Brandbergs' land where the great spruces still stood —1:34, it was called. The mosses grew out in the damp autumn air, drinking and swelling. The deciduous trees were thinning out, their colors vanishing, the leaves fading and displaying their skeletons of nerves. Here and there color flared, caused by the frost.

It was very quiet. He had expected to hear the clatter of game birds taking off, perhaps even see a large capercaillie cock flying between the trees with his heavy load of flesh.

The sound of an ax broke the silence, the rhythm that of someone chopping wood. Two, at the most three blows of the ax, then silence as he picked up the next log. One or two were stubborn. Duller sounds as he swung the ax and log onto the block. They were now so close that they could hear the dry sound of wood splitting as he twisted the two parts free with his hands.

They couldn't see him. He was probably behind the cookhouse he used as a woodshed. Johan was standing by the privy, now slowly being taken over by forest. Moss and lichen were growing in the cracks of the steps, grayish-black and green-spotted lichen covering the planking with a rough skin, the timber slowly decaying beneath it.

Birger had sat down on a stone, presumably to rest in order to be levelheaded when they confronted him. Perhaps he was wondering what to say. But Johan didn't really believe he was planning anything beforehand. He was used to plodding straight ahead, straight into misfortune.

The chopping stopped, but Björne didn't appear. It seemed to Johan that he was standing there, listening. Could he have heard them? Or could he sense them? Pick up their scent?

Björne was singular. Johan had been quite young when he realized it. There was something dark about Björne. He followed the brothers, moved just like them. But he was shapeless. No one could say Björne was like this or that—great talker, quick-witted, like Pekka, or competitive, like Per-Ola, unafraid of pain. Björne was the one who followed them.

Birger got up, went over, and shouted. Björne immediately appeared from behind the cookhouse. He held one hand in his pocket and was walking rather stiffly.

Then everything became quite ordinary. Birger and Björne greeted each other, the words falling as they should. Oh, yes, so you two're out an' about, are you? Yes, we thought we'd make our way up here. Did yer come across t'Area? Yes, Christ, there'll never be any forest there. Not many birds this year. Well, there's some, all right. But higher up. In t'thick forest.

They followed him indoors. There were rat droppings on the porch where he stored the firewood, and a rank smell. Maybe the stoat hunted there. When he opened the kitchen door, the air hit them like a sickly warm wall, reeking of coffee and snuff. Previously Björne had given off an earthy smell, but now the smell had sickened. The smell of old man, Johan thought. He's old. Not yet fifty, but old.

Björne put a log into the stove, picked up a battered, blackened coffee-pot, and tipped a scoop of water into it. Then he opened the window and threw out the water and the old grounds. Johan wondered what it looked like outside the window. All the time, as he scooped in fresh water, added the coffee, put out a loaf and a box of soft cheese, he said nothing, and that was quite usual. Björne usually said nothing when he was working. But at the moment he was using only one hand, the other still in his pocket.

"We've been to take a look at Johan's moped. The one you sank outside Tangen," said Birger after emptying his cup of coffee.

Björne looked up. The colorless blue eyes appeared. Then his face closed up again, as if it had no features. He was shapeless. Heavy rather than fat. The hair, once brown, had faded and thinned. There was a deep mark around his head where his cap had been, greasy, compressed hair at the base. His cheeks and chin were unshaven, the stubble gray and white. He was holding a slice of bread in a big hand spotted black where engine oil had penetrated.

"Hadn't you heard they'd pulled a moped up? When they were drag-ging for something fallen from the skies, or whatever it was."

He made a movement that might have been a shake of the head.

"Sleeping all right?" said Birger unexpectedly. Johan remembered Björne had been his patient.

"Not so well," said Björne. "Used to. But now 'tis hell. Usually put a buckler fern in t'bed. There's somethin' in ferns what makes you drop off. But you have t'watch it. You might drop off forever."

He dipped his slice of bread into his coffee and sucked into him the part that became too loose and was about to fall back into the coffee.

"Used to work so hard, a man jist fell in t'bed. A man slept then."

"I saw you when you were coming from the lake and had sunk the moped. You were pretending to fish with the long line and the otter board. Johan saw you going down in Vidart's Duett."

"Remember once cycling home, at night 'twas, and quite light. Been clearing above Alda's and decided to damn well finish before t'weekend. An' I did. But was so damn tired, I didn't think I'd make it home on t'bike. Then I felt it going by itself. 'Twas like if someone had his feet on the pedals and were pedaling for me."

His eyes glinted. He seemed to want to see the effect of his story. If they believed that he believed it.

"A man can get help," he said, and he grinned.

"Remember old man Annersa?" said Johan. "He didn't get any help."

Johan had been quite young when his brothers had told him about the old man in Vitstensviken. His name was Paul Annersa and he lived alone ten kilometers from Blackreed village. His cottage was on one side of the road and the stable and barn on the other. A great many people had seen the old man crossing the road, especially on autumn evenings before the snow had come. He was going to tend to his horse. He died late one autumn.

Sometimes he used to be away for a couple of weeks at a time, sleeping in forest cabins, his horse with him. So no one exactly gave it much thought when he hadn't been seen for quite a while.

It had been his appendix. The bottle of liquor and box of painkillers found on the floor by his bed showed that he must have suffered. The horse died of thirst. The old man never got to it. Its stall was kicked to pieces, but the iron chain had held.

The old man is very bent as he walks without looking where he's going. There's no need. One of the Brunström boys came driving at high speed around a corner. He didn't see the old man until it was too late and he had time to think, Christ Christ Christ almighty! But he drove right through the old man. He was like gray air.

The horse screamed and its kicks thundered on the wall of the stall. The wood splintered and broke. But its screams went unheard and the old man's body was lying still on the pullout sofa.

Ever since then, he crosses the road at dusk. He's going to see if his horse has water. He must have worried about it at the time, although he couldn't get out of bed. That is how strong the impulse was. And strongest in the autumn, at dusk.

"Do you remember him?"

Björne nodded.

"It hurts sometimes," said Johan.

" 'Tis why I haven't no woman," said Björne. "Haven't even a cat. No one after me."

It was growing dark outside. They would be sitting there getting nowhere with him. He would talk about things that made his strangeness and aloneness quite pleasing to his listener. But Björne was no oddball. Perhaps he's empty, Johan thought. Nothing but that inside him. He himself isn't there.

He had done it.

The event—ten, twenty savage knifings—came out of nothing. Out of the darkness that follows us. Perhaps he doesn't even remember it.

And when he's alone? He tried to imagine Björne alone in the cottage. The way he lit the oil lamp as he was doing now, still with only one hand. The way reflections began to appear in the windowpanes. There was a milking stool in the bedroom, a book lying on it. The thought of Björne lying on those dirty sheets reading at night was unbelievable. Johan got up and went to look at the book.

" 'Tis Nostradamus," said Björne. "Sent for it from Finland. There was an advertisement. Nostradamus is the only one to have predicted correctly."

He was hiding himself. He wanted them to think he was an oddball. A harmless, kindly old man of the forest. As folk were in the olden days. Perhaps he believed it himself. But that was no use. He was the son of one of the few in the village who had done well for himself. There was work for him. There was money and machines. He had no need to be there.

Birger took the oil lamp off the table and shone it down Björne's leg. There was a dark patch on the denim above the clenched hand in his pocket. As they were looking, the patch spread.

"Have you cut yourself?"

He nodded.

He had been frightened and cut himself when he heard us. Had he been frightened for eighteen years? And Annie Raft with her gun. How have people been living here? I got out, Johan thought. I slipped out.

Birger rummaged in the woodbox for a newspaper.

"Put your hand on this," he said.

Björne took out his left hand, the thumb clasped by the fingers. The blood seeping out was very dark. Birger got him to loosen the rigid fingers and straighten out his thumb. The wound gaped when he touched it and the blood started oozing faster.

"The rucksack, please, Johan."

He was still holding Björne's hand.

"Find the bandages I put in. There's some tablets, too."

"Don't want any," said Björne.

"They're calming. I don't think it'd be a bad idea. We must talk about what happened. And we must go down to the village to get that stitched. I've got my bag there."

When Johan had given him the packages of bandages, compresses, and cotton, he said:

"Go on out now, Johan. We'll have a talk while I do this."

"No, I don't want to," said Johan. "That's stupid."

"Do it anyhow."

He looked around. A shotgun hung on the wall by the kitchen cupboard. Björne had a knife in his belt.

"Don't want to."

"Go on."

Johan pulled on his jacket, trying to delay matters. They were sitting as before. Björne's head was hanging. Around the oil lamp was a pool of warm yellow light, in which Björne's and Birger's hands lay entwined. Birger nodded toward Johan. He had to go.

Outside, the darkness was not as compact as it had seemed through the window. It had begun to drizzle. He walked down toward the privy, stopping halfway to look back. The window was filled with the yellow light. He could see their heads and the lamp. It looked cozy, as always when you look into a room from outside in the dark and the rain. And Björne really did look like a kindly old man. An oddball.

"Did you know Lill-Ola Lennartsson had died?" said Birger.

"No."

"Had a heart attack. Maybe I missed something there."

He said the latter largely to himself, a thought with little energy behind it.

"He'd been living in Östersund since that business down by the Lobber. I suppose he didn't dare stay. Did you know he fainted when he saw it was his tent?"

"That bastard," said Björne.

Birger pressed the edges of the wound together and put a compress over it.

"Yes, he was a real shit. He fiddled all sorts of things. When they analyzed the feathers of the birds he burned, they were buzzards. Two of them. I saw the parcels in his freezer. Unplucked capercaillie, he'd written on them. He must have been scared the police would look into everything at his place because he had been up there. I'm going to bandage this quite tightly now. I'll have to stitch it when we get down to the village."

He thought about Johan out there in the semi-darkness. It was raining now, gusts of wind spattering the window with rain.

"You thought it was him, didn't you?"

"He drove up there himself. On the evening afore Midsummer. What business had he up there? I knew the buzzard had chicks. And a Dutch car had come earlier in the day. Now they're fetching them, I thought. He was taking the opportunity while they're all Midsummer partying. Goin' to sell the live chicks. As hunting hawks for some damn Arab."

"Did you go up to Alda's to see about Johan?"

"He was all right where he was. Anyhow, he'd gotten out of the well by the time I got there."

"You took the moped."

"I'd planned that all along. Take the car up an' I'd frighten the bastard. Thought of catchin' him on the path. The buzzard's nest's up on the cliff above the river."

"You recognized the tent?"

"Course."

"Why did you go about it so ferociously?"

He said nothing, just sat there with his head bowed, breathing heavily.

"Didn't mean to," he said. "I were just going to give him a thrashin'. But I saw his back. He was lyin' against the canvas. I could see his back. It bulged out. Then everything went black."

"It wasn't him."

"No."

He sat in silence again. Birger wondered if he remembered the rest. Perhaps it was just as he had said. Black. A hole. A hole he had circled around for what would soon be twenty years.

"Annie was on her way up to ask you about the moped."

"I weren't here. I were at Frösön. Admitted at t'end of April."

"Who was waiting for her?"

"I dunno."

"We must go down now. We must get that stitched. Then I'll take you back to Frösön. You must tell the doctor. It'll be best for you if you go to the police yourself."

Was he listening at all?

"Things won't be very different for you than they've been in recent years. You'll be given leaves and you'll be able to come here. It'll soon be twenty years ago. Nothing else on your record, is there? No assaults or fights?"

"No. Been mostly here on me own. Used to go and see Annie."

"Annie would have said what I've said," said Birger. "Go to the police yourself. That'd be best."

"They'll be here soon, I suppose."

"No, I haven't phoned them. And I'm not going to. I want you to come down with me and have that stitched. Then we'll go to Frösön."

He got up and opened the window.

"Johan!"

He had to call a couple of times. Johan wasn't all that wet when he came in.

"Has it stopped raining?"

"It's drizzling."

"We must go now before it gets too dark."

Johan's watchful eyes moved from Birger to Björne, still sitting at the table.

"We've talked about it all now. Annie probably came here to ask Björne about the moped. But he was in Frösön."

"Yes, I know he wasn't home," said Johan. "Mia and I were here early that morning. But Annie must have gone up to Gudrun to ask after you. Didn't she know you were in Frösön?"

"Let's go now," said Birger. His voice had turned thin. "Don't let's talk about it any longer."

Björne went over to the door and took his cap off the nail. He put it on, but didn't take a jacket. He was wearing a sweatshirt that had once been dark blue, but was now so faded it was grayish over the shoulders and back. They heard him putting on his boots on the porch. Birger collected up his things and put them back in the rucksack.

"Turn the lamp out."

Johan blew it out and the room turned dark. He had acted too soon: They had forgotten where they had put their jackets and started groping for them on the sofa.

"Hurry up, for Christ's sake," said Birger. "To hell with the jackets."

They stumbled over their boots and started pulling them on in the dark. They were in too much of a hurry and it all went wrong. Out on the porch, the door was open and swinging in the wind.

They shouted out his name, then consulted together in whispers. They ran to the cookhouse, then the privy, rushed back inside and lit the oil lamp, as if trying to attract a moth.

But he didn't come. They shouted and shouted, but there was no reply from the darkness. He was out there. Birger didn't dare guess what was in his mind, whether his thoughts were straight and cunning. Or whether there was nothing but darkness there. A hole.

But they had to get him in.

Johan and Birger sat opposite each other at the kitchen table, the lamp between them; the flame was burning too high and sooting up the glass. They didn't stay long.

"He'll take the car and drive down," said Birger. Yet how could he say that with any certainty? He had to decide on something he could believe in.

"We must go down."

"You don't think he'll come back here?"

"No."

But before they blew out the lamp and set off for the second time, Birger took the shotgun off the wall. He didn't know, after all. Björne might well come back and finish the whole thing off with the gun.

They started walking along the path. The rain came in little squalls on the gusts of wind. Their eyes got used to the dark. It could have been worse. They were no longer calling out. Birger noticed that Johan was also trying to walk as quietly as possible.

Walking was more difficult when they got out into the Area, but it was also a little lighter there. The sky seemed to give off some kind of light. They could see the swift-moving clouds as if they were lit up from inside. They tried to walk so that they had the river within earshot. Birger noticed he was relieved once they were out in the Area. He had been scared inside the forest. Only an hour before he had sat at the kitchen table with Björne and put everything right. He thought then that he knew what was going on in the man's mind. He had even told him. As people had probably always told Björne what he was thinking and what he had done. They had ordered him to fell the Area. Twenty years later, it was wrong to clear-fell like that. They let him do the wrong thing and then they told him so.

Now he was out there, not giving a damn for the oil lamp or Nostradamus. He was himself in the darkness.

They reached the car and Johan started it and drove away before Birger had had time to close the door on his side. Johan drove fast, the chassis striking hard in the potholes, the headlights flickering on the spruces. When they got down to the Strömgren homestead, there was no sign of Björne's car.

"Wasn't it parked a bit farther in? Toward the house."

They stared along the houses on the slope, but at first could distinguish nothing.

"I'll go out and have a look," said Johan.

He had taken a flashlight out of the glove compartment. Birger watched him go with some reluctance. His figure blurred, the torchlight a small yellow spot jumping and slowly growing fainter. Birger stared until the buildings down in the Strömgren homestead started flickering. Gray in gray, everything moving in the rain and gusts of wind.

"Wait! I'm coming, too," he shouted.

He caught up with Johan and they walked into the grass, now gone to seed and wetting their trousers right up to their thighs. The torchlight flickered over the uncut yellow grass. There were no car tracks. When they finally found them, they were far up by the road. The Saab had gone. He had gone.

"We'll have to drive on," said Birger. "Wish we'd taken my car. I've got a mobile phone."

Johan drove fast, the car bouncing in the potholes. It's the only thing we can do now, Birger thought. Drive fast. We've done wrong. Me and my officiousness. Johan and his thoughtless question. Though he wanted to know. He had been asking himself, and now he knows. Björne knows, too.

The dogs were barking in the Brandberg dog run. They stopped and saw them hurtling against the wire netting. Torsten had a bright light on at the end of the barn and it shone on them. The dog eyes caught the light from the headlights and looked like leaping pairs of dots. A more yellowish light was on in the porch, illuminating the dark hop leaves.

"Drive on up," said Birger.

Lights were on almost all over the house and the dogs went on barking as the car drove up. They saw Torsten come out on the steps and heard him quieting the dogs as they drove up. There was no car in the yard.

Johan did not get out. He wondered if Torsten could see who he was. He was standing up there in the light on the steps, trying to make out whose car it was.

"Has Björne been down?" Birger called out, and got out of the car.

Torsten didn't reply until he had seen who was asking.

"He's probably up at Nirsbuan," he said.

"Is Gudrun there?"

"She's at her evening class."

"Where?"

"At the school."

Before Birger shut the car door, he leaned in toward Johan.

"I'll go in here and wait. You must go down and fetch Gudrun. Take her to Annie's house and wait there with her."

"Are you going to phone the police now?"

"I must," said Birger. "I promised I wouldn't. But that was on the condition he went with me."

He himself thought it was odd to be standing there arguing the toss about his promise. Torsten was still standing in the strong light on the steps, trying to peer into the car.

"Who's that?" he said.

Women were on their way out to
their cars when he got down to the school. But the Audi was still there.
Johan drove up and parked as close to the steps as he could get. He wound
down the window and listened to them chatting as they came out two at a
time. He wondered what course they were taking this winter. Leather-
work? Genealogy? He marveled at her going there. At the way she struggled on, day by day.

Her everyday life was to be ruined now. No more chat. No more
coffee, lamplight, security. In a few moments, as soon as she looked up
from the handbag she was just zipping up. Then he realized that it would
take a little while. She wouldn't understand right away.

"So it's you?"

She didn't want to go with him at first.

"You must," he said. "Just leave the car here."

The other cars started up and he saw one or two people waving to her.
She was annoyed with him.

"Why on earth should I go up to Annie Raft's house?" she said.
"What business have I there?"

But in the end she had gotten into his car and then she could do
nothing about where they were going to go.

"You didn't really know her. You were never friends, were you?"

She said nothing, but she looked sideways at him. He drove straight
up there. The grass was wet and his wheels probably left ugly marks. But
he had to get her into the house.

"We're going to wait here," he said. "Birger Torbjörnsson is with Torsten. The police are on their way."

She asked no questions, but went ahead of him after he had unlocked the door. She was so small, her dark head level with his chest. He locked the outside door behind them.

"Wait," he said. "Don't switch on the light."

He went around, pulling down all the blinds, and when he turned the light on, she was standing in the middle of the kitchen floor, her face closed and guarded. Saddie had been sleeping in the bedroom and came lumbering out in all her deafness, sniffing at Gudrun's slacks with no real interest, her tail vaguely wagging.

"Take your coat off and go in and sit down," he said. "We may have to wait quite a while."

She sat down at the kitchen table. He wondered what she was feeling as she looked around. He could see the kitchen through her eyes. The batik cloth on the kitchen table was flimsy. A yellowed rice-paper shade hung from the ceiling. At least Mia had cleared away everything that had hung from the hood above the stove—a pair of pigeon feet, bunches of dried herbs, a birch fungus—all covered with cobwebs and dust.

"Birger Torbjörnsson and I did just what Annie did," he said. "We went to Nirsbuan to see Björne."

It was cold indoors, but he didn't want to light the stove. He figured he had to keep an eye on her all the time.

"We'd been down to take a look at my moped he'd sunk."

She didn't reply. She had put aside her bag but not unzipped her jacket. She was sitting straight up on the chair, her hands on the cloth in front of her. Her face was pale, but he had thought that every time he had seen her in recent years. Perhaps that was because she dyed her hair. He wondered whether she would now let it go gray.

This is where it all began, he thought. This is where Annie Raft stood looking out through the window and spotted me. How did she recognize me? No one knows.

She had thought she was seeing her child in the arms of a madman. A boy who had been insane or drunk and had plunged a knife over and over again into two people enclosed in a tent.

He suddenly noticed that Gudrun was cold. They had sat in silence for so long, and she hadn't shifted position, but she was shaking and her nose was running slightly. She kept sniffing, a nervous sound, the only sound in the house.

"I'll light the stove," he mumbled.

He fumbled with birch bark and matches. It was easier to talk to her when he wasn't looking at her.

"Björne has told Birger that he's the one who did that down by the Lobber. He was to come down with us, but he ran away. We were afraid he might come and hurt you. Now that he knows it was you."

He very carefully made a little pile of kindling before putting a match to the bark. A long time went by before she said anything. Then her voice was dry. Or hoarse.

"Björne?"

"Yes. Björne. Not me. You were wrong. Annie Raft was, too."

For a long spell she sat quite still, then he saw she was beginning to tremble.

"Hasn't she got electricity in here?"

She almost screamed it, her voice breaking. She had risen to her feet and wrapped her arms around herself. She was so cold she was shaking.

"Yes," he said. "Of course."

He rushed into the living room and switched on the lamps and the radiators. He found a blanket folded up on the bed.

"Here, put this around you. Sit on the sofa. It'll soon warm up. Birger's got some whiskey somewhere. Wait."

She wrapped the blanket around her and sat looking out of it at Annie Raft's room. The curtains were of unbleached cotton. A colorful paper monster floated below the ceiling. Must have been something the schoolchildren had made. She looked across at the bed and he thought about what she had said: "Hasn't she got electricity?" As if Annie Raft were still alive. And she looked as if she had never seen the room before. Yet she had gone in here with the key she had taken from the shed.

"Had Björne told you where she kept the key?"

She looked up and nodded. Absentmindedly, he would have called it. But it couldn't have been that.

"And the gun? That it was behind the bed?"

"Everyone knew that."

She looked so small, sitting there in that shapeless gray blanket. It hurt him to see her; it was painful. He had had no idea you could feel so much for another person, and for a moment he felt terror at having a child. If the child were injured—was this what he would feel like? Helpless and in pain.

His hands were uncertain as he poured whiskey out for her and he spilled some on the coffee table. She gazed vacantly at the little pool, and suddenly tears came into Johan's eyes and his throat contracted. Normally she would have gotten up to get a cloth. She was always quick to do that kind of thing. Now she just sat there, looking. She looked at him strangely as he wept. Guarded and timid. Almost frightened.

In the end he managed to control his tears. Gudrun sniffed again, that small, moist sound in her nose so neat and tidy beside his noisy sniveling. He had to go and fetch some kitchen towels and took the opportunity to put another log into the stove. I'll do what I have to, anyhow, he thought. In the past, she, too, had had the shell of habit and everyday routine around her. She did what she was supposed to do. Took courses. Joined search parties and went to the funeral, for that matter. Now it was over.

"What did Annie say when she came to you?"

"She asked about you."

"About that Midsummer Eve?"

She nodded.

"The moped," she said. "She had worked out that Björne had sunk it. I don't know how."

"You didn't know they'd pulled it up?"

She shook her head.

"It had been lying at Tangen for several years. Annie must have figured out it might have been the same one. She probably knew from Birger that Björne was on the lake that Midsummer Eve."

They heard a sound on the window and Johan jumped. It sounded like someone scraping on the pane. Then it was repeated more faintly and he recognized it—the rain hurtling in gusts against the pane.

He had been frightened and shown it. A moment ago, he had wept. He wished he could have been different now. But she was looking at him so strangely, maybe it did not cross her mind that he could help her. He was and remained a child to her.

She had seen her child threatened. So had Annie Raft. As soon as the two met, danger loomed. Neither of them had considered talking to us, handing over the problem.

If only it had been spontaneous at least. A reflex action, the way a cat lashes out with its paw. But she had arranged it. It was quickly done, but it was thorough. She had lured Annie Raft up to Nirsbuan. That gave her plenty of time. She wrote the note, fixed the thermos of coffee, and put buns in a plastic bag. The irony of such ordinariness.

"You never found her cartridges."

"She hadn't got any," she said.

"Yes, she had. Behind the clock radio."

For a moment he saw her face as it must have looked then, tense and calculating. But now she was calculating with hindsight. If only she had known. If only she had looked behind the radio. Just as swiftly, the expression vanished. She stared at the flimsy Oriental rug Saddie had rucked up, but she didn't seem to see it. She had lost interest in the house and Annie Raft. Her glass of whiskey was untouched, and he remembered now that she never drank spirits.

Somehow or other he recognized most of what she had done. She had arranged things for her family. She had brought her everyday competence to the tasks she had to carry out. The thermos. The buns. The written note. He remembered the times when she had brought him milk and sandwiches to his room. She never pretended it was anything special. Only an arrangement that would make things easier for everyone. She seldom sat the way she was sitting then.

Once he could remember her sitting on the bed in his room, her face pale. She had been staring out the window, chewing her bottom lip. She had had moments of doubt. But she did not yield to them.

He thought he could follow her in the everyday actions she had carried out that Saturday afternoon, with determination and without letting their irony get through to her.

But he couldn't picture her down at the Lobber.

And yet she had been there. It had been calculated. Annie Raft would have to cross the river at the ford when she came back from Nirsbuan. No matter how the paths wound and divided within the parcel of forest, that was the only place where she could get across the river. But Johan was incapable of picturing Gudrun there.

He could not picture her going up close, removing the safety catch, pulling the trigger, and firing. He wanted to ask, but the question could not be spoken aloud. It was too shameful and too emotional—as if there were still some decorum to adhere to.

How could you? That question would not pass his lips.

He remembered a night of wine drinking and talk. First, Mia had taken him to the library, where a famous old poet gave a reading of poems he'd written over five decades. Afterward, they had had wine and pizza and eventually had gone back to the home of one of her colleagues at the museum. There had been much talk, and quantities of cheap wine were consumed.

They had talked about the event by the Lobber. And about that mass rape outside Piteå. The old poet, a sensitive, gifted person, a conscience for them all, was able to describe it in detail. The way the last youth in the tent had cut up the unconscious girl with a broken bottle. How he had jammed it up her vagina.

They had been ordinary boys, boys who bought Mother's Day roses and Christmas presents. A consensus prevailed beneath the lamplight and the coils of smoke. Their eyes smarted. They were speaking rather indistinctly, but were in agreement on the influence of alcohol, on mass psychosis, and the crudeness of army life. On violations in childhood, poverty, and Rambo films. Then the old poet said:

"I think I would've been capable of doing that myself."

There was utter silence.

"Under those circumstances. The tent. Drink. Yes, I would have been capable of it myself."

And they could see beneath that bowl of yellow light and in the bluish coils of cigarette smoke that he was staring into himself. They realized that he could see backward to that event in the tent which they had not been able to make out in all their talk, and which still none of them could see clearly, could not even imagine at all. They had been very taken with his greatness and the depth of his humanity, and a long time went by before they had started talking again, and drinking wine and smoking.

But Johan had grasped Mia fiercely by the elbow and said that they were going home. She had been irritated and a bit cross, but she had gone with him. He had drawn a very deep breath out in the cold winter air and thought of the poet up there as an Antichrist.

"You didn't like him," said Mia.

"He made me sick."

"Why? Because he tells the truth about us?"

"Because what he says about himself is probably true."

They hadn't mentioned it again. It had been an open question between them, whether you can see into your own darkness and whether it actually is your responsibility to do so. Or whether you evoke the darkness and make it into your own by toying with it.

"re you still cold?"

Gudrun nodded.

"This may last quite a time. Wouldn't you like to lie down for a while?"

She shook her head. He got up and put more wood in the stove. Should he ask her if she wanted anything to eat? A sandwich or something? But it was late. Perhaps she was feeling sick.

"How could you think it was me?" he said.

That question had also been difficult to ask. But now he had asked it. She looked up with a trace of derision.

"Well, you're believing it of me."

Her face took on a little life from the irony, but it didn't last many moments.

"I had help, after all," she said.

"Björne?"

She nodded.

"What did he say?"

"I don't really remember. That he'd found your moped up where the path ended."

"Up by the river?"

"Yes."

"What a shit he is!"

"He's the only one of the brothers you've ever had anything in common with."

"I had nothing in common with him. How could I have?"

"He said you used to take turns in guarding the buzzard's nest. That you thought Lill-Ola had taken the chicks and was going to sell them. There'd been a Dutchman in the store that afternoon. And the chicks had gone. He thought you'd been . . . you'd just gone on stabbing. At the tent."

She fell abruptly silent, her face floating out in the lamplight. She had bent back her head with her mouth wide open. She looked as if she were in pain. He thought about birth pains. But she was quite quiet now.

"How could you have believed him?" he whispered. She didn't answer for a moment. Her lips looked stiff.

"We didn't talk about it all that much. No one at home wanted to say it straight out. We were trying to help you."

For a moment they looked each other right in the eye.

"Why didn't you tell us?" she cried. "You seemed to be afraid of being caught. Why did you agree to move to Langvasslien if you hadn't done anything!"

"I thought Torsten was fed up with me. I'm not even his son."

"*What* did you say?"

"I'm not his son. We'll have to talk about that sometime or other." She snorted.

"Are you laughing?"

"Well, what else can I do? Are you saying you're not Torsten's son?"

"I'm Oula Laras's son. The man you were with before Torsten."

She had clasped her hands and was moving her head, rocking it. Suddenly she reminded him of his grandmother, an old woman rocking her head.

"My dear child," she said. "I don't know whether to laugh or cry. Oula Laras! Of all people."

"Am I wrong?"

"Yes. I've never had anyone except Torsten."

She was looking at him as if she had never really seen him before. Her eyes slid over his pullover and tight leather trousers. She snorted again, almost imperceptibly this time. But it was ridicule. He could see every shift in her expression.

"Antelope trousers," she said. "Aren't they? Leather trousers. Made of South American antelope skin. Cost four thousand kronor. Oh, so you thought you were Sami? Totally? I ought to have known. The way you carried on about our people's old sacrificial places and all that."

424

She thrust her head forward and stared at him.

"You've never been right down in the shit."

He couldn't imagine her having been there, either. But he didn't dare say anything.

"We had to go into the privy to speak our own language. My teacher wasn't exactly on the right side. Not like yours, petting the dear little Lapp children. Telling them about the troll drums and all that stuff. When I went to school, they made you ashamed of being a Lapp, like having vermin or tuberculosis. And we didn't even own any reindeer. Dad was a drunk. Did you know that? Did you know your grandfather was a drunk? Well, now you know, anyhow. He sang and drank and talked shit. He wasn't violent. Only silly. I can't stand the way people are now collecting the Sami songs and all that. Singing and singing and singing. Do you know what it means to be poor, Johan? Piss poor. "Patch-pants Lapp, Lapps are crap," the kids used to say, turning their backsides on you. Oh, no, Johan. No ancient places of sacrifice. That isn't what we went around thinking about. But electricity! And patterned sweaters and a stainless-steel sink. Even your aunt Sakka dreamed Swedish dreams."

Sakka had read the weekly magazines. And saved them all up. Taken them with her up to Langvasslien in bundles tied up with string. The Pergutt and Johan had found them in the attic and Sakka had laughed. She remembered how she had tried to forget she had short little legs, a round bottom, and dead-straight hair.

"Sakka laughed at those magazine dreams," said Johan. "I know she did."

"She did a complete about-face as best she could when she married Per Dorj. Borrowed a silver collar for the wedding. Got herself a Sami costume, though it wasn't real wool. Now she's on every single committee there is and Per is chair of the Sami village. But that doesn't make the sun turn."

"I think they do it well," said Johan. "All the same."

"Sakka's southern Sami is spoken by a few hundred people. Did you know that? A few hundred!"

Yes, Sakka tried to get the sun to turn and the mountain birch to grow with its roots up in the air. She loved her language. But perhaps it had already been squeezed to death under the synthetic material. A stronger myth had swallowed hers. He had thought so himself, many a time. But living up there was so easy. For him it was a life of Sundays; winter life with the dogs, and branding the calves, fishing and walking in the summer.

"I suppose they do the best they can," he said. "Hanging on. Like everyone living here. There's no difference between the Sami and the others in that respect. They make do somehow. It can't be all that grand. They try to live a life that somehow connects to the past. And most of them want to remember. Not everyone can build roads for the company. Not everyone is involved in turning this into the Area."

"Yes, they are."

The treetops. The sleeping birds. Sparks between the trees. No more memory here, but a tumor, growing as fast as the destruction.

The Area has no paths. Here are steep slopes and rubbish, stones, log stacks, scrub. A network of roads out on the Area. A system of road networks running out to the cleared areas. Rubble after dynamiting along the roadside slopes. Shattered stony gravel. Dry root systems. Oil drums. Torsten has built the network of roads. Do you hate him for that? Do you hide in the treetops, creep along paths under capercaillie spruces that are no longer there? Then you're lost in the cancer that is called longing.

Hate you. Know what you did, what you took part in. It was the haste, nothing else. The great haste. Everyone was in such a hurry, hurrying toward death.

Paths run and disappear like roads, like forests. But it was fatal that it all went so quickly. Now you have only the presence and a hole of hunger.

Hate you.

Bend over your reflection in the water and hate.

She said it so quietly, he had to lean over toward her.

"Yes, everyone. You, too. And Annie Raft. Though she thought she was so much better than the rest of us. But all the same, she was involved in it."

"Did you hate her?"

What a word. She didn't reply.

But she does hate. I have never dared disturb my hatred. She touched on hers, and that was enough. It had been sleeping so lightly.

What shall we do with this hatred of ourselves—of the devastation? What shall we do? It fills our mouths. Rotten. Bitter. A taste we don't recognize. An unfamiliar vomit.

I would like to glide above it all like Ylja, with ridicule, with sarcasm, with affection. Like gliding above the treetops, above forests on fire, like vapor. Or just work, eyes closed, work to heal, like Birger. Healing. Assuaging.

But what do you do with the weather? You make forecasts. You provide a service. Five days at a time. Small bursts of controlled future. An ingratiating magic.

"It's over, Johan. A few hundred people. The northern Sami language will probably remain for a while. Nostalgia, it's called, so I've learned. That's all right for cultured people. Those who write and dance and carry on. But the reindeer owners drive their herds with scooters these days. That's not actually Sami culture. It's crude. It's Swedish. They search and drive with helicopters and move the creatures to summer grazing in long-distance trailers. They're living another life now. We're living another life. But we are alive."

"You took part in rejecting the old life," said Johan. "At least Sakka didn't do that. Apart from daydreaming over weekly magazines for a while, as a teenager."

"Yes, I took part. From shame. From compulsion. From a longing for something else as well. I was only human; perhaps human first and foremost. Even a Lapp can long for electricity. But you, you're a Sami. In antelope trousers."

"You don't have to mock me," he said. "I believed it."

"The time has come to stop now, then. Thank Torsten and the forest roads for the life you've been given. School and university and all. And that you were able to live with Sakka and Per. He has paid every day for you. I wasn't going to let one single insane event ruin your whole life. A sixteen-year-old. Who was frantic."

"But it wasn't me!"

"And I wasn't going to let that teacher destroy your whole life, either. When everything had gone so well. Just as I'd thought it would. As long as you had the chance to get away from all that, to forget it as if it had never happened."

"But you were wrong!"

She either didn't hear him or didn't want to listen any longer.

"She poked her nose into everything. Asking questions and digging up the past. You've no idea what she's been like here. How she's interfered in everything although she wasn't even born here. Out of curiosity, and because she thought she knew everything better than anyone else. When Magna Wilhelmsson told us at county fairs about Jonas in Brannberg, who was your great-grandfather, I'll have you know, she got up afterward and said that Magna had forgotten to mention that he had had children with both the sisters up there. His wife and her sister. And she said you mustn't forget the near starvation and the tuberculosis and the incest, when you talk about what it was like before. You couldn't just talk about what hardworking people they were, how fine Grandfather's stonemasonry was and the songs your auntie sang. Annie Raft poked and pried and interfered, and I don't think she ever grasped that these were the relatives of living people she was talking about. The truth must out, she said. We mustn't forget. And then she came and started digging into what had happened down at the Lobber!"

"She saw her daughter together with the person she thought had done it. She wanted to protect her child."

But that didn't get through to her. She's the only one with a child, he thought.

"Mia and I are going to have a baby," he said.

Then she really did look at him.

"That's impossible!"

Indeed, it was irretrievably difficult. Annie and Gudrun. The two grandmothers. Everything would come out over the years. It was too black. Too extreme. Condemning a child to such knowledge, even if it came trickling in late and perhaps diluted and falsified.

"It'll have to be possible," he said. He felt he didn't want to talk to her about it. It simply had nothing whatsoever to do with her.

Deliverance may come to the person who hates. Sakka's laughter. Her good-natured casualness. Johan seemed to see before him the piece of elastic that joined button and buttonhole in Mia's jeans. The way it stretched and bounced.

"Lie down on the sofa," he said to Gudrun. "Try to sleep for a while. It may be a long time before Birger Torbjörnsson phones."

She actually obeyed him. He drew the blanket over her, pulling it right up to her chin. When he brushed her hands, they were cold.

Things between Gudrun and him would be much as before, though he would be the one to go to see her occasionally. Torsten and she would probably have to move later, when she came back home. They would get older. Perhaps in a flat. Torsten would not live to old age there.

Torsten. He visualized him as he had seen him under the porch light beside the dark, shaggy wall of hops. Thinner, more worn, and grayer than he had thought it possible for him to become.

The person who hates may be delivered. In this incredibly untidy existence. And all the insanity we have been part of. To some, deliverance comes like a laugh. Well—good heavens! We have to make our way somehow.

But why doesn't it come to us all? he thought childishly. My mother. There's a hole where she used to be. A hole that is now closing.

He went around feeling the radiators. Saddie was lying in the hallway, staring silently at the door, and he realized she hadn't been out since Birger and he set off that afternoon. He let her out and quickly locked the door again.

He was frightened of Björne. He had no difficulty imagining him down at the Lobber. He had seen him slaughtering beasts. He had always been the one to do it. Pigs. Ram lambs. He could see his face as he thrust in the knife. A rigidity, teeth. It was called an archaic smile. Most people saw it only in museums. But it was alive and ecstatic.

Johan stood holding the blind in the kitchen slightly away from the window, watching Saddie squat and urinate for a long time a little way out on the grass. She wanted to come in again immediately.

When he went into the living room, Gudrun was lying with her eyes closed. It was impossible to know whether she was asleep. The tension had gone from her thin face, now smoothed out and childish. He could well imagine the girl who had read magazines, studying the pink-complexioned women with their hair en bouffant and in rigid waves. Sakka had also told him how they had read about film stars and tried to resemble them. They had gone for Ava Gardner. That was who they wanted to look like. They had wet their hair with pilsner and rolled it tightly onto Grandmother's chamois-leather curlers. They had painted their mouths with a moistened red crayon.

Gudrun's narrow little mouth with its tightly closed lips.

Sakka had laughed at it all. She had laughed so that her breasts bounced when she told him about it. But the other girl, with her terrible gravity, was now lying on Annie Raft's sofa under a gray blanket, looking as if nothing had happened to her since then.

Solitude. The pattering of mice. Clicks in the stove. Showers of rain on the metal roof. The birches shuddering in the sharp wind from the high mountain. Yellow leaves tearing loose and sticking to the cottage windows.

No shooting for Birger; silent solitude instead. Color prints of Jesus gave him meek and disturbed looks. He had leafed through Nostradamus, but had given up. Good grief! There was a pack of cards in the table drawer and he played the varieties of solitaire he could remember: round the clock, four queens.

Now I am myself, he thought. Whatever is inside here, that is me.

The Klöppen was gray and rough, the waves white-capped. He could just see it when the tops of the birches swayed and formed a gap. Ravens seemed to detach themselves from the sky, shrieking and chattering.

He had quite a lot of food with him, a rucksack full, and he was determined to stay until Björne came back. His car had been found just outside the village. He couldn't get anywhere. But Birger didn't want him to be met by police when he came back to the cottage. Then things might go crazy again.

The police didn't like Birger being there. But he never left the meadow and only seldom the cottage. He chopped a little firewood for himself and took it inside. Made kindling. Tore up birch bark. Went to the privy. Fetched two full buckets of water and heated a pan of water on the stove. Then he washed himself properly. He had put newspapers under the stool the washbasin was on. After that he made coffee.

He realized that this was how you did it. You divided up the day. The evening would come in the end. The radio worked faintly for the first two days, though the batteries were running out. Then it stopped. He was himself.

In the evening he could see the ridges beyond the Klöppen darkening in the autumn twilight. They still had some color and there was a great deal of gold among it all, dark gold. The greenery was the color of smoke and earth. There was a smell of smoke. The smoke from his own stove came down when the weather calmed and the landscape smelled like the colors. Twilight thickened more and more. Violet came into the earth and smoke. The clouds behind the ridges looked like gold that had been drawn out of the actual ground. The cookhouse windows glimmered.

He was reminded that there was supposed to be silver in the Klöppen. Down toward the church, just before the mouth of the Röbäck. A Lapp had seen the vein open one Christmas night. Good Lord!

Three panes were shiny in the cookhouse window, the fourth covered with a piece of cardboard. A crow circled above it all.

If he did not eat and divide the day up into chores, if he lay on the bed listening to what was not human—the clicks in the timber walls, the hissing of the sedge—then he would soon be on the borderline. But he didn't want that. He preferred to read Nostradamus. At least it had been written by a human being.

It was misty in the morning. He could see nothing, no ridges, none of the waters of the Klöppen, nothing. Out of the marsh rose two or three dense shapes, probably spruces. Anna Starr maintained she had seen Artur Fransa in the marsh water when there was a mist. That he showed himself there. Crazy old women, they must want to be able to see the dead. But why?

The wind blew up and the mist vanished. The dense shapes as well. So they hadn't been spruces. Maybe elks.

He looked at the patient forest beneath the northwest wind. The ragged surface of the water. The weeping windows of the cottage.

Find a lair. Crouch down. Creep in. Sooner or later, he was bound to come.

It was night. Birger had been awoken so many times by a rustling, thinking it was him. Now he rolled over and longed to return to his shallow, easily disturbed sleep.

The porch door creaked. Then he could faintly hear that he was standing there, sniffing the air. Yes, he could tell by the scent that someone was living there. Sausages had been fried, coffee brewed, and the stove was still a bit warm.

"It's only me," Birger said quietly.

He got up from the low bed and went out into the kitchen.

"Come on in."

Once he had the oil lamp lit, he could see him by the door. He was soaking wet. His clothes were dark with the wet dripping off him and running down to the floor. His hollow cheeks were covered with gray stubble. He had smeared something around his mouth.

"Where have you been?"

"In Klemmingsberg."

That was an old defense installation, dynamited out of Torsberg Mountain during the war and named after a major called Klemming. Birger had thought it had collapsed long ago.

"Let's have a look at your thumb."

He had wrapped a strip of shirt material around it and the package was stiff and brown.

"I've got the things with me now, so I can stitch it for you. But I wonder if it'll work. That wound must look damn nasty by now. I'll probably just have to bandage it up again. I'll make you something hot to drink. When I've done something about the wound, you can sleep. We won't be going down until morning."

Björne said nothing. He was swaying slightly. He couldn't get his boots off by himself. There was water inside them and Birger had to keep wrenching and pulling to get them off. He lit the stove and was glad of the few embers left inside. Then he helped him off with garment after garment until he stood naked on the floor in front of the stove.

A big man. His lower legs and hands were thickly scarred. His face was sunburned and so were his forearms; his forehead was white above the mark from the rim of his cap. His body was whitish-yellow, the skin slack across his belly. He had starved. The tuft of hair below his stomach had thinned out. Prematurely, Birger thought. Prematurely, too, his penis had shrunk and the scrotum shriveled.

He felt over him a little and listened to his heart. There was nothing wrong with it, he knew. The heart was pumping. The chest was being raised and lowered by his lungs. But Birger thought someone ought to touch him.

About the Author

KERSTIN EKMAN is one of Sweden's most prominent novelists. She was born in 1933 in Risinge, a small village in the middle of Sweden. She has written seventeen novels which have been widely published in the other Scandinavian languages, German, Finnish, Dutch, and French, and have won numerous prizes and awards. She became a member of the Swedish Academy of Arts and Letters in 1978, but resigned in 1989 when the Academy did not make a statement that she could approve of about the Rushdie case. She lives in Valsjöbyn, a small village in the north of Sweden.

Blackwater has been awarded the Swedish Crime Academy's Award for best crime novel, the August Prize, and the Nordic Council's Literary Prize.